A SONG
for her
ENEMIES

SHERRI STEWART

HERITAGE BEACON

FICTION

Heritage Beacon Fiction is an imprint of LPCBooks
a division of Iron Stream Media
100 Missionary Ridge, Birmingham, AL 35242
ShopLPC.com

Iron Stream Media serves its authors as they express their views, which may not express the views of the publisher.

This is a work of fiction. Names, characters, and incidents are all products of the author's imagination or are used for fictional purposes. Any mentioned brand names, places, and trademarks remain the property of their respective owners, bear no association with the author or the publisher, and are used for fictional purposes only.

All Scripture quotations, unless otherwise indicated, are taken from the Holy Bible, King James Version.

Library of Congress Control Number: 2020951556

ISBN-13: 978-1-64526-283-1
Ebook ISBN: 978-1-645526-284-8

Printed in the United States of America

PRAISE FOR *A SONG FOR HER ENEMIES*

It has been such a pleasure to read this. Once upon a time, years ago, there was a series called Zion Chronicles, and for us Jewish believers it was such a wonderful tool to use for giving to our unbelieving Jewish friends and family (I gave it to my mom). I wrote my book hoping to provide another such tool, and I believe yours will too. Your writing is elegant, dramatic, and filled with love.

~ Miriam Finesilver
Author of *Naomi, The Rabbi's Wife*

Sherri Stewart's gift for writing shines in *A Song for Her Enemies*, a gripping, emotional story of sacrifice, love, and hope. Tamar, a young Jewish singer with a promising future, discovers her talent is key to her survival. Neelie, an outspoken young woman, risks her life to put her Christian faith in action. Set in the Netherlands as World War Two expands across Europe, this beautifully written novel captivated me from the first page until the last line.

~ Pat Nichols
Award-winning author of the Willow Falls Series

A Song for Her Enemies grabbed me from the first page and pulled me into this heartwarming tale about survival and God's redemption. The characters are well-written and engaging. Tamar, Daniel, and Neelie's fight to live through one of the worst periods in human history came to life on the pages and had me rooting for them every step of the way. The love story that blooms between Tamar and Daniel is beautiful and filled with sweet interludes of tenderness backdropped by a world in chaos and a country torn apart by war.

Sherri Stewart's storytelling is gripping and poignant as she weaves a tale that will touch your very soul.

~**Mary Alford**
Bestselling author of the Courage Under Fire Series and
Love Inspired Suspense's Covert Amish Christmas

It was a joy to read *A Song for Her Enemies*. I felt as though I were a time traveler living through the eyes of a young Jewish opera singer in the Netherlands during World War II. Out of the evils of the Holocaust, Tamar loses not only a promising career but her freedom. This novel is a perfect reminder that God gives us beauty for ashes and praise in place of broken hearts.

~**Kimberly Grist**
Award-winning author of The Inspirational Brides of
Carrie Town, Texas

Sherri Stewart's well-developed characters and plot will transport readers to the challenging times of the Nazi takeover during World War II. Tamar Kaplan, a gifted singer, faces gut-wrenching choices and challenges with an engaging cast of characters in this fast-paced novel. From the outset, readers will admire and cheer for those caught in the dark web of persecution drawn from the pages of history. This story reminds us to face oppression and injustice with courage and faith.

~**Jan Powell**
Editor and ghostwriter

Sherri Stewart's superb writing drew me into the world of opera soprano Tamar Kapland from the first page to the epilogue. I shared the fears and hopes with the *Nederlanders* as they struggled against the onslaught of Nazi occupation. I cried at the end—tears of heartbreak for the agony they suffered, and tears of joy for their strength of faith in the Savior. I highly recommend this excellent historical fiction novel, which has a non-fiction truth flowing through its pages. Let us never forget what happened then.

~Janet Ramsdell Rockey
Award-winning author of *The God of Possible*

A fine, fact-based, historical novel, with a spiritual thread that reminded me of Corrie ten Boom and how her family hid people fleeing from the Nazis.

Experience this story through the eyes of a naïve, young vocalist for a local opera house in the Netherlands, whose voice is both a blessing and a curse.

~Nora St. Laurent
The Book Club Network Blog

ACKNOWLEDGMENTS

Many talented and knowledgeable people have lent their expertise to this book.

To my beta readers—Julie Russell, Dorothy Weber, Claudia Hamel, Marilyn DeSeno, Debbie Burton, and Mary Peoples. Thank you for your time and helpful comments. It takes more than a village to edit my books. *A Song for Her Enemies* is much better because of your constructive criticism.

I also want to thank the Orlando branch of Word Weavers International for your helpful comments. Constructive criticism is vital, though hard to take sometimes. I appreciate the sandwich method.

A special thank you to Mimi Finesilver who helped me with all things Jewish. I'm so grateful for your suggestions.

Thanks to my editors—Pat Nichols, who is a master at finding repeated words and nonessentials. She can certainly turn a phrase to make mine better. Thanks to Jan Powell, whom I have nicknamed *the slasher*, and she did, and the book is better because of her input. And to Denise Weimer, managing editor of Heritage Beacon Fiction. She is such an encouragement and helped me think through plot holes where I'd just assumed the reader could read my mind. Also thanks to LPC's initial proofreader, Steve Mathisen, for helping me make sure the timeline was historically correct.

A special thanks to my son, Joshua, who helped prop up my computer every time it quit on me. He knows his way around technology, and when he doesn't, he always reminds me to check Google. Because of Josh's handling of train schedules and directions around the Netherlands, I could concentrate on research. He's also much better at photography and videotaping than I am.

Finally, thank you to my launch teams in Michigan and in Florida. I'm grateful for your belief in me and your behind-the-scenes efforts. Thank you to Stacie Hatch for your help with navigating social media. You are all a blessing to me.

And finally, to you, the reader: Thank you for choosing this book, opening its cover, and reading it to the end. That takes work and perseverance. You have limited time and so many choices. I wrote *A Song for Her Enemies* for you, lest we forget. All reviews are appreciated, and I would love to connect with you on social media. I hope you enjoy this book from my heart to yours. May your life be full of adventure and love.

DEDICATION

To Bobby, my late husband, my love. You supported me through the writing of this book but did not live to see it published. Throughout our forty-two years together, you encouraged me to grow as an individual—through law school, through helping me prepare and tear down my classroom every year, through writing over a dozen books and traveling with me to visit my settings, for sacrificing our cruise so I could travel to Israel with my friend Twianne. I miss you. You still go with me on every trip. We'll talk later.

To my mother, Dorothy, who at 91.5 years has read all my books for the second time, and who still can find mistakes as I read my new books aloud to her.

CHAPTER ONE

"I've heard enough." Mr. Seligman's voice stopped Tamar Kaplan's aria mid-note.

Tamar avoided the ensemble members' eyes, cringing at the director's brusque words in front of the troupe. She thought she'd done well. Nerves hadn't prevented her from hitting the notes, and her voice sounded unstrained. Maybe her pitch was off.

"Why did you stop her? Miss Kaplan's perfect, especially at this eleventh hour." The producer, Mr. Van Cleef, gestured with dramatic flair. "Look, it's bad enough we have to scramble for a replacement mere hours before the show, but Miss Kaplan knows all of Violetta's songs. With her pure tone—"

The director removed his bowler hat and wiped his brow. "If you hadn't made that comment about Margot's waist being too thick for someone suffering from consumption, she wouldn't have stormed out of here. You know how sensitive she is about her weight."

"Yes, but during last night's performance, the audience snickered at her fake cough. We can't have people ridiculing Margot because she's too portly for a sick Violetta. They were laughing during her death scene."

Mr. Seligman waved a dismissive palm at the producer. "You still didn't have to bring it up in front of the troupe."

"We don't have time to bring someone in from Amsterdam." Mr. Van Cleef gestured toward Tamar. "Miss Kaplan has the body of a ballerina and the face of an angel. Her voice rivals Margot's any day."

Tamar dared a glance at the other members of the chorus. Greta winked at her. Hans quietly clapped his hands. Their support gave her confidence. She lifted her chin, refusing to react to the men's comments, spoken as if she weren't in the room.

Seligman's arms crossed over his ample middle section. "I agree, her tone is pure, but she's missing depth. How can a young woman her age understand Violetta's loss of everything she holds dear—her reputation, her possessions, her love, and ultimately her life? *La Traviata* requires angst, which Tamar doesn't grasp at her tender age."

Tamar tightened her lips to stifle her retort. *Depth? Angst?* How many times had she been overlooked when the producers forgot she *was* Margot's understudy—and brought in someone from Amsterdam? And loss? Hadn't Steffen just broken up with her when he discovered she was Jewish?

"One night, that's all. Margot will be back tomorrow, especially if she's so easily replaced." Mr. Van Cleef took Tamar's hands in his. "Will you sing Violetta's part tonight? Will you make us proud?"

"Oh, yes sir." Her voice rasped, making her sound more like a schoolgirl than a lead soprano.

"Good. Then after rehearsal, you'll need to be fitted for your costumes, dear girl."

Once the men departed, the chorus encircled Tamar. Heinrick's grin spread to his dimples. "If anyone deserves this chance, you do. *Mazel tov.*"

Anna, the head costume designer, squeezed her hand. "Come to my room right after rehearsal. We don't have much time."

Throughout the afternoon, Tamar glided from the stage to the wings and back. The songs came easily. She'd practiced them for months. Mr. Seligman didn't snap or roll his eyes, and Neelie Visser, her favorite violinist in the whole world whom she affectionately dubbed her *tante*, or aunt, stopped her after rehearsal.

"You'll make a beautiful Violetta, dear." The tall, matronly woman's smile was as generous as her heart. She squeezed Tamar's hands in hers.

"Oh, Tante, I'll never take Margot's place."

"Sweetie, don't try to be Margot. Make your own version of Violetta. You've prepared for this opportunity. This is your time. I'll be praying for you." Neelie pulled her into a warm hug, the kind that had brought Tamar comfort so many times before.

Later, Tamar forced herself to stand still while Anna and the other seamstresses hurried to shorten the hems and take in the seams of the five dresses for the performance. She bided her time by reveling in the day's turn of events.

Every singer dreams of this moment. Imagine playing the courtesan, Violetta, at the tender age of twenty-two. If only she had time before tonight to tell her parents and older brother. Of course, Papa and Mama attended whenever they could get away from the jewelry shop, but Seth hadn't come in a long time. He must have a new lady friend. Tamar understood why he kept her a secret. *Eema,* as they called their mother in the Hebrew tongue, would be delighted. She always teased him that if he didn't make her a grandmother shortly, she'd be sure to get one of her friends at their *shul* to find him a nice Jewish bride, one who attended their synagogue.

If Seth did have a girlfriend, though, he didn't seem overjoyed. Permanent lines framed his mouth, adding years to his twenty-nine, and he rarely made sarcastic comments about her wearing too much lipstick or eating too little. Tamar preferred his sarcasm to disregard, although she wouldn't have said the same thing five years ago when he presumed to check her homework, drill her on German conjugations, and make her practice scales *ad nauseam.*

"Stand straight, miss. We're almost done," Hedi mumbled through lips filled with straight pins. "Don't want a crooked hem."

"Sorry." It seemed a shame the three seamstresses missed their dinners because they had to take in Margot's costumes, and surely, she would return tomorrow morning ready to reclaim her role. Then all their work would have to be redone. Tamar would reprise her place in the first row of the chorus, ready to sing the "Brindisi."

Tonight, though, she'd give her all to Violetta.

Once the seamstresses' mouths were free of straight pins, they ushered her into Margot's dressing room for makeup and hair. On any other night, Tamar applied her own greasepaint and styled her hair, along with the dozen other chorus members who competed for the one common mirror. Tonight Eliza, the head makeup artist, created contoured cheekbones and applied a liberal amount of mascara and eyeshadow.

Tamar hardly recognized herself after Eliza eased the raven-colored wig over her blonde hair, and in a second, Tamar's innocent eyes and pale complexion transformed into the middle-aged face of a hard-living woman. So this is what thirty looked like.

"You should practice walking, Tamar. With this heavy wig, you won't be able to whip your head around. Practice turning your whole body instead of just your head." Eliza demonstrated. "Like this."

A stage boy peeked into the room. "Thirty minutes to curtain."

Tamar took measured breaths to calm her nerves. She needed her parents. Eliza was putting her cosmetics into a case, finished for the next few hours. Tamar took a chance. "I have a huge favor to ask. Would you go to my parents' jewelry shop and tell them I'm singing Violetta's part tonight? Their shop is on the *Barteljorisstraat*. Just two blocks past the church—no turns. Kaplan's. I'll pay you five guilders."

"Of course. I can understand you'd want your loved ones in the audience, and this might be your only chance." She moved behind Tamar and smoothed errant curls. "You look beautiful."

Her only chance. Tamar inwardly flinched at the reminder of her one-night assignment. She fished the coins from her purse and handed them to Eliza. "I appreciate you doing this. There might not be time for my parents to make it so close to curtain, but tell them to find my brother."

"Don't worry. You'll make a great Violetta." Eliza disappeared out the door.

With only twenty minutes before she'd stand in the wings, Tamar paced the room. Would she make a great Violetta? Mr. Seligman didn't think so. What was she besides a young *Nederland* girl who lived with her parents and brother? Sure, she could sing, but Seth should get the credit for preparing her for Verdi's aria in *La Traviata* tonight. Did being overlooked seven times and losing her one and only boyfriend create the angst she'd need to rise to the role? The audience would tell her with its applause or silence. Seth would certainly give his opinion—he'd go on and on. And tomorrow's dailies wouldn't mince words about her performance.

With fifteen minutes to go, she focused on her part. Violetta loved fine gowns and threw lavish parties. Eema had rolled her eyes when Tamar had described her.

"What don't I understand?" she'd asked.

Her mother had raised her shoulder. "Violetta's a kept woman, is all."

"What's a 'kept woman'?"

"Violetta lived a life Reb Frankl would disapprove of."

"What kind of life would the rabbi disapprove—oh." Then she'd understood. Violetta was what her mother called a floozy, which was why Alfredo couldn't marry her. His parents didn't approve of her courtesan lifestyle. By the time Alfredo realized what Violetta had sacrificed for him, he found her dying in a paupers' hospital.

Tamar understood Mr. Seligman's misgivings. Margot's sophistication made her better suited to play Violetta. And Margot was tough, usually concealing her soft side, though once she'd revealed it. The two of them had been waiting for the pianist to arrive.

She'd dabbed at a smudge on Tamar's cheek with a handkerchief. "Enjoy this time of life, sweetie," she'd said. "That hunger in your eyes. I remember it well. Time disappears like a feather in the breeze."

Tamar had wanted to ask what she meant, but Margot had roused herself and sailed off, calling for Pippa, her puppy, and the moment had passed.

If only Tamar had enough troubles in her life to communicate the angst Violetta experienced, then the audience would believe her performance. Besides being overlooked for the lead many times and losing her first boyfriend, the only trouble that came to mind was her name. *Tamar*.

Flashes of memories recalled times her name had brought puzzling reactions. Her teacher had covered her mouth upon hearing it for the first time. Tamar had wondered why, but shyness clamped her lips shut. A friend's father had looked surprised when introduced to her. He collected himself quickly, but Tamar noticed. Worst of all, during recess, Hilde had called out her name, and her so-called friends broke into fits of laughter.

That day, Tamar had waited until the supper dishes were washed and dried so she had her mother's full attention. "Eema, what's wrong with my name?"

"Nothing. It's a beautiful name from the Bible."

"But the girls made fun of it on the playground today. Why would they do that?"

"Later, when you're older, we'll discuss it." Then her mother bustled out of the room.

"Ten minutes."

Tamar roused herself. *Look at all the time I've wasted daydreaming.* God wouldn't listen to her—she hadn't prayed in a long time, so why should He? But she had to try. She'd pray for angst.

The audience roared its approval through four curtain calls. At first, her voice sounded tentative, but then Violetta's strong character emerged, and Tamar's voice took on the depth she'd prayed for. She curtsied again and accepted a bouquet of roses.

Mr. Seligman seemed pleased with her performance. A hint of a smile played on his lips. "Well done, young lady. You won over the audience … tonight. Margot is sure to return tomorrow, but next time, I won't forget what you did."

Next time. Warmth flooded Tamar's face at the words every singer in the chorus longed to hear. She couldn't wait to share the news with her family. She hoped they'd gotten to see her Violetta. Especially Seth.

Upon entering Margot's dressing room, Tamar locked the door. Eliza and Hedi would arrive soon enough to help her take off the costume, makeup, and wig. But she needed a few minutes alone to bask in the evening. She whirled as best she could with the wig anchored to her scalp.

Margot wouldn't be happy her understudy dared to invade her private dressing room. Tamar had always looked up to the lead soprano. How could she not? Every little girl in Haarlem aspired to sing like Margot. Hopefully, their relationship, though distant, wouldn't suffer because of tonight's performance.

Tamar surveyed the room—the brocade drapes, the framed pictures of Margot lining the walls, the satin hangers holding her numerous costumes. Now that she'd enjoyed a taste, she wanted the whole dessert. Could she still be happy singing "Brindisi" with the chorus? A twinge of guilt played at her conscience. Of course, she could. Maybe after tonight, she wouldn't have to experience despair to communicate it when parts opened up in the future.

An energetic rapping at the door almost caused her to trip on her way to unlock it. "Sorry." Tamar checked her wig. Still in place. "I needed a minute to myself." She opened the door to the excited faces of her mother and father, flanked by Seth and another fellow as tall as her brother. He'd stood outside her house before, waiting for Seth. In fact, Tamar had lingered at the window many times while searching for his handsome face.

Her mother pulled her into a hug. "Our little Tamar, you sang magnificently. I hardly recognized you."

"With the dark wig and all this makeup on, I don't look like you anymore, Eema." Everyone said she was the image of her mother, blonde and petite. She backed up. "Come in. You may as well enjoy Margot's dressing room. I only have it for another hour or so."

Her father kissed her cheek, his graying beard tickling her face. He was a man of average height, but his jovial personality made him seem taller than he was. "You brought a tear to my eye during that last scene. Wonderful job, daughter. Now, Seth, introduce your friend."

Her brother patted her shoulder. "You can thank me later, sis. All that *solfeggio* came to fruition tonight. Admit it."

She reverted to thirteen and rolled her eyes.

"Well?"

"You were right. I was wrong to want a social life." She remembered her manners and turned to face the bearded man with crinkly-edged brown eyes standing next to her brother. "I'm surprised Seth didn't jump onto the stage to take a bow."

"This is Dr. Daniel Feldman. A good friend to have, I must say, when my head hurts from listening to my sister sing scales. Doctor, my sister, Tamar."

She lowered her eyes for a moment at the sound of her name, then fought the urge and peered up.

He extended his hand. "Call me Daniel. I enjoyed your Violetta very much, Miss Kaplan."

"Thank you. It was a once-in-a-lifetime experience. Literally." A sudden twinge of self-consciousness assailed her, and she eyed the burgundy carpet in search of something smart to say. Everything sounded trite in her head. "How do you know Seth?"

Double trite.

"I met him at a rally. He persuaded me to join the group."

Tamar understood what he meant, at least a bit. She'd heard the words whispered—*the Resistance*. Maybe the *group* was what caused the hard lines around Seth's mouth.

Abba cleared his throat. "Dr. Feldman, how's your internship going?"

"Like a whirlwind, I'm afraid, Mr. Kaplan. Thirty-six hours on, eight off. I'm enjoying my pediatrics rotation."

Her mother's eyes darted between Tamar and the doctor. "Is that a specialty you might pursue?"

"It's a possibility, although I enjoyed the fast pace of emergency."

"It sounds fatiguing to me. I hope you'll carve out an hour to join us for supper some night."

Tamar would have shaken her head if she could've. Her mother's eyes had that matchmaking glint, but this time, not for Seth.

Daniel grinned. "That would be a welcome change from the tepid coffee and stale crackers I've been living on."

Eema linked arms with Seth. "If you could lasso this one to sit long enough for a good family meal, I'd make his favorite cake."

Seth gave her a wounded expression. "You don't have to bribe my friends to get me to sit for your famous *spekkoek*. Her spice cake is renowned in the neighborhood." He winked at Daniel and hugged Eema. "Sorry that I've been so busy."

"What have you been up to, son?"

His features darkened. "Nothing to worry about." He gestured toward Tamar with a flick of his thumb. "Maybe Miss Violetta here could join us for dinner as well. Unless she's too much of a diva to spend time with her family."

"I'll be back in the chorus tomorrow. And one performance doesn't make a diva."

"Good, your head's always been in the clouds. I can't imagine what heights of the heavens it would ascend to."

Tamar hit him on the arm. "Who's your new girlfriend?"

"What makes you think I have a new girlfriend?"

"You're never home. You have *your* head in the clouds. And you rush past me without a word every morning."

"I can assure you, I don't have time for romance. Not with our nation's current situation."

"Oh?" Abba pinched his beard. "I've heard some rumbling, especially at the store. Some of the congregation members have come into the shop, asking—no, begging—me to buy back their jewelry. What's going on that I don't know about?"

"It appears the occupation of our fair country is moving to the next level."

Sweeping his hand downward, Abba shook his head. "Not Nederland and certainly not Haarlem. The German soldiers have been here for three years, but as long as we don't make trouble, they don't bother us."

When Seth didn't answer, their father took out his pocket watch and glanced at it. "Let's talk about happier things. Our Tamar has become a star tonight, and I couldn't be prouder of her."

"Thanks, Abba."

He turned toward her mother. "And what do you think about our little girl, Odette?"

Her mother wrapped her arm around Tamar's waist. "She's worked hard for this."

After a tentative knock, Eliza peered around the door. "May we come in to help you out of your dress, miss?"

Tamar motioned her to enter. "I hope I didn't make you wait." Hedi and Eliza scurried in, their eyes darting from the commanding form of her brother to the handsome doctor. "Abba, Eema, would you leave us for a few minutes while they help me out of this costume?"

"We'll wait outside the door and walk you home," her father said. He nodded once, took his wife's hand, and stepped into the hall.

"We'll let the prima donna enjoy her last few minutes in this room." Seth feigned a weary expression. Tamar would have thrown her wig at him if the women weren't pulling pins out of her hair. "I have to attend a meeting of sorts, but Daniel has also offered to walk you home. Go easy on him, sis."

With Eliza behind her and Hedi to her side, she managed a wave in the men's direction. Through the mirror, the doctor locked eyes with her for more than a few moments before he donned his fedora and disappeared out the door.

What just happened? Was her brother playing *yenta*? With an eight-year age difference, Seth had never shown any interest in her social life, so why now? Tamar didn't have time to process his motives. The main things, though—she got to play Violetta, she didn't embarrass herself, and Mr. Seligman said she had a big future. Well, he hadn't actually said *big*, but he'd inferred it.

Once the cold cream dissolved years of sophistication and elegance and the gowns hung from satin hangers, Hedi and Eliza left her to put on her simple dress. With a furtive glance around Margot's dressing room, she joined her parents and Dr. Feldman outside the door.

Her father and Daniel chatted quietly about events in the newspaper. Words such as *Kristallnacht, pogroms,* and *atonement fee* unsettled her.

Her father harrumphed. "It's been five years since Crystal Night, but that occurred in Germany. I agree it's good to be cautious, but we *Nederlanders* are different. The Reich's not interested in our little country and certainly not in this little town."

Her mother's arm linked with hers. "Enough talk about such things. Let's enjoy the evening and celebrate Tamar's great performance."

The October wind bit through Tamar's jacket. Remnants of autumn's brown leaves swirled around her stockinged legs. She sniffed of the fall's crispness. Her father and the doctor had pulled ahead and appeared to be in a spirited conversation. She smiled at her mother and scanned the area. Most shops along the *Barteljorisstraat* slept, their neon signs turned off. In the morning, the street would be alive with activity once again—basket-carrying shoppers peering into display windows, the mix of cinnamon and freshly baked bread wafting in the air from the neighborhood bakeries, and shopkeepers sweeping the cobblestoned sidewalk in front of their stores.

"What do you think of the doctor?" her mother whispered.

"He's nice." What else could she say? He wasn't a hothead like Seth whenever he talked about politics. Dr. Feldman didn't brag or put on airs, and he didn't make fun of her. Tamar liked that.

"Give him a chance, sweetie."

Her mother stepped up her pace to join the men, who walked at a faster gait. Tamar didn't mind being left alone with her thoughts, although she'd hoped to have some time with Dr. Feldman. *Tomorrow I'll have to face the music or lack of it. Will Margot insult me in front of the producers and the ensemble? Will she insist I be fired?*

"Hope you don't mind." A deep voice interrupted her thoughts. The doctor strolled next to her, hands stuffed in his pockets. He nodded toward her parents. "Three's a crowd."

"Sorry. Of course." Tamar smiled, then veered off the sidewalk when a gust of winter wind blew her sideways. "Did my father wear out your ears, Dr. Feldman?"

He chuckled. "Daniel, please. He reminds me of my abba. Proud-to-the-bone Nederlanders, they are."

She cast a sideways glance at him. "You and Seth are involved in something big, aren't you? That's why he's been so secretive."

"You'll have to ask your brother." The smiling eyes returned. "Let's talk about you. How did it feel being up on that stage? You looked as though you were born to play that part."

"A kept woman—I hope not, Dr. Feldman." She giggled. "I've been preparing for Violetta for the last six months, and tonight I got to play her. Usually, I just stand in during technical rehearsals."

"Call me Daniel, please. You were magnificent. In truth, you seemed so much older and—"

Tamar laughed. "Sophisticated? No, I'm nothing like Violetta. Otherwise, my father and Seth would kill me."

"Seth can be a bit unyielding."

"By the way, I heard you tell Mother about the long hours you work. Do you enjoy it—working in the hospital?"

"Very much. I hope I don't sound like I feel sorry for myself. It's tough, but there's nothing better than helping patients, especially children."

"You have an important job. What's the hardest part, Doctor—I mean, Daniel?"

12

"A child dying from TB or cancer or typhus. I lost one this morning. It's hard losing one so young, even harder telling the parents."

"I can't imagine." They walked in silence for a few moments. "How *do* you tell them?"

"Most of my patients are Jewish, so it's not just the parents— it's the grandparents, aunts, uncles, and half the shul. There's a lot of support and a lot of crying."

They'd reached Tamar's home that looked out over the *Barteljorisstraat* from above the jewelry store. Her parents entered by the side door, but she lingered at the corner, not wanting their conversation to end. "Would you like to come up for some *warme chocola?*"

"Not this time. I have a six o'clock start tomorrow." The wind was picking up, but he seemed to want to stay. Then he shook his head. "I'm sorry. You're probably freezing." He led her toward the door. "This isn't the best time, but I'd like to see you—perform— again."

A warmth filled her despite the dropping temperature, a sensation she'd only experienced a few times before after the stagehand, Steffen, had first made eye contact with her. They hadn't really dated, but he'd walked her home most nights, they'd held hands, and he'd kissed her. Daniel was waiting for an answer.

"That would be nice," she said.

The wind snatched his fedora. When it landed on the street, she dove for it before the hat took wing again, then brushed the dry leaves off. She extended it with a gracious gesture. "Your hat, sir."

With a dramatic bow, he reclaimed it. "Thank you and good night." He walked her to the door and opened it for her.

"Wait." She inclined her head toward him. "My brother. What's he involved in?"

His eyes darted skyward, then he held her gaze. "It's not my place to tell you. Why don't you ask him?"

"He's never home. Could you at least tell me if he's in danger?"

The momentary gap between her question and his answer supplied what she needed to know.

"Times are difficult, but your brother's smart and resourceful." He tipped his hat and disappeared around the corner.

CHAPTER TWO

Neelie Visser placed a pot of coffee and a platter of *boterkoek* in the center of the table. "Eat up, Jan. Your sweater is hanging on you like a tent." She gestured toward the seat across from her. "I'm putting two extra sugar cubes in your cup."

"I'm eating enough, Mam. I've just been busy." He stuffed a bite of cake in his mouth. "Mmm. Still warm. You spoil me."

"If I don't, who will?" She pushed the plum preserves toward her son. "It wouldn't hurt you to come for dinner once in a while. Since your papa died, the house is so quiet." Neelie shuddered. "Too quiet."

"Is that why you bring home every person you meet on the street who needs a meal?"

Neelie lifted a shoulder. "Why wouldn't I? They need food and I need company. It's a fair exchange. Besides, the Lord tells us to take care of the hungry, and there are a lot now with fewer ration cards." She feigned spitting over her shoulder at the thought of the Nazis.

"Your hospitality will bring the Gestapo to the door. How can I protect you when you won't protect yourself?" He stood and took a last drink of his coffee—his dark eyes and features reminding her so much of her Frans. May he rest in peace.

"It's the least I can do for God's people. If everyone took care of the Jews, maybe the SS would leave them alone."

"If you really want to help, I have a suggestion." Her son rubbed his chin just as his father always had when he was considering some new idea. "A week ago, Hitler's people ransacked a Jewish orphanage in Amsterdam. Killed a hundred babies, but we—that is, some friends and I—were able to rescue a dozen. We need to provide temporary shelter for a baby or two until we can find permanent homes for them."

Her hand pressed her chest. "You could have been hurt—you and your friends." She waved a dismissive hand. "It's better I don't know." She noted his stricken expression and framed his face with her hands. "And I am proud of you. You are so much like your father."

"What about the babies, Mam?"

Her eyes lit up. "Of course, it would be an honor. Bring all of them here. My door will always be open."

"But you can't talk about what you're doing. The Gestapo's office sits a mere two blocks away. We can't ruin the work of the Resistance."

"So that's what you're involved in. I had a feeling." She frowned. "They break the law, don't they?"

Jan shook his head. "Whose law? The Third Reich's?" His fist hit the table, making the porcelain dishes jump. When her eyes popped open wide, he opened his hand. "I'm sorry, Mam. But we're not the bad guys."

She studied him. So handsome, so determined. He'd always been passionate about righting society's wrongs. Even in primary school, he championed the underdog. Maybe she needed to rethink things. "This could be exciting. I'll just say I'm babysitting."

"Mam, it's not exciting. It's dangerous. Don't think for a second this place won't be watched. And if they find out you're harboring a single Jew, even a baby, your fate will be the same as theirs."

"What fate, Jan? What has happened to our neighbors? They just seem to disappear."

"Labor camps, mainly, where they're worked to the bone. Just be careful. And I may need you to run messages. People are used to seeing you on the streets, so your presence won't send out alarms. But you can't keep on inviting everyone over to the house. We cannot trust everyone."

She was hardly listening. "You know, I still have your *kinderwagen* up in the attic. Why don't we bring it down?"

Jan fixed his gaze on his mother. "Good idea. You'll need a buggy to transport them. Let's go."

They took the spiral steps to the attic. Neelie was breathing heavily by the time they reached the third floor. Jan opened the door and pulled on the string for the single bulb, which provided a little light in the dark, dusty space filled with discarded clothes and furniture. Frans had always said, "We might need this someday." And then kept everything.

"I think it's in that corner. We haven't used it in twenty years." She squeezed his arm.

He waved his hand in front of his face, sweeping a cobweb aside. "I can't believe this clutter."

Neelie studied her appearance in the full-length mirror on one wall. A few gray hairs sprouted among her dark-brown tresses that hung straight on her shoulders. She always pulled them out. "You know, I'm forty-two. Won't people be suspicious of me, a woman of a certain age, having a baby? Especially the people in the orchestra. What will I do with the baby when I'm at work?"

Jan was busy restacking and moving the jungle of boxes to reach the corner. His head popped up from behind a crate. "Hadn't thought of that. I know you don't like lying. Just say you're babysitting. It's a baby and you are sitting with it." He grunted as he moved boxes. "Found it." He maneuvered the buggy through the path he'd made. "All we have to do is clean it up."

Neelie traced her fingers on its side. "Do you remember the long walks we took in the park every day in this?"

"Um, no. I was a baby?" Jan rubbed his chin, then knocked along the wall by the mirror.

"What are you doing?"

"This room is huge, but you don't need all this space. If we got rid of some of this stuff, maybe—"

"Maybe what?"

"Maybe we could create a small room with a false door. A place for the baby, just in case."

"Just in case?" But she knew. "Just in case a Nazi soldier comes calling, I could hide the baby."

Jan nodded. "If you agree, we could soundproof it. I have some friends who make rooms like this all over Haarlem. I can come over a few nights a week and see if we can make this work."

"And I can fatten you up a bit." She poked his ribs.

"All right." He traced the mirror's edge. "You know, this mirror could be the point of entry. Make it into a door. Nobody'd ever suspect."

"How can they kill precious babies?" She frowned at her reflection.

Jan leaned against the mirror. "They're not all bad. A few German soldiers have come to their senses. They've been a big help, at great risk to their lives. That's how we were able to save some of the orphans."

"I can't believe anyone dressed in those horrid green uniforms has an ounce of goodness in them."

Jan pushed away from the wall and linked arms with her. "I appreciate your zeal, but you must keep your thoughts to yourself, or you could put the whole work of my group in jeopardy. Almost forgot the buggy." He turned and retrieved the carriage. "I'll carry this down."

At the door, he stopped and stared at her, a groove forming between his eyebrows. Neelie, feeling like a scientific specimen, busied herself brushing dust off her skirt.

He said, "Don't be surprised if the baby arrives tonight."

"So soon?" She gasped and restrained herself from looking happy.

"You must control your excitement. The baby will only be with you for a few days while we search for a family in the country. Can we count on you?"

"Oh yes," she whispered, trying not to squeal with delight.

He kissed the top of her head. "Good. I have to get back. Thank you for your help."

Neelie locked the door behind him and fairly tripped over her feet rushing to the kitchen. She talked, as she often did, as if Frans were still there sitting at the table, smoking his pipe. "We'll need a place for it to sleep, and we'll need milk. Wonder if I have enough room on my ration card?" Her heart pounded with excitement as much as from the jaunt up and down the stairs. "I need to calm down. The age of forty-two means I have to watch my health."

Neelie peered into the pantry and the icebox, then groaned. "Where am I going to find milk? The ration card only allows one tin of powdered milk per month. That adds up to less than a cup a day." She could almost hear Frans telling her to drink black coffee and eat dry porridge. A baby was worth the sacrifice.

Hours later, when she pulled down her bed quilt, she heard a light knock on the door three floors below. She flew down the spiral stairs, ran to the door, and inched it open, but only darkness met her. Had she imagined the knock?

A slight mewing drew her eyes to the entryway floor. A picnic basket wobbled. Moses came to mind, but she hoped this wee one was a girl.

The infant couldn't be more than a few weeks old, with a crop of straight, black hair. The baby sucked on its fist with an intensity that made her wonder how she'd keep it fed. The basket also held a bottle and a half-dozen diapers. She hadn't thought about diapers. The washing machine had sat idle since ration cards limited the amount of detergent to a teaspoon a week. So she soaked her clothes in a bucket and hung them to dry from the fourth-floor rear windows.

"Oh, you're beautiful." Neelie picked the baby up and cuddled it against her cheek. "Mmm. I love the smell of babies—talcum powder and sour milk." She put the baby back, picked up the basket, and carried it to the kitchen. "I'm going to warm your bottle."

The baby yawned and its eyes closed.

Neelie rifled through the basket. "I bet you need changing." A folded paper swirled to the floor. "What's this?" She bent and read it. "'Meet Aletta Gochman, three weeks old.' It says you might be cranky at first, and there's a locket with your parents' photos— Moshe and Aviva. I'm going to call you Lettie and make sure your next family has your parents' photo."

She held the bottle under hot running water in the sink. At least she still had hot water. Then she snuggled Lettie and watched her suck hungrily. It had been two decades since she'd held a baby like this. God hadn't blessed her and Frans with another child.

Neelie could already feel Lettie tugging on her heart. Jan had warned her not to get too involved, but it would be hard. She'd heard the rumors. Gestapo breaking into houses of her Jewish neighbors at night, their possessions dashed on the floor as if the Nazi police took out their anger on plates and picture frames. She didn't understand such rage against the Jews. Her neighbors were gentle, hardworking people. Plates and picture frames could be replaced, so long as they didn't take out their anger on the people who owned them, but other Jewish neighbors had disappeared in the dark of the night.

Lettie's eyes drifted closed when the bottle was half empty. Neelie gently laid her in the basket. What an honor it was to care for this little one who was losing her parents at such a young age. If Frans were here, he'd insist they adopt her. And she'd be ecstatic, but of course, they'd make sure the child would grow up fully cognizant of her Jewish heritage. She'd pray that a good family would adopt her. *Oh, baby doll, you will be so loved.*

Neelie laid her violin case across the *kinderwagen*, masking her view of Lettie. It was the only way she could balance her instrument and manage the buggy over the cobblestones. She headed down the *Voldersgracht*, past the dairy, toward the central market where the opera house sat in the shadow of Saint Bavo's Cathedral. Always running late when it was just herself, she'd forgotten how much time it took to get a baby fed and diapered, especially since she had to cut a flannel sheet into squares.

Little Lettie's mewing during the night had kept Neelie from getting much sleep, not to mention the fact that her ration card was depleted, and she needed milk and baby supplies. A bike whizzed past her, almost knocking her off her feet. The church finally came into view, which meant she was getting close. Pieter Post, who was the first-chair violinist, would most certainly berate her for being late. Neelie prayed the rest of the way to work that the sweet music during rehearsal would lull Lettie to sleep.

Once she'd hung up her coat, Neelie flew down the aisle to the orchestra pit. Somehow, Lettie would have to sleep through rehearsal and later, the performance. She found a place near the stage to park the buggy, then hurried to her seat to the left of Pieter, took out her violin, and started to tune it. Pieter was talking to the conductor and didn't seem to notice her tardy arrival. She'd save her apology for the next time.

The tap of the conductor's wand called everyone to attention. Neelie glanced in the direction of the buggy, willing Lettie to sleep.

"Good morning, everyone. Let's get right to work. Last night's 'Sempre Libera' was a mite rough. Verdi wouldn't be happy. We can't let that happen again." He gestured with his eyes toward the diva on the stage behind and mouthed, *she's back*. "On three—"

Neelie's eyes were drawn to stage right, where Margot was having words with the costume director. The diva held up one of her gowns and was jabbing a finger at the waistline. By the stormy look on her face, this wasn't going to end well.

The orchestra made it through the song twice before Margot's voice exploded.

"You altered my costumes? They'll never fit properly again."

The costume manager flinched and retreated a step. Mr. Seligman joined them and tried to calm Margot down.

Music and every other sound came to a stop, waiting for the next outburst. Neelie knew it was coming. Margot had never been upstaged before, and by her understudy, no less.

21

"We had no choice, dear. There was a full house to think about, and—"

She cut Mr. Seligman off. "And I'm sure you didn't let the audience know until it was too late for them to get refunds." Her shrill voice ascended to the rafters.

Lettie responded with a gusty cry.

"Is that a baby I hear?" Margot faced the front of the stage.

Heads turned from side to side, searching for the source. Neelie stood, already cringing. Nothing good could come from this. She cleared her throat. "I'm sorry to disturb the rehearsal. The baby was sleeping. I couldn't find a babysitter at short notice. It won't happen again." She sat, praying for a gracious response.

Margot strode to the edge of the stage, hands on her hips, a storm on her face. "This is a business, *Mevrouw* Visser." The way Margot spewed out her proper name showed her disdain. "You can't bring babies to work. Fire Mrs. Visser or I quit."

Tamar stepped from the back where the chorus stood to the edge of the stage, her echoing footsteps breaking the silence. "You have no right to fire Neelie Visser. Fire me if you need someone to take out your wrath on. Neelie said it wouldn't happen again." She peered at Mr. Seligman.

Pippa trotted to the edge of the stage and stood on her hind legs next to Margot. She barked to get her mistress' attention. Margot bent to pick up the poodle and stroked its fur, her face softening. "That's my little girl."

Everyone but Margot laughed, and the tension disappeared like Seligman's cigar smoke.

"Let's pick up from 'Brindisi.' On three." The conductor tapped his baton.

Neelie positioned her violin for her cue. As soon as rehearsal was over, she'd have to find someone to watch Lettie. Here was another example of her taking on something without counting the cost. Worry crept in. Who would watch an infant while she worked at night? And where was she going to get ration cards to feed her?

Not now. The rest of the orchestra deserved her best. She'd think about it later.

Neelie stood outside Eva van Straat's house, her hands fidgeting. How the times had engendered distrust in neighbors and acquaintances. It was impossible to tell where each one's alliance lay. To the queen? To Hitler's new government? To God's people? Could she disclose Lettie's Jewish heritage to the former harpist who was on maternity leave? She didn't know Eva well enough to know if she'd agree to watch the child twice a day or not. But she'd prayed about her dilemma, and Eva's face had popped into her mind.

Neelie knocked on the door. She'd ask her to watch Lettie for the rest of the week. Jan had said the baby would only be with her until they found a place with a family, and she'd find a way to pay her. With the times as they were, Eva could use the money.

Eva's eyes grew wide when she opened the door. "Neelie Visser, come in. What a pleasant surprise to see you. I've missed the members of the orchestra so much. Adult conversation and all. Please tell everyone I miss them." She looked in both directions and ushered her into her house. "And who is this little one? I didn't know your son was married."

Neelie kissed her on each cheek once they were in the house. "He's not. Meet Lettie. She's three weeks old. I'm watching her for the time being. How are you doing, and how's little Bente?"

"My little girl is a joy. She's two months old on Sunday." Eva ran a finger over Lettie's cheek.

"It's just that these are such hard times. Do you think they'll be over soon?" Neelie attempted to gauge Eva's reaction to the Nazi occupation of their town.

Eva sighed. "Who knows? But enough somber talk. What brings you to my house today?"

Just like a Nederlander. To the point. Neelie swallowed against the lump in her throat. God would help her. She decided on the honest approach. "Lettie's a Jewish orphan seized by the Nazis from an orphanage in Amsterdam. Most were killed. She's with me temporarily. I expect to have more 'guests.' I need someone to watch her during rehearsals and performances."

Eva didn't seem surprised. "For how many days?"

Neelie opened her mouth to say, *for the rest of the week.* Instead, she said, "For as long as it takes, and there may be others after that." She stifled a gasp.

Eva said nothing at first.

Would she call the police? Would she chastise her with the admonishment to obey the law?

Finally, Eva leaned over the buggy and picked up the baby. "You smell so good. Just like my Bente. You two can become good friends as well as the others who follow."

"Then you'll do it?"

"There is one condition. I have a friend, Maarika Goldman. She needs a place to stay for a few nights, maybe longer. Her husband disappeared while she was at work at the hospital lab. She's a technician at the St. Elizabeth Gasthuis. Brilliant, but her head's in the clouds."

"She is welcome. My door is open to all who need a place of safety."

A baby mewed from another room. Eva handed Lettie to Neelie. "I'll be right back."

Where did that boldness to tell Eva the truth come from? She stifled a giggle, a huge weight lifted.

Eva returned, juggling a baby on her hip. Golden curls and fat cheeks. "And here is Bente."

"She's beautiful." The baby wrapped her fingers around Neelie's pointer finger.

"What if the Nazis find out about what you're doing?" Eva said.

Neelie lifted a shoulder. "God will have to keep me from making a mistake."

Eva hesitated.

Was she changing her mind? She'd come so close to a miracle. Neelie's shoulders deflated.

A smile spread across Eva's face. "All right, then. Bring little Lettie tonight." She opened the door for her. "Maarika can be difficult, but she's a fine woman, and she may provide the babysitting for your guests in the future. She lost her job at the hospital at the same time her husband disappeared, so she's grieving, but she'll have time to help you." Eva paused. "I appreciate what you're doing, but be careful. I'll be here for you as long as you need me."

Neelie thanked her more than a few times and shuffled out of Eva's house, then crossed the street to the park and lowered herself onto the closest bench. She grabbed onto the armrest to calm her shaking hands. Resistance work was hard on the heart. When the trembling dissipated, she trekked toward home, eager to share the good news with Jan.

As Neelie rounded the corner at the *Grote Markt*, a melodious voice from behind her caught her attention.

"Tante Neelie?"

She whirled and faced a pretty blonde, so tiny the wind could blow her away. Tamar Kaplan. "Hello there." She adjusted Lettie's blanket. "Thank you for sticking up for me at the rehearsal today."

"Of course. Why wouldn't I defend my favorite aunt?" She leaned over the buggy. "Whose baby is this?"

Neelie almost blurted out the truth but stopped herself. Jan had warned her not to trust anyone. Yet this was Tamar, with whom she shared lunch so many times, and the young girl was so full of questions about faith and God and—how could she not trust her with the truth? "This is Lettie. God is so good. He just answered my prayer so much bigger than I expected."

Tamar ran a finger over the baby's cheek. "What was your prayer?"

"For a sitter for the week. God gave me a babysitter for as long as I need one."

"Your faith is so big compared to mine. I have so many doubts." A furrow formed between Tamar's brows. She straightened and shook her head.

At that moment, two teenagers whizzed by on bicycles, almost bowling them over. They jumped back onto the sidewalk, pulling the buggy close. The large, cobblestoned square, dominated by the cathedral, was full of pedestrians and people on their bicycles, crisscrossing from one side of the road to the other, and the ever-present German soldiers, standing on corners, tapping their sidearms, watching.

"These are hard times," Neelie said. "I understand why the world around us brings doubt, but if you look at God, it's easy. And no, my faith is smaller than a mustard seed." She gazed at the young soprano's pretty face. "You know, I've always loved your name. It's from one of the spicier stories from the book of Genesis. God didn't mince words. I love that about Him, don't you?"

"You love my name? Would you tell me about the original Tamar? I asked my mother, but she dodges me every time."

Neelie pointed at a bench by the church, and they sat together with the baby carriage beside them. "There were actually two Tamars—one the daughter of King David. Her story is a sad one, I'm afraid. She must have been a pretty girl like you. Her stepbrother Amnon became obsessed with her. He pretended to be sick to persuade her to tend to him, then raped her. It came at a time when jealousy and ambition tore the house of David apart, and when the king didn't act quickly enough to avenge his daughter, Tamar's other brother Absalom killed Amnon, which led to a tragic battle between father and son."

Tamar's brows furrowed. "Not only a victim once, but she had to live with her brother's death. How very, very sad. Who's the other Tamar?"

Neelie patted her hand. "Are you sure you want to know?"

"It's time I find out about my namesake."

"The Tamar in Genesis married the oldest of Judah's three sons.

An evil man, he died, leaving her a young widow. Tradition said that the surviving brother had to marry the widow, so the second brother did, but he died as well. The third brother was too young to marry, so Judah arranged for Tamar to live as a widow until the third son grew up."

Tamar crossed her stockinged ankles. "Imagine that. Treating women like property."

"It gets worse. Years passed, the third son grew into manhood, but Judah forgot about his daughter-in-law, so she decided to act. She disguised herself as a woman of the night and had relations with Judah, who gave her his signet ring as surety. Soon she became pregnant with twins."

Tamar stifled a soft gasp.

"When Judah heard that Tamar had acted like a prostitute, he sought to kill her, but when the widow showed him the signet ring, he said, 'She is more righteous than I.'"

They sat in silence, then Tamar cocked her head to the side. "Do you believe names determine character?"

"It seemed to be so in the Bible, but I don't think so nowadays."

"Both women were victims of family members. That won't happen to me, though—not with my family."

Hopefully, the growing threats in their nation wouldn't shatter the young woman's sense of security. Her innocence. Brushing off her tweed skirt, Neelie rose from the bench. "I've only met your parents a few times, but I can tell they're good people." A smile erupted. "Do you want to know something really neat?"

"Yes, please give me some good news."

"One of the twins Tamar bore, Perez, is in the messianic line. What does that tell you?"

She thought for a minute. "That God uses damaged people?"

"Yes. It wasn't easy being a woman in those days."

"Well, I am Tamar, but I refuse to be a victim like my namesakes."

Neelie gave her a hand up. "After the way you defended me today against Margot's diatribe, I can see you're no victim."

"I'm happily back in the chorus where I belong. So … it seems we'll both keep our jobs."

"Give my best to your parents."

"I will. Thank you, Tante."

When Neelie arrived home, Jan sat in the parlor with a second baby.

After parking the carriage inside the door and picking up Lettie, she exclaimed with delight and clasped her hands together. "Who do we have here?"

"Meet Rachael. We're not sure what her last name is. Could you take on another? Just for a week or two."

The child followed Neelie's movements with teary, petulant eyes. She sat on the table between Jan's large, supporting hands, her thumb firmly ensconced in her mouth.

Neelie laid Lettie in her carriage and picked up the new baby. "Hello, pretty Rachael." She posted the girl on her hip and swayed back and forth. "Of course, but I'm almost out of food and milk. Wait until you hear what happened." She filled him on Eva's proposition. "So, I have babysitting help while I'm at work, and maybe even a live-in babysitter if Mevrouw Goldman moves in."

They stared wide-eyed at each other, then Jan said, "It must be God's doing." A crafty smile crept over his face. He reached into his jacket pocket and pulled out a stack of ration cards and fanned them. "Here's six. Don't ask where I got them. They should last a month if you're careful." He stood and stretched. "Well, I'd better get to work."

"What do you mean? I know the Reich closed your college down temporarily. Did you find a job?"

"I'm going to start cleaning out the attic. And no, I don't want your help because you'll want to keep everything."

Neelie chuckled. "Papa was the pack rat. Just save heirlooms and things I can use with these little ones. There should be a crib and some of your baby toys up there."

"All right, Mam. But then I have to start building that room.

You have to be ready to move the children into the attic at a moment's notice. And the fewer toys and children's things down here, the better. Otherwise, the Nazis will ransack the place until they find the babies."

As the clock ticked in the silence, the seriousness of their actions dawned on Neelie. This was no adventure. A glance at Jan's face informed her he felt the same.

"We're looking for a home for little Aletta. It may be a week or so, then you'll be given instructions about where to take her."

Neelie retrieved a blanket from the guest bedroom, laid it on the floor, and placed Rachael on it, then picked up Lettie, who was fussing in her carriage. "I'll miss this little one." A tinge of sadness overcame her. Would she become so attached to each guest that it felt like ripping a bandage off a fresh wound when they left?

CHAPTER THREE

The house was a beehive of activity this afternoon. A new toddler, Sophie Maislin, careened around the room as she perfected her walking. Lettie and Rachael tried to win the battle of the loudest crier. Neelie picked up Lettie and bounced her on her hip while unsuccessfully trying to soothe Rachael with her words. Chaos prevailed. From the empty bottles and scattered toys on the floor to Jan's attic pounding, it was too much. Was she truly cut out for Resistance work?

"Maarika, would you come and help with Rachael? She needs a bottle or something."

"Sorry, I'm busy at the moment," came from the kitchen.

She should have known. While Neelie's maternal instincts were rose-colored, based on raising one docile boy twenty years ago, Maarika lacked even an ounce of doting motherhood. While Maarika pored over medical textbooks she'd borrowed from the hospital library, Neelie peeked through the curtains, wiping her wet face, hoping against hope Maarika's husband would come walking down the street.

The overhead hammering had Maarika shaking a fist at the ceiling from the doorway. "Can't you stop that awful noise? I'm trying to study." Her tall presence and dour expression were more pronounced by the black clothing she wore from head to foot.

Neelie approached her with caution, placed a hand on her arm, then jerked back when she noted her annoyance. "Please be patient, Maarika. Jan is working as fast as he can. It's for the protection of you and the babies."

"I didn't bargain for this when I agreed to move in."

Neelie held her tongue. It had only been three weeks, and they were still getting used to living with each other. She told herself to concentrate on the good things. While Maarika was as prickly as a cactus, her presence did allow Neelie to keep her night job at the opera, as long as the children were fed and diapered before she left.

The unrelenting noise caused Neelie's head to pound. She'd take an aspirin if it weren't for their need to conserve pain relievers for real sickness. "Why don't you take a piece of cake up to Jan? I'd do it, but I can't leave the babies. And cut a piece for yourself." Anything to bring a smile to that stern face.

Maarika nodded and disappeared into the kitchen. "We have enough for a few days, but you'll have to make more soon," she yelled.

"I will." It didn't occur to Maarika to help with the baking though she was living free at Neelie's house. Neelie's growing resentment festered below the surface, but she tried to lighten the mood. "The neighbors must wonder what's going on here." When Maarika reappeared, Neelie put Lettie down and took the tray. "You go back to your studies." She headed up the stairs, which seemed to become steeper and narrower each year.

While the sawdust made her eyes water, and she disliked the noise, Neelie swallowed her pride for the greater good. If God needed her attic, so be it.

Jan was stirring a can of white paint when Neelie entered. Newspapers covered the wooden floor, and masking tape framed the mirror.

"A quick coffee break, son?"

He wiped his hands on his pants. "Thanks, Mam. I'm done, except for painting." Jan motioned toward the mirror. "Have a look at yourself." He stood by the portrait of her grandparents that graced the wall next to the mirror. He touched the top left corner of its frame. The mirror moved to the right, exposing an empty area the size of a large closet.

She covered her mouth. "It's like magic. Like a haunted house. I expect to see Oma's eyes follow me from the picture."

"Yup, like the Mona Lisa. I still have to soundproof the room, then we'll fill it with a crib or two, and I'll see if I can get some powdered milk to keep up here for the babies. Then your job begins."

"Explain, please." Wasn't she already doing quite a job?

"One of you ladies will have to carry the babies up here, and the other will have to remove any evidence of them."

Oh, he meant if there was trouble. "Sounds easy enough," she said.

Jan's dark eyes narrowed. "Believe me, it will be extremely difficult. If the SS officers come to the door, you have to get rid of any remnants of the babies' presence—the garbage has to be emptied, toys have to be picked up—anything that might let them know you're harboring Jewish orphans. They're experts at finding secret places."

"I hadn't realized. What about the buggy and the stroller?" Reality chinked away at the adventure she'd been imagining. In its place, the responsibility of her charges' lives bore down on her. "This is more challenging than I thought."

He took a bite of the cake. "That's a hard one. Why don't you take Eva's daughter for a walk? If you take care of her child one day a week, you'd have a reason for the stroller and buggy."

"This job is growing beyond what I pictured. It's an honor to take care of the babies, but like always, I didn't count the cost. How many more babies will there be?"

Jan shrugged. He lightly pushed a button on the side of the frame, and the mirror slid shut. "Are you ready for all this?"

She nodded more slowly this time.

"At least you have Maarika."

Oh, but did she? Would the unyielding woman prove more of a help or hindrance should trouble come knocking?

CHAPTER FOUR

Tamar stared at the stage floor. Margot was upset again. Everyone in the troupe froze in place, not wanting to draw her attention.

Everything bothered Margot today—her costume made her itch, the footlights provided so much heat her makeup dripped onto her neckline, and the dust affected her high notes. Her manicured finger poked at Van Cleef's chest. "If you don't get this dump cleaned up, you can find yourself a new Violetta."

"But Margot, dear, we brought in extra crew to dust the opera house just last night."

She took a handkerchief from her clutch bag, swiped it over the piano's surface, then thrust it at the producer's face. "See?"

He wiped his forehead with his own handkerchief. Tamar glanced at everyone's faces. The troupe members' eyes focused on Van Cleef. Would he stand up to Margot and risk losing her forever, or acquiesce to her criticism with the promise of a new gown or a puppy? Margot had earned the right to be difficult. The public came to see her sing, unaware of her behavior during rehearsals.

Van Cleef glanced at Seligman, who nodded, his lips tightened. The producer cleared his throat, his face tentative. "The place is as clean as it's going to get. Everybody knows about that snuffbox you hide in the folds of your costume. Perhaps if you refrained from using it, the notes would be easier to hit." His eyes widened, and he took a step back.

Bravo, Mr. Van Cleef. Tamar inwardly clapped and suppressed a chuckle. The producer had said what needed to be said, but this wouldn't end well.

Margot spun as fast as her ermine cloak allowed. "That's it. Find yourself another Violetta." Her voice rose with every stride toward Mr. Seligman. "When I finish telling the newspapers of the dirty conditions you subject your leading lady to, you'll be lucky to sell a single ticket." Then Margot's eyes landed on her. "Do you think this child from the chorus can carry *La Traviata* as I can?"

Tamar clamped her lips closed. As much as she longed to play Violetta, it wasn't worth an argument over dust. If only the trapdoor would open and help her disappear.

"A mere flower—a tulip—here for a few weeks in the spring, then gone." The leading soprano gave a jaunty shake of her head. "Nothing personal, honey, but I give you two performances before the show closes. If you're smart, you'll get out while you can."

Tamar's conversation with Neelie surged to mind. She would not be a victim like her namesake. "I'm no flower," she murmured.

"What did you say?"

"I said, 'I'm no flower.'"

Margot's eyes narrowed, and she circled like a panther ready to pounce. Instead, she turned on the cluster of managers. "And I demand a new seamstress. The little one—what's her name—oh, yes, Hedi. She took too much off the seam. I could hardly breathe last night. Get me a new one or I quit."

Tamar glanced at Hedi cowering behind the curtain. The woman's husband had been sick for the last few months. Despite herself, Tamar stepped forward. "No."

"You really dare to speak to me again?" Margot's eyes shot darts, almost making her flinch and back up.

Tamar swallowed. "Hedi is a wonderful seamstress, and she's worked here for twenty years. Her family depends on her earnings. She deserves another chance."

Loud noises came from the entrance. Footsteps. The doors were usually locked during rehearsal unless the producers opened them to the public for special occasions. Had Margot anticipated today's conflict and brought reinforcements?

"What's going on? Were the doors not locked?" Mr. Van Cleef's arms unfolded, and he strained to see what was causing the interruption.

"I thought so." The harried stage manager rushed up the aisle. When he reached the curtains leading into the lobby, three SS soldiers blocked his path and shoved him out of the way.

With every syncopated footstep toward the stage, Tamar blinked. Tension and fear were palpable in the air. She'd heard rumors, Seth's warnings.

Three men stood at attention at the orchestra level of the stage—charcoal-metal helmets, the SS insignia of a lightning bolt on their collars—all staring straight ahead without a hint of emotion. An officer holding his hat sauntered down the aisle, blond hair, piercing blue eyes. He couldn't be more than twenty-five. A scar sliced his upper lip, creating a permanent scowl. "At ease, men."

"I'm Mr. Van Cleef, the producer. May I help you?" His voice cracked as if he already knew the answer.

"You know of the ban? The Reich forbids further meeting of all groups," the officer said.

"Haarlem's opera company is a legitimate business."

Margot planted a fist on her hip and sashayed forward. "Perhaps you should come to tonight's performance. I'm sure the seats in the box could be made available if you—"

"Silence." The officer's strident tone sliced through her words.

No one in the troupe had ever dared interrupt her. She stepped back. Tamar caught a flash of intrigue in her eyes.

Mr. Seligman had inched backward into the folds of the burgundy velvet curtain, having shed his recent bravado. Tempted to join him, Tamar held her ground. If she remained still, maybe the officer wouldn't notice her heritage.

"This opera is shut down until further notice." The officer gestured with his chin at his three assistants. As if choreographed, one pivoted to the left, one to the right, and the middle officer climbed onto the stage, his Luger trained on the troupe.

"But what about tonight's performance?" Margot asked, clearly no longer concerned with dust.

The officer dismissed her question with a flick of his hand. "You'll have thirty minutes to gather your belongings. This is a temporary proclamation unless you disobey orders." Then he turned on his heel and strode toward the exit.

At least it was only temporary. Tamar squeezed into the single line of choristers, making sure she didn't take up the rear, and left the stage.

Britt, one of the altos, bumped into her from behind. "Sorry," Britt whispered, "gun."

A somber mood permeated the dressing room where they gathered makeup, street clothes, and other personal belongings. Tamar removed her family photo from its place on the mirror. Would this be her last chance to sing with the opera? Due to the town's small size, this was the only company. Maybe she'd have to move to Amsterdam to find work. The thought unnerved her.

The soldier blocked the door, his presence thwarting any conversation. Instead, sniffles and the rustle of fabric were the only sounds, each of the singers silenced by their own thoughts and the threat of the soldier's gun.

Margot's toy poodle, Pippa, scurried into the room, oblivious to the heavy tension. Tamar's breath caught in her throat when the dog approached the soldier and sniffed at his boots.

"Pippa?" Margot ran into the room but stopped when she saw her dog at the soldier's feet.

He frowned at Margot's outburst, then knelt down, petted the dog, and tickled its chin. "What a pretty puppy you are. I have one like you at home."

Margot tittered at the soldier's words, then moved, even sashaying her hips a bit, to pick up the dog.

Tamar relaxed until she noticed the man's sidearm still pointed at the group.

To think that a mere hour ago, she'd prepared to play Violetta once more. Now, in a single pronouncement, she had no job. The other performers dabbed at tears and stuffed cosmetics into bags. How would they feed their children with no income? Somehow, Tamar felt responsible. Because of her people, the Nazis had shut down businesses, clubs, and organizations. Only a handful of the troupe was Jewish, yet all would suffer.

No, Tamar chided herself. Her people had done nothing to deserve this. The SS officers were to blame. Like playground bullies, they'd grown into men who still needed victims.

If justice prevailed in the world, they'd be put in their place before long, and life would return to normal. She almost longed for Margot's whining about dust. Tamar hugged Britt and the others and waited for the SS soldier to open the side door.

As she buttoned her jacket to keep the wind out, Tamar noticed the scrawled sign across the box office window. *Closed until further notice*. At least she still lived with her parents, but were they in danger?

Tamar hurried down the *Barteljorisstraat* to her home, numb from the frigid November wind and from what had just happened.

Until now, the presence of the Gestapo hadn't touched her life. Sure, uniformed soldiers stood on corners of busy intersections, and she'd even noticed the same *Closed until further notice* signs on a few businesses between the theatre and her home but dismissed their closure as due to the economic situation more than the political one. Now, near the end of 1943, she looked more closely at those darkened shops.

She scanned the area for Gestapo officers. Seeing none, Tamar cupped her hands around her eyes and peered in the window of a closed dry cleaner. The counter still looked like it always had. An order pad leaned against the cash register, clothes hung from a circular bar, and the glass bowl sat half full of sweets—the ones she always grabbed when dropping off her father's shirts. A small pile of rumpled clothes rested on the counter as if a customer had been quickly called away.

Spirited away. That's how her father had described the disappearance of their neighbors from the bakery across the street. How she missed the wonderful aroma of freshly baked bread. For years, the fragrance had wafted into her bedroom window each morning until the Betz family vanished one night. In response to her question, her father had explained they were called away by an aunt's death, but six months had passed, and they hadn't returned.

Tamar remembered the shattered shop windows, the flour covering the landing, their cooking utensils and pans scattered on the sidewalk the morning after their disappearance. Her father had said the burglars had wasted no time. Then he grabbed a broom and swept up the debris. She'd believed Papa. Now the truth screamed silently at her.

Six months ago, Seth had started staying out until all hours, and he'd become consistently glum—even more irritable than normal. Probably about the time he'd started working with that underground group she'd heard about from one of the younger tenors in the chorus—the one who'd taken a leave of absence but didn't give a reason. Others put a name to the group ... the Resistance.

Her brother was munching on an apple and poring over a newspaper when Tamar entered the kitchen.

"What are you doing home?" She wriggled out of her coat and hung it on the peg in the closet at the top of the stairs.

He opened his hand on the table. "Can you believe this nonsense?"

"What nonsense?"

"Do you know what propaganda is?"

Tamar plopped down on the chair next to him. "Isn't it a form of advertising?"

"More than that. It's a calculated method of using the media to sway public opinion. This paper's full of lies." He peered up for the first time. "What are *you* doing home? Aren't you supposed to be at rehearsal?"

"The show's closed until further notice."

"The Third Reich?"

Tamar nodded. "We're considered a group, so we can't meet, although the SS officer said it would be temporary."

"So they say." He huffed and threw the paper on the table.

The ticking of the rooster clock was the only sound. Her eyes brimmed with tears despite her effort to stop them. She'd been so naïve to think life was normal when the signs were everywhere.

A tear fell on the corner of the newspaper and widened. Seth's arm circled her shoulder, and she sobbed into his shirt. "Why are they doing this?"

"I wish I could tell you it'll get better, but I'm not going to cover what's happening with sugar like Abba does."

"Tell me."

His lips tightened as he tapped the paper's front page. "This article blames the Jews for the economic collapse in Europe. Prices are high because we're supposedly hoarding all the world's wealth. We're depicted as subhuman creatures, parasites, even. People believe this garbage." He flipped the pages and pointed at a comic strip on the back page. It showed a tarantula sporting a Semitic face.

"Isn't that against the law? Why don't people stop it?"

"It's all about money. The Great War devastated the German economy, and the people need someone to blame. They blame us."

"But it's not our fault." Her eyes took in the kitchen, hardly the dwelling of a subhuman creature. Familiar sights. The smell of polished wood mixed with remnants of last night's herring. The regular drip of the sink faucet. The menorah sitting on the shelf with her mother's cookbooks.

He folded the paper. "It's not the first time." He tapped his finger on the wooden table, then shifted to face her. "I'm not going to lie to you. Things are going to get worse."

Anxiety made Tamar's stomach clench. "Can we go somewhere else? To America?"

His eyes darted around the kitchen. "Can you keep a secret?"

"Yes."

"No, I mean swear that you won't tell anyone. Lives could be in danger if you do."

"I won't tell." Maybe now Seth would tell her what had taken him away so much. "Are you involved in the Resistance?"

"Call it what you want. We don't reduce it to a name. If we did, then it becomes a group the Reich will close down." Seth stood and paced the narrow room, then stopped. "Let me give you a breakdown of what's coming, but remember, you can't tell Abba or Eema. I'll do that when the time is right. They're having a hard time accepting what's happening to our country."

Suddenly cold, she rubbed her arms.

"Are you familiar with the ten steps of genocide?"

"No."

"The first step is classification. According to the Nuremberg laws of 1935, anyone having two Jewish grandparents is a *Jid* even if their parents aren't. So, my dear sister, we are classified as Jews through and through."

She straightened. "I'm proud of my heritage."

He rested a hand on her shoulder. "The next step is symbolization, which means we'll be forced to identify ourselves as Jews."

"The yellow star armbands. Abba and Eema wear theirs whenever they're at the shop or out in the streets, but they told me I didn't have to wear mine."

"Good for now. That gives me an idea, but let me enlighten you a bit more. You've encountered the next three steps today. The articles, movies, and comics describe the Jewish people as animals and vermin, out to destroy the world. And the Gestapo on every corner are examples of a concerted effort to subjugate us."

She shook her head. "Why do people target the Jews? What did we ever do to them?"

"They're not all bad, Tam. I've met a lot of Gentiles who are putting their lives on the line for us. Right here in our neighborhood." Seth adopted the professorial voice he'd used whenever teaching her. "There's one more step I'll mention today—polarization. Soon we'll be forced to live in ghettos."

"What are those?"

"Tight quarters in an enclosed area, and we won't be able to leave to go to school or work outside of the area. It may happen as soon as this week."

Her world was falling apart around her, yet all she could do was sit there, stunned. "Will we have to move?"

"Who knows? Maybe this will become the ghetto since so many Jews already live in this neighborhood, but soon they'll close all businesses and schools."

"And of course, they'll close down shul." Tamar traced a finger over the newspaper. "How are you involved in all this?"

"We help people in danger move to safety."

"Is that why the Betzes have been gone for so long—because you helped 'spirit them away,' as Abba said?"

"No, but it was their disappearance that spurred me to join the underground."

"What do you do?"

"Whatever needs doing." Footsteps and the rustle of paper bags came up the stairs. "Eema's home." He held a finger to his lips. "We'll talk later."

Eema breezed into the room and plunked two heavy bags of groceries on the counter. "There, we're officially out of ration cards, so go light on the milk, Seth."

Out of work, out of food. What next?

"Tamar, dear, put the canned goods in the pantry, please." Her mother whirled to hand the bag to Tamar but stopped mid-circle. "Oh my, you're so pale. Is that why you're home at this hour?"

"No." Tamar sat up straighter and managed to offer a weak smile. "I'm fine. The show closed today."

"I knew it." Eema gestured to the ceiling. "If you'd had a chance to play Violetta for more than a night, the play would still be a hit."

"It's not that. The Nazis shut us down ... temporarily."

"Temporarily? Did they say what that means? A week? Three days? What?"

Seth covered his sister's hand. "Tamar doesn't know."

Eema wrapped her arms around Tamar's shoulders. "I'm sorry, sweetheart. I know how much you love it, but you know, I never liked that opera. Imagine the leading lady being a floozy." Eema put the milk and brisket in the icebox, then lined up three boxes of cereal on the yellow shelf she had added to make the room cheerier. "That cut of meat will have to last all week or longer. We need to stretch it. Who knows when I can get another ration card." Her mother regarded Tamar for a moment. "Now you can help out in the store. It will be fun, you'll see."

Seth stood. "Don't worry about the ration cards. I'll try to get more. Can I borrow Tamar for a few minutes?"

Their mother made a rolling motion with her hand. "Don't tell me where you get the cards. I don't want to know, and yes, you can borrow her."

Seth retrieved Tamar's coat, tossed it to her, and put on his own. "Let's go for a walk."

She felt honored—it had been years since Seth wanted to spend time with his little sister. There was more to the story about his recent activities. Tamar needed to know it all.

They hurried down the outside steps.

"Do you want to go to the park? We can talk privately there." Before Tamar answered, he seized her hand and headed toward the river.

"Slow down," she said, trying to match his long stride.

"Sorry." He released her hand and halted, seeming to study the leaves swirling at their feet. "You asked what I do. Okay, I'll tell you, but you must keep quiet. Promise?"

Tamar held up two fingers.

"The most important thing is getting the Jews out of here before Hitler and his cronies enforce their plan."

"What plan?"

He turned to face her. "To destroy us."

"Oh." She picked up a pebble from the side of the path and threw it at the closest thing—a poplar. Had this whole day been one long bad dream?

"Because I have Aryan features—blond hair, fair skin, blue eyes, I can move around where others can't." He tipped her chin up, forcing her to look into his eyes. "And so can you."

"What do you mean?"

"You look like a *shiksa*. You'll be safe. As I said, they're going to limit Jewish movement in and out of the ghetto soon. You're used to walking the streets without wearing the star on your arm, so you won't be noticed if we should ask you to take a message someplace."

She blinked at him. "Is it legal?"

"By whose laws—the Nazis'? No. But by Nederland's and God's law—absolutely."

"What do we do?"

Seth guided her to a park bench. The wooden boards felt cold beneath her dress. Her teeth chattered despite her efforts to stop them, and she crossed her arms for warmth and comfort.

Her brother's knee bumped hers as he angled toward her. "A whole lot of people are working to find safe places for the Jews until we line up sponsors in other countries. Our goal is to get them on boats to England or America or Switzerland until the war is over."

"How do you find those places?" Just then, a woman walked by with her dog on a leash. Tamar clamped her lips and stared at the ripples of the water in the canal. Normal sights. They waited until the dog had done its business and the woman had moved on before resuming their conversation.

"I don't know how we find places. That's someone else's job.

I deliver messages, find ration cards, and transport people in a variety of ways."

"Such as?" She tilted her head.

"We've moved people in garbage cans, cardboard boxes, and trunks of cars to approved local houses. Then we arrange transportation out of the country."

Like spy work. Tamar's middle tightened. "It sounds dangerous."

"It is. I don't want to forget the risk, or I'll grow careless."

"How many have you saved so far?"

"It's getting colder." He blew into his gloved hands. "I couldn't say exactly—dozens for me, but thousands through the group." With his pointer finger, he lifted her chin. "This is where you come in."

"What can I do?"

"I'll introduce you to my people."

"I don't know if I'm ready for this."

"It could be our parents next. The Nazis target business owners. They come in the night. Destroy everything. Take what they want. And since they think we're worse than animals, you can be sure they won't treat us well."

Once the opera closed, Neelie needed to bring in an income. Since the people of Haarlem could hardly manage to feed themselves on ration cards, they certainly didn't spend money on the extras, so she had to figure out another way to use her skill as a violinist to earn money. Then it came to her—if she couldn't play in an orchestra, she could teach the instrument and do minor repairs.

To drum up business, she posted flyers at the Grote Markt and on church bulletin boards. Every day, she went to a different area to advertise. If she could get three or four students a week, it would provide enough money for the monthly bills. She could teach them at home in the foyer, provided Maarika could keep the babies quiet.

On an overcast Wednesday a few days after posting flyers, Neelie trudged home from the canal. No one had contacted her for lessons or repairs. It disheartened her, but she understood. People didn't think of music when they were living at survival level. Yet she had to keep trying.

She opened the door to chaos. The babies were screaming to be held. Little Sophie had climbed up on the table, knocked over the last of the flowers Neelie had picked from the front garden, and was drinking the remaining water from the vase. And Maarika was playing the piano, oblivious to the noise.

Once Neelie quieted the babies and redirected Sophie, she summoned her patience and waited for Maarika to end the song. "Maarika, we have to keep the babies quiet, or our neighbors will turn us in."

Maarika sprang off the piano seat. "I'm not their mother, and I certainly don't have the time or patience for such tasks when a war's going on. Good day." She stormed up the stairs, slamming her bedroom door behind her.

After a long day of toddling around the dining room and the parlor, Sophie whined, rubbing tired eyes with her fists. How Neelie wished she could take the children to the park to play, an impossible task with the Nazis' daily impromptu investigations of houses in their neighborhood. More and more of their Jewish neighbors' houses were either unoccupied or had closed curtains, so Neelie couldn't tell which ones were abandoned.

What drastic changes had come so swiftly. The sign was still posted across the opera house box office—*Closed until further notice*. How were the others doing? No doubt, Tamar Kaplan was working in her parents' store, but how long could it stay open? So many boarded-up windows. No longer did people stop and chat on the sidewalks. Instead, they rushed past each other, hands stuffed in pockets, eyes straight ahead.

A knock at the front entrance made her breath catch. She closed the kitchen door, hoping the babies couldn't be heard from the dining room. Neelie gulped and opened the door halfway to a man wearing an overcoat and a young girl with braids.

"May I help you?"

The man didn't smile but handed her one of her flyers. "This is my daughter, Ilse. She would like to take violin lessons. Are you the teacher?"

Neelie had to work hard to keep her voice modulated and professional. Finally, a job. Now if she could just convince the babies to sleep on command and Maarika to watch them.

CHAPTER FIVE

Tamar loosened her scarf and let it drape around her neck. A wintry November gust of wind blew strands of blonde hair across her face. She let it. The guards didn't give her a second glance. She hurried toward the intersection that divided the newly formed ghetto in Haarlem's Jewish section from the rest of the town. Solemn-faced soldiers kept traffic from crossing the red line.

Their Lugers seemed larger with every step. Should she avert her eyes or meet their hollow, soulless stares? Best to keep her expression impassive. Seth had counseled her to walk with confidence, not to let the Nazi soldiers catch a whiff of fear, or they'd pounce like feral beasts.

Seth had been right. The changes to her world came with an immediacy that shocked everyone on the Barteljorisstraat. Nazi guards stalked every sidewalk. They checked pedestrians for yellow stars. Tamar kept hers stuffed in her pocket in case someone asked, but no one had.

Her blonde hair and blue eyes allowed her to leave the ghetto with little scrutiny, so her brother had enlisted her to deliver messages to neighboring towns. If the distance exceeded eight kilometers, Seth let her borrow his bike, but she usually travelled on foot, taking the backroads to avoid the trucks full of boisterous soldiers sporting swastikas, roving eyes, and rude comments.

Today's destination—Zandvoort, a seven-kilometer walk in the icy wind. Happy memories of long-ago trips to its beach made the journey bearable. Building sandcastles at the feet of her parents as they enjoyed the newest novels on Sunday afternoons. Summer days lazing next to her girlfriends on sandy towels.

Now, as Tamar approached the beach, she slowed in deference

to its desolate condition. Gone were the sunshine and the joyous shrieks of children. Even the lapping waves remained mute against the seashore, as if they didn't want to draw attention to themselves. Not a single person strolled along the boardwalk. The Germans had demolished roads, taken over resorts for their personal residences, and forbidden access to the beach. Only a lone seagull dared to fly low across the roiling water.

A block from the sea, she pretended to stroll along the remains of the boardwalk. Not an easy task, since much of the concrete lay in rubble. A contact would pass her at the appointed time, pretending to be an old friend. They'd hand off a message when they shook hands.

Her mind went numb. She had to do her small part for the movement, and numbness worked better than dwelling on the danger. Her thoughts reverted to the silent movie filmed on this very site back in her parents' day, *The Misadventure of a French Gentleman Without Pants at the Zandvoort Beach*. Tamar and her friends had laughed so hard when they watched it at the Paathe Theater.

The note, folded to fit her palm, crinkled in her grasp. She hadn't dared to read any of the messages entrusted to her. Just a simple hand-to-hand exchange with the contact. Sometimes the other person passed a communication back.

Enemy eyes watched everywhere, and the slightest false move would arouse the German soldiers' suspicion. At first, her involvement had seemed like an adventure—doing something for her country, for her people. She imagined the messages contained information about available safehouses in the country or directions to hidden boats that would take the refugees to safety.

More neighbors vanished during the night, either by force or by choice. She pretended the events were part of a temporary nightmare, not touching her or her family. Soon Tamar would be back at the opera practicing with the chorus, dreaming of singing an aria—such an innocent fantasy.

Dark gray clouds mottled the milky sky. Funny, how she'd

always thought of Zandvoort as a sunny place—a happy reminder of childhood and family. Now the dark sky shaded those memories. Why did they have to destroy the beach? What possible motive could they have for ruining beauty?

A distant figure approached, hands stuffed in trench-coat pockets, head down. Tamar rallied her spirits, reminding herself of her role on this stage of sorts. If successful, she could save lives and render a second performance. If she failed to be convincing, not only would a message not be transmitted, but her life and that of the contact would be over.

Tamar strolled toward the person, who resembled her brother—tall, in a hurry. Upon getting closer, she recognized the sparkling dark eyes. Could it be?

"Daniel?"

"Tamar Kaplan." He took her hands in his and stared at her. He'd lost weight. Lines framed his eyes. Whenever her brother came home, she'd hurry to meet him, hoping that Daniel stood with him, but he never did.

"What are you doing here in Zandvoort? What about your work at the hospital?"

He shrugged and peered over her shoulder at the billowing waves. "Jewish doctors can no longer work at the hospitals." His hands still held hers. "I heard about the opera closing."

"It's been hard. So you're working with Seth? You're my contact?"

"I assume so, since I was to meet up with mine on the boardwalk." He glanced around. "When there's a medical need, they send me to help, but I can't easily cross ghetto lines because of my Semitic looks." Daniel gestured toward the path, and they walked side by side. For the first time, the numbness vanished, and her heart dared to hope for a normal relationship with a normal man.

"Do you have a message for me?" His little finger intertwined with hers. "It should be the address of the ones needing medical attention."

"I have one in my pocket, though I haven't read it. How do I get it to you without looking obvious?"

"Would you be offended if I hugged you? You can extract the note from your pocket and pass it to me."

"Not at all." Oh, if it were only real. She'd imagined his arms around her since the night he walked her home. When he didn't come for dinner and her brother didn't mention Daniel's name, she tamped down the thoughts as those of a schoolgirl crush. He must be at least five years older than she was. Maybe he had a girlfriend, or worse, a fiancée. Besides, if Daniel had any interest in her, he would have found a way to see her again.

Her arms looped around his neck, awkward and stiff like a preteen at a school dance. "Like this?"

"Yes, you smell good. Like lilacs." His hand moved slowly toward her pocket. "I'm going to take the note." His eyes were brown, smiling eyes that seemed to understand her malaise and sought to make her feel more comfortable. "I've thought of you often."

"You have?"

"If it were a different time, who knows?"

"What do you mean?"

Parallel lines formed between his eyebrows. "We're living on a precipice. Even this. In a moment, we could be hauled away, arrested."

She closed her eyes for a moment. "I need hope."

"God gives us hope—and strength, power, wisdom. He's our hope."

"It just feels like the bad guys are winning. Where is God in Nederland?"

Daniel pointed at her heart, then at his. "In the Psalms, He promises to walk with us through the valleys, but they're still there in front of us, like this place."

The sea wind kicked up, and Daniel gathered her closer. Her head rested against the rough twill of his coat. After a few moments, he gently pushed her away. "We should be going. It's not safe. Would you like to come with me to visit the patient noted on this piece of paper? I don't suppose it would blow our cover, since we're obviously more than acquaintances."

"I have to be back before curfew—when darkness descends around six."

"As do I, but I can use the excuse that a medical emergency pulled us away and you offered to be my assistant. We should go."

She peered behind her. "What goes on in those two white towers? They weren't there when I came here as a kid."

"The Germans built those as lookout posts to guard the sea. You can bet they've got guns trained on any possible enemy infiltration along the shores. They also watch for small boats trying to ferry people out of the country."

At the end of the boardwalk, a weeping willow bowed over the remnants of the pathway, its leaves touching the ground. Where was hope when weeping willows gave up?

Daniel glanced at the address, then pointed ahead to a forest. "It's not a house; it's a boat moored close to the water about a kilometer from here. We'll have to travel through the forest. A young woman due with twins. Do you want to come?"

"Yes, but won't I be in the way?"

"Not at all." He took her hand, and they hopped over felled tree trunks. "These people are looking for a ray of hope in an otherwise bleak existence, so smile, play with the kids, offer encouragement."

"How did they end up on a boat?"

"Probably one of the safehouses. It's becoming more difficult to find places to conceal those waiting to leave the country."

She held her coat lapels together with one hand and balanced over a fallen bough. "My neighborhood is almost empty. What happens to all the families who leave?"

Daniel shrugged. "Some have connections who'll sponsor them in other countries, but most leave under the cover of darkness. Others are forced out."

She feared the answer but needed to know. "That's what happened to our neighbors, the Betzes. Their shop was looted. My father said the place had been burglarized, but I knew better. I saw the word on the sidewalk. Do you know where they might have been taken?"

"Do you really want to know?"

She brushed aside a strand of hair that blew in her eyes. "I'm not a flower. I can handle it."

His lips tightened. He stared off into the distance. "There are places—mostly in Poland and Germany—called labor camps. Bergen-Belsen, Auschwitz-Birkenau, Dachau, Vught closer to home."

"So … it's like serving time in one of the worst prisons?"

"You could say that." They came upon a clearing. He put out an arm to prevent her from moving forward. "I always feel like a deer during hunting season when I come to the tree line." He took out mini binoculars and scanned the area. "I think we're safe."

He took her hand. They skirted the trees until they reached an alcove hidden by a thatch of foliage descending into the water. "Here it is. Ready?" If anyone had been walking by, they would have thought the boat had met its death on a mound of rocks. It looked more like a capsized pile of waterlogged wood than a residence.

The door, concealed by fallen branches, creaked open an inch. Daniel passed the message through the space. The door opened wider.

Peeking in, she gasped. A dozen people sat on the floor in the darkness, reading to children sitting on their laps or resting their heads against others' shoulders. Only the wavering light of a few candles lit the space.

She had to lower her head to fit through the doorway and then stand behind Daniel as he conversed with the gatekeeper. Stale air mixed with kerosene made her eyes water.

"The girl's in here." A man carrying a lantern gestured from a curtained door. Daniel motioned for Tamar to follow. She smiled at a woman nursing her child. The woman smiled back.

The room had only a mattress and a small can in the corner. A girl barely out of her teens writhed from side to side. An older woman wiped her forehead with a rag.

"Bubbe, make it stop," the girl moaned.

"How far along is she?" Daniel asked.

"She's been at ten centimeters for hours, but the babies aren't crowning."

Daniel knelt and checked the young woman's pulse. He pressed carefully on her belly. "We have to move fast." He rose to his feet and whispered to Tamar, "Get me a knife and some antiseptic—alcohol or something strong—brandy if there's nothing else. I'll also need some cloths and fresh water. Can you do it?"

"Of course." Tamar spun to leave. Would they even have the items in such a desolate place?

"And I'll need thread, needle, and scissors."

She rushed out of the room and found a woman with wiry hair in the small galley, rinsing clothes in a pail of gray water. Tamar relayed Daniel's instructions. Without a word, the woman grabbed diapers from an overhead clothesline, emptied the murky water through a hole in the floor, and handed her a chipped pitcher.

"This is all the water we have for now, so don't waste it." The old woman opened a cubby above the porthole and fished out a bottle of red wine from among orange emergency vests. She managed a smile, and with it, her face lost twenty years. "Here's a knife. A little dull, but it should do."

"We also need a needle and thread and a pair of scissors."

"One moment." She limped to the door and motioned to a middle-aged female in widow's black sitting in the corner. "Maryam, could I borrow your needle and some thread and your scissors, please? I'll make sure you get them back."

Maryam's stormy eyes darted from the woman to Tamar, then she heaved a sigh and retrieved some string and a needle from her bra. The scissors came from a pocket.

"Thank you." The woman returned to her pail. "Possessions become vastly important when one has so few." She handed the items to Tamar. "Maryam unraveled a discarded shirt for the thread. Use what you need and return it to her."

"Thank you for your help—" Tamar paused. "I'm sorry. I don't know your name."

"There are more important things than names." The woman patted her shoulder and turned back to her work.

The pregnant girl's face was ashen. She mumbled incoherent words. A woman with a ponytail of gray hair squatted behind her, lips moving with eyes closed.

Tamar knelt next to Daniel, who was taking the girl's vitals. "Here's everything. This is all the water they had, so try not to use it all. And this is the last of their wine."

He glanced up. "Thanks. Would you be up to assisting me?"

"Gladly, but I don't know how."

He squeezed her shoulder. "I'll tell you what to do. You'll be fine." He uncorked the wine, speaking to Tamar in a low voice. "We need to wash our hands, the knife, scissors, and needle. Since water is at a premium, let's pour a splash of wine over our hands, then rinse with a splash of water. We don't want the mother or the babies to catch an infection from us. We'll do the same for the surgical instruments."

Tamar held out her hands. "Are you going to do surgery?"

"I'm going to have to perform a C-section as soon as possible. Give the mother some wine. She's going to have to go through this without anesthesia. I'll ask you to pass me things, and you'll use the cloths to stanch the blood."

He turned to the expectant mother, whose damp hair pasted against her cheeks. "What's your name?"

"Sarah."

"Sarah, I'm Dr. Feldman. Your babies are in distress. We're going to have to take them by C-section. It's going to be painful, but it's the only way. I'll hurry as fast as I can. Do you understand?"

The girl nodded, then issued an excruciating shriek from another bout of labor pains. "Whatever it takes. Save … my … babies."

Daniel addressed the praying woman. "Ma'am, are you the grandmother?"

"Yes, Doctor."

"Will you hold Sarah's hands? Let her squeeze them as hard as she can?"

"Yes." She kissed the agonized girl's temple. "You scream as much as you want, dear one. Don't worry about the others. God is good. He'll bring your babies into the world."

Daniel deftly cut across the girl's belly. Tamar shielded her eyes and passed Daniel whatever he asked for. Sarah's screams were so loud Tamar feared the Nazi soldiers from the two white towers would come knocking on the door.

At one point, when it seemed every child in the small boat wailed, Daniel glanced up at Tamar. "Will you sing?"

"What?"

"It's too tense in here."

Sweat streamed into Daniel's eyes. Why hadn't she noticed before? She tore a piece of cloth from the hem of her blouse, wiped his face, then broke into a rousing rendition of "*Wilhelmus*," the national anthem of Nederland.

A collective gasp surrounded her, then voice after voice joined hers, and soon all the crying stopped. She glanced through a hole in the curtain into the other room. The people stood and sang, placing their hands on their hearts. They faced the same direction, singing with tears streaming down their cheeks.

After the anthem, she sang "*Opa Bakkebaard*," a favorite children's song. Giggles and claps emanated from the other room. Daniel lifted the first baby out—red-faced and frowning. He placed the boy on the mother's chest. Then he lifted the second baby, a sleeping, pale girl. Daniel lightly patted her bottom, but she didn't respond.

"She's choking on amniotic fluid." He used his finger to wipe out her mouth, then patted her back. "Come on, little one. Cough it up."

Tamar's singing trailed off. "What can I do?"

"I have to finish with the mother, or sepsis will enter. Take the baby and pat her lightly on the back like this." He demonstrated. "If she doesn't start breathing on her own, breathe into her mouth in little spurts. I'm going to close up the mother."

The child couldn't weigh more than a kilogram. Tamar felt ill-equipped. She patted the baby's back. *Oh Lord, please, please bring breath to this baby's lungs. Only You can give her breath.* When the baby's lips began to turn blue, Tamar whispered, "She's dying. Help me."

"Breathe into her lips with two little breaths and then depress her chest lightly," Daniel said under his breath. He cut the cords attached to both twins, pulled out something unidentifiable, and threw it in the can in the corner. "Do it now."

Tamar placed her lips over the baby's and blew. The infant coughed and let out a lusty cry. "Yes! I've never been so eager to hear a baby cry." She wrapped the infant in one of the cloths and handed it to the grandmother.

The singing had stopped, but Tamar's heart swelled. *"Gadol Adonai"* surged from her lips. Soon voices joined hers with clapping. Even Daniel sang along while he sutured the girl's stomach. Sarah merely winced, her full attention on her babies.

When the singing ended and Daniel cleaned the area, Tamar leaned close. "You did wonderfully."

"Thank you, but I couldn't have done it without you." His eyes locked on hers. "We're a good team."

"That we are."

"And you're right. You're no flower."

"I take that as a compliment." She took the needle and scissors and rinsed them in a small amount of wine and water, then gathered the borrowed items and returned them to the woman in the kitchen, stopping on the way to hand the scissors, needle, and thread to Maryam.

Tamar hurried back for another glimpse of the twins. The baby girl, whose cheeks had gained some color, sucked on her fist, her face contorting into a grimace, while her brother slept in his grandmother's arms. Not wanting to disturb the babies, Tamar waved at the grandmother, then turned to leave.

"What is your name, miss?"

Tamar touched her chest. "My name? I'm Tamar."

"Then Tamar will be her name." She gestured with the tilt of her head toward the sleeping baby boy. "And this one is little Daniel."

Tamar clasped her hands together. "I'm honored."

"I am too." Daniel moved to the side of the bed and took Sarah's hand. "You did very well."

With one more glimpse of the babies, Tamar followed Daniel to the door.

A wizened man shook his hand. "Thank you for risking your lives to help our Sarah. May God be with you."

Daniel tipped his cap. "It was our pleasure. Tell me, what's the safest and quickest way to return to Haarlem?"

"I'd take to the forest if I was you. Them SS officers are a mean bunch at this late hour. Just follow the path on the left out of here, and you'll hit the main road in two clicks."

"I appreciate it, sir." Daniel took Tamar's hand and helped her onto the path that ran up the hill. They stayed close to the tree line until they reached the other side of the clearing. "We have to hurry," he whispered. "Are you ready for a trek through the forest?"

"If it will keep us safe."

"There may be some bogs. I'm afraid you'll get your boots wet."

"I'm not—"

"—a flower, I know." Daniel elbowed her. "And I'm so glad. What do you think of being my assistant? You have a natural way with the patients, and you're not squeamish."

"I just didn't look too close. Do you think we'll ever see our namesakes again?"

"Who knows? Maybe someday when all this craziness is over."

"And yes, I'd like to be your assistant, but I don't know what I'm doing."

"Did you hear their singing? In a single moment, you changed the whole atmosphere of that forlorn place. I'll never forget what you did."

For the first time in weeks, her heart brimmed with hope, and the buds of attraction grew in her for this man. Tamar peered up at him and reddened when he caught her glance and winked at her, as though she was merely the little sister of a friend.

They walked in silence, attentive to the hidden ruts and branches in the pathway.

A rustle of leaves to their right caused her eyes to dart in that direction. She peered up at Daniel. His eyebrows furrowed. He put out an arm to hold her back. Tamar froze, on alert for further sounds from the thatch of trees close enough to touch but dense enough to conceal anything or anyone.

Another rustle. Squirrels scurry, larger animals trudge, but the start-and-stop sounds bespeak a more deliberate animal—the kind that carries a gun.

Daniel seized her hand and veered away from the hidden sounds. "Time to leave the forest," he whispered, his long strides making her run to keep up. "Just a hundred meters and we'll reach the road."

The rustling matched their pace.

Tamar dug her fingers into Daniel's hand. They were reaching the point where the source of the sound would intersect their path.

Truck lights whizzed past the opening in the trees. If they could make it to the road, they'd be free, but they'd be exchanging one danger for another.

A creature with a panting tongue, huge ears, and light-brown eyes stared at them from the shadows next to the path. Tamar would have frozen if Daniel hadn't pulled her toward him.

"It's just a dune fox. See? He means no harm." He made a kissing sound with his lips. "That's a good boy." The animal studied them, then turned and trotted back into the dark of the woods.

"Wait, I need to catch my breath." She lowered herself to a log.

Daniel dropped down next to her. "One minute and we have to be going, or we won't make curfew. *Canus Nazicus* are a lot more dangerous than dune foxes."

As they followed the curve toward Haarlem, Tamar's heart rate slowed, and she asked, "Is it always so wonderful to bring babies into the world? I haven't felt this good since playing Violetta."

"Most of the time, yes. But I don't just deliver babies. People hiding out have no access to medicine. Malnourished children, the elderly with their chronic problems, and people with fresh injuries need a doctor's touch."

"I didn't think. I'm sorry."

His arm rested on her shoulder. "I don't want you to get the wrong impression. If you're going to help me, you'll see some atrocious things." He paused for a moment. "Do you still want to be my assistant?"

She took a sobering breath. "Of course, and I'll remember our namesakes whenever it gets to be too much."

The lights of Haarlem gradually appeared as they rounded the hill toward town. Tamar checked her watch. Five forty-five. "We have fifteen minutes to make it."

"It'll be close."

"If you look Jewish, how do you get through?"

He removed a card from his coat pocket. "False ID. It says my name is Dr. Witt, but I choose times when the lines at the exit are long so the guards don't look too closely at the picture."

She studied the photo. "There's a resemblance, but the red beard is a dead giveaway. Where do you keep your yellow star?"

He pulled it from his pants pocket. "I put this on once I'm out of the guards' view."

Bitterness at being forced to such subterfuge roiled in her gut. "Don't you just hate them?"

Daniel stuffed the yellow patch and identification card back in his pocket. "Hate isn't something I allow myself to feel. If I do, I might as well surrender."

"But look what they've done to our homes, to our people."

He shrugged. "Someone I respect said, 'forgive them for they know not what they do.'"

Swinging her arms to help her match his pace, she almost stumbled at his reply. "Are you one of those?"

"One of those what?"

"Jews who believe in the Gentile Jesus?"

With a quick glance, he nodded.

"Oh. Does Seth know? He has strong opinions about—"

"Yes, he does. Your brother thinks I'm something between a reprobate and a heathen."

"But you're still friends?"

"I'm still a *Jid*, born and bred, and proud to be one. My family's firmly entrenched in *Yiddishkeit*. He knows that. We just don't talk about my faith."

She stared at his profile, a sadness filling her as hope for a future with this man ebbed away. "How can you align yourself with men like Hitler?"

He rolled his eyes. "Hitler's no believer. None of his followers are. They couldn't do what they're doing and be believers."

"But he calls himself a Christian."

"The monster is a liar and a murderer." He pointed to his chest. "I'm a Jew through and through, but I also believe that another *Jid*, Yeshua, fulfills every single messianic prophecy in the Bible."

They slowed down and joined the line waiting to enter the ghetto. Eight people stood before them. "I have a lot more questions for you later, but what do I say now?"

"Just play along."

They reached the guard station. A portly man in a green coat and helmet stood in the door, barely looking up. "Your card?"

Daniel handed him his. "She's with me."

The man's mottled nose sniffed. "Why are you returning so late?"

"I had to deliver twins near Zandvoort. It takes longer for twins." He gestured with his head toward St. Elizabeth Gasthuis, towering above the other buildings three blocks ahead. "The hospital."

"And this one?" When the guard hooked a thumb at her, Tamar kept her gaze level.

"I needed her to assist."

"Where are your uniforms?"

Daniel shook his head. "Things are scarce at the hospital. We do what we can."

The guard handed back Daniel's ID card. "You may pass."

She let go of the breath she was holding after they moved well past the checkpoint. "That was close."

Darkness was descending, and with it, a bitter chill hung in the air. They headed down the narrow street toward Tamar's home. People stepped into the street to pass them on the narrow sidewalk, then scurried ahead, their yellow stars discernible even in the dark. Bicycles took over the streets. It was rare to see a car since petrol was no longer available.

"Okay, you're officially my assistant. Unless you've changed your mind." They veered into an alley between the two buildings on their right. Daniel pulled her in front of him and turned his back to the sidewalk to block curious eyes. They took out their stars.

"I haven't changed my mind. How will you notify me?"

"Seth will let you know." He pinned her star on her lapel, put his own on, then took her fingers in his. "It's been quite a day. Thank you." His eyes locked with hers.

A familiar voice sounded behind them, coming from the sidewalk. "Well, look who's hiding in the shadows." Margot had entered the alley and stood smiling, arms linked with an SS officer's. "If it isn't the little chorus girl who tried to replace me."

Tamar pulled her hands away and hid them in the folds of her coat. "How have you been, Margot?"

The woman's rheumy eyes studied her, an ermine stole hanging loose around her jewel-bedecked neck. "Never been better. Who's your boyfriend?"

"This … is … Daniel." Tamar stared at her shoes. "Margot's the principal soprano at our opera company."

"You bet. I was the best Violetta they ever had, but they didn't appreciate me, and now who knows if I'll ever get a chance to sing again?" She glanced at the yellow star on Tamar's lapel for the first time, then her manicured finger bore into Tamar's chest. "Look what we got here. One of those … those—what did you call them, Heinz?"

The officer's nostrils flared over his bushy, graying mustache. "Vermin." He feigned an exaggerated chill.

Margot cackled, her voice loud. "They're the reason the opera closed down." She flicked her fingers as though ridding herself of debris. "It's starting to smell around here. Thanks for the tour around the ghetto. Now let's go get a drink." Tossing her curls, she whirled around and linked arms with the officer.

Tamar took a step back and bit her tongue to keep quiet. When Margot and her escort had flounced past, she looked up. "I want to wipe that fake beauty mark off her cheek. How could that woman lower herself to date a Nazi? Even for Margot, that was a descent."

Daniel glanced after the couple. "They're loaded."

"What do you mean?"

"They take whatever they want when they break into stores and houses."

"A bunch of thieves."

Daniel's eyes narrowed. "You've got quite a temper. That could get you in trouble. Be careful, Tamar."

The softness that remained in his expression communicated concern rather than anger, but Tamar's sense of justice flared. How could he criticize her and not them? "It's so wrong. How can you stand by and not get angry?"

He shrugged. "I get angry, too, but I try to channel it into positive avenues." His hand pressed on her back, reminding her of the time. "I'll walk you home."

The cathedral, St. Bavo's, appeared abandoned, and the market square stood empty except for a dog sniffing through trash dumped in the gutter. Nederland people prided themselves on cleanliness. Colorful pots of flowers used to bloom from balconies, windows, and front entries. Now the fetid smells in the air made Tamar sick to her stomach.

"Can you believe how everything has fallen apart in just a few weeks? Why don't we stand up for ourselves?"

"We're outnumbered, but our time will come."

"Do you believe that?"

"I do. The Jews have been down many times. We always come back, in God's time."

Daniel's unfailing patience was beginning to grate on her nerves. "God's time? Why doesn't He protect us now?"

Daniel didn't answer. The only sound was the echo of their boots on the cobblestones, accentuated every so often by distant gunshots.

CHAPTER SIX

Tamar wriggled into the white pinafore, three sizes too big for her small frame, then pulled the sash taut around her waist. With a mouthful of bobby pins, she anchored the white cap on her head. Daniel had said it was time to dress the part, and he'd managed to find her a nurse's uniform. Tamar held back her questions. With the few minutes she had left, she primped before her bedroom mirror.

Seth made her so mad. He'd mentioned this morning between bites of porridge that Daniel needed her to accompany him to Bloemendaal for a medical visit and would pick her up at seven-thirty.

She'd slapped his arm. "Why didn't you tell me earlier?"

He'd shrugged and continued to read the newspaper. "Slipped my mind."

Slipped my mind? Thirteen minutes to get ready for Daniel.

With renewed vigor, she brushed her teeth, then glanced at her reflection one last time. The long treks to deliver messages and assist Daniel had given her cheeks a healthy glow. She dabbed her mother's *Coque D'or* behind her ears just in case, then berated herself. Now wasn't the time to focus on the crush she had on the doctor. Not with the country on a precipice.

She grabbed her cape and bounded down the stairs toward his knock. She hoped today's trip would be more pleasant than the one to help the man with the gangrenous toe. The memory brought shivers—more from the procedure than the toe itself. Without anesthesia, Daniel had amputated it while the man clenched her arm. Only now, two weeks later, were the bruises from his fingers starting to fade.

She opened the door to Daniel's handsome face. "Good morning, Doctor."

"Good morning to you. It's a brisk one, but the sun will make our three-kilometer jaunt pleasant." He offered his elbow. "My lady?"

For all his good-natured chivalry, Tamar still didn't know where she stood with him. Sometimes, it was hard being a female, having to wait for a man's advances, which with Daniel had amounted to none. She donned her light and airy face. "So … who do we visit today?"

"All I know is, the family has a lot of children." He surveyed the cloudless sky. "Isn't it a glorious day?"

Tamar sniffed. "It even smells good." She remembered herself as they neared the guards and slowed. One of these days, they'd figure out the picture on her new identification card appeared at least twenty years older than she. In the years past, before Nazi soldiers goose-stepped past her parents' shop, Tamar would have prayed the guards wouldn't notice the difference, but God seemed too distant. Maybe He had abandoned Nederland.

Daniel must have read her thoughts because he squeezed her hand. "God will see us past the guards. He has every other time."

Tamar gulped down her fear and kept her eyes lowered, then handed the guard her card. Daniel had told her people lost their ability to see individual identities when they wore uniforms, so she needn't worry about the guard noticing the twenty-year difference.

The guard whisked them through with a perfunctory glance. Once beyond sight of their station, her shoulders relaxed, her steps became lighter, and laughter came easy. They followed the canal to the outskirts of Haarlem, and soon neat and tidy farms replaced the suburbs, although weeds overtook some properties.

Tamar inhaled deeply of the alfalfa and clover. "Tell me about your childhood, Daniel. Why did you become a doctor?"

"Nothing much to tell. I grew up in Santpoort-Zuid, not too far from Haarlem. My father is a country doctor. When I was a kid,

I accompanied him to the hospital on weekends when he made his rounds. I've wanted to be a doctor since childhood because of those trips. My sister, Ana, always went with my mother to her work. She volunteers as a docent at the Brederode Castle. Do you know it?"

"Of course. In primary school, we visited there on a field trip. It's a ruin, isn't it?"

"Yes. My mother usually works in the gift shop or the ticket office but is often called upon to lead tours." He grinned at her. "See? We were meant to meet."

Warmth trickled through her like sweet syrup. What did he mean by that? She peered up at him. "How old are you?"

"Twenty-five. What about you?"

"Twenty-two. I thought you were my brother's age. He's eight years older than I."

"I'm not ready for the grave yet." He took her hand, and in that single move, everything changed. Gone was the wondering, the uncertainty. Had she not been held to the ground by that hand, Tamar would have floated away like a balloon in the wind.

"By the way, my brother forgot to tell me about today's assignment. I didn't know until thirteen minutes before you arrived."

"I wish they hadn't taken away our telephones. There's no other way except to go through Seth, and he has bigger things on his mind."

They passed a lonely looking windmill on the road to Bloemendaal. It saddened her to see these landmarks in such a state of disrepair. "I remember this town. My family and I spent an afternoon at the beach and went sailing."

"You have a wonderful family."

"I do, but they shelter me too much, and I'm not a flower that needs to be protected."

"If you were, you'd be the hardiest flower ever smelled, like a *muscliola*."

"There's no such—" She slapped his arm. "You're mocking me."

66

"I wouldn't dare." He removed two protective masks from his pocket when they reached the town limits. "I'm not sure what's awaiting us, but if this family has a lot of children, I don't want us to catch a virus." He glanced at the address. "Bloemendaal looks like a ghost town, except for the intruders." A Nazi motorcycle flanked by a sidecar zipped past. "Keep your head down. They'll be watching us."

It became tedious to have to act whenever they were out in public. But difficult times trumped personal well-being. They arrived at a three-story residence, the once-bright paint on its façade fading like the rest of the town. Daniel knocked lightly. The door inched open to reveal the lined face of a man too young to have wrinkles.

"Come in, Doctor."

A small candle lit the darkened room. The high-quality furniture showed signs of wear, though its former glory shone through the patina and scratches. The candle's flicker showed a mother holding a coughing toddler. Two small girls wrapped in blankets shared the sofa. They coughed as well.

The woman slowly rose and shuffled over to join them at the door. "Thank you for coming so quickly. We didn't know what to do, seeing as we can't take the children to the hospital."

Daniel felt the child's forehead. "He has a fever. What seems to be the problem?"

Dark smudges appeared under the mother's bloodshot eyes. Her pale face and thin hair showed a woman who needed care herself. "It started over a week ago with chills and fevers for all three kids. I assumed they'd come down with the flu because they were nauseous, complained of headaches, and lost their appetites. But when rashes broke out on their chests, well—" She shrugged. "We can't take them to the doctor. We'll be arrested if we do."

"Let me have a look."

The woman laid the child on the dining room table, which made him cry. "Please, David, this is a doctor. He's going to make you feel better." She pulled up the boy's shirt to reveal spots covering his stomach.

Daniel remained quiet as he listened to the boy's chest, checked his ears, and felt his glands, then he pulled the child's shirt down and covered him with the blanket. "Could I examine your daughters?"

"Of course," the father said and gestured toward the sofa. "Can we get you something to eat or drink? I'm sorry we don't have any way to pay you." His eyes reddened. "We've always paid our way, but now with no income, and not even able to walk down our streets—"

"Don't worry about the money." Daniel pulled the mask from his pocket and put it over his mouth, kneeling by the sofa. "Tamar, put your mask on."

Taking a tiny step forward, the mother twisted her hands together. "What is it, Doctor?"

Daniel peered up at the woman. "Give me a minute to check the girls, then we'll talk."

He felt the girls' foreheads, then lifted their shirts.

Why didn't he say something?

He rose to his feet, then approached the parents, looping his mask over his wrist. "At first, I thought the children had a simple case of measles, but because the chills and fever and other symptoms preceded the rash by more than a week, it's possible the kids have a form of typhus."

"Typhus?" the mother gasped. "That's deadly, isn't it?"

"It can be, but children have a way of rebounding more quickly than adults, which means you'll have to wear these masks until their symptoms are gone." He handed his to the father and indicated Tamar should give hers to the mother.

She accepted it with solemn thanks. "But how did they catch it? We haven't been out of the house in a month."

Daniel shook his head and sighed. "It's borne by insects— mainly ticks, mites, and lice." He touched the mother's arm. She averted her eyes. "It's not your fault. Since the sanitation system in town is not working, these infestations find their way into homes."

The father coughed. "What can we do for our children?"

"I brought a small amount of tetracycline. It's not enough for three children, but it will have to do. Keep them comfortable, and the symptoms should abate in a few days. But it would be best to boil your clothes as well as the bedding."

The mother lifted her palms toward the ceiling. "They turned off our electricity. The only thing we can do is heat water over the fire, but smoke from the chimney will draw the attention of the German police. They've already taken our neighbors." She stared at the girls now sleeping on the sofa. "What would happen to these little ones?"

"I understand." Daniel glanced at Tamar, the agony on his face confirming that he'd run out of answers. Except one. "Could we pray with you before we leave?"

The man took the prayer shawl from the sideboard and covered his head. Daniel covered his head with his hand, then prayed for healing and protection for the family. Did Tamar imagine it, or did a sense of peace descend in the dimly lit room?

"Thank you, Doctor. From your lips to His ears." The father inched open the door, glanced in both directions, then opened it wider. "One can never be too careful."

Conversation lulled on their way back to Haarlem. It seemed as though everything in their lives was on hold. Like the little boy in the legend, her people were trying to stem the deluge of water by poking fingers into holes in the dikes. But how long could they keep that up? Daniel was right. They were standing on the edge of a precipice with no hope of rescue in sight.

"Daniel, is there any end to this?"

He rested his arm on her shoulder. "Honest answer? Not for a long time—years, maybe. And we haven't seen the worst."

"That's what Seth says all the time."

"There will come a time when we'll have to move like the others."

She stopped walking and faced him. "How long do we have?"

"A month, weeks, days."

"I … I don't think I can—" She stifled a chill.

He pulled her close, tipped her chin up, and met her lips with his. For a few moments, Tamar lost herself in the sanctuary of his gentle touch, the warmth of his coat, the security of his arms.

The low rumble of an approaching motor brought her back to the stark street. She peered over his shoulder and stiffened. A Nazi soldier pulled his motorcycle to a stop next to them. An SS officer seated in the sidecar trained a Wehrmacht's rifle at Daniel's back.

"Uh-oh," she whispered and stepped back. Her heart thudded.

"Your papers," the driver ordered.

"Yes sir." Daniel removed his hospital identification card from his pocket. She did the same. The driver handed them to the officer, whose cigarette dangled from thin lips.

"Dr. Witt, I didn't realize the hospital in Haarlem did house calls this far away. Perhaps I should call them."

"If you must, but this has nothing to do with the hospital. We—"

Tamar glanced at Daniel. Would he tell them about their secret mission?

"Enough talk. Witt. A German name. *Sprechen sie Deutsch?*"

"*Ya, ich spreche Deutsche.*" Tamar caught the gist of their conversation. She'd have to thank Seth for drilling German vocabulary into her. They talked about the weather and the local economy, and Daniel seemed to have no difficulty keeping up.

"Well, Dr. Witt, your German is better than most, but you speak with a low-Dutch accent."

"My mother's from the lowlands."

The officer eyed Tamar. "And your girlfriend? Does she speak German?"

Daniel seized her hand. "*Meine freundin …*"

"*Ich spreche ein bisschen,*" Tamar managed through dry lips. Keeping her face impassive and her posture ramrod-straight, Tamar looked him straight in the eyes. She had the impression the officer batted them around like a cat paws a mouse.

The man's smile exposed a gap between his teeth. "Very good." His gaze shifted back to Daniel. "I'm surprised, Doctor. I haven't seen you at St. Elisabeth Gasthuis. What department do you work in?"

"I'm completing my residency in pediatrics."

"Ah. Well, my advice to both of you is to stick closer to home. The next one of my colleagues might not be so tolerant of high school German. Good day." The man returned their papers, touched the brim of his hat, and left in a cloud of smoke and dust.

Tamar stood silent, shaken to the core. Daniel took her hand. "Come. We should heed the man's advice."

They headed toward Haarlem, passing kilometers of nature's unspoiled fields, now turned yellow with the approaching winter. The air was crisp, but the sun warmed their pathway. A cow stared at them from the other side of a wire fence.

"I don't think I've ever been so scared, but you didn't seem nervous at all."

Daniel's face twisted. "I hate lying."

"About your mother being German and working at the hospital?"

"All half-truths. My mother is partly German, and I'm still assigned to the hospital, but I'm definitely not Peter Witt." He grinned at her. "And I told the man you were my girlfriend."

"I heard you."

He squeezed her hand. "What do you think?"

"About what?" She could feel a smile playing on her lips.

"About being my girlfriend?"

"I thought you weren't interested, since we're living on the edge of a precipice."

"'Beauty out of ashes.'"

"Now I'm confused."

His arm went around her waist. "It's one of the promises I

cling to—to bring beauty out of ashes. Something wonderful out of the despicable."

"Ah. I like that, but if God can do anything, why doesn't He stop this madness?"

Daniel shrugged. "He didn't create us to be robots, like the one in the German film, *Metropolis*. He created us with the ability to choose, so even though I'd like the Nazis to jump into a grave and bury themselves alive, I have to concede their choice to do evil."

"I don't think I could ever tolerate evil."

He frowned at her. "I don't tolerate evil. But if it's between being a robot with no freedom of choice or a person with a free will, I choose free will every time."

Her thoughts jumbled from thinking so much. "I still don't understand, but I love the poetic feel of beauty from ashes, and yes, I'd be honored to be your girlfriend for whatever time we have left on this precipice."

They locked eyes. She loved how his crinkled—laughing eyes, kind eyes.

At the guard's gate, they joined the line. To quell her nerves, she whispered the question that had bothered her. "Isn't it okay to lie to certain people?"

"Like whom?"

She nodded toward the front of the line. "My father used to put a sign up in the jewelry store's window—*Beware of Dog*—but we didn't have a dog. Abba said it's okay to lie to burglars."

He shrugged one shoulder. "We have to be true to our conscience. By the way, where'd you learn German?"

"From Seth. I wanted to take French because my mother comes from Belgium. That's where I get my blonde hair and blue eyes. Her first language is French, so she made sure we spoke French at home when we were young, but Seth insisted I learn German. It's almost as if he had a premonition about this." Tamar motioned to the guard who questioned the couple in front of them. Once they made it through, she blew out a breath. "Whew. I don't know how many of those interrogations I can endure before I crack."

"Me too. You were saying about the premonition?"

Tamar sighed. "It just seems as though Seth has been preparing me for the last few years. Since Germany invaded Poland at the start of the war. It's as if he knew Nederland's time was coming, and he wanted me to be equipped."

"Seth's a wise man. He's rescued a lot of people." Daniel ran his fingers through his hair and checked his reflection in a window. "Are your parents at home?"

"They should be. Why?"

"If we're going to be courting, I'd like to get their blessing."

She smiled. Beauty for ashes.

Shattered glass on the sidewalk in front of the shop told her there'd be more ashes. Tamar raced inside to the crunch of showcase glass under her feet. "Eema, Abba?" Chaos. The effects of sheer rage. Overturned tables. Someone had taken a blunt object to the glass counters and grabbed the rings, watches, and necklaces. The cash register drawer sat open—empty.

"Mother? Where are you?" Desperate and high-pitched.

The halls echoed her words.

She trembled. Daniel's concern showed in his eyes. Tamar didn't want concern; she wanted her life back. "Where did they take them?"

When he didn't answer, she rushed up the steps. "Are you up here? Answer me. It's Tamar."

The kitchen, untouched, looked as it had this morning. Seth's porridge bowl sat in the sink, and her mother's red lipstick smudged the rim of a coffee cup. Normal things.

Daniel gently squeezed her shoulder. "We have to go."

"I can't leave. What if they come back, and I'm not here?"

"You can bet the soldiers will return for the remaining jewelry.

Grab a small bag and put a few things in it. We'll take what jewelry's left. It's yours by rights."

"You don't think my parents will be back?"

"No, and they'd want you to take what's left in the store. It might come in handy."

Tamar scanned the kitchen and other rooms for anything of value and grabbed the framed picture of her grandparents. She entered her parents' bedroom. Her mother's brush set. Her father's pipe. She needed tangible mementos. She gathered the items in one place on the bed, unable to decide. Maybe this was all a big mistake and her parents would return tonight. She grabbed a suitcase from the closet and placed the items in it.

Daniel waited by the bedroom door, and she turned to him with a misty gaze.

"Where will we go?"

"We need to avoid the main street, so we'll stick to the alleys. We'll go to my place and make a plan." He stared at her, his voice calm and his gaze full of sympathy, but his posture and the way his eyes darted to the hall bespoke urgency. "Do you have a bag for me to collect what's left downstairs?"

Tamar ran into her brother's bedroom and returned with a canvas bag, which she handed him, then let her arms drop to her sides. "Could you carry my suitcase into my room? I'll collect my toiletries. There's so much stuff up here. I don't know what to take and what to leave."

"Hurry. The looters will be back." Daniel grabbed her suitcase, then his footsteps clattered down the stairs, followed by clinking and clacking as he presumably packed what remained of the jewelry.

Her feet refused to move. Where was Seth? Were her parents still alive? Dread rooted her to the spot.

Daniel's voice rose from the floor below. "Tamar. We have to go."

She roused herself and ran to her room to find the suitcase open on her bed. She threw a dress, her nightgown, and a few pairs of underclothes into it, then closed it up and shouldered a warm coat and her purse. With a last tearful look, she grabbed a much-loved stuffed bunny from her childhood and hurried down the stairs, the suitcase banging against the wall with every step.

CHAPTER SEVEN

The early afternoon wind, invasive and bitter, numbed Tamar's limbs. Daniel carried her suitcase and the heavy bag of jewelry, letting her grip her purse and her bunny. He'd glanced at it and rolled his eyes, then smiled.

As they'd set out, he'd said a quiet and quick prayer for protection for her parents … and for them. They kept to the alleys and small lanes—he appeared to know them all. Tamar said little. She drifted behind him, imagining the worst scenarios for her parents.

Finally, she moved beside him and whispered, "Do you think they're at the Gestapo station? Tell me the truth."

His mouth worked before words came out. "They may be, or they may have already been sent to a different location."

"Where?"

He shrugged. "A transit camp—Vught, Amersfoort, Westerbork. They'll stay there temporarily until space opens up in another camp."

"And then what?"

"Hopefully, the queen will return and rescue the people from the camps. Until then, we'll pray that God puts a hedge of protection around your parents."

"What good will it do to pray if they're already there? Isn't it too late?"

"Worry won't help. God's power is bigger than the Nazis'. You watch what He does for His people."

Tamar peered up at Daniel's face. If only she could borrow his faith and cover herself with it like a shield. He leaned toward her, a line forming between his eyebrows.

"Everything will work out. Just watch."

When they reached an intersection, Daniel blocked her while he peeked around the corner of a brick bank. The rising-pitched roar of airplanes followed by sporadic bombs sounded in the distance. The smell of garbage wafted on the alley air. Tamar covered her nose with the crook of her arm. He motioned for her to hurry across the small street to the alley on the opposite side.

She'd never been to his apartment. What would her father say? Would she ever hear her abba's voice again? All she wanted was a quiet place to sleep and forget this day had ever happened.

A voice called out.

No! Already caught. Too late.

She swiveled on her heels. Daniel gripped her sleeve. "Pretend you didn't hear. Keep going."

"Tamar?" That voice again. Familiar. She whirled toward it, and a figure rounded the intersection they'd just passed.

"Tante Neelie." With a sigh of relief, she ran toward the middle-aged woman and threw her arms around her neck. "My parents are gone. The shop raided. What am I going to do?"

The woman rubbed her back and brushed the hair away from her cheeks. "Oh, dear girl, dear girl." She enveloped her in her arms and prayed softly.

Daniel interrupted. "We have to get out of the street."

Neelie stiffened. "Who is this young man?"

"Daniel Feldman. He's a doctor and … my friend." Tamar calmed her quivering lips and managed a weak smile. "Daniel, this is Neelie Visser. She's not really my aunt, but I've always called her Tante Neelie. She played the violin at the opera, and we ate lunch together almost every day."

Neelie thrust her hand in Daniel's direction. "Are you one of God's people?"

He removed his hat and shook her hand. "That I am."

Her gaze darted between them. "Then you're in danger too."

"Yes." Frown lines furrowed between his eyes. "We have to go into hiding."

"I know a place where you two will be safe. Come. Follow me." Neelie spun and scurried across the street. "We'll stay in the alleys. Don't worry. Watch and see what our Father does."

Daniel's eyes widened. "Double witness," he whispered as they crossed the street.

"What's a double witness?" Tamar asked.

He shifted her suitcase to his other hand and hoisted the bag of jewels over his shoulder. "Weren't we just talking about seeing what God does? Then this woman says the same thing. Double witness. Jewish law requires two witnesses. See how quickly He answered?"

Tamar nodded, but she still had her doubts. Wasn't God too detached or otherwise busy to give them a *double witness*, as Daniel called it, when bombs were going off and her parents were missing?

As they hurried after Neelie, Daniel murmured, "Tell me about Mevrouw Visser."

"Tante Neelie is a widow. Her husband was our orchestra's pianist, but he died a year ago. It's been hard for her. She seems to be in touch with God more than others, and I love talking to her."

Surprisingly swift and silent, with frequent glances over her shoulder, Neelie stayed a half a block ahead. When they caught up, Daniel lowered the suitcase and the bag of jewels and wiped his forehead. "Stop, please. Where are you taking us, Mevrouw Visser?"

"It's not too much farther. And call me Neelie." She glanced at Tamar. "While you catch your breath a moment, tell me what happened."

"We returned from a short trip to Bloemendaal, and—"

"How did you get past the guards?"

Tamar shot Daniel a questioning look. Seth had said they shouldn't trust anyone, even neighbors. Yet Tante Neelie was different. She talked about God as if He stood right next to her.

Tamar had to trust someone. When Daniel nodded, she released a tremendous sigh and answered. "We have fake identification cards. Daniel makes medical visits out of town. I help as best I can."

"I see. So you returned and—?"

"The door to the shop was wide open. Broken glass everywhere. Displays shattered and most of the jewelry stolen. The word *Jood* was written across the sidewalk in front of the shop."

"And your parents were gone."

Her voice failed. She nodded.

"Well, dearest, we'll do our best to keep you and your young man safe. That's what they would want." Tante Neelie waved them forward again.

The cold wind sprinkled rain on their path. Tamar tucked her stuffed bunny inside her coat. If the Nazi soldiers saw a tall man carrying a suitcase, flanked by two women, they'd surely arrest them on the spot. She shuddered. What had Abba and Eema endured when the Nazis entered their shop? Had they forced them to lie down on the broken glass as they looted the place? Some of those soldiers were hardly out of adolescence. Were they driven by a thirst for power? Riches? Envy? Hatred? She had to stop the alarming thoughts.

Neelie paused at the edge of the street and peered up and down its visible length. Tamar stood on tiptoe behind her. The once-busy neighborhood was devoid of cars, carriages, and bicycles. Silence hung heavily like a thick fog in the normally busy afternoon. Gone were the chuckles and greetings, the bicycle squeaks, the honks and whistles and barks. A pair of black dogs sniffed the littered sidewalk for scraps. Faraway bombs beat a regular rhythm too distant to worry about.

"Follow closely. Act as though we just met up for a nice walk," their guide said.

They hurried across the street, pretending to carry on a jovial conversation, and stopped in front of a brownstone house facing the canal.

"This is the place. Head to the back door. I'll go in the front to avoid suspicion." Neelie raised her voice for the benefit of anyone watching. "All right, then, Daniel. Nice to meet you, Tamar. See you soon." She waved from the doorway and slipped inside.

Tamar waved back. "Okay." She shielded her eyes against the sun and peered up. Neelie's home, though dwarfed by taller structures on each side, sat regally overlooking the canal. "Isn't it beautiful? I've only visited once when she invited me for tea."

Daniel surveyed the buildings. "These old houses have been here for centuries. I hope the SS doesn't destroy them like they did in Rotterdam." He squinted upward. "Looks as though it's three stories with an attic on the fourth." He touched her elbow. "We should head to the back."

"Neelie said it's been in her late husband's family since the 1700s." Outwardly, like all the houses in the neighborhood, it showed no sign of life, yet didn't appear bereft like the others. Sad how quickly shops and houses adopted an abandoned, forlorn appearance when their humans were gone. Tamar's family's store already looked that way.

They strolled to the corner and headed to the alley behind the row of houses. Daniel put the bag and suitcase against the wall, then backed up to get a better look. "Can you believe this place? I love these old houses. Looks like there's even a balcony off the roof."

She followed his gaze, then looked full at him, matching her low tone to his. "I can't believe Tante Neelie is willing to put her family in danger because of us."

"Seth told me about her son, Jan."

Seth. "Really? What did he say?" Her tremors remained inside.

His fingers massaged her shoulder. "He works for the Resistance, or whatever it's called. He's in charge of moving the babies who were rescued from the orphanage in Amsterdam."

"But the Vissers aren't Jewish. I think they're Reformed. Why would they put themselves in danger? Won't they suffer the same fate?"

"There are good people throughout Nederland, and—"

The door inched open.

"Come in, come in. Welcome to my home." Neelie stood aside as Daniel lifted their bags inside and they passed in front of her. The minute the door was closed, Neelie's arms circled Tamar's shoulders and drew her into her thin frame. "I am so sorry, dear. We'll pray a hedge of protection around your family."

A hedge of protection. Tamar glanced up at Daniel, and he nodded. Another double witness.

They stood in a cloakroom that also held supplies and food. Ahead stood a closed door. To the left, three stairs led to a door that opened to what looked like the kitchen.

Neelie studied Daniel. "How did you two meet?" It seemed Neelie was trying to ascertain their relationship.

Tamar blushed at the assumption they were a couple, but the words warmed her heart. "Daniel is a friend of my brother, Seth. Now that the opera's closed, I'm assisting him on house calls."

"House calls?" Neelie's eyes widened and darted back to Daniel's face.

"I was completing my residency at the hospital before they forbade Jews from working there, so I've been running 'errands' to help those in need." He smiled at Tamar. "We bumped into each other on one of my trips, and she's been helping ever since."

Neelie offered her hand. "Welcome to our home, Dr. Feldman."

"Please, call me Daniel."

Neelie linked arms with Tamar. "Let me give you a tour." She gestured with her hand. "This was my late husband's house, and it's been in his family since the eighteenth century."

"All these houses on the canal are majestic. I'm glad they survived over time." Daniel grasped Tamar's hand.

Neelie noticed and grinned. "Well, this mudroom isn't so majestic. Frans' great-grandfather and his grandfather were physicians and had their office on this floor. Where we're standing was the family's private entrance. Follow me." An inner door opened to a larger room. "This was the examination room. As you can see, it's now used for the Christmas tree and skis and suitcases." Another door led to an ample room with a round, marble table in the center and a cabinet on the side. "This was the waiting room, but after Opa Visser retired, we changed it into a foyer. Now I use it to meet violin clients."

Tamar's eyes widened, and she linked arms with Daniel. "You have a business?"

"Had to after the opera closed. Bills still need to be paid. I meet with my violin students here in the foyer, and I also repair violins. This provides a bit of privacy from the rest of the house."

"Privacy?" Tamar and Daniel said at the same time.

"You'll understand in a few minutes." Neelie gestured for them to follow, and they retraced their steps to a staircase.

The three steps took them to a door that opened into the kitchen and a dining room, separated by an arched wall. The same type of rooster clock as the one in her parents' kitchen hung above the sink, framed by colorful curtains. A large, covered pot bubbled, and the smell of turnips and bacon filled the room. Baby bottles lined the sink on one side—for the same baby from the opera?

A glance at the dining room showed a table set for five but with room for more. A highchair sat at one end. Five settings, *hmm*. Daniel must have noticed, too, because his eyes caught Tamar's.

Neelie smiled. "I'm afraid our ration card doesn't stretch too far, but we do what we can, and it's healthy fare."

"We're grateful for your hospitality. Sorry that we're putting more of a burden on you." Daniel ducked his head under the low beam framing the casement.

"My son brings me extra ration cards when he can, but sometimes, they show up in the most interesting places. One day, I found one slipped under the back door. Another time, one fell out of the basket that—" Leaving her sentence to dangle, Neelie lifted a shoulder. "God is good."

A fresh round of tears arose, but Tamar sniffed them back. To keep her emotions at bay, she focused on Neelie's words—*hedge of protection*. Tamar visualized tall, thick shrubs, the kind that formed mazes where she and her friends had enjoyed playing hide-and-seek during the autumn. She pictured her parents and brother hidden safe within.

They ascended a set of steep, spiral stairs that opened into a large parlor. As her eyes adjusted to the dim light, Tamar stifled a gasp at the number of people. A couple huddled at the end of a sofa, and a woman in black held a baby in her arms, while another baby mewed from a cradle and a toddler with a pacifier careened into furniture around the parlor. "Oh, you have company. I'm so sorry we've interrupted."

Neelie emitted a sweet, musical giggle. "These are our guests, as you are now." She took Tamar's hand. "Let me introduce you. Maarika, may I present Daniel Feldman and my friend from work, Tamar Kaplan. Maybe she'll grace us with a song. Tamar's an opera singer."

Neelie pivoted to the frowning woman in black. "Daniel, Tamar, this is Maarika Goldman. Maybe you've seen her at the hospital. She works in the lab." Neelie clapped her hands. "I feel better already having two medically minded people in the house. And, Maarika, you play the piano, don't you? Maybe we can have a night of music."

Maarika cocked her head to the side. "Doctors and lab rats have little contact. I don't deal with people, just test tubes. And since my husband just went missing, I hardly feel like 'a night of music,' as you say."

Neelie's hand covered her mouth. "I'm sorry. I wasn't thinking—"

"But if you insist, I'd be willing to play a song or two."

Neelie beamed. "I could play the violin, and I have enough flour to make a *boterkoek*."

Daniel's eyes widened. "Did someone say *boterkoek*?"

"Yes, Daniel." She indicated the babies and introduced them.

Maarika said, "I'm glad you're here. There will be more hands to keep these little ones quiet, and I can return to my books." She focused on Daniel. "What type of doctor are you, Feldman?"

Daniel sighed so softly, only Tamar probably heard. "Haven't decided yet, ma'am. I'm completing my residency at St. Elizabeth's. Since then, I've been making ... house calls outside the ghetto."

As he spoke, Tamar gripped the back of the nearest chair to keep from falling. She hadn't had a bite of food since lunch the day before.

Neelie touched her shoulder. "You look so pale. After what you've been through today, no wonder." She indicated Tamar should take a seat. "Sit here. I'll bring you some tea."

Tamar sank onto the chair. "I'll be okay in a few minutes. I haven't sat down since ... this morning." Daniel moved a chair next to hers and covered her hand with his. The simple act brought some comfort, but worry for her parents welled up.

He whispered, "Hope for the best."

"How can I if what you say is true about the labor camps?"

"There's a verse in the Christian Bible that says God will provide a way of escape for the trials that accost us."

She shook her head. "It's better to prevent the trials in the first place."

Returning on her quick, silent feet, Neelie placed a cup of tea in front of her. "Here, this will warm your spirits. We don't understand what is going on around us, but we must not give up hope."

Tamar's shaky hand lifted the cup. The tea helped, as did her friend's and Daniel's encouragement, yet a small part of her resisted their words. Neither of them had lost anyone to the war. Would they speak so easily if their family members were taken by the Nazis? Yet they meant well. She offered a weak smile and stood. "I'm ready to see the rest of your house if it won't be too much trouble."

Neelie, who'd posted the toddler on her hip, nodded toward the couple at the end of the table whom Tamar had overlooked in her moment of distress. "Wonderful, but first, may I present

Job and Carina Hamel? Their art gallery is three blocks from here. Tamar, you must have visited it."

"Of course. I didn't recognize you at first." Tamar forced a faltering smile. "I used to peek in your window on my way home from school to see if you had any new pictures on display. One of my favorite times of the day."

The woman, so faded she seemed to blend in with her husband's twill jacket, nodded in Tamar's direction but said nothing. Her husband barely lifted his eyes from his newspaper. Tamar longed to ask if their art gallery had met the same fate as her parents' shop but didn't.

Neelie reached for Tamar's hand. "This room is where we spend our days as well as the dining room next to the kitchen downstairs." A menorah sat on the top shelf of a hutch, and plants lined the windowsill facing the street. "Tamar, I will move you to one of the bedrooms upstairs, but Daniel, you will have to sleep down here."

Her tone contained an apology that Daniel brushed aside with a slight move of his hand. It warmed Tamar's heart that Neelie cared for her people.

After Tamar took a last sip of tea and set the cup on a doily, they headed to another set of stairs.

"Amazing." Daniel slid his hand along the rich wood of the banister.

Neelie reached the landing and turned. "Everyone has chores to do. Cleaning, taking care of the babies, cooking."

"Of course. Whatever you need," Daniel and Tamar said at the same time and laughed for the first time since that morning. It felt good to think about something other than her own problems.

"Very good. Tamar, would you rather mop or wash and iron clothes?"

She brushed a tendril of hair from her eye. "Oh, I'll do both. It's better to keep busy, and we owe you so much." This woman had opened her door at great risk to herself. Helping with chores was the least she could do.

Daniel nodded. "I'll do whatever you want. Like Tamar, I'd rather stay busy. I'm not used to being idle."

Neelie studied him. "This might be a trial for you, sitting in the parlor all day." She winked. "I may have a solution of sorts."

"What would that be?"

"One guest is reluctant to clean the bathroom. I hesitate to let her win the battle, but for the time being, would you assume that responsibility? And empty the trash?"

"Those would be my pleasure."

"Pleasure, indeed." Neelie rolled her eyes before continuing the spiral ascent to the third floor. "And you'll get plenty of exercise climbing these stairs. This level has two bedrooms and the bathroom. I've put a sign-up sheet on the bathroom door for mornings and evenings. Of course, keep your water use to a minimum. Now we have one more flight of stairs, but it's a short one."

"This house is so tall and spacious." Tamar took measured breaths to slow her heart when they reached the fourth floor.

"Yes, my husband's great-grandfather bought this house, and it's tall like the others in the area because the government taxed the owners based on the width."

"You have the perfect setup for hiding guests." Tamar eyed the small hall with a door at each end.

"Agreed. Little did Great-great-grandfather Visser know his purchase would be a godsend a hundred and fifty years later." She stopped and opened a door to the right of the stairs. "This will be your bedroom, Tamar. It's Jan's room when he's here, but he'll have to sleep in the parlor with Daniel. I share a room with Maarika, and the Hamels have the other room."

"Where do the babies stay? They can sleep in my room," Tamar said, wanting to repay Neelie and Jan for their sacrifice.

"That won't be necessary, but they are on this floor." Neelie headed to the other end of the hall, opened the door, and turned on the attic light. One side was cluttered to the ceiling. A path on the right led to a small door. Neelie pointed to the full-length mirror on the wall. "Watch this." She pressed on the upper corner of a portrait, and the mirror slid to the side, revealing a closet-sized room with three cribs. "This is where the babies sleep. We leave the doors open most of the time so we can hear them."

Tamar and Daniel entered and had to lower their heads and walk sideways to fit between the cribs.

"So this is where you hide the babies if—" His Adam's apple bobbed. "I just hope—"

Tamar had been reading a framed verse on the wall. "Daniel, your face is so white. Hope what?"

"That we won't have to stay in this room for too long. It's closing in on me."

With a little grin, Tamar pointed at him. "Ah, so you are afraid of something."

His eyes crinkled. "You found me out."

Neelie poked her head in the door. "So what do you think of our tiny room? It's soundproofed."

Daniel joined her at the door. "We're grateful that you went to the trouble of having this built. I hope you won't have to use it, though. Will we all fit in?"

"It will be tight, but I think we can." Neelie extended her arm to indicate they could exit.

Tamar followed Daniel out. "How long does it take to get everyone in?"

"We've practiced. Just under two minutes, but we often make mistakes, like not picking up the toys or moving the diapers. If everyone can do something to remove the evidence and hurry to get in here, it will make our job faster. I'll show you the rest of the place, and then we'll have supper."

After Neelie closed the mirror, she led them to the small door at the other end of the attic. "This leads to a small balcony."

The few minutes Tamar stood in the enclosed room increased

her appreciation of the fresh air. She breathed deeply.

"Now I'll share a secret. This is where I come for privacy and quiet time." Neelie grinned. "You can use the balcony too."

Daniel peered down on the roofs that surrounded them. "We'll have to be careful. A neighbor from an adjacent building could see us. In times like these, it's difficult to distinguish friend from foe."

"And soldiers patrol the back alleys, so yes, we must be careful." Neelie swiveled to face her roof. "See that alcove in the roof? When Frans' father was still alive and we wanted some privacy, we'd climb up there." She winked at them. "At my age, it's too hard for me to maneuver this body over there, so now it's your space."

Tamar hugged her. "Oh, Tante, you are a wonder."

Neelie shrugged. "It gets crowded after a while … if you know what I mean." She pushed away from the railing and headed in. "I must get dinner ready. Maybe you could carry the food to the table?"

"We'd be happy to," Daniel said.

They followed her down three sets of stairs.

For the first time since Tamar discovered her parents had vanished, the dark despair in her heart ebbed to create a small space for the goodness of this family. She and Daniel were safe for the moment.

But something else. In the few minutes they were in the crib room, she memorized part of the verse on the wall— "… in the secret of his tabernacle shall he hide me." Although her faith didn't match Tante Neelie's or Daniel's, it wouldn't hurt to pray for God to keep His promise and hide her parents in the secret of His tabernacle.

As Tamar poured water from a pitcher into the glasses around the oval dining room table, she thought about that promise, then all the ones she'd broken throughout her life. Words came easy, but follow-through always seemed hard.

No, she had to believe that Neelie and Daniel knew what they were talking about—that God cared and that He kept His promises.

Eema had told her one time that faith was like closing your eyes and letting your father lead you. Easy when you're in a park but more difficult when crossing a busy street. The father she spoke of hadn't changed, just the circumstances.

CHAPTER EIGHT

L ife took on a new normal tempo, and Tamar found comfort in the daily routines. The house was considered huge compared to most other houses in Nederland since it sat with the other Grande Dames along the canal. Maarika had seized the biggest bedroom, apparently without permission, from the way the others responded to her. It seemed she had a way of snatching what she wanted, and Neelie was loath to stop her.

Sometimes, Tamar joined Neelie for prayers at night, content to listen as Neelie prayed, quoting God's promises, even the one from the attic wall. Tamar had never prayed like that—conversational, yet reverent. She'd always recited memorized prayers from childhood. It wouldn't have entered her mind to talk to God like Neelie did, but it pleased her.

The days began before dawn. Tamar woke at half-past four, earlier than the rest of the household to enjoy fifteen minutes for herself in the bathroom without someone knocking on the door. She filled a bowl a quarter full of water to wash up and brush her teeth. She used the same water to rinse out one of her two outfits, then laid it on the balcony floor to dry, safe from the eyes of curious passersby. After running a comb through her thick, curly hair, she tied it up in a ponytail. Then she tiptoed down the narrow steps to the kitchen, made a fire, and put on a large pot of water for coffee, tea, and porridge.

During the first few days, Tamar floated aimlessly from room to room, like the ghost from Dickens' *A Christmas Carol*. Not smiling, not reacting, not talking to anyone. The others left her alone—even Daniel. He'd squeeze her arm and offer a smile from time to time yet also seemed to need space to acclimate himself to this captive, interior life filled with baby sounds.

Each day, to help out and keep busy, Daniel collected trash from the rooms and scrubbed the bathroom. When he sat, his knee moved at a fast clip, and often he'd stride to the window to peek out, especially at the sound of rhythmic goosesteps pounding the pavement on the street below. This stifled routine must be hard, remaining idle when he was used to traveling dangerous paths far from the ghetto to care for patients. Here, life was safe and ordered, and nobody needed him.

After a few days, Daniel smiled more easily. He played chess with Job Hamel and conversed with Maarika about medical issues and the events that led to the queen leaving Nederland to live in England, and of course, the Nazi infiltration of their vulnerable country.

One night a week, they each took turns teaching a lesson. The group was an educated one—that became obvious. Maarika spoke about microbiology, didactic but informative. Daniel chose various interesting aspects of medicine, which led to a plethora of questions about personal health issues. Neelie taught how to sight-read music, and Carina Hamel instructed them in art history.

Finally, one evening, their eyes shifted to Tamar.

"Teach us about the opera," Jan, who showed up a few times a week, requested.

Her hand traveled to her neck, which seemed warmer than the rest of her. "I don't know what I can tell you."

"We heard you sang the lead in *La Traviata*," Mr. Hamel said.

"Only once. Usually, I sing—sang … in the chorus. But that once, when I played the part of Violetta, it was exhilarating and scary at the same time. I felt sure my voice would betray me on the high notes." She shivered at the memory of staring out at the audience that night, hoping they wouldn't laugh, or worse—get up and leave.

Daniel squeezed her hand. "I saw the show that night—the first time I'd ever seen Tamar. She played a captivating Violetta. I don't think I ever told you this, Tamar. You scared me." His eyes lingered on her for a moment, then he peered at the others. "When her brother, Seth, introduced us, I couldn't believe how Tamar differed from Violetta."

Tamar gave a little laugh. "You're right, Daniel, I'm nothing like Violetta. I'm the cautious type, while she lives according to her own rules, although she loves fiercely and sacrifices everything for the one she loves." Fierce love and sacrifice—worthy goals for her to aspire to.

Maarika flipped her book shut and *tsk*ed. "How can you play a character so contrary to God's statutes? What did your parents say?"

Tamar lowered her eyes. "I guess I didn't think of it that way. My parents thought it was a great opportunity to further my career."

Mr. Hamel spoke up. "History and even the Torah contain stories about people who go against God's law, but that doesn't mean we must avoid those stories. They teach us about life and the ensuing consequences when we don't follow God's teachings."

Maarika scowled. "It doesn't mean we should pay good money to be entertained by them."

"Through opera, we learn about life," Neelie said quietly. "Tamar, what happened to your Violetta in the end?"

"She died in a paupers' hospital, with her fiancé at her side."

"So sad." Daniel reached over and took Tamar's hand. "The longest death scene I've ever witnessed."

Neelie retrieved a plate of cookies from the credenza and placed it on the coffee table. "And you've seen a lot, Doctor."

He nodded. "More than my share."

"Will you sing for us, Tamar?" Carina Hamel, who'd rarely spoken before, raised her eyebrows. "When you feel up to it?"

Others added their assent to the shy woman's question.

Was she up to it? Tamar had been dragging through each day ever since her parents disappeared. She needed to take a tiny step toward rejoining the world. "I haven't practiced in weeks, rarely since the opera house closed. But yes, I'd be honored to sing for you sometime soon."

"Your violin won't be ready for two weeks. Maybe a month." Her hands behind her back, Neelie studied the young man in the green uniform she'd just admitted to her foyer when he came to check on the status of his repair. "It's hard to get the parts we need when the mail comes so slowly." She couldn't keep the sarcastic tone from filtering into her voice.

The officer's fingers tapped the Art Deco table Frans had bought her for her birthday two years ago, his eyes taking in the portraits on the wall. Then he noticed the violin on the chair in the corner. "Is that a Stradivarius? My father just purchased two of those—"

"Purchased? Or stolen from families forced to flee?" Oh, that mouth of hers. When would she learn to keep her thoughts to herself? Neelie held her breath.

The soldier removed his hat and smoothed his reddish hair. His lips pursed. His eyes slitted, and for a moment, he reminded her of a Gila monster she'd seen at the zoo in Amsterdam. Then a smile spread across his face. "I like a woman who speaks her mind. The situations to which you refer are the result of what happens to people who defy patriotism."

It was all Neelie could do not to spew out a retort. She composed herself. "It will cost twenty guilders. The cost of parts has increased in the last few months."

"Money is of no concern." His eyes shifted to the grandfather clock in the corner. "Is that a Huygens?" He approached it slowly, his fingers caressing its rich woodwork. "It is the most beautiful I have ever seen. Would you consider selling it?" He pivoted toward her.

"I'm afraid not, Lieutenant Bergman. It's been in my husband's family for more than one hundred years."

"I understand and respect your loyalty to your family. However, everything and everyone has a price, Mevrouw Visser. Especially now. What is your price?"

How dare he? Before Neelie could reply, Tamar's sweet, pure voice floated from the kitchen. Neelie hurried to close the door that separated the foyer from the stairs to the kitchen.

"Wait."

Neelie stopped, squeezed her eyes shut, sent a silent plea for help, then turned toward him. Everything was out of her hands now.

"I have never heard such a haunting and pure rendition of 'O Mio Babbino Caro.' Who is singing?"

What Neelie said next would change everything. Somehow, she'd avoided lying to the Nazis in her dealings in the city. Now the officer forced her to confront the dilemma of half-truths. Managing a shaky intake of breath, she said, "My niece."

"I must meet her. What is her name?" His gaze remained on the open door. "I have not heard beauty like that since—"

"I'm sure she's too busy." Neelie hurried to the pad of paper that sat on the Amsterdam School Art Deco cabinet she'd set up in the foyer for clients picking up their violins. "Here is the receipt for your instrument. Two to four weeks, Lieutenant Bergman."

"*Nein,* Mevrouw Visser. It will only take a minute to tell your niece how much I appreciate her voice. One minute is all I need."

"As you wish." Neelie inched toward the door, wishing there was a way to lock it without him hearing the click. When would she ever learn to be more careful? It had slipped her mind to close the door between the foyer and the stairs leading to the kitchen while Tamar scrubbed the floor.

A scarf held back Tamar's hair, but curly tendrils fell into her eyes. Her singing came to an abrupt halt when Neelie appeared in the doorway. "Oh, you scared me." She blew an errant lock away from her face, removed the scarf, and retied her ponytail. Her *blonde* ponytail.

"Quick, take off that apron and the scarf and come with me." Neelie offered a hand to help her to her feet.

"What is it, Tante? What's wrong?"

"Good. Call me Tante. Pretend I'm your real aunt." Neelie took a handkerchief from her pocket and dabbed at a smudge on Tamar's cheek. "A customer, a Nazi officer, heard your singing and insists on meeting you."

"No." She breathed. "I'm sorry. I didn't think."

"We have to go." Whispering, Neelie took her hand and tugged her forward. "I told him you were my niece. I'll introduce you, then you make some excuse and leave. I'll handle the rest."

Before heading down the stairs, Neelie stopped, took a deep breath, and smoothed her hair. Then she pasted on her public smile and opened the door. Lieutenant Bergman was examining the grandfather clock in the corner, his back turned to them. He whirled, his eyes widening at the sight of Tamar.

He approached with his eyes locked on her face. For once, the lieutenant seemed at a loss for words. He took her hand in his gloved one and brought it to his lips. "You are as beautiful as your voice is enchanting. The gods have created a stellar masterpiece."

"This is my niece. Tamar. And this is Lieutenant Bergman."

He held onto her hand despite Tamar's obvious discomfort. "A pleasure to meet you. As lovely as your rendition of Puccini's aria. It mesmerized me. I had to meet the source of such a pure tone."

Tamar took a faltering step backward. Her pure voice now cracked. "Thank you. Please excuse me now. I'm afraid my aunt has me doing many chores."

"Tamar? An interesting name. Isn't it Hebrew? If I remember right from my early religious education, Tamar's story didn't end well, did it? But of course, you are not the same."

She refused to look away. "No, sir, I'm nothing like her. I should be going."

"With your aunt's permission, I would like to take you to the opera in Amsterdam. It's the only one still operating. I have associates there who would be interested in hearing you sing. We could enjoy dinner afterward." His eyes darted to Neelie. "Would it be all right with you?"

She managed a pasted smile at the tenacious man. "Thank you for your offer, Lieutenant Bergman, but that would not be possible since I cannot speak for Tamar's parents."

"Well, then, I'll speak with Tamar's parents myself. Will you arrange this for me, Vrouw Visser? I would love the chance to get to know Tamar better." His gaze remained fixed on her.

Tamar folded her hands in front of her sprigged muslin dress. "I thank you for your generous offer, but I am already spoken for."

His face visibly fell, except for a slight tic of his lower lip, then he roused himself. "I see. Well, I still would like you to meet my associate about your singing. Your fiancé will accompany us, and Mevrouw Visser, you are welcome to attend the opera with us as well. I will return with further details. Good day." With one last glance at Tamar, he strode out of the house.

Neelie stared at the door he shut behind him, then sighed. "What a fine kettle of herring."

Tamar turned to her, her mouth falling open. "What are we going to do?"

"You simply cannot go." Neelie shook her head, touching the back of her hand to her forehead. "When he returns in two weeks to pick up his violin, I'll make some excuse. Say you're sick or you've gone away."

"Do you think he'll figure out I'm Jewish?"

"Not with that hair. But one thing I do know is you cannot go with him. Lucky for us, he didn't ask for your last name."

"I'm so sorry. Never in a thousand years would I want to cause you trouble."

Neelie hastened to admit her guilt, taking both Tamar's hands in her own. "I shouldn't have left the kitchen door open. Don't worry. God will provide a way of escape as He has promised."

"How?" Tamar's wild eyes looked more desperate than hopeful.

"I don't know yet. But from now on, we must keep songs to the upper rooms."

CHAPTER NINE

The brisk wind of January 1944 mellowed into warmer February temperatures. Tamar found time every afternoon to climb onto the roof's alcove and let the breeze wash over her. Oh, to be outside whenever she wanted. They'd been at Neelie's house since late November, and never again would she take fresh air for granted. Sometimes, she fell asleep, an unwise choice because a soldier or a nosy neighbor might glance up and see her.

Ensconced among the daily chores were hours of free time. Sometimes she played hide-and-seek with Sophie. The turnover of the orphan babies had halted, and only three remained. Jan said available homes in the country had dried up.

Two new guests had arrived at the end of January in the middle of the night. Both strapping young men in their twenties, Lars and Bram had been part of the group who helped move people. Both looked like they needed a bath. Now they needed a place to stay. Daniel spent hours huddled with them, all three speaking in hushed tones.

Tamar knew what they talked about. Hopefully, Daniel's restlessness wouldn't lead to foolhardy behavior. She had to find out about her brother, so she approached them one evening. "Do you know of a man named Seth?"

Lars' eyes darted to Daniel. "I know a few with that name."

"He's my brother. Blond hair like mine. Tall like Daniel. Have you seen him?"

Bram nodded. "Don't you remember, Lars? He was at the general meeting last week, the man who talked about the boat being shot at near The Hague."

"He seemed okay to me, but I've never met him. We try not to get too close. Too many secrets."

Tamar managed a smile. If she could trust what they said, Seth was still alive. It gave her a thread of hope to cling to.

Since their little group in hiding had remained static, they'd learned to coexist—except for Maarika, who still refused to help. In fact, her quick-witted excuses to avoid doing chores became so legendary that Daniel, Bram, and Lars bet their evening desserts on the battle of words between Neelie and the woman.

Tamar still hadn't told Daniel about the soldier, although from the way his eyes lingered on her, he suspected that something had disturbed her.

One morning as she finished wiping the last breakfast plate, he came up behind her and whispered, "Meet me on the roof." Then he left.

She glanced around the kitchen. Neelie had gone to shop for food, and Maarika was reading one of her germ books with a finger trailing over the back of the toddler who played on the kitchen floor. Tamar removed her apron and hurried up the stairs before anyone noticed.

Daniel sat in the alcove, squeezing to one side to make room for her. A robin tweeted nearby. Farther away, the ever-present bombs boomed and zoomed. His arm circled her shoulders. She rested her head against his strength.

"Why we don't meet here every day is beyond me," he murmured.

"Me too." She rubbed her arms for warmth under the chill of the wind. He pulled her closer.

"So, what's wrong?" he asked.

"What do you mean?" He had enough on his mind without adding her worries.

"We need to be honest with each other. Please, tell me."

He was right. Honesty had to be the foundation of their relationship, or it would flounder. She needed one good thing in her life, even if they lived on a precipice. She swallowed. "A week ago, a Nazi soldier came into the shop and heard me singing from the kitchen. He insisted on meeting me, so Neelie introduced me as her niece."

He leaned his head forward to look at her. "Did he find out you were Jewish?"

She sighed. "No, Neelie didn't tell him my last name, but he commented on my first name being Hebrew."

"That's not good."

"There's more. He asked if he could take me to an opera in Amsterdam. Said he wanted to introduce me to an associate." She shifted to face him.

A craggy furrow formed between his eyebrows. "What did you say?"

Tamar studied her fingernails, torn and frayed by the harsh ammonia she used to clean with. "I told him I couldn't go because I was … already spoken for. I'm sorry I lied, but I didn't know what else to say." She waited for his reaction, hoping for a small smile or a smoothing of the lines on his forehead. Nothing. She should have listened to that little voice within that told her to omit that part.

He let out a discernable breath. "Then what happened?"

A fresh wave of despair filled her. "He invited you and Neelie to come along and said he would return with more information." Her eyes implored him to forgive her. "I'm so sorry my singing put everyone in danger. Neelie said his violin would be tuned and ready to pick up in a week or two, so he will come back."

Daniel traced a finger along her cheek. "You are spoken for if you want to be."

She allowed a tiny gasp to escape. "What do you mean?"

"I mean, I care about you … deeply." He brushed stray hairs from her cheeks. "These are such uncertain times, and I don't want to force a commitment from you when we can't be sure what's going to happen. I just know that if things were different, I'd court you like crazy."

Just as quickly as it entered, despair fled. The dull ache of loss had pulled her under the waves of her inner life, but moments like this with Daniel brought spurts of joy. She clung to them like a lifesaver.

The lines on his forehead smoothed, and his eyes regained a glint of humor. He brought her hand to his lips and kissed each knuckle. She winced. "What's wrong?"

"Washing so many dishes has made my hands rough and red."

He examined her hand with an exaggerated frown. "I'm a doctor, and all I see is a lovely hand." The frown dissolved. "And a face I want to kiss."

Her lips trembled. The depth of her emotions matched his, but could she trust her growing feelings for Daniel, or were they the result of living in uncertain times? She'd heard about soldiers marrying girls they'd just met before shipping out the next morning.

She nodded. Times would always be uncertain somewhere.

Tamar met him halfway, lightly framing his bearded cheeks with her hands, then wrapping them around his neck. His lips met hers, soft but firm at the same time, commanding but gentle. Oh, she could stay like this forever. He kissed her nose, each eyelid, her forehead, then his lips met hers again, this time more urgent, as if time were of the essence. Then he pulled back.

Startled, she opened her eyes to find him smiling at her.

"Well?"

"The kiss was quite nice." *Quite nice. How formal. Like when Great-aunt Anna describes a cookie.*

A coy smile played on his lips. "Funny. You're making this difficult on purpose, aren't you?"

"Oh, you were referring to courting me like crazy." She shrugged. "Well, if my Nazi suitor doesn't pan out, I'd be delighted to … court you right back."

"Don't joke about that. Going with him could put you in a lot of danger." He circled his arms around his knees and stared at the alley below.

"Neelie will tell him I've gone away or that I'm not feeling well. It will be all right."

"I don't know. Something's off—I can feel it."

The eleven residents became restless after more than two months of confinement. Close proximity day and night and the lack of fresh air and activity fostered arguments about the most mundane subjects. Fifteen-month-old Sophie had managed to sit quietly each day, although her young legs must be bursting with stored-up energy. Maarika complained about the noise, but her loud voice often woke up the babies.

How Neelie wished she could take the babies out for a walk along the canal to see the seagulls and the boats, but now they were filled with German soldiers. With the frequent staccato of goosesteps, outside activity presented too much of a risk. Then an idea struck her—something to move all the guests off their seats and onto their feet. And laughter would fill the house once again.

Spijkerpoepen. Neelie shared her idea with Tamar after lunch as Neelie washed the dishes and Tamar dried.

She responded with an immediate giggle and a *yes*. "And we could add some other games. How about a scavenger hunt? We could create teams." Tamar carried the stack of wiped soup bowls to the cupboard.

"Brilliant. I could start with Adam and Eve and go through the Bible. And we could play hide-and-seek with the little ones. I foresee a whole night of games, the best Spijkerpoepen ever. Imagine Maarika with a string on her backside, trying to fit it into a beer bottle! Do you think she'd do it?"

Tamar rolled her eyes. "Who can tell with that lady? Though sometimes, she surprises me."

"I can't wait to get started. I'll make up the games today, and we can play tonight. When Jan comes, I'll see if he can find the shuffleboard in the attic so we can play *Sjoelbak*."

Tamar clasped her hands. "This will be great. And lift our spirits. We need to laugh."

That evening after everyone gathered in the parlor, Neelie and Tamar shared the plan with Daniel first.

His response was less than enthusiastic. "Spijkerpoepen?" He motioned with his eyes toward Maarika. She was running a distracted finger over the shoulder of Lettie, who was teething.

"Come on. We need to laugh and have fun. Even God has a sense of humor. Just look at the platypus." Tamar begged with her eyes. "I learned that in a high school biology class."

Daniel finally relented, agreeing they needed to move around.

The interaction between the two young lovers brought back memories of the many times Neelie had used her own feminine wiles to convince Frans of something she wanted. As with Tamar's face, Neelie's could always erase Frans' frown.

When Maarika rolled her eyes at the idea of searching the house for Bible clues, Neelie didn't dare bring up the sophomoric game of Spijkerpoepen. "You want us to act like street urchins running all over the house looking for bits of paper? What the point of that?" Maarika stood, stepped over Lettie, and walked over to the end table next to the sofa to get her book.

"It will be good for morale," Neelie coaxed.

"All right, but I only agree because the children are driving everyone crazy." Maarika stepped back as Rachael toddled too close and gripped her skirt to keep from falling.

"Perfect." Neelie gave each guest either a red or blue homemade nametag. "Each team will be given the first clue of ten. You'll find the second clue with the first item. Both teams will take a different path to the tenth clue so that we won't bowl into each other. Reds meet in the kitchen, blues can stay in here. Daniel, will you be the captain of the blue team? And Jan, you be the head of the reds?"

Jan, standing with Lars in the corner, grinned. "Be glad to."

"Me, too," Daniel said from the sofa where he sat next to Tamar.

"All of us must participate in some way. Questions?" Neelie's eyes darted from guest to guest.

"What's the prize?" Bram leaned against the arched entry to the parlor, smoking a pipe. A man of few words, he normally just observed the group's conversation, but the idea of a game seemed to pique his interest. "A trip to Venice, a bag of gold nuggets?"

"An extra helping of turnips tomorrow will be your prize." Daniel joined him at the entry and pretended to pummel his arm.

Teams met, and laughter abounded as they rushed to find the next clue. Since Tamar and Neelie couldn't take part in the scavenger hunt because they had hidden the clues, they went to the kitchen to enjoy tea and a cookie from the batch Neelie had made earlier in the day.

Neelie sipped her tea and leaned her head against the wall, her hand rocking the buggy holding the babies. "Why didn't we think of this weeks ago? It's such a great way to form friendships. I'm glad Jan could join us. He needs to smile, as well."

Tamar nibbled a bit of her cookie. "We were so busy keeping everyone fed and safe, it didn't occur to us."

Footsteps sounded from above, accompanied by gales of laughter. Neelie glanced at the ceiling. "I hope all this noise doesn't irritate the neighbors or attract the curiosity of a passing soldier."

Tamar poured more hot water from the kettle into Neelie's cup and her own. "You're right. It's easy to become complacent."

"From your lips." Neelie winced at a loud noise from above. "Sounds as if the teams should be finished soon. I hope they don't tear apart the rooms looking for clues. We should head up to the parlor. That's where the last clue is."

"What did you write?" Tamar rose from her chair at the small table.

"The clue is about the Angel Michael. So where do you think I hid the plate of cookies?"

Tamar rubbed her earlobe—a habit of hers Neelie had noticed

many times since she'd lived there, whenever the girl fell deep into thought. "I know. That porcelain angel in the parlor."

"You're right. It's on the top shelf. I hope they don't break a vase pulling it down."

Maarika's nasal voice came from above. "I was here first."

"Get off my foot!" a man exclaimed in protest.

Tamar hurried to carry the teacups to the sink just as three people squeezed through the kitchen door and bumped into her, which caused some of the tea to spill on her dress. "Oh no!"

Neelie stood. "What's going on?"

Maarika wiped her hand on her skirt. "I was reaching for the cookies on the bookshelf when that rapscallion grabbed it out of my hands."

Jan's eyes opened wide. "Rapscallion? You were nowhere near the cookies. Mam, our group got there first."

"Now, now," Job said, his urging hardly discernible among the raised voices of his team. "We must get along."

Tamar blotted at the tea stain on her bodice with a napkin, then turned to Neelie. "Do you have any more clues? It sounds as though they are in need of a playoff."

Hmmph. Neelie held in a huff. Leave it to Maarika to ruin all the work she'd put into creating the game. "No, but we have more games. Come. Let's meet in the parlor." She passed the cluster of guests and headed up the stairs to the room where everyone normally congregated during the day, followed by agitated cries of "go red" and "go blue."

After they gathered, Neelie clapped her hands to get their attention. "I can see we were overdue in organizing games." Her eyes fell on the chipped plate on the floor and cookies strewn over the carpeting by the bookshelf. "I guess nobody gets the prize unless you're happy with crumbs."

Lars looked crestfallen, and Maarika looked judgmental.

They needed to change the mood back to something more pleasant. "Let's take a break and enjoy some music. Maarika, would you accompany us on the piano?"

She scowled but went to the piano bench.

Neelie smiled. This was the first time the woman had agreed to play the piano. "Something quiet and lovely. Ideas?"

Bram raised a tentative hand. "I managed to grab a violin before coming here. I could play a song."

"Oh, please." When he opened a suitcase he'd hidden under the highboy and gently took out the instrument, Neelie approached and peered over his shoulder. "Is that a Rombouts? May I touch it?" When he nodded, she slid her fingers over the wood. "What beautiful craftsmanship. This looks like spruce. Is it?"

"Perhaps. I'm not sure." He shrugged. "I'm a simple man and don't require such a fine instrument, but one of the people we rescued asked me to keep it safe. Days later, the woman's house was ransacked. So ... I keep it for her ... until she returns." He positioned the violin under his chin and took up his bow. "I hope you like Saint Saëns' 'The Carnival of the Animals.' Which animal do you think this is?" While Bram played the haunting song, the group sat mesmerized. When he finished, he prompted them. "Well?"

Daniel scrunched his face. "Something small. A cat?"

"What else is gentle and glides through the water?"

"A duck," Carina Hamel said.

"Bigger."

"A swan." Her face lit up when Bram nodded and everyone clapped.

Catching the vision, Maarika made her fingers plod over the low piano keys. "Guess which animal this is."

"It's an elephant. What a delightful idea. Another," Carina said and clapped.

"I only have one more." Bram brought the violin to its proper position. "Guess this one. Think about the way the song moves."

Maarika's head bobbed to the music. "I got it. A powerful tiger."

"Close. What else stalks like a tiger?"

"A lion."

"Excellent." The young man put the violin back in its case and returned to his seat.

Neelie clasped her hands together, grateful that the group's enthusiasm had returned. "Thank you, Bram. Maarika. Now who else will bless us with music?"

"I will sing if you'll accompany me, Maarika." Tamar rose and whispered in Maarika's ear.

Neelie fairly held her breath until Maarika responded with a vigorous nod. Oh, this was good. Anything to pull Maarika into the group.

Tamar waited for the opening bars, then began *"Wilhelmus,"* the national anthem of Nederland.

The mood changed immediately. Mr. Hamel stood, then everyone joined him. Moisture brimmed in Jan's eyes as he placed his hand over his heart. Tears washed Neelie's cheeks, but she didn't care. The song lifted her soul.

"Again," Daniel said, and they repeated the words in unison.

It felt good to sing for their country instead of having to listen to the German anthem that played on the radio nonstop and sounded in the streets as the regime's truck passed the house.

Then someone knocked on the door.

Nobody moved at first. Then a flurry of activity ensued as guests picked up what they could carry and raced up the stairs. Jan pushed the chairs in, grabbed a book, and pretended to leaf through it. Tamar brushed the cookie crumbs onto the chipped plate and carried it into the kitchen. Neelie hurried down the stairs to the foyer and opened the door.

Her neighbor, Lenore Frank, stood there in her robe and slippers. "Neelie, the whole neighborhood can hear your guests singing. You're going to get us all killed. Please, tell them to quiet down."

"I am sorry, Lenore. We didn't realize. Of course, we will keep the noise down." Once the door closed, Neelie leaned against it and waited for her heartbeat to slow to a normal pace. She climbed the four flights to the top floor and opened the mirror. "False alarm."

Everyone climbed out and brushed off their clothes.

"Who was at the door?" Bram asked, his usual carefully groomed dark hair in disarray.

"My neighbor, telling me our singing was too loud. The whole neighborhood heard."

"Oh, I'm sorry." Tamar's hand hovered near her mouth. "I should have known everyone would join in."

Neelie picked up Lettie, who'd begun to cry. "Don't be sorry. You chose the best song. We'll keep it down next time."

Maarika shook her head. "I warned you not to play childish games."

They descended the stairs to the parlor. "At least, we know there are still neighbors we can trust," Neelie said.

One week plodded into the next. Fewer students came for lessons. It didn't surprise Neelie. Most people in the neighborhood had lost their positions and were scraping by on their weekly ration card, which forbade more than the essentials. A few people left their violins at her back door—beautiful violins but rarely accompanied with a note.

She'd keep them safe, vowing not to profit from the owners' misfortunes, no matter how hard things became. But Neelie still had to feed eight adults and three babies, and the food amount and choice diminished with their waistlines. Worry filled her heart until she remembered how God had always provided.

She was dusting the cabinet in the foyer when Lieutenant Bergman's invoice glared back at her. Three weeks had passed, and the German man hadn't returned. Maybe the young officer had second thoughts about taking Tamar, her fiancé, and herself to the opera in Amsterdam. Or he couldn't procure the tickets. It was fine with her if he never came back for his violin. Lieutenant Bergman had leeched into her every thought. His return played continually in the back of her mind, tingeing each moment with dread.

Someone knocked on the door—so close to where she stood, it made her jump. Through the door's window, Lieutenant Bergman waited, as if on cue. Neelie took a fortifying breath and opened the door.

"*Goedemorgen*, Mevrouw Visser."

"Good morning to you, sir. I was just looking at your invoice. You're here for your violin. I'll go get it." Happy to leave the room, Neelie made sure the door to the hallway was locked, then leaned against the wall to steady her nerves. Acting had never been her forté. Frans always said her face expressed her emotions so much that she didn't need to say a word. But now she needed to make her face impassive. Worse. She might need to lie.

Oh, Father, if that man asks Tamar to go out with him, I don't want to say yes, and I don't want to lie. He's out there. I need a miracle. Please put the words in my mouth. That young girl's life and all of ours might depend on it. Amen.

Neelie smoothed her hair and unlocked the cabinet where his violin was kept. Returning to the foyer with a pleasant expression, she opened the case on the round table and removed the instrument. "Here it is. I had to drill the holes a bit to make them larger. It should make the strings move easier. I also replaced some of your steel strings with gut, but it will take longer to break in, so let the instrument set for a week before using it. Of course, I lubricated the nuts and pegs." She handed the violin to him.

"Thank you, Mevrouw Visser." He slid a hand over the wooden surface, then returned the instrument to its case and snapped it shut.

She went to the cabinet to get his invoice, then turned to give it to him but stopped at the stare with which he pinned her. This was not good.

"I would love the opportunity to take your lovely niece to meet with my associate about her future with his opera. I have tomorrow night off. Will that work for Tamar?"

"I'm not her parent, so I cannot speak for her." What else could she say? Neelie dangled the invoice in front of him until he took it.

Without looking at the paper, he placed several bills on her table. "I appreciate your concern for your niece, but Tamar is an adult. Let her speak for herself."

Neelie swallowed to quell the nerves that brought a tremble to her voice. "Normally, that would be the case, but for something as momentous as a potential move to Amsterdam, my niece's parents would want to be included in that decision—even the initial visit there—and would blame me for not insisting upon it."

"Tamar said she was spoken for. I can only assume that means she's engaged. It would seem to me her fiancé would have a bigger stake in Tamar's future than her parents."

Neelie met his colorless eyes—dead eyes, she thought. "Tamar is from a close-knit, protective family. I would not presume to speak for them."

"It's not as if Amsterdam sits on the other side of the world—at most, twenty kilometers from here." When Neelie didn't respond, his lips thinned into a single line, and a vein twitched on his neck. She swallowed the lump that formed. This man did not allow people to say no to him. Yet she marveled that she hadn't yet uttered a single lie. "Let the young woman speak for herself."

Neelie couldn't expose Tamar to the wolf. "Come back tomorrow and we'll have an answer for you."

"Very well." He hefted his violin case, then strode out the door. "Good day, Mevrouw."

Neelie released a breath. She'd bought them some time, but what would happen when he returned?

Time for a group meeting.

Fifteen minutes later, the guests congregated in the dining room as did Jan, who was conferring with Lars and Bram.

Neelie cleared her throat to get everyone's attention. "We've called you together because we've had an upsetting situation arise that may impact all of us. We need your input to make the right decision. Jan, would you lead us in prayer to begin?"

After he prayed, she said, "Three weeks ago, a Nazi officer brought his violin to the house to be repaired."

Maarika slammed her fist on the table. "How can you deal with those pigs? You've put us all in danger."

"As I was saying, through my fault, I left the foyer door open, and the man heard Tamar singing." Neelie told them the rest of the story.

"Do you see what I mean? Look at what's happened because you continue to deal with a Nazi." Maarika's face reddened with each word. A few others nodded.

"In my mother's defense, we can't control who comes to the door for lessons or tune-ups." Jan spread his hands. "How else will we be able to provide food for the group?"

Neelie continued. "There's more. He came back today." She told them about her conversation with Lieutenant Bergman.

"Why didn't you just say no?" Maarika asked, her words curt.

Neelie shrugged. "I finally convinced him to agree to come back tomorrow morning, and I'd have an answer for him. This is why I need your collective wisdom."

Silent, the group stared straight ahead. Meanwhile, Neelie prayed for clarity. A verse she'd studied that morning came to mind—Proverbs 11:14. *Where no counsel is, the people fall: but in the multitude of counsellors there is safety.* Her answer, despite Maarika's harsh words.

Mr. Hamel stood. "We simply cannot let the young girl leave this place and go with that man. It wouldn't be right."

Tamar spoke for the first time. "First, I am sorry I caused all this trouble. My singing has been a blessing and a curse. How I wish I could relive that day, but I can't. So far, the man only knows my first name, but if he heard my last name was Kaplan, it would put us all in jeopardy." She peered at Daniel. "I could handle a simple trip to meet his associate about a job. The problem is, before I came here, I used a fake identification card to pass by the guards at the ghetto station. I'm afraid one of them will recognize me."

Daniel tapped the table. "Tamar's right. They're used to seeing her with me when we pass through the gate, so I should go with her. At least, I'd be there to protect her."

Maarika snorted. "Have you looked at yourself lately? You don't exactly have blond hair and blue eyes."

"I can't do anything about my face, but I can dye my beard or wear a hat. And, Tamar, we safely made it through many times before. We can do it again."

Red splotches appeared on Tamar's neck. She must be anxious, Neelie thought. "Remember, my ID card shows a woman twenty years older with the name Anna Jansen. I told Lieutenant Bergman my name was Tamar."

Maarika shook her head. "Why don't you just announce to the world you're holed up with a houseful of Jews?"

"No, this might just work." Lars stood and leaned two hands on the table. "Tamar, you should insist that Daniel accompany you. He'll keep you safe, and his presence might discourage the lieutenant from asking you out again. Take your identification cards to get by the guards. Maybe you won't even have to use them since you'll be with an officer from the Reich. Keep them hidden."

More welts appeared on Tamar's neck. She brushed a hand against them. "What if I do have to show my ID, and Lieutenant Bergman sees it isn't me?"

"I don't like this at all. It's too dangerous." Job Hamel sliced his hand down. "Neelie, you must tell Lieutenant Bergman that Tamar cannot go. That's all there is to it."

Bram pushed to his feet. "I agree with Job. There are too many unforeseen paths Tamar and Daniel could be forced to travel. It's too dangerous."

When nobody argued with Bram, Neelie had her answer.

Five minutes after nine, Lieutenant Bergman knocked on the door. Tendrils of fear enveloped Neelie's throat like fast-growing vines. The adventure she'd envisioned when they'd built the attic room had lost its excitement. This adventure kept sleep at bay. But now was not the time to bow to fear. Neelie straightened her shoulders and opened the door halfway, hoping for a short meeting. "Good morning, Lieutenant."

He pushed past her, slapping his gloves against one hand. "Good morning to you, Mevrouw Visser. Lovely day, isn't it? Have you made your decision?"

"Yes, sir, I have." Neelie summoned what strength she had and moved to the far side of the table in the middle of the foyer, steeling herself for a volatile reaction. "As I said yesterday, I don't feel right about discussing Tamar's future without her parents' input, and she also wants them present." She took a breath. "So, until they return, the answer is no." Neelie winced, expecting a fist to pound the table, a strident reprimand that she'd overstepped her bounds by not bowing to the request of a high-ranking officer of the Reich.

He tipped his hat and smiled. "Well, then, good day."

Relief fell like a gentle rain over her shoulders until the man reached the door and pivoted to face her. "One more thing. I noticed you've made more than a few trips to the market and to the grocer's store in the past weeks. How are you able to buy so much on one weekly ration card?"

Payback. Despair hit with a thud in her stomach. "I buy what we need, that's all."

"I followed you not one time but two in the same week. Your ration stamps seemed to stretch farther than the other residents' cards."

She stared at the table in front of her as the full realization of his words hit her like an anvil. This officer knew about their guests. Or was he just toying with her like a predator with its prey? Maybe he only implied that he knew she had ration cards. Whatever the answer, their guests' safety lay in her hands.

She gathered what little strength remained. "What time will you be picking up Tamar and her fiancé?"

CHAPTER TEN

Tamar glanced at her face in the bathroom mirror. Not that there was anything to do about her appearance except dab at the smudges on her cheek and the stain on her blouse. In her haste to vacate her home, she'd forgotten to pack any toiletries other than a toothbrush. It didn't matter what the Nazi officer thought about her; in fact, the less he thought, the better. But if playing the role of an aspiring opera singer would buy her fellow guests more time, Tamar would give an award-winning performance. A drawer held a tube of lipstick. She applied a layer to her lips and rubbed a dot on each cheek.

When she reached the parlor, Daniel pulled her to a corner. "Are you ready for this?"

"Could we go over the plans one more time? What do I say if the lieutenant reads my identification card?"

"Tell him you lost yours and that someone gave you this one. We needed it to travel to nearby towns to provide medical help. It's the truth."

"What if he asks me medical questions? How do I answer?"

He rubbed his chin. "Just give a vague response. I'll be there if you don't know the answer."

"And I can tell him I'm new to nursing, only having gone with you on a few house calls." Tamar straightened his tie, then smoothed a curly lock that had fallen over his forehead. "You look so different without your beard." His new look would take some getting used to, but she actually preferred his smooth cheeks and was tempted to glide her fingers over them.

"I didn't recognize myself in the mirror. Do you think I'll fool anyone?"

"Sure you will," Tamar said in a tone brighter than she felt. "But maybe you should keep your hat on."

They returned to the table where Maarika pored over a book on viruses, Lars and Bram argued over a crossword-puzzle word, Carina played solitaire, and Sophie colored a picture. They stopped what they were doing and peered at Tamar and Daniel.

"I'll be praying for you," Carina Hamel said.

"We all will," said Lars. "Be safe."

Neelie was showing a violin to the lieutenant, dressed in full regalia, when they entered the foyer. "This Stainer belonged to my husband's father. Its tone is quite pure."

"I recognize it. We have one at my father's home. And—"

"Oh, here you are." Neelie spun toward them, her eyes registering relief at their presence. Yet new lines appeared on her forehead. "Let me introduce my niece's fiancé. Daniel, Lieutenant Bergman."

Bergman shifted his gaze from the violin to Daniel. A smile spread across his face. He moved toward Daniel and thrust out his hand.

Tamar winced at Daniel's old-fashioned suit. Since he hadn't had the opportunity to return to his apartment to gather his belongings, Daniel wore one of Neelie's husband's suits. She'd let out the hem on the trousers and taken in the waist, but nothing could be done for the short length of the jacket sleeves.

Daniel squirmed, his discomfort palpable.

"Tamar's intended. A pleasure to meet you. What a lucky man you are, Daniel—?"

"Pleased to meet you, Captain." His hand remained on Tamar's back.

"Lieutenant." He pointed to the two stripes on his epaulet.

To bridge the awkward moment, Tamar smiled at the man. "It was generous of you to arrange a visit with your colleague, but I am surprised the opera is still open in light of the war."

Lieutenant Bergman turned toward her and took her hands. "You look lovely, my dear. Our officers need a chance to relax amid all this dreariness, and you are just the one to help them. We should be on our way. Mevrouw Visser, are you coming?"

"No, I have work to do. Godspeed." Neelie appeared to be tightening the violin's strings. Tamar noticed her pursed lips, the slight tremble of her fingers. The men upstairs had convinced her not to go. "How can I sacrifice this young dove to the beasts?" Neelie argued when Daniel urged her to stay home.

Maarika had waved off her worry. "Leave her be, woman. Doctor Feldman is her intended. Let *him* take care of Tamar."

Lieutenant Bergman led them to a shiny Mercedes parked at the curb and opened the passenger door. "We can all fit in the front." He helped Tamar into the seat, then rounded the car to the driver's side while Daniel slid in next to Tamar.

Except for Bergman's whistling, they rode in silence. Tamar clenched the identification card in her pocket at their approach to the guard's gate. Daniel pressed against her arm.

Lieutenant Bergman slowed down and waved, but the guard raised his palm. "Halt."

Her breath caught when the man leaned in and frowned at them.

Bergman lit a cigarette. "Good job. We must be on our way. *Heil* Hitler."

Daniel squeezed her hand as they left the ghetto behind.

When they'd crossed the canal, Tamar struggled to think of a question to fill the silence. "Do you attend the opera often?"

The lieutenant cast a sideways glance at her. "My parents used to take me to the *Opern* in Frankfort. I favored Wagner, and I especially liked Mozart's *Magic Flute*. But sadly, as most of the singers were unpatriotic to the Führer, it closed down years ago. And you?"

"My parents took me as a child too. *Rigoletto* and *La Bohème*. *Faust* scared me to death." She managed a weak chuckle. "I decided then and there that I didn't want to go to hell."

"Lucky for you, hell doesn't exist except in the minds of the unenlightened." He accelerated once they'd left the suburbs of Haarlem, and they easily sped along the roadway connecting the two cities. Hardly a car passed them since gasoline remained a rare commodity. Only drab olive-green trucks and motorcycles traveled between the two cities.

Tamar gazed out at a small village that flew by. Two boys kicked a ball in the yard while their mother removed white bedsheets from the clothesline. Normal activities.

They approached the outskirts of Amsterdam. Tamar stared at the city she'd loved to visit as a teenager. The city where she and her friends shopped for clothes because the stores had a wider selection than Haarlem's boutiques. The city where they'd strolled through Vondelpark, crisscrossed the canals in water taxis, and biked along the manicured paths of the Jordaan district. Now the gray sky reflected the stark condition of a city gone to waste.

"How about you, Daniel—isn't it? Do you frequent the opera?" Lieutenant Bergman said.

"Not as a child. My interests tended toward the sciences more than the arts."

Bergman slowed but still had to swerve to miss a young girl whose bicycle veered into the street. He spewed out German words Seth hadn't taught Tamar. "I'm sorry. I missed what you said. Something about science. Are you a scientist, Daniel?"

"Of sorts. I'm a physician."

"That's wonderful. I respect a man with a good mind. And what hospital do you work in? Or do you have a private practice?"

"The hospital in Haarlem—St. Elizabeth Gasthuis."

"And your specialty, Doctor?"

"When the war is finished, I'll decide on a specialty."

"Oh, so you're still a medical student?"

"A resident, yes. I still have two rotations to go."

Tamar cast a sideways glance at Daniel. Had he said too much? It wouldn't take the officer long to check on his credentials at the hospital. How she wished they'd arrive at the opera house and get this over with. Until then, she tried to focus on the city outside her window.

Memories floated back of Amsterdam. Memories of attending her first opera with Bubbe as a teenager. This same drive with her grandmother but at a slower pace. They'd seen *Saffo*, one of the few original productions in the low-Dutch language. The exquisite opera house with its gilded ceiling and private boxes appeared more elegant than the one in Haarlem. It had sparked her imagination. The sound of her own language in the *libretto* engendered her love of all things operatic.

Now the streets evoked nothing but disgust at the sight of broken shop windows with glass littering the sidewalks. She raised a finger to cover her nose from the stench of garbage filling the gutters that wafted through the windows. Thin dogs foraged through their contents. The few pedestrians who walked along the sidewalks hurried as if they were late—their downcast faces reflecting the mood of the gray skies.

"How it's changed," she mumbled.

"How has what changed?" The lieutenant's eyes raked over her.

"This. The city. It used to be so colorful and clean, but now—"

"It's no wonder—the spoils of war."

Daniel pressed his fist against her leg, so she held her retort between pinched lips.

They stopped in front of a quaint restaurant, *de Silverin Spiegel* written over tall windows. Guards in green uniforms stood on either side of the entrance. A valet in the same green rushed out to open the driver's door. He saluted when Lieutenant Bergman alighted from the car. Once Bergman reached the entrance, the valet approached their door, but Daniel had already opened it. They stepped out and huddled together on the sidewalk.

Tamar had heard of this place, renowned for being the oldest restaurant in Amsterdam. But this wasn't the opera house she'd attended with her bubbe. A sideways glimpse of Bergman gave her no clue why they'd stopped here. Operas always started at seven, and the clocks had chimed a cacophonous six times at the shop. Curiosity won over constraint. "This isn't the opera house I attended with my grandmother as a teenager. Has it moved?"

He lit a cigarette and blew out a stream of smoke. "My friend is meeting us here. We should go in."

Daniel touched her elbow, and they followed Bergman into the building. The officer stopped and chatted with others lining the hallway, holding beers or cocktails.

"Hermann, how's that little boy of yours? He must be in school now." Bergman slapped a tall, uniformed man on the back.

"Yes, Lieutenant, he's growing like a tree."

"Just like his father. Well, you take care of him. They grow up so quickly."

A heavy layer of smoke hung in the air and stung Tamar's eyes. Meters of khaki green. Hundreds of uniformed Nazi officers chatted in small clusters or nursed drinks at the bar. Boisterous laughter and loud arguments indicated the party had started hours before.

Tamar gripped Daniel's arm. Her breath came in stops and starts. Daniel's eyes remained impassive, but his tensed muscle let her know how he felt.

They entered the main dining area. Tables circled the wooden floor where a dozen couples danced cheek to cheek. An inebriated officer staggered among the dancers, his cocktail sloshing onto the floor. A woman in a blue sequined dress with peacock feathers adorning her platinum hair belted out a German song from a small stage. The crowd leaning at the bar waved their steins in the air and sang along with her.

Where was the associate she was supposed to meet? Tamar summoned her strength when Bergman finished his conversation with another officer and beckoned them to follow. He hadn't introduced her to any of them. "Will we leave soon for the opera?"

"I'm sorry, but it closed down a month ago." He took her hand. "It's all right. My associate told me to meet him here."

He had lied about the opera. What else had he lied about? Tendrils of fear enveloped her throat. Daniel stood so close the slight odor of mothballs mixed with cinnamon wafted toward her. They'd added the spice to mask the mothballs. His veiled lids made him appear disinterested in his surroundings, yet his eyes darted around him. Tamar couldn't imagine a worse place for two Jews than a restaurant filled with hundreds of drunken Nazis. Would they make it out with their lives?

Bergman led them to the bar. "Would you like a beer or a glass of wine?"

She shook her head. "No, thank you."

"You don't drink?"

Think fast, Tamar. Was accepting a drink a German custom? "I want to keep my head clear for the conversation with your associate."

"Good thinking," he said.

He whispered something to the bartender, who nodded and slid a large beer toward Bergman. "Here you go." He turned toward Daniel, a tic belying the lieutenant's cheerful exterior. "You don't need a clear head, do you?" He laughed.

Daniel accepted the drink. When Bergman eyed him, he took a sip. "*Bedankt.*" Bergman clinked his glass against Daniel's, signaling him to take another drink.

The woman at the microphone stopped singing, threw a kiss to the officers, and stepped down from the stage. She headed to the bar.

Tamar whirled to speak to Daniel when her eyes landed on Lieutenant Bergman approaching with a rail-thin man with a pencil-mustache and hair like patent leather, parted down the middle. The mustachioed man eyed her and nodded. His immaculate suit stood out among the drab green uniforms.

Bergman touched her arm, its imprint burning her skin. She swallowed her revulsion.

"This is the man I told you about. Herr Klaus Sneider, I present Tamar—sorry, I don't know your last name."

The eyes of the three men focused on her. "Visser. It's Visser." *Lie one*. What had she agreed to? The opera, and this was nothing of the sort.

"Don't be nervous, young lady. And call me *Meneer* Sneider or Klaus. I'm a Nederlander, as are you." Sneider studied her with appraising eyes. "Nerves will affect your voice, and I'm eager to hear you sing. Won't you honor us with a performance while the singer enjoys her break?"

What? Singing in front of Hitler's followers? "This doesn't seem like the kind of audience who would appreciate opera. Would you like me to sing something else?"

He raised a shoulder. "Them? They're too drunk to notice. Do you know any German songs?"

"Just '*Liebestod*' from *Tristan e Isolde,* but it's not appropriate for a place like this."

He eyed her. "This is just the place for a dirge like that. These men have been away from their families for months. 'Liebestod' is more than appropriate." He gestured toward the stage.

It had been a while since Tamar had sung the aria, and never had she performed without at least a piano. She summoned her courage. "Is there someone to accompany me?"

"Not that I know of. Please, the singer will be back in a few minutes."

This too shall pass. Tamar repeated the phrase one of her Gentile friends had recited before every test at school. She cleared her throat prior to approaching the microphone. *Lord, help me to forget where I am and sing as though my life depended on it. Because it might.*

The first few words came out raspy, but the noise of the crowd concealed them. Fine. Tamar closed her eyes to block out the green uniforms and the man with the thin mustache nodding in her direction. Then the song took over. She sang for the love between the two young people who were destined to die away from their homes. Daniel's face replaced Tristan's. Like Tristan and Isolde, she and Daniel lived as victims in an angry world, away from their loved ones.

When the song finished, silence greeted her. What had she done? She opened her eyes to see everyone staring at her, a few with mouths agape. A woman's weeping broke the silence. Tamar muttered a quick "thank you" and jumped off the stage.

Applause erupted. She couldn't believe it. Were these Germans moved by the song?

Meneer Sneider clapped, his eyes kinder now. "A remarkable performance, Mevrouw Visser. I would like to hire you, but the opera companies in this part of the world have been temporarily discontinued. When this crazy war is over, I hope you'll let me help guide your career. You have the makings of a prima donna." He bowed. "Good day. I will be in touch."

Tamar thanked him, then released a sigh of relief. She leaned close to Daniel's ear. "I'm so glad that's over and—"

"Mevrouw Visser?" Mr. Sneider touched her arm. She spun to face him.

"Sir?"

"I meant to tell you … I've heard your voice before. I just can't remember where. It will come to me. *Tot ziens*, Mevrouw Visser."

CHAPTER ELEVEN

U tter despair replaced Tamar's momentary euphoria. Violetta came back to haunt her. Meneer Sneider had probably been in the audience the night she took Margot's place. He'd remember soon enough. Lieutenant Bergman and Sneider would compare notes; he'd find out where she lived and tell the authorities about the soprano who lived under an assumed name in a house on the canal in Haarlem.

Somebody once told her bad things came in threes. The second came as they were leaving the restaurant.

"If it isn't Tamar Kaplan." A female voice rang behind her just outside the exit. "You're the last person I expected to see here."

Tamar's gaze darted to Margot's heavily painted face. She leaned against the doorway, alone, a drink tottering in her hand. Like those of most leading ladies, her voice carried across large areas. Tamar cringed and hurried to her side, hoping Margot's volume would diminish with less space between them.

Meanwhile, for the first time, Daniel engaged Lieutenant Bergman in a conversation while they waited for the Mercedes to be brought to the front of the restaurant.

"How are you, Margot?" Tamar managed.

"Never been better. What's a Jew from Haarlem doing in a place like this?"

"I'm leaving and I won't return." She backed up.

"It should have been me up there on the stage. I could've sung 'Liebestod' if someone had asked me." She slurred her words.

"And you *should* sing it. The crowd misses opera. Ask the manager. I'm sure he'll beg you to sing when he hears your voice."

The car pulled up to the curb. "I have to go." Tamar didn't wait for a response.

Margot's voice trailed behind her, but Tamar jumped into the front seat and closed her eyes. With any luck, she'd wake up tomorrow morning and find this had all been a bad dream.

"Who was that woman you were talking to?" Bergman's question forced her back to her present reality.

"An old acquaintance. She's—"

Resting his hand on her knee, he didn't wait for her to finish. "You did very well, Tamar. Herr Sneider raved about your performance. I assume you'll be open to future singing engagements."

Number three.

"You should have heard her sing. In a matter of seconds, our own Tamar Kaplan closed the mouths of a hundred drunken Nazi officers. The applause broke my eardrums." Daniel stood at the head of the dining room table, regaling the guests and host who'd gathered to hear about the evening's events.

Tamar, standing next to Daniel, removed her hat and suppressed a desire to roll her eyes. She'd never been good at accepting compliments, and Daniel was exaggerating. Everyone's eyes turned to her for a response. She swallowed. "No doubt, the hardest audition I've ever experienced. I had to sing a German aria in a minor key with no accompaniment. The singer before me wore sequins and peacock feathers. And me in this simple outfit."

"Weren't you petrified?" Job put his old newspaper aside. Tamar was sure he'd read the same one over and over, but they only received outside news during one of Jan's sporadic visits.

She closed her eyes for a moment. "At first, I thought my voice pitchy, and I couldn't remember some of the words. It's been so long since I sang *Tristan e Isolde*. Then I went into my imaginary world, focused on the story, and forgot the crowd."

"Daniel, did you have a good time?" Lars looked up from cleaning his pipe.

"Good time? Hardly." Daniel blew out a dismissive breath. "I just tried to keep my mouth shut and blend into the background. With this dark hair, I had to keep my hat on all night."

Tamar nodded. "Lieutenant Bergman baited him all the way to Amsterdam, but he kept his composure and didn't react like I would have. And Bergman didn't even take us to the opera house—more like a German dance hall."

Neelie returned from the kitchen with a small butter cake and a stack of plates, which she placed on the table. "Well, now we can put it all behind us. So many different things could have happened. God took care of you two."

Tamar cast a furtive glance at Daniel. "It may not be entirely behind us. The man, Meneer Sneider, asked for my last name. I said *Visser*—it just leaped out of my mouth."

"Well, you are a niece to me." Neelie cut the cake into eight pieces and placed them on the plates.

"And Bergman made a point of saying he'd have other singing engagements for Tamar." Daniel accepted a piece from Neelie. "It's not over."

"No, it's not." Tamar waved off the offered slice of cake and coughed. "Sorry. Margot, the lead singer of my opera company, saw me as we were leaving and made sure the whole neighborhood heard I was Jewish. I thought Lieutenant Bergman would arrest us, but Daniel kept him from hearing her."

Daniel lifted his pointer finger. "Oh, and let's not forget that Bergman thinks I work at the hospital, and Sneider thinks he's heard you sing before."

The mood changed from festive to fearful in a moment. Even little Sophie stared straight ahead as if she could sense the tension in the air. The bandits were circling their wagons, as an American wrote in the newspaper. The journalist had referred to London, but the same could be said of this house on the canal.

Neelie clapped twice. "Come on, folks. We cannot let fear swallow us up. Everyone is safe. We have a hiding place if we're searched. Let's have a night of music." She eyed Maarika. "Quiet singing."

What Tamar wanted more than anything was to sleep and put the night's events behind her, but she had a duty to these people. Her voice had put their lives in danger. That singing—a blessing and a curse. A curse that crushed the hope in the guests' eyes, replaced with fear.

Carina stood to her full height, which was even shorter than Tamar's mother, and asked with her shy voice, "Tamar, would you sing for us?" She was "coming out of her shell," as Tamar had heard an American announcer say on the radio.

"As you wish, but maybe not Nederland's national anthem this time." She offered a gentle, apologetic smile. "Why don't we move into the parlor?"

Once they'd all taken seats on the sofa and chairs, and Neelie had finished riffling through the scores in the piano bench, she took a seat. "How about *Tristan e Isolde*, since you just mentioned it? It's haunting but beautiful, and I have the *libretto*." She waved it like a flag.

Tamar's nerves didn't flare up as they had at the restaurant, and she sang from the heart, picturing the face of each guest behind her closed eyes. Each guest in need of a blessing she could provide. Thunderous applause erupted when she finished. "Thank you," she whispered and pressed down her hands to lower the volume.

Lars and Bram offered a rousing version of a Yiddish song Tamar had learned at shul. Everyone laughed and joined in, swaying from side to side. The swaying and the heat of the room made Tamar dizzy. She loosened her collar and tried to keep up her enthusiasm, but her throat hurt, and black spots danced in front of her.

She reached for the chair back too late.

When Tamar opened her eyes, three concerned faces stared down at her. Neelie wiped her forehead with a damp cloth, and Carina drew circles on her wrist.

"What happened?"

"You fainted, dear," Carina said, a crease etched between her dark eyebrows.

Lines furrowed Daniel's forehead. "You've endured a lot tonight. It's no wonder."

She tried to sit up, but her head reeled. "I don't know what's wrong. I must be coming down with the flu. My throat hurts and I'm dizzy."

Neelie wiped Tamar's cheeks with the damp cloth. It felt good. "Can you make it up the stairs? If not, you can rest on the sofa."

"No, I'll be okay. Just a glass of water would be nice. It's hot in here."

Neelie felt her forehead with the back of her hand. "She's burning up. Daniel, do we have any aspirin?"

"A few. I'll go get them after we put her to bed."

Neelie and Daniel eased her to a standing position.

Her head spun. Never had she felt so weak. Every part of her ached. She leaned on Daniel, who wrapped his arm around her waist and slowly helped her climb the stairs. She gripped the banister, taking one slow step at a time. Halfway up to the third floor, she stopped and shook her head.

"I'll carry you." Daniel scooped her into his arms. She sagged against his chest, the smell of cinnamon easing her mind.

He gently laid her on the bed and promised to return with an aspirin. She lay motionless in the dark, unwilling to turn on the bedside lamp. The dark felt better.

Between disturbing dreams, she felt Neelie remove her shoes and cover her with a blanket. Daniel coaxed her to sit long enough to swallow a pill with a sip of water, but it lodged in her throat, which had narrowed to the smallest, rawest size. It finally worked its way down.

The next morning seemed no better. The cough that started during the night aggravated her sore throat, and now chills and teeth chattering intermingled with oppressive heat. She vacillated between huddling under the blanket and kicking it aside.

What a problem she was—her fault the others were in danger, and yet every guest, including Maarika Goldman, climbed the stairs for a brief visit. Job sang another song in Hebrew from shul. Neelie brought her soothing hot tea with honey.

Daniel stayed the longest. He held her hand and sang in an off-key but charming voice. "I gave Jan the key to my apartment, and he brought me my medical bag." He held up the thermometer and took her temperature while he told her a funny story from the hospital, then took out the stethoscope to listen to her chest.

That evening, he listened again. "I hear a lot of crackling. Does your chest hurt when you cough?"

"It didn't last night, but it does now. What do I—" A coughing fit interrupted her.

"Are you bringing up anything?" He put away his stethoscope.

She nodded and frowned when she tried to swallow. "An ugly chartreuse. So what is it? Am I going to die?"

He smiled and brushed strands of hair away from her face. "Hardly. I'm not positive, but you may have bronchitis. You haven't been sleeping well, have you?"

"No, I've been worried about Bergman's invitation for a while."

"All right, this should pass in a few days with a lot of rest and tea with honey. I'm sorry I don't have any medication for you."

"Where do you think I caught it? I haven't been out of the house in weeks."

"I have no idea. Infections take a few days up to a week to incubate, so we can't blame the Nazis this time."

She yawned. "I feel guilty lying here when everyone else has to do chores."

He brushed a stray strand of damp hair from her forehead. "You've done more than your share. Maybe we can get Maarika to take your place. Try to get some rest."

She slept on and off for the next twenty-four hours, hardly

aware of people coming in and out of the room. At times, her own heavy coughing jarred her awake.

Neelie entered the room with a fresh pot of tea and a cool cloth. She went to the window and pulled the draperies apart to let in the morning sunshine. "Thought you could use some light in this room. Shall I open the window to let in some fresh air? It's a bit stuffy in here."

"Please." Tamar couldn't help but notice Neelie's gray pallor. She remembered what Daniel had said about her own illness the day before. "Are you getting sick, Tante? Did I give you bronchitis?"

"Of course not, dear. It's just a little cough. It will pass." She sat on the edge of the bed. "Your color's coming back. How's your throat?"

Tamar pushed to a seated position and forced herself to swallow. "It still feels like a billiard ball is stuck in there, but it's not raw, and I'm not coughing as much." She touched Neelie's cheek. "Your color isn't so good. Maybe you need this tea more than I do."

"I have to admit, I'm tired. Climbing the stairs from the kitchen to my bedroom is like climbing the Alps."

"Go get some sleep. You need your strength," Tamar urged, knowing Neelie wouldn't heed her advice.

"I'll be fine. By the way, Lieutenant Bergman stopped by today. He invited you to join him tomorrow night at a different place in Amsterdam, and then one this weekend in Rotterdam."

Tamar hugged her knees to her chest. "I can't. I just can't."

"Nor shall you," Neelie said, patting her hand. "I told him you were sick in bed with bronchitis."

"But even when I get better, I won't go." Her heart raced. The very thought filled her with dread. "Oh, Tante, when is this all going to end?"

"God tells us to keep our eyes on him instead of our circumstances. So don't worry. God will take care of Lieutenant Bergman."

Tamar stared at her hands. "I don't know how to stop worrying."

"When your father took you on a trip out of town, who carried your suitcase?"

"My abba, of course, although I carried a little one."

Neelie lumbered to her feet. "Precisely, so if our problems are heavy, let's allow our heavenly Father to carry them for us."

"Where did you get so wise, Tante?"

"I heard the suitcase story from a friend at church—Cornelia ten Boom. Do you know her?"

A smile broke across her face, the first in many days. "She lives on my street. Abba says she's the only licensed female watchmaker in Nederland."

"Corrie ten Boom has been an inspiration to me. I miss seeing her and her sister, Betsie, at church." A coughing fit smothered her words. She covered her mouth with a handkerchief. "I may take your advice and fit in a catnap."

"Let me help you to your room."

"Nonsense, I'll be fine. You're probably still weak. Stay in bed until you feel stronger."

Tamar had lain around enough. Her coughing remained, but the chills and fever ended, replaced by a growing restlessness. Three long days had passed since she'd ended up in this bed, and she longed to do something other than lie around.

Daniel tapped at the door and peeked in. "How are you doing?"

"Fine. This bed rest is becoming tedious. Can I join the human race again, doctor?"

"If you're ready." He sat on the edge of her bed and felt her forehead. "Say 'ah.'"

When he finished checking her throat, she swung her legs to the floor and stood. "There. I need some fresh air. Could we go out on the roof? It will do me a lot of good."

"Absolutely. I've always been a proponent of fresh air."

"Good. Let me get cleaned up, and I'll meet you in twenty minutes in the alcove."

"And I'll check on Neelie. She's been coughing like you did at first."

Her heart heavy that Neelie continued to worsen, Tamar changed into her one clean outfit and ran a brush through her hair. She stood too quickly from tying her boots, and a fresh wave of vertigo assaulted her. With hands gripping the sink's edge, she waited for it to abate. Maybe it was too early to join the human race just yet.

She wobbled to the roof alcove on weak legs. Daniel moved over to make a space for her. The brisk wind took her breath away at first, but she closed her eyes and lifted her face to the sun, enjoying the fresh breeze against her cheeks. Daniel's arm circled her shoulder. Tamar leaned back and basked in his sweater's warmth. "This feels so good. Aren't you worried about catching my bronchitis?"

"No, I've built up a strong immunity from my time at the hospital." He clasped her hand and kissed her knuckle. "There. If I get sick, it will be all your fault."

"Did you hear that Bergman asked me out again? Will he never give up?" Revulsion and dread wrung out her insides.

"I'm glad you were too sick to go."

"Me too. Once I get my strength back, should I say yes?"

Daniel's shudder traveled to her. "No, but let's not think of that right now." He shielded her after a gust of wind made her shiver. "I've had a lot of time to think, and I want to talk about what I've decided."

"Decided?"

He shifted to face her and brushed a tendril of hair from her eyes, the strand that made them water when gravity pulled it down. She liked it when he played with her hair.

"Whether the war ends and we walk out the front door, or the war continues and the worst happens, I want you to know that I love you. If we ever get out of this mess, will you consider being my … nurse?"

"You need a nurse?" She blinked several times.

"Sorry. Nerves." Screwing up his mouth, he gave a rapid shake of his head. "I meant to say *my wife*—and nurse, too, if you want."

Warmth flooded her. Tamar wrapped her arms around his neck. "Yes, yes, and yes. I love you, too, Daniel, and I want you in my life forever and ever. I wish we could get married right now." She expelled a sigh. "It's scary not knowing what's to come. I feel as if we're suspended in time and place, waiting for something terrible to happen."

"God will keep us in the palm of His hand. That's what Neelie always says. Let's just enjoy each other in the present, and the moment we leave—" He kissed her forehead.

She pulled away. "The moment we leave, what?"

"We'll have such a wedding." He smiled and kissed her nose. "Until then, we can dream. I see our apartment above my office. The sweet smell of your *pindakoeken* wafting through the vents, and all my patients salivating and demanding the recipe."

Tamar giggled. "I've never made cookies in my life."

He put up a hand. "Don't interrupt my dream. Then you'll bring a plate of pindakoeken down for me, I'll put the *closed* sign on the door, and I'll kiss the crumbs off your face."

She nudged him with her elbow. "And then you'll frown when you take a bite of one of them, and I'll have to nurse you back to health."

"Okay, you ruined my dream. Tell me yours."

Tamar closed her eyes and lifted her chin to the cold breeze. "It's spring, and we're strolling through the Vondelpark. Rows of tulips, crocuses, and hyacinths line the pathway. It's warm but not too warm. We have the whole park to ourselves, and no guards are watching our every step." She breathed in through her nose, imagining the scent of spring flowers. "I can almost smell them." She opened her eyes.

He gazed at her. "What a lovely dream. Let's remember them—your park with its flowers and my office with your delicious cookies."

But for some reason she couldn't understand, a sense of foreboding filled her. Those dreams seemed too far away.

CHAPTER TWELVE

The nap only made Neelie groggy. She plodded down the stairs to the front door, her legs feeling like blocks of concrete. Someone was knocking, and she was the only one who could answer. Who could it be? If she were lucky, someone had seen her ad for violin lessons.

A coughing attack left her windless. She pulled the sweater tight around her shoulders against the chill in the air. Their supply of firewood was almost depleted, and Jan had suggested they use the rest in the parlor where the guests spent most of their time and in the kitchen for the oven. "Soon it will be spring, and we won't need much wood," he'd said. Still, she worried about the babies catching cold in the attic.

The late February chill in the air seemed to penetrate her skin. The frigid foyer made her shiver as much as her bedroom did. Why hadn't she grabbed a warm robe or her winter coat?

The bell rang again and again. Hopefully, it wouldn't be someone needing a lot of her time. Despite her bad attitude, Neelie managed a weak smile and opened the door.

Lieutenant Bergman stood on the stoop, shifting from foot to foot.

"Good day, Lieutenant, may I help you?" She had to hold back what she really wanted to say to the man.

"Mevrouw Visser, may I come in?"

"Yes, pardon my manners. It's just that I've been ill—" She stepped aside to let him in.

His eyes swept over the small foyer and the door that remained closed. "Is Tamar feeling better? I'd like to see her, please."

"She's a bit better but still confined to bed. I don't think it would be a good idea to visit her today. I seemed to have caught what Tamar has, so she must be contagious." Neelie pushed past him to the entry door and opened it. "I'm sorry, but today isn't good."

A baby's cry pierced the ceiling from the floor above. Lieutenant Bergman's eyes widened. His head leaned toward the sound. Another baby howled. He spun to face her. "Do you have babies in there?"

"I sometimes watch the daughter of the harpist from the opera house. She's on maternity leave and money is tight. I should check on the infant. Good day, Lieutenant."

He grabbed her arm. "I hear two babies."

"You must be mistaken. These walls are so old they echo at times." Horrified by his touch, she struggled to wrestle her arm free. "I must be going. Good day, Lieutenant."

He tightened his grip. "Something's not right. I'll be back this afternoon. Seventeen hundred. Make sure Tamar is ready to see me." He spun and strode out of the house.

Neelie lifted a trembling hand to her lips. Cold eyes. That's what power did to people. Once her heart rate slowed to normal, she made her way to the kitchen, stopping on the stairs to wait for her breath to catch up. A coughing fit erupted when she opened the door.

Carina paused from stirring a large pot of soup on the stove. "Neelie, you're gray. You need to go to bed now."

"The man—" she managed between coughs.

"I'll lock up. Don't you worry." Carina helped her to the stairs that led up to her bedroom.

"No, Lieutenant Bergman insists on visiting Tamar at five." Her hand went to her chest.

"I can handle him. I'll pretend to be your cousin. You go to bed." Carina pointed to the top of the stairs.

"I have a bad feeling about this. If we let Bergman in, he'll harass her, and he'll keep coming back."

"You go to bed, Neelie. I'll talk with Daniel and the other men. They'll take care of him."

Neelie trudged up the stairs, stopping every few steps to catch her breath. With so much work to do, she didn't have time for naps. Carina had assumed much of the responsibility when Tamar fell ill, but Maarika still failed to help. Carina put up a brave front, although she, too, had become more fragile. While she never complained, her olive skin had taken on an unhealthy jaundiced pallor, and it seemed a breeze could pick her up and carry her away like a balloon.

When she finally reached her room, Neelie wilted into bed. The quilt felt comforting and blocked the chill in the air. Carina was right. A short nap would do her good. A robin chirped outside her window. Spring approached. She couldn't wait to put the gray skies and blustery wind behind her ...

Lieutenant Bergman returned to the house and stood in the foyer but didn't remove his hat. A clock from the parlor chimed five times. A proper man always takes off his hat when he enters, so this proved the officer was uncouth. Something moved in his hat. Did he realize it? It seemed to be getting taller.

"Sir, your hat's growing."

"Yes, my name is Bergman, silly woman, and I've come to collect your niece."

"I will get her for you, but first tell me what causes your hat to grow so tall."

"It's my mountain, of course. Now hurry. I don't have much time."

"Oh, I understand now. Bergman means mountain man *in low Dutch. How perfectly wonderful."*

As Neelie turned to call Tamar to the door, she gasped at the sight of the gun pointed at her. "Surely, I cannot easily call Tamar if you shoot me."

Bergman held the gun steady. "You have one minute."

Neelie clutched the rim of the table to keep from falling. So Bergman was a man of the mountains, ready to kill his prey. She would not show fear. "I have to protect her. She's Jewish."

"Everybody knows that—"

Neelie woke with a start to the sound of harsh voices arguing. Had one of the guests opened the door without her permission? Footsteps clamored up the stairs. She put on her slippers and plodded to the door.

A clock tolled five as Maarika hurried past her up the stairs to the attic, carrying Lettie and a book.

Something was wrong. "What's happening?"

Maarika shook her head but didn't say anything. A confused expression covered her face. Job and Carina caught up to her, both carrying a child. They practically rammed into each other when Maarika dropped her book.

The dream. Five o'clock. Bergman. He knew about the babies from this morning. Neelie had to reach the others to tell them not to open the door to him. She ignored the dizziness and made it to the hall outside her bedroom and called down. "Lars … Daniel, don't open the—" She tried to yell, but a spasm of coughing forced her to lean against the banister until it stopped.

The crash of splintered wood. The door was being forced open. Too late.

Male voices shouted. German voices. More than one.

Bram's voice. He asked what they wanted.

"Where are the babies?"

"What do you mean?" Lars' voice.

"Where are you hiding them?" German accent.

Noise from above reached Neelie's ears. Bumping against the attic walls. Footsteps. If she didn't get downstairs, those below would come looking for what caused the footsteps, but Neelie had a feeling once she was downstairs, she'd never return to her room.

Had all the guests made it in time? In the crush of people passing her, Neelie didn't recall seeing Daniel or Tamar. *God preserve them.*

The soldiers would be up soon if she didn't hurry. What to take? She turned back into her room and donned her overcoat. Her eyes landed on the picture of Frans, her favorite hairbrush, her Bible. She lumbered to the closet by the door, placed the small, framed picture in her pocket, reached for the Bible, and headed downstairs. She clutched the book like a shield against her chest.

A squat man in a green uniform stood in the foyer.

"What do you want?"

"Where are you hiding the babies?"

"Nowhere." Her breath stopped at her throat. Prolonged coughing forced her to prop a hand on the wall to catch a breath. "I'm sick," she gasped.

With the back of his hand, he struck her hard across the face. Blood spurted from her nose. The Bible flew out of her hands. She bounced off the wall and slid slowly to the floor.

He loomed over her, his face an ugly mask of hatred. "Where are you hiding the babies?" Saliva spewed with every accented word.

She pushed herself up to sit. "Look all you want. You'll find no babies here."

He marched past her, then climbed the steps to the kitchen. The sound of glass breaking, then more footsteps and conversation. The man was talking to someone in German.

Oh, Father, please preserve the babies and the others. Call the officers away or blind them to everything. Keep the group from uttering a sound.

The Nazi officer reappeared and jerked her to her feet, his hand ready to slap her again. She squeezed her eyes shut and waited.

"We'll have none of that." Dutch with a German accent.

She opened her eyes to a squint. Lieutenant Bergman came from the kitchen, his gloves in one hand, a glass baby bottle in the other. He strolled toward her. His voice was polite and even-toned. "You're lying, Frau Visser. You know what the Führer does to liars. Where did you send the babies?"

"I don't know where they take them," she whispered.

He lifted her chin with a finger. "A little persuasion will help you remember."

Footsteps came from the stairs. The squat officer entered the foyer. "*Keine babys da oben.*"

She understood enough German to know they hadn't found them. *God is good.*

Lieutenant Bergman held the bottle as if it were contaminated. "Take her out with the others."

Oh, they'd already captured Tamar and the three men, and it was her fault. She'd promised Tamar and Daniel a place of safety. She'd left the door open, so Bergman heard her singing. Mistakes she'd made. The air deflated in her lungs.

A German soldier jabbed a rifle in her ribs, pushing her off-balance. Anger filled her at the sight of the damaged door on its side, but it wouldn't do to be enraged, not if an interrogation loomed ahead. Neelie straightened her back and lifted her quivering chin, defying them in her mind if not with her words. God allowed this for some reason; these soldiers were merely Satan's pawns.

"You're a liar, Frau Visser." The officer pulled her toward him and stood nose to nose with her. His breath made her eyes water. Beer, onions, garlic. If this were the perfect race, they'd better learn about oral hygiene. His eyes held disgust, but she stood up to his gaze.

Jesus said nothing. She said nothing.

The little rooster of a man shoved her toward the door. "Lying to the Reich is a capital offense."

A crowd gathered outside the shop, ready for the show. Some Neelie recognized—Mrs. Rogowski, the widow who lived above the flower shop. The bus driver, whose eyes showed sympathy. Others whom Neelie didn't recognize looked on impassively, as though they were watching a sideshow at the carnival that came to town every fall.

Lieutenant Bergman stood apart from the crowd as if he didn't want to contaminate himself. He'd betrayed them all because he wasn't granted another date with Tamar. And she had not prevented it when she could have.

Regret welled up in her. Overwhelming despair added weight to the load. How could she have been so foolish as to advertise violin lessons and repairs? The guilt lay too heavy to bear. Whatever happened, the survival of the babies in the attic and the others who'd entrusted their lives to her weighed down her sagging shoulders. *No, Neelie. Do not carry guilt you don't own. Stand strong.* Wise words. Corrie ten Boom's words. Neelie needed every bit of strength her body and soul could muster.

Neelie didn't appreciate the spectators, especially Lieutenant Bergman and his squat friend, yet she seized one last opportunity to smile at the neighbors she knew. Their faces registered the grief she felt. "Don't worry," she said to Mrs. Rogowski and the bus driver.

"Shut your trap, old woman," a voice behind her snapped.

A green truck with a canvas tarp over the top sat at the curb. A soldier prodded Neelie toward the back of it. A half moon was stenciled on the back below the single opening, but no other markings gave away the truck's identity. Another harsh jab sent her reeling. She straightened to keep from falling. Why did they have to treat her like a sheep or a goat?

The soldier pointed to the rear of the vehicle. Though it was dark, she could see movement inside. Maybe Daniel and the others were there. A few onlookers lost interest and left. Neelie struggled to pull herself up. In one quick move, the soldier shoved her through the opening like a sack of potatoes.

She landed in a not-so-graceful heap with a grunt. A half dozen people huddled around the periphery. One person lay in the center, unconscious or asleep.

Neelie found Lars and Bram. A bruise darkened on Bram's cheek, and one eye swelled. Lars held a blood-soaked handkerchief against his lips. Neelie pulled a clean one from her pocket and blotted at the blood on Lars' nose. "What did they do to you?"

"It will heal in no time. We're a pair, aren't we?" Bram jerked his head toward Lars.

Out of the corner of her eye, she watched Bergman stride across the street, brushing his hands together, another job complete. Neelie hoped they'd never meet again. She glanced at the others. No Daniel or Tamar. "Where are the other two?" she whispered.

Bram shook his head. "What happened upstairs?"

She knew what he was asking, but the truck was full of ears. "I'd just woken up. I had this weird dream about Lieutenant Bergman with a mountain in his hat. There's more to the dream, but I'll tell you later. I hurried downstairs, and the rest of the story is up in the air." Neelie tried to smile at the double meaning. What she wouldn't do for a sip of water.

"Then there's reason to rejoice." Lars gave a firm nod. He understood.

Neelie shifted to glance at Brams' puffy eye. "Only you could rejoice at a time like this."

"Think of it, Neelie. They're safe," he mouthed.

"No thanks to me. We're on the truck because I let Bergman in the house one too many times."

"Don't say that. You did nothing wrong," Lars said through his damaged lips.

She sighed and slumped against the truck wall. "I don't remember Tamar and Daniel passing me on the stairway."

"The palm of His hand. We must not worry." Bram tipped his head back to stem the tide of blood from his nose.

The truck jerked forward. Neelie waved to the neighbors still standing by her door with unabashed tears streaming down their faces. Neighbors who'd been part of the Vissers' lives since her husband was a child. Would this be the last time she'd see them? Was that why they cried?

Her eyes traveled back to her beloved house on the canal. Would they ever see it again? Would Maarika and the rest escape without harm, or were all her efforts for naught?

"Neelie, don't worry." Lars' voice. "He'll protect us."

For the first time since she'd embarked on this dangerous

venture, doubt nearly strangled her. "How? Here we sit in the back of a truck going who knows where."

"Whether He protects us in this life or takes us home to a better one with his Son, we'll come out of this rejoicing." She'd forgotten Lars believed in her messiah.

She dragged in a difficult breath. "I know this to be true. It's just—"

The truck jerked to a halt, flinging them off-balance. They were still within two blocks of her home. The train station stood just around the corner. If Neelie craned her neck to the right, she could see the top floor of the house—the attic door that opened onto the roof—her hiding place. "I can see our house from here." Neelie pointed behind. "See, Bram, Lars? The door is open. The soldiers must have been in the attic." She could only pray that the mirror was in place. But where were Tamar and Daniel?

CHAPTER THIRTEEN

They stared at each other, Daniel's finger lightly tracing a line on her cheek. Tamar had sprayed some lavender oil on her neck, and it seemed to be working. He didn't pull his eyes away. Never had she been able to stare at someone so long, even during the childhood game she and her friends used to play, the one where the person who blinked first would lose. But this was no game. For the first time, she understood how Violetta felt about Alfredo.

Daniel kissed the space between each of her fingers. It tickled and thrilled her. "Where do you want to go on our first date when we get out of this place?"

She shrugged and grinned. Their daily game of imagining future times together helped relieve the tedium of their situation. "It's summer, and the sky's a glorious blue with fluffy white clouds but not too many to shield the sun. We're in one of those swan-shaped paddleboats on the lake. You chose a black one. We're paddling at a leisurely pace—the waves are making it easy. Other paddleboats pass us, and we wave. The smell of warm sand and marine scents waft through the air. You make a joke, and it's funny this time."

"What do you mean, 'funny this time'?" Daniel poked her in the arm. "My jokes are always funny."

"Just a test to see if you were paying attention—" Pounding footsteps and loud voices. Tamar jolted upright. "What should we do?"

Daniel tensed and grasped her arm. More footsteps. A German voice on the stairs. He shot to his feet. "It's time."

"Should we chance going in?"

He pulled her up. "It's too late. We can't." He scanned the area. "We have to climb down. Are you up to it?"

She nodded, but … "How?" Not to mention, her legs were already weak from the illness, and now, also shaky with fear.

"Jump down onto the neighbor's balcony." He pointed at the third-floor window. "We'll go through there."

"What if it's locked?"

Daniel peered around. "We'll break in. Then sneak down the stairs and leave by the back door."

"What if the Nazis—"

"Enough *what ifs*." They climbed down from the alcove and got as close as they could to the adjacent roof, which fairly touched theirs, but the balcony was a ten-meter drop. "I'll go first, then I'll help you down." He leaped down onto the neighbor's balcony, an easy feat for his long legs, then he turned and reached up for her. "Grab my hand."

Fear made her dig her fingers into the grooves of the roof tiles. "I don't think I can make it."

"Trust me."

A coughing spell engulfed her. Not now. Tamar squeezed her eyes shut and thrust her hand toward him. Though she held back for a few moments, Daniel kept talking, and finally, she let herself go.

His breath expelled in a whoosh when she slammed into his chest.

"Sorry."

They rested a moment, then he whispered, "I can hear German soldiers. They'll be out on the balcony any moment. We need to move."

Necessity spurred her to action. Consequences didn't matter. The window was locked. Daniel kicked it hard. The glass gave way. He reached inside and opened the window. "We don't know if anyone's living here, so we have to be quiet. I'll go in first."

Harsh voices came from her house. German voices. Did the babies and the others make it to the room? Bergman's voice. A single glance to the side and they'd see her standing alone on the balcony, broken glass at her feet.

Daniel cleared away the sharp edges, then thrust his hand through the window. "Lower yourself through. I'll help you."

Tamar didn't need convincing. A shard of glass pierced the palm of her hand, but she hardly noticed the sting or the blood. She stepped into a bedroom with a single bed, a lamp, and a robe laid neatly on its quilt. Whoever owned that robe didn't deserve their intrusion. Tamar would come back and pay for the window with interest, as Abba had taught her.

Daniel put his finger to his lips, grabbed a handkerchief from the bureau, and wrapped her hand. She'd replace it as well and add two more. He gestured toward the door. They started down the stairs, stopping at each step, listening for voices. One step creaked. They waited for seconds that seemed like minutes.

The smell of cigar smoke and the rustle of fabric. They weren't alone. Daniel sniffed and held her back. Maybe the woman who owned that robe was in the parlor or the kitchen, but *men* smoked cigars.

They crept down the last few steps, then stopped at the bottom. Nothing moved. No one talked. The front door stood mere meters away, but Daniel inched toward the rear of the house. He'd been in the Resistance movement longer than she. Tamar put her second guesses aside.

As she caught sight of the back door, her shoulders relaxed. Until her gaze landed on a slight, white-haired woman who sat huddled in a chair placed in the center of the kitchen. Gnarled hands twisting a handkerchief was the only movement in the still-life portrait of the cozy room.

The woman straightened when their eyes met. Again, a tiny movement where there should have been more. Was that a slight shake of her head?

Daniel stopped, pressing Tamar behind him. The tick of a clock and the drip of the faucet echoed an incongruous rhythm. Why didn't the old woman speak?

Then an officer with a wide face and features stretched into an ugly grin stepped from behind the kitchen door. From his lips hung a cigar, and in his hand, a Luger. "Well, look what we have here. Two interlopers—*Juden*, no doubt." He gestured with his gun toward the hallway wall.

A coughing fit racked Tamar. She bent over to catch her breath. "The only thing worse than a Jew is a sick Jew." His gun dug into Tamar's shoulder. Its cold metal on her back caused the paroxysm to stop, and she straightened.

The officer pushed her to the wall, then turned her around to face him. He ordered Daniel to face the wall and place his hands on his head. "Don't try anything or your wife dies."

The man patted down the inside of Daniel's legs, then felt around his waist and pockets. A ripple of fear or anger vibrated Daniel's shoulders—she wondered which. They'd been so close, inches from escaping. He must be feeling outrage, yet Daniel revealed nothing.

The officer focused his weapon on Daniel and ordered Tamar to spread her legs and place her palms on her head. His hands touched above her knees and moved up, slowly, like a creeping mantis. A game for the squat man. A horrid little power game, but she dared not object. She swallowed the bile filling her mouth. His hand reached her underwear, and judging by his expression, he was enjoying her reaction. His hand traveled down her other leg. If he wanted a reaction, he'd get the opposite. Through narrowed eyes, she stared right back at his bloated face, refusing to flinch. No flower here.

When the officer moved away, Tamar glanced back at the elderly woman's eyes, which fixed on her. Why didn't the woman do something—create a diversion, or at least try to escape? But a hint of a smile and slight shake of her head communicated something. Sympathy?

Tamar didn't need a glimpse of Daniel's face. She felt it—the tight lips, the deepening groove framing his mouth, and the white-knuckled clench of his fist.

A soldier entered by the front door and spoke in German, too fast to follow. The taller, younger man in uniform motioned toward the door he'd just entered, shaking his head with vehemence, then strode to the back door and threw it open.

Tamar breathed as the vile officer's lecherous hands now rested on his wide hips. He screamed into the kitchen. "Move, Frau."

When she didn't react, he reached her in three steps, grabbed her arm, and threw her toward the hall. She lost her balance and fell to the floor, expelling a sob. Daniel rushed to her and helped her to her feet. The woman offered him a grateful smile.

Tamar failed to suppress a warning gasp. In a flash, the officer swiped his gun against Daniel's head. Blood spurted. He fell face-first to the kitchen floor.

"Who told you to move?" He kicked him in the side. "Get up. We have to leave."

Still holding his head, Daniel struggled, faltered on one knee, then slowly stood. He winked at her as the little man shoved him forward. When he joined her, Tamar slipped the handkerchief she'd been using into his hand. Daniel spoke his gratitude with a squeeze of her little finger.

The old woman shuffled to join them in the hall. Small and thin as a sparrow, she had to be near ninety. Her housedress hung on her shoulders like a tent. A glance at the pristine counter made Tamar wonder … had the woman been slowly starving? Would someone her age even have access to ration cards?

The taller officer marched them, single file, out the door into the alley. Tamar glanced back at the Visser house. What had happened to Tante Neelie and her guests? Had they made it to the attic room in time? All she'd heard were the footsteps on the stairs and German voices. A sense of loss filled her. She and Daniel should have been there to help.

No, she had to believe they'd reached the attic room before the soldiers found them. In her haste, Tamar had forgotten to pray. Neelie would be praying, but did God hear? Did He even care?

The old woman shuffled ahead of her. Daniel took up the front, with the two officers flanking them on either side, spitting orders Tamar didn't understand. Each time the old woman faltered or stumbled, the tall officer nudged her hard with his weapon.

When they reached a side street, they stopped. The soldier who had taken the lead pointed toward a green truck parked a block away. The officer shoved Daniel toward it. He caught himself before he fell to the sidewalk, brushed off his pants, and grabbed Tamar's hand.

So … this was it.

They trudged toward the truck, which loomed ahead like a firing squad. Panic of the unknown threatened to choke any hope. She remembered what Tante Neelie said when they washed dishes.

"When fearful thoughts knock at the door, ignore them. Don't let them in."

Okay. Maybe she'd finally see her parents, wherever they had taken them. A cough threatened. Tamar swallowed to keep it buried. She focused on the truck. A half a dozen faces appeared through the opening in the back. None whom she recognized. That was good.

The soldier swore when the old woman tripped over a groove in the sidewalk. She lurched face-first onto the brick sidewalk. With a grunt, the man kicked her in the hip.

Daniel knelt to gently assist her to her feet, not stopping to seek permission.

When the woman stood, she turned to the soldier and spit at his feet. "You bring dishonor to your mother."

The soldier's eyes widened. Everything stopped. Even nature around them seemed to suspend activity. Daniel stepped in front of her, mere centimeters separating the two men. Then the soldier laughed. "Get on the truck, old woman." He shook his head and turned away.

Bravo, Tamar thought. Bravo for both of them. Despite the horror surrounding her, Tamar's heart filled with love for her man's bravery and goodness and the old woman's hubris.

Daniel whispered in the woman's ear and lifted her. He heaved her through the hole into someone's arms. Then he reached down with one hand and pulled Tamar onto the truck.

A dozen people sat in clusters, staring ahead, clinging to one another—a few old women, two children, an old man. Someone stretched out face-down in the center. Tamar surveyed the group for familiar faces, then lighted on Neelie, Bram, and Lars. Oh, they didn't make it to the attic. "I'm so sorry," she mouthed.

Tamar crept toward her friends, but Neelie frowned and gave a slight shake of her head. Why did she stop her?

Caked blood covered Lars' nose and lips, and Bram's right eye was swollen shut. Neelie managed a crooked smile. Tamar's hand went to her mouth. She bit her finger to stop the trembling. How dare the Nazi creatures touch these wonderful people?

"Where are the others?" Tamar mouthed.

Neelie shrugged. "Safe, we think," she whispered.

A soldier hopped up and trained a rifle on them. As the vehicle lumbered forward, Daniel pulled her next to him and held her hand.

When the soldier focused elsewhere in the truck, Neelie peered at the woman at Daniel's side. "Mrs. Weinstein?"

The old woman managed a weak smile and rubbed her hip, her breath coming in spurts.

Once the soldier's back was turned, Neelie crept over to the old woman and brushed loose white hairs from her face. "I'm so sorry. God is sorry too." The old woman leaned her head against Neelie's shoulder and closed her eyes.

The truck jerked to a stop, causing the group to lurch forward. More people joined them. The vehicle filled to the point they sat shoulder to shoulder. They remained quiet except for fits of coughing from Neelie, Tamar, and a young boy. At one point, the old woman Tante Neelie had called Mrs. Weinstein keeled forward into someone's back.

Daniel crept to the woman. "Give her room." He eased her into a prone position. "Tante Neelie, hold her head." The crowded conditions and pothole-filled streets made it hard for Daniel to kneel next to her. He felt her wrist for a moment and leaned over to check her breathing. Then he began pressing on her chest and counted.

The soldier bent to get a closer look, his weapon bumping against Tamar's shoulder as he spoke in broken Dutch. "What are you doing? Let the old widow die. It will be better for her."

Daniel ignored him, listened again for a breath, then kept pressing the old woman's chest at quick, regular intervals.

Pity swelled in Tamar's chest. "Do you need help?"

"Take over for me while I check her vitals." He showed her what to do, then she took over. "I wish I had my medical bag."

"Are you a doctor?" A trail of smoke rose from the soldier's cigarette.

"Yes, do you have any medical supplies on the truck?"

He rolled his eyes. "That would hardly suit our purposes." He guffawed. "Let the woman die. Better here than where you're going."

Daniel leaned down to listen again before addressing Tamar. "She's not breathing. My guess is, she's suffered a heart attack. Keep pressing on her chest five times, then rest, and so on."

She did as instructed. "She's so thin, Tante. How has Mrs. Weinstein stayed alive?"

"We took her food whenever we could. Our neighbor's always been a wee one." Neelie grasped Mrs. Weinstein's hand. "What can I do?"

"Does anyone have any water and some clean hankies?" Daniel whirled slowly.

Eyes turned away.

Neelie covered both the old woman's hands and bowed her head. "Lord, Mrs. Weinstein needs Your tender care. Wrap her in the precious arms of Your love."

Just then, Mrs. Weinstein's eyes flicked open. "Where ... am ... I?"

"Thank you, Lord," Neelie said, smiling up at Tamar's wide eyes. Then she patted the widow's hand. "You're with us, Mrs. Weinstein. You just rest." She glanced at Tamar again and chuckled. "Close your mouth, Tamar. You'll catch a fly." Neelie ducked her head and whispered to her, "Why didn't you hide with the others?"

Tamar felt her face warm, even in the cool dusk of the evening. "We were out on the roof."

"And you couldn't get back in time."

Tamar nodded, glancing at the soldier who stared ahead, smoke trailing from his lips. She lowered her voice. "We jumped onto Mrs. Weinstein's balcony, but when we reached the first floor, a German officer caught us." Remorse surged in unannounced. "We shouldn't have been out there. Bad decision."

"Don't say that. Regrets are weights we can't afford to carry. Let them go."

"Where are they taking—?" A spasm overtook Tamar. She averted her head and coughed into her sleeve.

"I don't know, but it's almost dark, so hopefully, we'll arrive shortly."

Tamar peered around the truck, then eased toward the opening when the guard appeared to be nodding off. The dark February sky had descended like a heavy curtain. The silhouettes of windmills loomed like dark monsters on either side of the road. February twenty-ninth, 1944. Leap year—the extra day. They could have done without it, she mused and moved back to sit next to Daniel.

The truck pulled to a sudden stop, throwing them forward. Tamar caught herself before she landed on Mrs. Weinstein. Searchlights moved from left to right. Someone said they'd seen a sign for Westerbork a few meters back.

They were moving again. The truck bounced along a pockmarked road until it jerked to a stop.

The soldier bolted up. "Everyone off." People struggled to their feet and limped toward the opening where the guard stood. "Hurry, off, off, off," he spat. With a sweep of his arm, he thrust a child and his mother off the truck.

One after another lowered themselves to the ground, but their progress was too slow for the soldier. He pushed an old couple toward the opening. Tamar helped Daniel lift Mrs. Weinstein to her feet. The woman leaned against his shoulder, her eyes remaining closed. She wouldn't make it through the night.

Daniel jumped to the ground, lifted the old woman from the truck, then helped Neelie and Tamar down. Tamar landed in a puddle on a heavily rutted, muddy road next to railroad tracks. Bram and Lars jumped down and assisted the final old man.

Tamar looked around. A high fence topped with barbed wire stood on one side. Dark silhouettes of watchtowers lined the fence at regular intervals. A few identical buildings stood by the tracks. Chaos everywhere. Darkness. Cries and screams. More trucks pulled up. People pushing and shoving, looking for their loved ones. Guards shouting in German. Bedlam. They stood in hell, lacking only the heat.

In the distance, golden light glowed from a large house on the free side of the fence, a mocking reminder of safety and warmth.

Tamar shivered and rubbed her arms against the cold night, panic niggling in. She'd lost sight of Daniel. She and Neelie scanned the crowds.

"Men to the left. Women to the right." Guards accentuated their commands with pokes from sidearms.

Daniel's voice behind Tamar made her gasp. Before she could turn, he said, "Remember that I love you."

"I love you too. Where's Mrs. Weinstein?"

He kissed the top of her head. "I carried her to the entrance of the building and left her there."

She spun, but he'd already vanished into the shadows. Tamar's hand went to her head, to that last touch of his lips. Would she ever see him again? How would they survive without the protection of the men they knew?

Neelie stood next to her until a guard jabbed a gun in their direction. A coughing jag erupted, and Neelie couldn't catch her breath.

"My tante needs a doctor," Tamar said to a female guard who looked less harsh.

"Move on," she responded.

Women of all ages were herded through the door of one of the single-story buildings. Inside, a row of people in uniforms sat at a table that stretched the length of the room. Tamar and Neelie took their places at the end of the line. The men had apparently been directed to another building.

So this was Westerbork. Tamar's first impression of this building was the lack of color. Gray and stark. Despair threatened to envelop her. She had to keep positive—maybe they wouldn't be held long, and maybe her parents were here. Tamar clung to that thought.

CHAPTER FOURTEEN

Neelie fingered the burning tattoo on her arm. She'd bitten her tongue to keep from screaming at the pain. Could the day get any worse? At least the guards let her keep her coat and her things. Four uniformed female guards flanked the line of women exiting the building and marched them single-file past one building after another—at least four rows of them—all the same. It reminded her of summer camp, without the fun.

Finally, the guards stopped at the door of the seventh—or was it the eighth?—building. Neelie had lost count. Nothing happened. Nobody said anything. She glanced back. Tamar was behind. Neelie nodded, afraid to say anything out loud. At least she and Tamar would be in the same building.

After five minutes, the door opened, and the guards yelled something in German that she assumed meant *move forward* since the guards were poking them onward with their sticks. Neelie moved inside and faced a woman with a clipboard.

"Name?"

"Neelie Visser."

The woman pointed to the left. "Cell six."

Neelie followed the guard who'd waited for her past a long row of cells along one side of the corridor. Dark gray, all the same, with small windows in metal doors. The guard moved in front of her to unlock the one that would be hers. She glanced back. Tamar was being funneled in the opposite direction.

The dust in the air made Neelie cough. "Water," she rasped.

The guard shoved her in. The jarring bolt on the door slid shut behind her, locking her into a small, square, and very dark room.

So this was her new home. A lone wooden cot sat against the right wall. A slop bucket sat by the door. In the dim light, everything appeared ... what else? Gray.

Conversations burbled from other cells—women housed together. Why did they put her in solitary confinement? She'd sacrifice comfort for company. It must have been her coughing. Tamar and Mrs. Weinstein? Maybe they were isolated as well.

Lumpy and uneven, the thin mattress reeked of sweat and dirt. When she flipped it over, a billow of dust rose, causing another coughing ordeal. Bone-tired, she lowered herself onto it. The straw pillow smelled of rotting vegetables. Reluctantly, she eased her head against it, holding her breath. The thin blanket did little to ward off the icy draft. Her hands dug into her coat pockets to get warm. What was that? Something metallic with corners. Frans' picture. A grateful sigh escaped. She took it out, kissed it, and hid it under the pillow.

Hours later, when harsh lights came on, she shielded her eyes. The bolt slid open with a resounding metallic clang. A guard carried in a tray of food. Thin, beige-colored broth and a hunk of bread. Black coffee.

The guard peered in the empty slop bucket. "I'll be back to pick up the tray. Hurry and eat because you'll be visiting the doctor."

The doctor. That explained her solitary cell. Neelie sipped the soup. Tasteless, saltless, yet the warmth of the bowl felt comforting in her hands. She dipped the bread in the soup and savored each bite, then sipped the tepid coffee, which matched the color of the room. Oh to make it last. She thought about the rich soups and homemade breads slathered with butter and homemade jam, and the cakes and cookies at home.

No, she would not allow her mind to wander to warm rooms and delicious meals. God had given her this new assignment. She'd forgotten to say a blessing. She thanked Him for the meal, and her heart almost meant it.

Despite the uncomfortable bed, she fell into a deep sleep, waking to the jarring sound of the cell door opening. A tall, erect guard walked in. "Good. You're wearing your coat. Follow me."

"Where to?" Neelie increased her pace to match the guard's strides.

"The consultation bureau."

When they exited the building, the fresh, early-morning sunshine splayed against her face. She closed her eyes for a moment and basked in its light.

A black car waited for her. Two other prisoners sat in the back, a pale woman and a sleeping man. She eased in next to them, while the driver and the guard climbed in the front seat. The car bounced over the train tracks that stopped in front of the building where they'd stood in line. The word *Westerbork* appeared above the arched egress through which they exited.

Sunshine bathed the road. The Hooghalen village sign welcomed them. Normal sights. A church. A bakery. A young boy carrying a book bag peered into the shop window. A horse-drawn buggy. A truck. A woman wearing a fur coat entered a bank. Ordinary activities. Did these people know what went on just outside their city?

Neelie didn't mind the wait in the warm consultation bureau. Maybe twenty minutes passed before a nurse called her to her desk.

"Name, please."

"Neelie Visser."

Unsmiling, businesslike, the nurse asked more questions, then stood. "Follow me to the WC." She pointed at the scale.

Neelie stepped on, amazed to see she'd lost five kilograms even with her coat and shoes on.

"Do you need anything?" The nurse's voice barely reached above a whisper.

Their eyes met. "What do you mean?"

"Soap, paper, cigarettes—anything?"

"Could you get me a Bible? And a pencil. And soap, and a needle and thread—anything you can think of. Please?" A dozen more things came to mind—a clean blanket, a towel—but she didn't want to annoy the woman. When Neelie looked up, the nurse smiled at her—a compassionate face. So unexpected after the harsh treatment from the guards last night.

The nurse led her to an examining room.

The doctor listened to her breathing, then said, "It sounds like pleurisy with effusion. Pre-tubercular. You'll need to go to the hospital. I hope a hospital visit helps you." Neelie didn't know what pleurisy was, but a hospital room sounded better than that cold cell.

Before opening the door, the nurse hugged her and slid a small bag into her pocket. "Hope you feel better soon." Then she led her to the guard who waited by the exit.

Neelie fingered the small bag and marveled at her good fortune. She'd been so astonished by the nurse's interest in her that she failed to say thank you, and even forgot to ask her name. The intensity of the last twenty-four hours had sapped her of good manners. Had it only been one day since Lieutenant Bergman had entered the shop demanding to know where she kept the babies?

Neelie climbed in the backseat with the other two prisoners. Would they be taking her to the hospital now? Mixed feelings filled her. Relief at getting proper help for her illness but unease at being separated from Tamar and the others. Should she say something to the staff at the hospital about the conditions at Westerbork? Could the staff be trusted?

The woman next to her snored, her head bobbing like a yo-yo. The sparse-haired man stared straight ahead. Neelie gazed out the window. The village streets were busier now. A mother pushed a buggy, stopping to peruse the wares in a shop display window. Two frolicking teenagers shoved each other, but when a green-uniformed officer crossed their path, they stuffed their hands in their pockets and hurried away.

When the car stopped at the Westerbork entrance gate, the driver spoke to a guard who waved them ahead, so they didn't go directly to the hospital. Neelie disliked being under someone else's control.

Her thoughts went to Maarika, whose strong will rivaled hers, but they'd reached a standoff of sorts. How were the babies? Had they remained in the attic room? Since the Hamels and Maarika hadn't been in the truck, Neelie chose to believe they'd made it. Jan would sneak them out when safe to do so. At least part of the plan had succeeded—the most important part.

They pulled up to the prison building. The guard escorted them back to their cubicles. Were Tamar and Mrs. Weinstein in any of the cells they passed? The small window on each door prevented a view of the rooms. How were Daniel and Lars and Bram?

The metallic bolt of her cage slid open. Neelie entered the cell, dismal and chilly without the sunshine's presence. The only window offered a patch of blue sky if she stood in the middle and craned her neck. She ventured a question. "When will I be going to the hospital?"

The guard frowned. "You don't need a hospital. Your temperature isn't high enough."

"But the doctor said—"

The door clanged shut. At least, the bag of surprises gave her something to look forward to. She'd take her time to enjoy each gift like her family did at Christmas. The uneven cot creaked under her weight. Neelie pulled out the bag.

She closed her eyes and fingered the items in its interior. Bless the nurse. Something felt smooth and waxy. A sliver of soap. Used sparingly, it would last a long time. Now she could wash her clothes.

Next came a nail. What a strange thing to put in the bag. She shrugged. With God, nothing was an accident. She closed her eyes and pulled out a small pad of paper and a pencil, its eraser almost gone. And something else in the bag. She pulled out a few pages from a Bible. Matthew. The nurse must have torn it out of her own book. *Thank You, Lord, and thank you, nurse with no name.* Neelie had no idea what the future held, but verses from this small section of the Gospels would stabilize her, entertain her, and enrich this gray cell. And she'd share its precious words with others whenever the opportunity arose.

The bolt sprang open. Neelie swept the gifts under her pillow and rested her head against it. The way the nurse had slid the bag into her pocket made it clear that the guards wouldn't allow prisoners to receive gifts.

A thin woman with hard lines etching her cheeks entered, dressed in a different uniform than the other guards. "I'm here to take your temperature."

With a little gasp of effort, Neelie sat up. "Good. I feel feverish, and I coughed up blood."

"That's why you're in solitary, so you won't give others your germs." The nurse approached. "Put this thermometer under your armpit." Neelie began to object that it wouldn't give an accurate reading, but the woman held up her hand. After a minute, she pulled the thermometer out and read it.

"Slightly above normal. You're fine."

"But I spit up blood."

The nurse shrugged and turned away. "Get some rest. You'll feel better soon." She pivoted back at the door. "I'm Hannie Kroes. I've been here for a year now. You're in for a long stay. Get used to it."

Neelie gaped at her. "So you're a prisoner too?"

Hannie gave a brusque nod. "If you need anything, I can find it for a price. Cigarettes, playing cards, extra bread. Let me know."

"But I don't have any money."

"There are ways. I also take trades."

Wobbling slightly, Neelie rose to her feet. "I have friends here. Lars and Bram. Not sure of their last names. Also, Tamar and Daniel Feldman. He's a doctor. Have you seen them?"

"A doctor, you say." Hannie's eyebrows lifted. "I'll see what I can find out."

Once the door clanged shut, Neelie sat back down, a sliver of hope edging her despair aside. This nurse, this prisoner, could be an ally who could bring her news.

For the first time, Neelie noticed a dish and a hunk of bread that sat on the floor by the door. Food would give her strength, and it would give her something to do. She picked up the bowl and bread. Colorless gruel. It didn't matter. The cold mush filled her stomach. Neelie gulped it, then remembered to slow down. It wouldn't do to throw it up.

Now that she felt better, she stared at the wall above her bed. No clocks were near to toll the hour like the choir of timepieces at home. The only way to judge the passing of time was by the blue of the sky outside the window. Like the prisoner in *The Count of Monte Cristo*, she'd have to etch the walls with the passing days. But how? Her gaze drifted to her pillow and the items it hid. Ah, the nail.

Neelie almost giggled. Maarika would roll her eyes at Neelie finding the good in a bad situation. She teetered on her cot and used the nail to fashion a rudimentary calendar on the wall. The nail penetrated the plaster with ease.

Was that a knock on the other side? Another living soul separated from her by a thin wall. She rapped twice and almost lost her balance when two knocks responded. "Hello? What's your name?" The knocking moved to her left. Neelie kept up the two raps until they reached the corner. A crack appeared where the two walls met. If Neelie pressed against the wall, she could see movement on the other side. "Hello? I'm Neelie. Who are you?"

"Tante Neelie? I heard you talking to that nurse. It's Tamar."

A squeal escaped. "Tamar. How are you? I thought you were at the other end of the hall."

Tamar's lower lip appeared in the crack. "I'm fine … I mean … I can't stop coughing."

Neelie flattened her hand against the wall, almost as if she could touch her young friend. "It's the dust. Do you have others in your cell?"

"I was in a different cell at first, but they moved me here because my coughing bothered the other women."

It must have happened while she was gone to the doctor. "Oh, it's so good to hear your voice, to know that you're—"

"Now we don't need to be alone, Tante."

"Wait a minute." Neelie ran to her pillow, removed a piece of soap, and rushed back. "I don't know why I'm hurrying. I'm not going anywhere." She broke off a small piece of soap and forced it through the largest gap in the wall.

A gasp answered her effort. "Where did you get the soap?"

"They sent me to a health office this morning—the consultation bureau. They said I had pleurisy with effusion. I met the nicest nurse. There are still good people in Nederland." Neelie glanced at the little pad of paper on the pillow. "Wait, Tamar." She grabbed a page from Matthew 5 and a piece of paper from the pad and scribbled some words on it, then stuffed the two papers through the gap in the wall. "Here."

"What is this, Neelie?"

"A page from the book of Matthew and a Bible verse. If you can't read my scribbles, it says, 'He shall cover you with His feathers, and under His wings shalt thou trust.' It's a verse from Psalm 91. A promise. God always keeps His promises."

"Thanks. Any news about the others?"

"No." A moan escaped. Every time Neelie's mind went to the babies and the others at her house, and Jan—wherever he was— her joy faltered under the blanket of despair. *Without God, Neelie. You worry when you forget about God.*

"I hear footsteps. Until later."

Neelie nodded as if Tamar could see her and returned to the cot. The mattress had taken on new bumps with the creation of the calendar, but she smiled despite herself. Imagine having Tamar Kaplan as a neighbor. God had given her a gift, and she needed to trust Him with what little reserve remained.

CHAPTER FIFTEEN

A fresh spasm of coughing racked Tamar. If only someone could bring her relief—a lozenge, a hot compress, anything. But the unheated room and thin blanket offered little shelter from the cold. She picked up the wedge of soap and sniffed it. Clean smells. She'd hold it to her nose to ward off the odor wafting from the pillow.

She smiled. Neelie's God had taken care of her. Not just Neelie's God, her God. *Yahweh*. Tamar traced a finger over the small paper the size of a note card. It wouldn't hurt to memorize the verse. And Daniel would be proud of her. She'd ask Neelie for more verses to memorize because she had nothing else to do with her time.

Daniel. With one more sniff of the soap, Tamar closed her eyes. Daniel smelled like clean soap. Her neck cricked at his height, but she loved his warm lips against hers, the slight cinnamon of his breath, the scratch of his beard. Nothing could ever steal the sensations of Daniel from her. Every sniff of the soap would remind her of him.

The slide of the bolt made her sit up straight. With her hand behind her back, Tamar slid the paper and the soap under the blanket. If discovered, the guard would confiscate them. Why? Because she could. A matronly woman entered, carrying a tray of food. Porridge the color of the cell, and a gray-black liquid. At least, the coffee was warm and would help renew her strength.

"Thank you," Tamar said, then her eyes widened. She covered her mouth to contain the gasp at the man standing near the door, holding a large box. "Daniel."

He shook his head slightly, then frowned when the guard turned around.

"Doctor, will you see to this woman's cough?"

Daniel nodded and approached Tamar, not making eye contact with her. "Open your mouth wide." He peered down her throat, frowning. His hand felt cool against her forehead. "She has a fever." He shook a thermometer. Tamar opened her mouth. "No, under the arm, miss. You wouldn't want this in your mouth." His eyes peered at her through long, dark lashes. Smiling eyes. He winked and slid her a peppermint.

With the thermometer under her armpit, she said, "Are the men as sick as the women, Doctor?"

"No, miss. Most of the men are fine."

Good. She needn't worry about Bram and Lars. "Did you see Neelie next door?" she asked under her breath.

"No," he whispered. "I'm sorry. They told us not to waste our time on older people, but I'll—"

"Enough talk." The guard's shriek made Daniel drop the thermometer on the cement floor. He scooped it up and wiped it on his shirt. "If you can't be quicker and less careless, doctor, we'll get someone who can."

He didn't react, but a note fell next to Tamar's lap. She inched her fingers forward to cover it as, with a wistful, parting smile, Daniel stood and then retreated from her cell.

The moment the bolt clanged into place, she picked up the crumpled piece of paper, no bigger than the palm of her hand. *Bram and Lars released. I love you.*

Released! Yes. Joy shot through her, and a giggle made her stomach wobble at the memory of Daniel saying he wanted her to be his nurse.

If they made it out of Westerbork, they'd marry. Nothing lavish. A civil ceremony, and later on, when her parents and brother returned and the jewelry shop was restored, Tamar would get her Jewish wedding. Of course, her mother would insist on a proper one with caviar and the *hora*. Tamar imagined Daniel with his gangly legs delicately balancing on a chair held up high. Thinking about the wedding gave her hope.

Her prison cell looked a little less desolate. Daniel was mobile. Maybe when she felt better, Tamar could join him as his assistant, but first things first. The gruel looked unappetizing, but she'd take care of herself. She gulped down the insipid mixture and made her plan.

One, work on becoming strong of spirit. Begin each day by reading five verses. Commit them to memory if they held a lesson or a promise. Neelie was always offering words of comfort or advice from the Bible. More than pithy sayings, the verses seemed to have a certain power to settle an issue—to settle a heart.

Two, work on becoming strong of body. Instead of feeling sorry for herself, she'd get up and walk or run around the cell. For a few weeks, the long walks to visit patients had invigorated her, but since her confinement at the Visser house, she hadn't managed any physical activity except hustling up and down the stairs. Now her skin resembled the color of a moth, and her limbs trembled with exertion. No more. The wall would become a barre on which to perform the daily exercises she'd learned in early ballet classes. And the room would become a gym to do calisthenics—lunges, squats, and push-ups.

Three, work on becoming strong of mind. Instead of worrying about her family and friends, she would concentrate on what she did know—the things Daniel had taught her about working with patients. Her bit of experience might become useful if the guards let her nurse prisoners. Also, she'd review the German Seth had forced on her as an adolescent. With the guards passing by her cell, she'd listen to their conversations, try to make sense of them, and memorize words. And there was music to practice—arias, scales, Dutch ballads.

She would begin now.

The sun shone through the small, slanted windows, narrowing into a circle in the middle of the floor. Tamar stood in that circle, head tilted to the light, eyes closed. She remained there, content for the moment. A few steps to the wall for support, then she worked her way through barre exercises from her teen years. *Grands* and *petits battements, relevés,* and a few *ronds de jambe.* Her legs groaned their disapproval, yet she kept at it, doing five more, then ten.

Despite the tightness in the back of her legs, the pain felt good—as if she was doing something positive for the first time since her parents had disappeared. She circled the cell in a walk, in a trot, and then as fast as she could run in the small room. Her breath came in spurts after a dozen circles, and at twenty, she doubled over, coughing. When she caught her breath, she slowed to a walk—toe, heel, toe, heel—the way they'd taught her in ballet.

She managed a few twirls, then lowered herself to the floor to stretch. Stiff as a piece of wood, she forced her nose to the floor, refusing to think of the cement's dirty condition. Slowly resuming a seated position, she raised her arms above her head and hummed a Yiddish ditty from Shabbat school.

Hums turned to soft melodies of songs she'd learned at school. Simple songs that evoked memories. Lullabies and folk ballads and songs from shul. Without realizing it, Tamar raised her voice to hit the high notes.

A knock on the wall separating her from Tante Neelie had Tamar scrambling to the slit.

Neelie's lips moved. "You sound lovely, my dear—" She lowered her voice. "But you must be careful or the guards will hear you."

"I'm sorry, Tante. I don't want to get us in trouble."

"Keep on singing, child. You bring beauty to the prison with your melodies, but keep the volume down."

"Guess what?" Tamar widened her eyes, squeezing her fingers into a fist. "I saw Daniel. He came with a guard to take my temperature."

Neelie's lashes fluttered. "That's wonderful. Did he say anything?"

Tamar held her breath for a second. "Lars and Bram have been released."

"Oh, this is very good. I wonder if that means we might be released." Hope purled into Neelie's voice, and she nodded.

"Please, keep singing."

"I will. But first, I have a question."

Fabric rustled. "Yes. Ask anything."

"What happened yesterday?" Had it truly only been yesterday? It felt a lifetime ago. So much had changed. "Daniel and I were out on the roof, and we heard the German voices."

"Lieutenant Bergman came by." The pause that followed held meaning.

Her Lieutenant Bergman. If it hadn't been for her singing, he would have been nothing more than a client getting his violin repaired. Tamar's shoulders drooped. "Oh."

"Don't, Tamar. It's not your fault. When Bergman was there, two of the babies cried. He heard and demanded to know whose they were. That's why we are here and our guests are not. We can rejoice in that much. Keep singing, Tamar. It's a gift to me."

After weeks of calisthenics and kilometers of circles around the cell, Tamar's coughing subsided. Her arms and legs, though thinner, were firm and strong. She felt better than she had in a long time.

It occurred to her she'd been floating through life since the opera closed, not thinking too much, living in the urgent—her way of protecting herself when one freedom after another was ripped away. Then her parents disappeared, and her life became a nearly comatose walk. But now, with each stretch, with each song, Tamar took charge. No longer picturing herself as a victim, she'd look for opportunities to act. For what? Only God knew.

Ten *pliés* at the barre increased to two hundred. At first, her legs burned, but now she thought of other things. Such as subterfuge. Tamar had learned a few things from watching her brother and accompanying Daniel to visit sick patients. And of course, the hidden attic room. She'd get herself in good shape and see what doors opened.

One morning, Tamar woke to the rustling of paper. A note lay near the door from a prisoner who had been part of the Resistance, telling her that Seth had gone into hiding. Tamar breathed out a *thank you*.

Daniel also used his position as a doctor to convey messages and medicine. He'd visited her cell twice since the first time. Always with more peppermints or a pencil or something pretty. Always with an apology that he couldn't give her more.

Messages changed hands when the guard turned away. With the pencil's lead almost gone, Tamar wrote sparse notes to him on one of the pages of verses Neelie had stuffed through the corner gap. Daniel passed a note under the door another time. He'd written that Mrs. Weinstein had died ten days after arriving at Westerbork. She was with the Lord, Daniel wrote. *With the Lord.* Tamar had never heard those words before. They comforted her. But each time Daniel left her, her spirit chafed at her confinement.

Danger lurked in the unknown, but she could do nothing sitting in this cell.

She had one key that had opened unexpected doors in the past … her voice. That evening, Tamar stood under the window, warmed up with some scales, and then chose "*L'ho Perduta*," Mozart's work from *The Marriage of Figaro*. The little dictator who hated Jews came from Austria, as Mozart had.

Next, she launched into another song from *Figaro*—"*Voi Che Sapete*," a lilting tune designed for a mezzo-soprano. A fun song to sing as she circled the room.

Tante Neelie rapped on the wall, her cue to meet her at the corner slit. Through the crack, part of Neelie's lip was visible as it moved. "What are you doing, singing so loudly?"

"I don't know." Tamar bounced on her toes and wiggled her fingers to keep the blood flowing. "But I need to get out of here, and maybe my singing will help."

"I can't fault you, my dear. Just be careful. We're not dealing with normal people here. They're evil and disdainful. Such intense hatred for your people cannot come from this world."

"Then cover me with your prayers. I know God answers yours."

"That He does, but not always the way I want Him to."

She pressed her narrowed eye to the slit and whispered fiercely, "I still don't understand why God—if He loves us—would allow us to be here."

Neelie frowned. "I'm not good at explaining things. But God is good. He never promised life would be easy. But He did promise to go with us through the valleys, and my God and yours does not lie."

An unbidden sigh leaked out.

"Will you be careful, Tamar?"

She stepped back a bit. "Yes, and you will pray?"

"I will, dear girl."

"And Neelie?"

"Yes?"

Tamar breathed in, hating to relay the news. "I heard about Mrs. Weinstein."

"She died?"

"Yes, Tante. Ten days after we arrived here. That's all I know."

Neelie released a soft breath. "She's with her husband now. Mrs. Weinstein was a believer."

Tamar started to ask what that meant—a believer—as if that determined where Mrs. Weinstein went. It reminded her of the certainty Daniel had of his future. Could anyone be certain of what they couldn't see? "Good night, Tante," was all she said.

The next day, Tamar sang a song for Tante Neelie, but "*Exsultate, Jubilate*" led to the bolt sliding to the left. The matronly guard entered the cell, followed by a soldier in green garb. "Come with us, Visser."

Good. They still didn't know her true identity. She'd given the name *Visser* to the *ober* when they'd registered that first night at Westerbork. So much the better. Her Jewish heritage was still a secret. Visser would fare better than Kaplan.

Subterfuge.

Her eyes went to her bed. They'd find the soap—her precious soap, and the pages of verses that she'd come to appreciate. Lucky for her, she'd had time to stuff them under her pillow before the guard entered.

"Lice," Tamar said.

The matron's eyes narrowed. "What did you say?"

She pointed. "Lice in the bed." A lie, or maybe not. Hadn't she awakened scratching her scalp? Lice or lack of washing her hair in over a month. At any rate, lice would keep the guards away from her bed.

Tamar followed the soldier, the guard taking up the rear. Where were they taking her? Neelie had mentioned being taken to the consultation bureau, but Tamar felt better now.

Outside, the colors filled her with delight. How she'd ever taken nature's sights for granted made no sense now. Tamar breathed in deeply of fresh, frigid air—the first time in over a month. Was it March? No, more likely the beginning of April—she'd lost track after a few nights. Neelie would know. She lifted her face to the sunny breeze.

A cumulus cloud formed the shape of a rabbit. She took in the gloomy sameness of the red-brick buildings around her and realized the enemy could control the surroundings, but they couldn't keep the cloud from forming into a bunny. God gave her that as a present. God again. She thought about Him more often lately.

The courtyard was devoid of humanity. Their little procession headed toward a building on the other side. Tamar hurried to keep up with the officer's long strides. She longed to ask him where they were going, but he wouldn't tell her, or worse, he'd respond with the back of his hand. Germans didn't talk to those they considered as low as rodents or skunks.

Although the rows of barracks looked identical, the one they entered was different. It buzzed with activity and noise—the busyness of an office. Typewriter keys clicked. Footsteps echoed. The staticky voice of the Führer mixed with the other sounds in a syncopated rhythm. How she hungered for rhythm. It smelled better here, not like the fetid air of her building. Officers—both female and male—passed the lobby at a fast clip. Normal people doing what appeared to be normal jobs.

Tamar peered behind her at the guard. The woman frowned and nudged her forward. The officer had stopped at a receptionist window, then motioned for her and the guard to follow him. Not knowing made her anxious. Would she be punished for singing? What could be worse than solitary confinement? Death ... for a song?

They stopped beside a door at the end of the hall. The officer opened the door, motioned her in, then stood back. "Frau Meier will be meeting you in a few minutes." He clicked his heels, then closed the door.

Alone in the silent room, she surveyed her surroundings. Rows of dresses and fur coats lined the wall on the left. Tamar approached the first row, lifting a satin sleeve. The musty smell of humid attics and dank cellars filled her nose. She refused to think where these dresses—some stylish and expensive—came from. Her hand slid over the soft fur of one of the dozens of mink coats and stoles.

Racks of leather boots and high-heeled shoes covered the back wall. A wide assortment of hats with feathers and veils crowded the shelves above the racks. It reminded her of the costume rooms of the Haarlem Opera, although this room held ten times as many garments. Maybe they'd heard her sing and brought her here to perform. If so, her plan had succeeded. So why was she not ecstatic? Far from it, she had the distinct impression she was walking into a trap.

"*Ach*, there you are." A portly woman, dressed in an emerald frock and a sequined cap with a peacock feather, bustled into the room and waved dramatic red fingernails at her. Her eyes flashed with delight, a great and unexpected contrast to the dead and aloof eyes of the guards and officers. "Come, child, let's get you fitted."

The woman circled Tamar, punctuated with *ja* and *zehr gut*. "I have just the thing."

"Why am I here?" Tamar asked, under her breath in case the woman didn't want her questions.

"You don't know? But of course, you're here to sing." The woman grabbed her face in one hand and examined it, turning it left to right. "You'll do very well, sweetie."

A sense of guarded excitement filled Tamar, not unlike the feeling she'd felt when Anna and Eliza had prepared her to play Violetta months ago. Had it only been months? Her life had changed so much, it seemed like decades. If it was April, then six months had passed since she played Violetta. She had been guarded that night, but more idealistic—believing her performance of Violetta could lead to a future as a lead soprano. Small dreams, selfish aspirations.

The frau took her hand and studied her long, broken nails. Tamar bit her lip, grateful for the gentle touch, so foreign since she'd arrived at Westerbork.

"You can soak these while I work on your face, but first, you'll need a shower. Then we'll trim your nails, style your hair, and select your outfit."

Tamar's eyes widened. A shower? Maybe there'd be soap and privacy. Warm water might be too much to hope for. A tinge of guilt entered unbidden. Neelie should be here to take a shower more than she. But if what Daniel said was true, the older prisoners were overlooked for any favor.

"Come on, child. We must hurry."

"What are we preparing for?" Tamar steeled herself for a cuff to the side of her head.

"Don't you know? You're performing for the celebration tonight. It's the Führer's birthday." She handed her a towel and soap. "Get out of those clothes. We'll burn them. I've got a lovely blue ball gown that will look beautiful with your blonde hair."

Tamar stopped midstream. "Is he coming here?"

The frau guffawed. "Of course not, he's much too busy for

a transit camp like Westerbork. But celebrations will occur everywhere tonight. Now get going."

She entered a large room with at least a dozen showerheads. What kind of establishment would offer a communal shower like this? A camp? A prison? Tamar picked the one closest to the corner. Warm water sprayed over her face, her shoulders, her hair. Tamar used the soap to wash her thick curls for the first time in … who knew how long? If only she could stay here for hours. Her vigorous scrubbing left red welts on her legs and arms. Never had she appreciated a shower more. When the water ran cold, she dried and wrapped the towel around her head, then waited for the woman to return.

"Come, dear." The German woman peeked around the corner, beckoned to her, then disappeared.

Tamar removed the towel from her head and wrapped it around her midsection before following the woman back to the dressing room.

The frau handed her a luxurious satin robe with Oriental drawings. Tamar put it on and hurried to the seat facing a large mirror.

"Do you have curly hair, dear?" she asked, dabbing her fingers in pomade and rubbing it on her palms.

"Yes, ma'am, it's naturally curly. May I ask you some questions?"

"Of course, but I highly doubt I'll know the answers. I'm simply the wardrobe monitor." After massaging the pomade through her hair, the woman grabbed a wide-toothed comb and teased through Tamar's curls. "Your hair is a marvel. We'll add a few twigs of baby's breath. That's all you'll need." She twisted the chair around to face her. "Let's add some color to your cheeks and lips. You don't need a lot."

While the woman added a touch of rouge to her cheeks, Tamar ventured a question. "What is your name?"

"My name? I'm Gisela Meier. What's yours?"

"Tamar Ka—Visser. Do you know what I'll be singing?"

"I'm sure I don't know. But when you leave here, the man in charge will give you the information you seek. We don't have time to dry your hair. We'll let nature take its course. Come with me."

Frau Meier whirled the chair around and strode away at a fast clip. Tamar jumped up and hurried to catch up. Somehow, she knew this woman was an ally. And she needed one.

"Here it is. The blue gown I had in mind for you." Frau Meier held the dress against Tamar's frame. "You're so thin, girl. You must eat like a bird to keep your figure so lithe."

"I—I—"

"We don't have time to take in the waist, so I'll use safety pins. Is it not beautiful against your blonde hair? Yes, they'll like you. They'll like you very much."

"Who, Frau Meier? The guard told me nothing. Who will I be singing for?"

"Why, the officers, dear. It gets a little dreary around here at times. The men need some fun. You know men. They're missing their families. I don't blame them."

Tamar grimaced. Her hand clutched her chest. Her horrified expression must have caught the woman's attention.

"Now don't you worry. They need someone pretty to listen to and look at. That's all." She patted Tamar on the shoulder. "Now go put this on." The woman pointed to a Japanese room divider.

Behind it, Tamar couldn't help but rub the smooth, cool satin of the gown against her face. Sapphire blue, simple lines. Slipping it over her head, it fell with no resistance. She'd definitely lost weight—ten kilograms. Her hands bunched the extra inches of fabric on either side of her waist, and she regarded herself in the mirror from all sides.

"How does it look, dearie?"

"It's a lovely dress, but it needs taking in."

"Didn't I tell you?" Frau Meier peeked around the corner. "Nothing a few pins can't fix. Come with me, child." In no time, the dress took on a waistline, and the bodice no longer sagged.

"Now have a look at these three-quarter length gloves and pretty shoes. Put them on and return to the makeup table. I have a surprise for you."

Everything happened so fast. Tamar felt out of control but trusted this woman. She regained her seat before the mirror.

"I'm going to pull the side strands of your hair back with baby's breath and let the curls hang down your back. How's that?" The woman stared at her through the mirror's reflection.

"Nice."

"Good. I think so too. Now here's the surprise." The wardrobe monitor handed her a plum-colored, rectangular box embossed with the name *Bron*—a famous jewelry company. As a tremulous breath escaped Tamar, Frau Meier frowned. "What's wrong?"

"My parents—my parents' shop kept a few necklaces and bracelets from Bron Jewelers for some of their clients." Each costing more than the average person could afford in ten years. "It just brought back … memories."

"Well, now you'll get to wear them. That's my surprise. Open it."

Tamar removed the tight-fitted lid. A diamond necklace and matching earrings twinkled on smooth, mauve satin. "They're lovely."

"Glad you like them. They'll bring out the rich blue of the dress. Here, let me help."

Head spinning from the rapid—and drastic—turn of events, Tamar closed her eyes while Frau Meier added more pink to her cheeks. She was wearing confiscated jewels. She would be performing for the men who might have stolen them. It made her sick.

Frau Meier must know the jewels came to this room by force, even violence. The woman maintained her sunny disposition, not digging too deep, not asking anything more than basic questions. Tamar must do likewise for now, forcing the horrible thoughts from her mind.

"Stand, dear." Frau Meier clasped her hands like a proud parent. "You'll be a big hit. Now let's go meet the man in charge."

Tamar almost tripped over the woman when she came to a quick stop and rapped three times on a door at the other end of the corridor.

"Come in," answered an impatient voice.

Frau Meier glanced up at Tamar, wet her finger, and swiped it against Tamar's cheek. "You'll do fine. I'll be in the wings watching. Don't be nervous." She smiled warmly, then bustled away.

Tamar buoyed her nerves with a deep breath and entered the office. Her eyes widened at the man behind the desk. Glossy black hair, pencil-thin mustache. Thin. Elegantly dressed. Sneider. The man from the Amsterdam restaurant who'd asked her to sing. The one who'd said he remembered her voice from somewhere.

CHAPTER SIXTEEN

The man's eyes met hers. He sprang to his feet. "Tamar Visser. What a nice surprise. I hadn't expected to see you here. I hoped to follow your career, even arranged a performance at a private club, but Lieutenant Bergman said he lost track of you. How delighted I am to see you once again." He rounded the desk and took her hands in his. "What are you doing at Westerbork?"

"I'm … a guest." She kept her face impassive.

His head cocked to the side. "Guest? Of whom?"

What could she say that would satisfy him? Tamar mumbled a few words about a friend and managed a smile. He took her elbow and guided her through another door to a large, Rococo-style room with a dozen rows of ornamental chairs facing a baby grand piano.

She took in the whole space—so ornate it suffocated her. Cherubs playing hide-and-seek amidst fluffy clouds covered the ceiling. The gilded walls displayed framed paintings on every panel. One caught her eye—the lady in yellow with the violin. Tamar had seen it a dozen times adorning the wall of the gallery she'd passed on the way home from school—the Hamels' gallery. Now it hung on the wall of this stifling room.

"Come this way, Mevrouw Visser. The accompanist isn't here yet, but I can play the part. I suggest one aria and one ballad. German would be best in honor of the Führer's birthday."

She clasped her gloved hands in front of her. "Whatever you suggest. Will I be the only one singing?"

"No, there'll be some burlesque numbers, a comedian, and a magician. You won't be alone."

"That is good. I must tell you I've been sick of late and may be rusty. What songs do you suggest?"

"Herr Bergman said you'd been sick. He may be in the audience tonight. I'm sure he'd love to see you." Bergman in the audience. He studied her as Tamar held her breath, willing her face to remain impassive. "Well, we don't have long to rehearse. Something lighthearted like 'Lili Marlene.' Are you familiar with it?"

How could she sing in front of that—? She focused. Meneer Sneider was waiting for an answer. "Yes, that's a good choice. And what about the operatic piece?"

"Again, something lighthearted. *'Frühlingsstimmen'* by Strauss. Would you like to try it?"

She nodded. "It's a challenge in the high register, but I'll try."

Sneider took a seat at the piano, the polish of his hair catching the chandelier light. He played through the Strauss piece with its *oompah* beat. Tamar had spent six months perfecting the aria with her vocal coach, and her brother had made her sing it until every note hit the mark and every German word was pronounced with no mistakes. It had been a few years since she'd thought of the song. If only she could ask Neelie to pray for her to remember the words.

Husky at first, her voice strained—from nerves or disuse, she didn't know. Sneider had to start over a few times, but he said nothing. Finally, when Tamar forced herself to calm down and forget the peril, the words and phrasing came back.

Finally, Meneer Sneider rested his hands in his lap. "There, Tamar—may I call you by your given name? You're ready. I noticed something different in your voice this time, but I can't put my finger on it."

She brought a knuckle to her lips. "I'm sorry. As I said, I've been out of practice."

"What sickness did you have? I hope I'm not being too forward."

"It came almost immediately after performing in Amsterdam. Pneumonia or bronchitis. I'm over it now."

Swiveling on the piano bench, he pulled her hand away from

her lips and held it in his. She stared at it, not knowing what to do. "That certainly is good news. But the difference in your voice runs deeper than that. A newfound pathos. Angst. There are layers that only one who is attuned to the subtleties of tone and phrase would note. It's a compliment, Tamar. You own your voice now."

"Th-thank you." It was what she had wanted so badly before singing Violetta. And now, apparently, she had it. But at what cost? And to what end?

He blinked, cocking his head. "Has this war been hard on you?"

Hard? Her breath caught in her throat. She could feel the words ready to spew out of her mouth. About her parents disappearing. About people she loved being denied treatment because of their age. Although Sneider's eyes filled with concern, she didn't trust him. "It has been hard on us all, Meneer Sneider."

"Klaus."

She nodded but kept her eyes on the piano keys.

"Well." His hand slowly moved away, and he stood. "Your voice is crystal clear and your diction exquisite for someone who doesn't speak German."

"Thank you."

He bowed. "The guests will begin showing up in minutes. You can wait in the adjoining room or return to the costuming area. Your choice."

"May I see the room?"

He pointed at a door, almost concealed by a small table holding a bust of some military figure. "Help yourself."

She entered the room, desperately wanting some space from this man who covered her hand, who seemed to read her thoughts. The early evening sun illuminated the space—a waiting room of sorts. Hangers littered the tapestry rug, and ladies' gowns and men's tuxedos lay over the backs of chairs. An upright piano sat next to a door with an exit sign over it, an overflowing ashtray littering the high keys. This was too dangerous with Bergman in the audience. Her cell suddenly looked inviting. Heading toward the stage door, Tamar almost ran out of the room, then stopped. This was her precipice. If only Daniel were here to advise her. Even Seth, who'd punctuate each sentence with reprimands.

If her fiancé or brother or Neelie couldn't be here, she'd be strong like the new Tamar, no longer the victim. Lowering herself into one of the wingback chairs, Tamar faced the window. Dust particles floated in the stale air. She smoothed the wrinkles from her gown.

I'm here because I can sing. This is what I do. Much better this than wallowing in my cell.

What could go wrong? Many things. Sneider might figure out where he'd heard her sing before. Maybe he'd attended *La Traviata* that night. Saw her Violetta. He hadn't asked about her fiancé. How much did the man know about her? What had Bergman said? She felt like that mouse again, and tonight she would sing before the very felines who had torn her life and the lives of her loved ones apart. So many things could go wrong.

Neelie had once said something about praying a hedge of protection around her parents. The prayer had comforted her. She needed that hedge around her tonight.

Voices came from the Rococo room. The guests must be arriving. Little time remained.

Lord, right now, I need Your help with that hedge of protection Neelie talked about. I'll be singing before the enemies of my people. Your people. I trust You.

The door squeaked open, and Frau Meier flounced in. "There you are. Let me check everything, just to be sure. Are you nervous?"

"Yes ma'am." Tamar calmed her breathing as the woman bustled around her, straightening her neckline and touching up her lipstick.

"You look fetching, my dear. Herr Sneider said to be ready at the door." She took Tamar's hand and led her to it. "Wait here. Don't be afraid. I always like to think the officers are merely somebody's sons, somebody's grandchildren."

Tamar nodded. "Thank you, Frau Meier. You're very kind."

"Don't mention it." Then she left.

Tamar peeked through the small opening. Although the lights were dimmed, she could tell that uniformed officers occupied most of the seats. A few women in evening gowns fanned themselves. A short, tuxedo-clad man spoke in fast German at the mic. The sudden bursts of laughter led her to conclude he was the comedian. He sat at the piano and played the "Happy Birthday" tune. Everyone stood and raised their hand, palm down, and sang in unison, "*Zum Geburtstag viel Glück.*"

Whew! Had she been asked to sing that, Tamar would have stumbled over the words. The little man stood and bowed, and the crowd applauded. How could she follow a comedian? Would the audience be stifling yawns, or worse, would they fall asleep?

Meneer Sneider went to the piano, clapping as he walked. He said something that drew laughter. The German she'd learned in high school didn't help here. The name *Visser* reached her ears.

Like a phantom, Tamar glided out to the crowd's polite applause. She bowed, then approached the microphone, set too low for her, and bent to reach it. This wouldn't do.

When Meneer Sneider hurried over to adjust it, the static made her wince. He said something else, and the audience tittered—a comment about Dutch people. A new pianist had taken a seat at the piano, waiting for her signal.

To have to perform for the very people who thought her less than human was unadulterated evil.

In the presence of my enemies. Words she'd heard in shul now took on new meaning.

In broken German, Tamar said, "Good evening. I am happy to sing for you tonight. I begin with Strauss." She nodded toward the pianist and breathed in. *In, out. In, out. Hedge of protection.*

Her voice took flight.

Tamar had not thought about the lyrics since all her energies had focused on learning the German by sound rather than meaning, but now she concentrated on the words:

Spring in all its splendor rises,
ah, all hardship is over,
sorrow becomes milder,
good expectations,
the belief in happiness returns;
sunshine, you warm us,
ah, all is laughing, oh, oh awakes.

Despite the harsh conditions, spring always made everything look better, feel better. Tulips appeared, a harbinger of warmer temperatures. The dull, crusty snow, short days, and endless nights gave way to sunshine, and with it, hope. Did she dare hope? The music brought hope. It lifted her spirits, and for the first time in months, fear disappeared and the melody took over. Without effort, her voice took on a fanciful tone. Entranced in the rhythm, the high notes came easy—even lighthearted and fun.

Tamar glanced at the audience. Their heads swayed in unison to the rhythm, as though they were joined together through this song. She sensed their delight, saw the rapture in their eyes despite the dimmed lighting. With the last chords, the crowd sprang to their feet, their applause generous. A few *bravos* punctuated their acceptance. It occurred to her in a flash that music had the power to unite. Tamar bowed, then smiled her gratitude.

After she curtsied twice more, the audience finally took their seats. The pianist began "Lili Marlene." Tamar gave her whole self to the song, taking risks with trills and octave changes. The audience joined in on the refrain with rousing voices. They demanded an encore, which she gladly gave them, the applause deafening. She bowed, then disappeared into the waiting room, closing the door behind her.

She leaned against it, waiting for her heartbeat to return to normal. How she missed the opera and the interaction with the audience. Her part in the chorus had given her a tiny piece of what it was like to connect with the audience, but tonight she consumed the whole cake.

Fatigue struck like a sudden shower. She'd forgotten how performances depleted her strength. Perhaps now that she was finished, she could sneak away to her cell for a much-needed nap and a chat with Tante Neelie later.

"You were magnificent." She jumped at the sound of a male voice behind her.

CHAPTER SEVENTEEN

Tamar waited for her eyes to acclimate to the dim room. A slight movement and rustle of fabric made her freeze—and the silhouette of a man in the corner wingback chair, the one that had been covered with garments. His voice sounded familiar, a slight German accent, a tone used to being obeyed. He rose and ambled toward her.

Lieutenant Bergman.

"Why are you here?" She inched backward, tamping down the fluster.

"The Führer's birthday, of course. How are you, Tamar?" He moved toward her with a panther's ease, his gaze locked on hers. If she didn't know better, she could almost imagine he cared. His eyes held a glint of emotion—remorse, compassion, tenderness. But no, this man had betrayed Neelie Visser and her guests. He was not to be trusted.

"I am fine." She backed against the door. "I should go."

"You did such a lovely job. Your voice is still above everyone's."

She managed a polite smile and turned to leave.

"Don't. We have much to talk about. I want to discuss your career, your future."

She faced him, her fingers touching the safety of wood behind her. There was no way she could evade his grasp if she tried to reach the exit door on the far wall. She had to choose. Leave via the stage in the middle of the magician's act or stay in this isolated room with the man responsible for her imprisonment. An easy decision. "Nice to see you again," she whispered, then slipped through the narrow gap in the door.

The tuxedoed magician held up a deck of cards. All eyes focused on his every move, which worked to her advantage. Tamar tiptoed around the baby grand, not sure where to go. She scanned the side walls for Frau Meier but didn't see her. She couldn't go back to the prison barrack in this gown. Imagine waiting outside the cell for them to unlock the door dressed like this. She almost laughed at the absurdity of her situation, which was fraught with layers of unseen danger.

Tamar searched for an empty seat on the end of a row so she could sneak out of the room—in case Lieutenant Bergman spied her. She spotted a vacant seat in the second row on the right and headed toward it. Her eyes took in her surroundings—every exit. Guards stood at each one. The crowd laughed and applauded at the magician's antics. She sat and forced her hands to relax. For the moment, it felt easy to be part of a crowd. To just be.

Her conscience accused her. How could she sit with these Nazi sympathizers, pretending to celebrate the Führer's birthday? What would her parents say? What would Seth say? Guilt's tendrils twisted inside her like ivy.

In the presence of my enemies. Neelie had said those words often, followed by, *I will fear no evil for thou art with me*. If this group dressed in minks and regalia knew they sat close to a Jewess, she'd become easy prey. She didn't look the part in this elegant gown, her blonde curls cascading down her shoulders.

No. No guilt. Her parents would want her to save herself, and if pretending to be a Gentile provided the only way to safety, it was the right thing to do.

Two comedians followed the magician, slapstick their specialty. She had never appreciated vaudeville, but the audience did. They doubled over in laughter at the men's pokes and shoves. Tamar hardly noticed, lost in her thoughts. Funny—in the quiet of her cell these last few weeks, thoughts had tumbled in wild disorder, but here, amidst the clamor, her mind cleared.

The importance of a name came to mind. Her mother had often said one's name determined their character. She'd learned from Neelie what Tamar really meant. Why hadn't her mother told her?

Memories of what Neelie had said on the bench replayed—was it just six months ago? The Tamar in Genesis, the one widowed twice with no children. The one who had maneuvered Judah into her bed. Shameful? Yes. So why had her own parents given her a shameful name?

Then Tamar remembered something else Neelie had told her. One of Tamar's twins, Perez, appeared in the messianic line. *Beauty from ashes.* Something wonderful could come out of the shameful.

The second Tamar came to mind—the princess raped. Both Tamars had been victimized, but the first refused to be a victim—a prime lesson for her. And though *victim* appeared in the numbers tattooed on her arm, she—the new Tamar—also refused to be one. Luckily, Frau Meier hadn't mentioned the tattoo if she'd seen it, and now white gloves concealed the numbers from the people seated around her.

The vaudeville act finished, and a tall, Marlene Dietrich look-alike sidled up to the microphone. She belted out a German song, her hat jauntily covering one eye, a cigarette holder waving from her fingers like a wand. It took Tamar a few minutes to discover the singer was a man. The impersonator held the audience in his palm.

Just then, the officer sitting next to Tamar rested his hand on her leg. She stiffened. Victimized again. She hazarded a glance at the old man. He seemed enthralled with the singer. She crossed her legs away from him. The hand remained. She pushed to her feet. He pulled her down, the same hand clutching her wrist.

"Stay," the man said through clenched teeth. She didn't want to make a scene, especially in enemy territory. Meneer Sneider stood in the corner, his attention on the singer. Tamar glanced sideways at the man sitting next to her. A red, bulbous nose. A sparse shock of white hair combed sideways covered a bald spot. Although his attention seemed to focus on the willowy singer, his grip on Tamar's wrist didn't loosen. His flushed face held a sheen of perspiration, and the collar dug into his thick neck. Regalia covered his uniform, indicating a man used to getting what he wanted.

Not this time, officer.

The man sitting on the other side glanced at her clutched wrist. He shook his head, believing the worst about her. Marlene took a final curtsy. Tamar tried to wrestle her hand free while the people were otherwise distracted.

"I must go," she said, low enough for him to hear. Tamar sprang to her feet, but his fist tightened on her wrist.

"The night is young, Miss Visser. I enjoyed your singing very much." The smell of alcohol wafted toward her. His thick eyelids reminded her of a bullfrog's. She half expected a tongue to whip out of his mouth to catch her as his fly.

"I need to speak with Meneer Sneider. Now." She wiggled her hand loose. "Please. Let. Me. Go."

The audience had taken their seats, and the lights came on. Her last, emphatic words had attracted the attention of those seated around her.

The woman with a large hat in front of her turned, then giggled when she saw the man's hand encircling Tamar's wrist. "You could do worse, honey." Then she whirled to chat with her seatmate.

What a fine mess she'd made. Tamar sat back. The man couldn't keep the pressure on her wrist forever. The second he loosened his grip, she'd bolt. Some of the guests rose to leave, while others remained in their seats, talking in small clusters. Meneer Sneider chatted with a middle-aged woman draped with a mink stole. Was Lieutenant Bergman still waiting in that room?

A weight crashed into her shoulder. She shrieked, causing all eyes to swivel toward her. The man fell sideways into her lap. And finally, his grip loosened.

"What happened?" the woman with the hat gasped.

"Is he dead?" asked her companion.

"What did you do to him?" someone from behind said.

Tamar glanced down, acid rising in her throat. She pulled her hand free and scanned the faces surrounding her. "I don't know.

He must have passed out."

"Check his pulse," the officer on the other side of the man directed.

Tamar gingerly pressed two fingers against his wrist, as she'd seen Daniel do. Nothing, but what did she know about pulses, anyway? Daniel had also touched a patient's neck. She did the same. His skin felt clammy and cold. The red on his face had changed to a mottling tableau of pale colors. "I don't feel a pulse."

"Someone, send for a medic." Meneer Sneider strode toward them, his face stormy.

Tamar peered around. Though the room had almost emptied, including a couple of men who ran for the exit at Sneider's command, those remaining centered their attention on the commotion surrounding her. She caught a few of the German words nearby. "He's with the girl. Ask her."

Sneider glared at her. "Well, Mevrouw Visser, what happened?"

Her lips refused to work, but the man's question necessitated a response. Tamar peered at the white wisps of hair of the man sprawled across her lap. "I ... I don't know him. He seemed fine, then he fell against my shoulder. I smelled alcohol. Maybe he passed out."

A woman in a dazzling red dress and white stole linked arms with Sneider. "If it isn't the little Jewess." Margot. Was the diva stalking her? Was this her way of getting revenge for standing up to her?

"Jewess?" Sneider's eyes darted from the fallen officer to Margot.

Margot lifted her shoulder. "I thought I recognized her voice, but she's so thin. The little Hebrew tried to upstage me in *La Traviata*. Now she's even trying to upstage the Führer."

"Haarlem. That's where I heard you sing." Furrows formed between Sneider's brows. "This is not good. Not good at all." He shook his head. "A fine ending to the Führer's birthday celebration. Tamar Visser, why are you even out here?"

"The little killer's last name is Kaplan." Margot smirked, the corners of her blood-red lips curling up.

"Kaplan?" Sneider's eyes flashed to her.

Tamar took in a breath. The man's weight lay heavy against her. "Could you please move him?"

"It's best to stay where you are until the authorities have a chance to investigate."

"But what if he's still alive? Shouldn't we do something to help him?"

"The medic will be here shortly. Again, what were you doing sitting out here?"

Should she mention Lieutenant Bergman's presence in the waiting room? No, he'd probably gone out the back exit after she resisted his advances. That would just make her even more of a victim. "I came out to wait for Frau Meier to help me change out of my costume." Tamar took a chance. "May I go?"

"Of course not, you're a witness to what happened to Major Goetz."

Margot sneered. "If not the cause." She folded her arms across her ample bosom, the smirk on her face and toss of her red curls revealing that she was enjoying this turn of events very much.

Sneider's face was unreadable. "It won't be long now," he said.

Tamar's neck prickled at the dead man's proximity. "Could you check and see if he's still alive?"

Sneider didn't answer her, his focus on the major two seats away, whose accusing scowl and pointing thumb informed her he was speaking about her. German babbled all around her, above her level of expertise, so she couldn't defend herself.

A commotion of footsteps and an authoritative Dutch voice sounded from behind. An officer with four stripes on his epaulet strode forward, clapping his hands brusquely. "Everybody out except you, you, and you." He pointed at her, the major, and Sneider. "Clear the area now." The row of attendees in front of her rose, muttering under their breath. Margot flung her mink stole over one shoulder, jerked her chin up, and ambled away.

Hopefully, this would all be over soon, and Tamar could go. Her austere cell seemed more inviting with each passing minute. The officer adopted the expression of the major, his eyes accusing her of loose morals.

A nurse appeared from the front, followed by a tall man carrying a stretcher.

Daniel.

CHAPTER EIGHTEEN

R elief arrived when Tamar saw that face, then shame. A flicker of recognition, then surprise in the eyes she loved so much. She hung her head. How this must look to him.

The major expounded in guttural grunts and pointed at her lap. The officer standing in front of her scowled as if convinced of her guilt. Daniel's head shook a bit, so subtle a movement Tamar almost missed it, but she understood. They would pretend to be strangers.

Daniel approached the man, felt for a pulse, then said, "He's dead."

Tamar stiffened, her gaze lifting to the ceiling—anywhere but at the man—as the officers finally pulled him upright. A circle of saliva remained on the center of her lap.

"I'm Commandant Van Winkel, Head of Westerbork. What happened?" He moved close—so close his breath made her flinch. "What's your name?"

She leaned back. "Tamar ... Tamar Visser." Now that Margot was gone, she had a chance of preserving her cover ... if Sneider would allow it.

"So you're Dutch. And you are here for what reason?" His words were a mixture of German and Dutch.

"I sang for the celebration."

He leaned closer, their noses almost touching. "And yet you sit in the audience."

She nodded. "After I finished, I wanted to see the other performers. This seat was unoccupied, so I took it." She pressed her lips together. Tamar would allow no apologies to escape.

"So why was the officer's face in your lap? What did you do to him?"

Her wide eyes darted from Daniel to the commander questioning her. "He grabbed my hand. Forced me to stay when I tried to leave."

"She's lying." The officer two seats from hers sprang to his feet. "The girl insinuated herself into that seat, toyed with his affections, and invited his advances. I saw the whole thing."

Tamar shivered, unsure of what to say next.

Daniel bent down next to the deceased officer and took his hand. "Look at his fingernails. They're gray-blue, as well as his lips. It shows he wasn't getting oxygen. This man died of a heart attack. The woman had nothing to do with it."

The three officers remained silent for a few moments, then headed for the door. One glanced over his shoulder. "Take him to the morgue, Doctor."

Sneider smoothed his cummerbund. "Well, I'm glad that's handled. Mevrouw Visser?" He tipped his hat and strode through the door by the piano. He'd called her *Visser* instead of *Kaplan*. Perhaps her secret was safe with him. At least, for now.

When she and Daniel were the only occupants of the room, he took one look at her. "Ravishing. I can't believe how beautiful you look."

She flicked her hand against his chest. "How can you say that? I almost got arrested. Again."

He peered around, grabbed her hand midair, and brought it to his lips, his eyes closed at the contact. "What are you doing here?"

"I couldn't stand it anymore in that cell. The walls were closing in on me. So I sang. It's what I do to calm myself."

"And they heard you."

"Yes. I must admit that I also wanted to get out of the cell, and I was hoping my singing would give me that chance, as medicine has you. It was exciting to sing again and fun dressing up like the old days."

"But you could have been hurt." He stroked her cheek, his gaze so tender it sent shivers through her.

"I'm not a—"

"Flower," they said at the same time and laughed. It felt good to laugh.

"It's just that your medical training has allowed you some degree of freedom, and I thought maybe my singing could do the same for me." She rose, shaking out her skirt. "I should get back to the wardrobe room to return this dress."

"Ahem," he cleared his throat. "I need your help." Rising, he indicated the dead officer whose head had tilted to the side. "How *did* he end up on your lap?"

"He wouldn't leave me alone. Then he just fell over." When Daniel still looked askance at her, Tamar sucked in a deep breath. Apparently, he, too, needed the whole story. "After I sang my two songs, I left through that door to the waiting room." She pointed. "You'll never guess who was waiting for me."

"Who?" Daniel drew the stretcher closer. "Could you help me lay the man on here?"

"Lieutenant Bergman. Sitting in the dark. Scared me to death." She knelt to take the man's legs while Daniel maneuvered his torso off the chair and onto the stretcher.

His eyes flashed up at her. "Whoa. That must have been a shock. So that's why you preferred to watch the show."

"Yes, but I couldn't tell them that." She struggled to lift one end of the stretcher while he took the other, then they headed toward the entrance. "The old man grabbed my hand and wouldn't let go. Why do these things always happen to me?"

"Have you looked in a mirror lately? He probably died a happy man."

"Stop it." Then she blew out a breath. "Do I have to go to the morgue?"

He glanced back, a teasing smile playing on his lips. "It takes two. Plus, we haven't had any time alone in weeks."

"Not exactly my idea of a date."

"But a date just the same. We'll look back at this and laugh."

They left the building for the darkness. A few giggles wafted in the distance. Probably Margot or someone like her. Otherwise, calmness prevailed. She surveyed the area. "How hard would it be to escape?"

"Very hard. Barbed wire sits atop high fences that surround the place, and guard towers are everywhere."

"I wouldn't want to leave Neelie, anyway. Not after what she did for us."

They stopped at a double set of black metal doors that led into a building that was different than the ones the prisoners stayed in. Daniel propped one door open with his foot. "Believe me, I'm always alert for opportunities to leave this establishment, and you'll be the first to know once I hatch a plan."

They made their way through an ominous, tunnel-like corridor and stopped at a door marked *Mortuarium*. He turned to her. "Are you ready for this? I've never been in here before, so I can't prepare you." He opened the door and flipped on the light.

I am not a flower, she repeated to herself. Tamar drew a breath and nodded.

The long room contained eight surgical tables located in a single row. Sheets covered the silhouettes of bodies on six of them. Under a row of cabinets, a dozen gurneys lined the far wall. Along the side walls were the outlines of drawers with handles. A pungent odor permeated the air. It didn't take a medical license to know what the drawers contained.

"Let's transfer the officer to one of the gurneys."

She nodded her assent, her eyes still on the squares.

He glanced at her. "You're wondering about Mrs. Weinstein, aren't you?"

Tamar nodded, the words coming hard. It had been such an emotional day, and she'd reached her limit. Even non-flowers had limits.

"She would have come through here. They probably buried her in a local cemetery months ago."

She looked up. "They didn't send her back to Haarlem?"

"No, they didn't even know her identity until I told them. Bram and Lars had already been released."

Tamar started to open her mouth, but he stopped her. "I know what you're going to say, but you have to remember. I'm a prisoner here too. I gave the powers that be her name, then had to leave."

They maneuvered the body onto a gurney, then Daniel said he'd go search for a sheet to cover the corpse. Meanwhile, she studied the stark walls, the covered tables. Could she work in an infirmary, handling life-and-death matters daily? She thought back to their visits to neighboring towns. He returned, covered the major, and motioned toward the door. "Let's get out of here. Gives me the creeps."

They headed down the cavernous tunnel to the door outside. She inhaled the crisp air. "Are we prisoners? Is this what they call a labor camp? Because we're not doing a lot of labor."

"Westerbork is designed to hold prisoners until room opens up in a labor camp."

"Then things aren't going to get better."

"Don't think like that, Tamar. Hope. We must hope no matter what."

She let out a breath. "You're right. Just spending time with you, even if surrounded by corpses—well, it's a good end to a terrible day. The idea of returning to that cell makes me—" She gasped when Daniel took her hands.

"Let's tuck in here for a minute." He pulled her into an alcove, then held her close to his chest. "Mm. You smell so good." His cheek brushed next to her hair. "Whatever that woman put in your hair makes me want to—" He kissed her temples, her cheek. They stood so close she could feel his heart beating next to hers. Then he tipped her chin and kissed her with an intensity that matched her own. Their kiss became more heated, more urgent, as if their hunger knew no bounds. She never wanted it to end. "I love you so much," he whispered between kisses. "So very much."

"I love you … too." Then Tamar kissed him again with the same urgency.

When they pulled apart, she touched her swollen lips and smiled. "Well, well, well," was all she could think of to say.

He blew out a breath. "'Well' is right. You—" He smiled. "I can't wait to marry you."

"Me neither. You know, if you helped me get a job as your assistant, we could enjoy more of these stolen moments. Do you think you could?"

"I'll do what I can, but it's not as though I have any authority as a prisoner." He brought her hand to his lips, and they rested there for a moment. "We need to get back. They'll wonder where we went."

They reached the administration building where she'd first come for wardrobe. She moved toward the door and waved. Her gait had lost its leadenness, replaced with a buoyancy she hadn't felt in a long time. Maybe God would work through Daniel to get them together.

CHAPTER NINETEEN

Voices and rapid footsteps startled Neelie from a deep sleep. She bolted up. The blanket lay bunched at her feet due to the night's heat.

A female guard shook the metal door and yelled, "Everyone put on clothing."

No. Neelie roused herself by shaking her head. She'd heard the guards' conversations outside her cell. How often Westerbork's departing trains led to the east to Poland. Auschwitz and Bergen-Belsen were names she often heard. It was the camp's way of making room for new people. *I mustn't think like that. Maybe it isn't the end but the beginning. Could liberation be imminent? Oh, to sleep in my own bed. No, I can't get my hopes up. It could be anything—an untimely drill or some sort of evil punishment for being alive.*

Neelie surveyed her few belongings. How to carry them? The pillowcase would make an adequate bag, although the straw inside had poked through the worn fabric in places, tickling her neck and making it hard to get comfortable.

"Tante Neelie?" came a whisper from the crack in the wall.

"Yes, child. Do you know what's happening?"

"They said everyone should prepare to leave and take all belongings. Do you think we're going to be freed?"

"From your lips." No sense in sharing her thoughts about Poland. "I heard the guards talking yesterday. The Allies arrived in France last week. Maybe they're demanding that all prisoners be set free."

"Oh, this is good news." Tamar's voice sang the short, breathy phrase.

"But we don't know for sure. We do know that God will watch over us." She rubbed her hands. "All right, then. I'll see you soon, really soon."

The halls, usually quiet except when the guards passed, came to life. What time was it, anyway? The high window showed a cloud passing the moon. Neelie peered at the makeshift calendar and counted the days since she'd etched a star on the sixth of the month. It must be the Allies coming for them. Hope energized her to pack quickly, not that there was much to pack.

Only small things—four cough drops, which she'd managed to make last for two months, a safety pin, the colorful threads she'd pulled from a tea towel, and the precious needle Hannie had smuggled in. Should she leave her treasures for the next person who'd need to while away the day? No, the guards wouldn't consider them treasures and would throw them away.

She pulled the straw out from the pillow, which made her sneeze when a plume of dust erupted. Neelie wouldn't miss the foul-smelling straw. She wrapped crumpled papers from her small notebook in patches of material from the lining of her coat and hid them in the shoulder pads. Then she wrapped the rest of her goodies in her slip.

Too hot to wear her heavy coat, she stuffed it in the pillowcase. That didn't work. The pillowcase strained under its weight, so she removed the coat.

She scanned the room, then took a seat on the cot—maybe for the last time. She'd hurried to get ready, and now she waited. Minutes turned into hours. Just like Westerbork. No news. No information. Just commands and jabs on the door. The guards were probably running scared knowing the Allies were on their way. *Stop that, Neelie. Stop raising your hopes.* It could be a million things.

It was still dark when the guards threw off the bolts and yelled, "Everybody out. No time to waste."

With one last glance, Neelie shouldered her coat and pillowcase and walked through the open door. *Freedom.* For the first time in four months, she saw her neighbors, assembling in the narrow hall. Tired, confused, thin, but eyes wide with the hint of a sparkle.

Hannie, who had sneaked her extra treats, joined her. Her somber face stood in contrast to the other faces in the hall.

"Aren't you happy, Hannie? This could mean liberation."

Hannie waved her hand, and the number tattooed on her arm peeked out of her sleeve. It was one of the lower numbers—which meant she'd been a prisoner longer than most. "Put your hope away. I don't trust it. We're probably leaving the country. People leave and don't come back."

Every hopeful thought shattered. "At least we're out of solitary confinement. I'm thankful for that."

Tamar came out and fell into her arms. "Tante."

The embrace made words unnecessary. Neelie squeezed her tight, delighted finally to find a familiar face. Tamar had lost so much weight that Neelie felt the bones of her back through the material of her dress.

The girl drew back, her eyes misty. "Do you think we're going home?"

Neelie refused to look at Hannie. "I don't know. But we're together. And you'll see your Daniel soon."

"Form lines of five." A guard strode past, batting them with her stick. They crammed into two adjacent lines in the narrow hall.

It felt good to walk, to move her limbs beyond the small space of the cell. The humid breeze swept over her face. Another form of freedom—the first time outside in months. Neelie inhaled deeply and climbed into one of the huge vans that lined the road known as *Boulevard des Misères*. Boulevard of Miseries.

She took a seat next to Tamar and two rows behind Hannie and peered out the dirty window. The guards jammed their Lugers into the prisoners' backs to hurry them along. What was the rush? It couldn't be more than three in the morning. Maybe the guards realized the Allies were coming and were anxious to get rid of the evidence. She chose to focus on her version of the truth rather than Hannie's.

The convoy of vans and buses passed through the arched entry and drove the short distance to what looked like a train station in the center of a village. This was good. At least, they weren't loaded onto the trains that connected Boulevard des Misères with Poland's camps. The guards ushered the prisoners off the bus with the usual threats and pokes.

The moment Neelie's feet touched the ground, crowds pressed around her and separated her from Hannie and Tamar, the mob of women pulling her away like a wave. The nurse's head bobbed above the mass. "Hannie," she screamed, not caring if the guards jabbed her in the back. She jostled her way through the crowd and finally reached her. Though Hannie favored negative thinking, she knew how to land on her feet.

"C'mon." Hannie took her arm, her expression lighter than when they'd left the camp. "Let's get a spot by the window. This will be much better than the cattle cars I thought we'd be taking."

And hopefully, Tamar had found Daniel.

The group behind them pressed toward a train with real seats and windows. They found places with a view, and soon Hannie was up walking the aisles, trading what was in her pockets for information. She came back and lit a cigarette.

Neelie straightened in her seat. "Did you find out what's going on?"

"Looks like we're going to Vught." Long-faced, Hannie stood over her, puffing smoke.

"Is that a good thing?"

"Could be. It's a labor camp, but at least we'll be in Nederland."

The question burned on her tongue. Not knowing was sometimes better, but the desire to know was just as strong. "Is it a death camp?"

Hannie's eyes scanned the train car. She didn't answer at first. "Yes and no."

"What does that mean?"

"Means there's a gas chamber, but they don't use it all the time." She swung herself down into the seat and folded one leg in front of her.

"Oh."

They traveled for an hour or so in silence and darkness, except for lights along the aisle floor. They came to a stop with such squealing gears that Neelie winced. A glance out the window showed no train station, just darkness.

"Everybody off." A voice in the dark repeated the command.

They stepped down into nothingness. Only the light of the stars and a sliver of moon illuminated the silhouette of the woods next to the tracks. She and Hannie stood with the others until searchlights forced them to shield their eyes. Soldiers circled the crowd and leveled weapons at them.

They trudged through a narrow forest path, tripping over roots and other unseen obstacles. Curses prodded them like cattle. With one hand, Neelie held the pillowcase, and with her other, she gripped Hannie's sleeve. The last thing she wanted was to get separated. Hannie urged her on when soldiers kicked women around them who stumbled.

Neelie searched for something positive to say amidst the grunts and groans around them. "Isn't it wonderful that we get to navigate the woods in warm weather? Imagine what this would be like in December."

Hannie just released a gusty sigh.

After what seemed like hours, they entered a lit-up courtyard. The women were funneled toward one building, the smaller group of men herded toward another.

Because she and Hannie had been on the farthest train from the registration building, they brought up the end of a long queue. When they finally entered the stark-walled, single-story building, male guards yelled, "Clothes off. Into the showers. Twenty at a time."

Blessed sounds of running water confirmed these were real showers, but when it became clear the guards enjoyed watching the women remove their clothes and stand naked in the line, Neelie locked eyes with Hannie. "I cannot do this." The men strolled by, their eyes lingering on the group in front of them. Where was Tamar? She hadn't been on their train. Neelie hoped the men weren't ogling the pretty young woman.

Hannie jerked her head toward a guard who couldn't be more than eighteen. "Don't let them get to you. They can smell fear. Let's concentrate on taking showers for the first time in months." She waved her hand in front of her face.

Hannie was right. They weren't much to look at, anyway. Dirty women who'd been starved for months, who'd endured all kinds of sicknesses, were no feast for the eyes. Still. *Lord, make it stop.*

In the next breath, "Keep your clothes on," came the command. "We're out of uniforms."

"How He does it, I'll never know," she whispered to herself as sweet relief spiraled through her. They were herded toward a long table where they were to give their names, place of birth, and status to a row of women in uniforms.

Status? Neelie shook her head.

The woman grabbed her arm and rolled up her sleeve to see her tattoo. "Political." She waved her hand toward the woman behind her. "Next."

Hannie caught up with her, and they followed the row of women out the door and across a courtyard to a barrack, one of dozens in three rows. Inside, a three-tiered maze of bunkbeds filled one side of the room. On the other side stood rows of tables and benches. Women had already grabbed the lower bunks and stared at the newcomers with disinterest. Some spread their arms across the bunks to keep newcomers from trespassing.

The women who'd had to shower and change into overalls clamored for the closest second-level bunks. The blue-striped uniforms they wore featured a red stripe down the back and a blue-and-white polka-dotted neckerchief. Not a bad-looking outfit and certainly better than the ragged dress she'd been wearing for the last few months.

The sound of a stick hitting the side of the beds silenced the noise.

"Welcome to Vught," a twentyish woman said. "You will call me The General. All one hundred fifty of you must follow my commands to the letter. It will not go well for the group if a single person in this barrack disobeys my orders. Tomorrow, roll call starts at six outside. Beds must be perfectly made. Tardiness will not be excused." The General's eyes narrowed, and her mouth dragged down at the corner.

So young and yet so full of bitterness, this woman barely out of school looked at them as if they were rodents. What had happened to fill her with so much hate?

She pounded the wooden bedframe twice with a stick and whipped around. Her eyes lit on a toddler who played under the lowest tier.

Neelie held her breath.

"Hi, there, little one. What are you doing under there?" The General leaned down and picked up the child, who grabbed at the phoenix insignia on the brim of her hat.

Nobody made a sound. Neelie glanced at Hannie, speechless. A woman, most likely the child's mother, took a step forward, but The General's glare and raised palm made her step back. The General cooed a bit more, then set the child down and marched toward the exit. Once she'd turned and scanned the room with narrowed eyes, then disappeared out the single door, the mother rushed forward and whisked the child into her arms. Collective breaths released around the room. Neelie expelled a sigh. Maybe the *Aufseherin* had a scrap of humanity after all. Minutes later, the room became a beehive of activity.

Hannie grabbed her arm. "If we don't hurry, we'll be forced to take the uppermost bunks."

Neelie tried to keep up with Hannie, who dashed to a corner

and climbed a wooden ladder to the second tier. At least, they were together. A folded blanket sat at the end of the straw mattress that sagged in the middle, its stench reminiscent of her pillow at Westerbork.

"Well, second tier is better than the top bunk, but we're not by a window. I'll see what I can trade to get better beds." Hannie jumped down.

"It seems every bed is filled. I don't mind this. It's quieter and we have some privacy." But Hannie was already gone.

Neelie spread out her possessions. How Vught differed from Westerbork. From quiet solitude, where Neelie had hungered for human communication and had so prized moments of chatter with Tamar, to a room rumbling with over a hundred voices and many languages at the same time—as though the quiet could no longer be suppressed but spewed out because it could.

When Hannie returned, Neelie asked, "Did you find anything?"

"Not yet. A lot of them don't speak Dutch."

"I wonder where Tamar went. She stood behind me when I got off the bus, then the crowd separated us. I hope she's okay." Neelie scanned the room, but her position in the middle of three bunks in a corner offered little perspective.

"That cute little thing in the cell next to yours? She can sing, can't she?"

"Yes, she was with the Haarlem opera."

Hannie rolled her eyes. "Not a lot of demand for that type of work in this place."

Hannie was a dear soul but so bitter about her life. She'd have to give her reasons to hope. Undaunted, Neelie climbed to the top tier and called Tamar's name. Several faces turned toward her, none of them Tamar's.

"Maybe tomorrow," she told Hannie as she returned to her bunk and stifled a yawn. "We should sleep. Six a.m. will come before we know it."

What seemed like minutes later, loud, accented words broke the silence. "Everyone up. You have ten minutes to line up outside."

No light from any windows reached their bed in the corner. In their haste to find a bunk, Neelie hadn't thought of the fresh air or the light available to those closest to the window. She smoothed the blanket, threw on her coat, and hurried down the ladder, stopping to help the woman down from the bed above Hannie's.

They scurried through the door that was flanked by The General and another female guard. "Out, out," she yelled, her voice strident. "Six rows of twenty-five." She beat the ground with her stick for emphasis.

After chaotic moments of tripping and bumping into one another, the women lined up as ordered. A glimpse across the courtyard showed rows of men standing in front of a barrack. Many women stood on their tiptoes to catch a view of husbands, sons, or boyfriends.

Roll call took over an hour as the guards called out name after name, then checked them against their numbers. Neelie didn't mind. The sunrise slipped over the roof of the men's barrack, an orange, pinkish sphere. Its rays reminded her of the ones she'd drawn as a primary student. Simpler days.

The General mutilated the names and became enraged when their owners didn't step forward. One woman's fainting incited The General's anger. She shrieked German invectives with each contact of her boot to the woman's torso.

Neelie felt the woman next to her sway and grabbed her hand, holding it taut against her side. When Hannie tried to stop her, Neelie stayed her. "We're here for a purpose," she whispered.

Hannie's eyes narrowed. "If we can make it through."

The General dismissed them, saying their work would start the next morning.

A free day? Neelie couldn't remember her last one outside

solitary confinement. She squeezed the frail hand of the woman she'd helped to remain standing. "What a gift. I think it's Sunday. A true day of rest."

Neelie remained outside, walking along the barbed wire fence, which stood in contrast to the field of wildflowers on the other side. Mounds of grass provided a place to sit and reflect on the past few months without the deafening noise of the barrack.

A young woman with a long, dark braid, wearing a threadbare dress, stopped and knelt next to them. "Excuse me. We are holding a service between the two barracks on the left. Join us."

Neelie's nod was enough. She followed the girl to a grassy knoll where a woman read from a New Testament the size of her hand. Then they joined hands and sang hymn after hymn in reverent tones. Her heart filled with joy. It had been so different at Westerbork. Would they be able to meet every Sunday like this? Oh, let it be so. They ended with collective prayer, so sorrowful, so deep, about husbands, children, and lost loved ones.

Before they adjourned, the girl who had invited her asked if she would share her thoughts the following Sunday if allowed to meet. Of course, Neelie agreed. The group had so much to discuss. How to frame their time at the camp. What to expect when they were released. How to help one another when conditions became overwhelming.

The rest of the day was like a piece of paradise. Birds chirped from birch tree branches. The blue sky met the woodlands in the distance. A small farm nestled in the valley. Did its inhabitants know what occurred so close to its property line?

As Neelie rested in the grass, Tamar walked past, running her finger along the fence.

"Tamar, over here," Neelie called out.

She whirled around. "Oh, it's good to *see* you for a change." Tamar dropped to her knees and hugged her.

"Where are you staying?" Neelie smoothed strands of Tamar's hair that were blowing in the breeze.

"Barrack 24. How about you?"

Neelie's eyes popped open wide. "The same. Hannie and I are in the far corner away from the window. You're welcome to join us. The bunk above is empty. Then we'll be together."

"Oh, that would be wonderful. The ladies around me have such loud, complaining voices. Although I detested it at the time, Westerbork has taught me to appreciate quiet." She glanced over her shoulder.

"What are you looking for?"

Her cheeks pinked. "Daniel. Because of his height, it was easy to pick him out of the rows of men across the courtyard at roll call, but then I lost sight of him. Hopefully, he'll find me soon." She folded her legs beside her and twirled a dandelion between her thumb and finger. "Having you and Daniel here makes everything brighter."

Neelie suppressed a laugh when Tamar gasped, pulled to her feet from behind her by a tall man with an impish smile. He wrapped his arms around her and kissed her temple. Tamar glanced up, then swiped a swift palm at Daniel's shoulder. "You almost caused me to have heart palpitations."

"Well, then, it's good to have a doctor at arm's length, isn't it, Tante?"

Neelie smiled but glanced at Tamar, whose eyes were fastened on her fiancé. She could tell the young woman was eager for some quiet time with her beau.

Daniel, too, only had eyes for his intended. "Will you excuse us, Tante Neelie? My girl and I have some walking to do." With a brief bow, Daniel took Tamar's hand and led her away.

"Young love." Neelie sighed. She remembered those hungry feelings from her earlier years, when her thoughts were solely upon Frans. *They're so young, at the beginning of their lives, really. I hope this place doesn't rob them of their innocence.*

CHAPTER TWENTY

After shivering in roll call line for an hour, Neelie and the others endured an extra hour while the guards handed out job assignments. They were poked, prodded, and eyed by guards and officers half their age. Anything to make them feel less human—like pieces of weathered meat.

Hannie was busy trading with an Armenian, their bartering becoming so loud a guard prodded her away with her stick. Tamar headed to the infirmary to begin her job as a medic, a position suggested by Daniel, no doubt.

A tall girl with a perpetual scowl inspected Neelie, turning her chin from one side to the other with the tip of her forefinger. Then the woman examined her hands, pressing the calluses on her fingertips. "Where did you get these?"

Neelie lifted her chin a fraction. "I'm a violinist."

The woman's nose scrunched as though she'd smelled something rotten. "Brabant Building." She motioned with her head toward a one-story building tucked between two of the men's barracks. Neelie looked around. All the other prisoners lined up to head toward their new workplaces.

A prod to the back. "Go now."

When she righted herself, Neelie hurried to the building. It had a few windows and didn't look as dreary as the rows of barracks. Should she knock? She peered in the window. The room was empty except for two clusters of wooden chairs, an upright piano, and a chalkboard. Papers were scattered over the floor.

"What are you looking at, vrouw? Are you one of our musicians?"

Neelie spun around to see a wizened old fellow. Bent over, he peered up at her with the bluest of eyes, uncharacteristic for someone his age. "Sorry, I don't know why I've been sent here. The guard noted my calluses and told me to come. I am a violinist and was with the opera in Haarlem."

The bushy white brows shot up. "Fantastic. I'm a pianist. Come. The others will be here shortly." He held the door open for her.

"So this labor camp has an orchestra?" The notion seemed to defy logic. "Are there instruments?" Stepping onto the scuffed hardwood floor—cement in places—she whirled around to face the man. "I'm Neelie Visser."

"And I am Wolf Drukker from Amsterdam."

"*The* Wolf Drukker? Aren't you the pianist who plays the music for silent films?"

He nodded. "I was. I'm surprised anyone knows that."

"My Frans and I watched you play rather than the moving picture at *The Sea Wolf.* Much more interesting."

"You're most kind." His eyes traveled to the door. "Ah, here are the two others. With you, we have a proper quartet. Meet Katja ten Pas. She's our cellist." A woman with a lovely smile greeted her with a handshake. "And Felix Niel, our flautist." A young man in his thirties, his dark glasses held together with white tape, bowed in Neelie's direction. "And this is the newest member of our ensemble. Meet Neelie Visser on the violin."

Katja linked arms with her. "*Ensemble* is an ambitious description, but I'm happy to have another female to chat with. Wolf and Felix are wonderful, but sometimes it's nice to talk about other things than politics." She chuckled and motioned toward one of the four chairs, each with its own music stand.

Neelie took a seat, frowning her confusion at the empty stand before her. "What exactly do we do?"

Katja scooted closer to her, tilting her head, her dark hair swept into a chignon. Pronounced cheekbones and striking green eyes evoked the image of a beautiful cat. She had the face of a model that graced the cover of a fashion magazine. "Well, the *kapo*, a trustee—a prisoner like us—brings in the instruments, and we spend the day practicing pieces we've scribbled down on paper. They have no music to give us, and the instruments aren't in the best shape. We're quite sure they were confiscated from other prisoners." Katja waved her hand. "When we've asked Arend—that's the kapo's name—he tells us we'll know in good time." She shrugged. "So we scribble and practice and smoke and chat for eleven hours, six days a week. It's not bad—breaks up the tedium of the place." She leaned forward. "Now tell me about yourself."

Neelie had become so wary of the people around her—even her neighbors and friends—since the Nazis had occupied Haarlem, it was hard to trust strangers, even fellow prisoners, but she had to start sometime. "I played second chair violin for the Haarlem opera for many years. Then they closed us down."

"Good." Katja squeezed her arm. "You'll bring some new music to the group. Do tell, what are your favorite operas? I—"

A door opened, and a man with a white mustache and wiry hair strode in, carrying two leather cases as he headed to the piano.

"Wolf, grab the cello and give it to Katya, then gather around the piano." He handed a battered flute case to Felix. "I just received information about an upcoming performance and maybe more."

Katja took the cello from Wolf, leaned it against her chair, and ambled toward the piano, a smirk on her full lips. "A performance? For free? When you gonna pay us, Kapo? We work our fingers to the bones." She motioned toward Neelie. "Kapo, meet the newest member of the ensemble, violinist Neelie Visser. She'll need a violin. Do you have one in your stash?"

The kapo nodded in Neelie's direction. "Pleased to meet you. Lots of violins in my 'stash,' as you called it. I'll bring one in shortly." He waited until Wolf stopped playing arpeggios on the piano in dire need of a tune-up. "The commandant has determined that music will be played two afternoons a week at an outside location. Dates to be determined as soon as the commandant gives me more information. Could be weeks. Could be months, but it would be good to have a nice selection of pieces ready."

"What are we supposed to play, and who are we playing for?" Wolf threw his hands open. "And how do I play the piano outside?"

Felix had taken the flute out of its case and was examining it. He glanced up. "Yeah, what's the occasion? Is it for the prisoners or the—?"

The kapo waved a dismissive hand. "Don't know. Just start preparing. I'll be back with a violin." He headed to the door. It slammed behind him.

Felix made an obscene gesture with his hand, then tuned his flute.

Katya must have noticed Neelie's wide eyes. "The kapo is one of us, but somehow he worked his way into the good graces of the powers that be, and he gets to order us around now. There's a lot of kapos in here. Be careful what you say."

Minutes later, the kapo returned with a violin and handed it to Neelie. "Here. I'm not sure what kind of shape it's in. I brought the best one I could find."

Neelie thanked him. She opened the case as if it were a cherished Christmas present. Who would have thought that two nights ago she was in solitary confinement, and now she was going to spend her days doing what she loved? She opened the case and ran her hand over the smooth surface. One of the strings was missing and some were loose, but she'd do what she could to tighten them.

Wolf clapped to get their attention. "We'd better get to work. Let's tune the instruments and be ready to start in five. 'Per Lei,' Nabucco, 'Milonga Sentimental.' Are you familiar with the pieces, Neelie?"

She hesitated, then removed the bow from the case. "I'm a bit rusty, but I'm a quick learner." Her heart clenched with joy at the first rich sounds of the strings.

Katja's long fingers settled on her shoulder. "Neelie plays violin for the opera. Shall we add an opera piece to our list?"

Wolf rippled out a minor scale. "What would you suggest,

Vrouw Visser?"

She glanced around. "I'm not sure. What's our purpose? Do you want uplifting or something in more of a minor tone?"

Katja stood and crossed her arms across her slim chest. "Something Dutch. We'll show those Krauts a thing or two about Nederland pride."

"How about *Bacchus, 'Ceres en Venus,'* or *'Heer Halewijn'*?" Neelie suggested.

"Both," the three said in unison. "Let's get started."

Vught, compared to Westerbork, nearly bordered on being pleasant. The walks near the beautiful meadows outside the fence and the gorgeous, sunlit blue sky—she had dreamed of such walks sitting in her cell at Westerbork.

The closeness of other people in the dormitory and the ensemble was a welcome change after the deafening silence of solitary confinement, although change came with an underbelly of flaws. The noise of the same six records replaying at the loudest volume. The women's profanity and complaining. And something intangible Neelie hadn't been able to grasp yet—an undercurrent of duplicity, perhaps.

The laughter at the mistakes they made as they practiced for the performance made the work environment easy. But when the kapo was out of earshot, the ribald humor reminded Neelie of high school. Whenever he left the room, rehearsal halted and books, letters, and handiwork came out of pockets.

When she asked Katja about the lack of work ethic, the cellist lifted a shoulder. "Why would we want to do our best for these people who'd just as soon kill us as look at us? We do the least we can for them."

When footsteps approached, books and needlework returned to pockets, conversation stopped, and everyone picked up their instruments.

All in all, belonging to the ensemble pleased Neelie, although eleven-hour workdays preceded by long roll calls left everyone tired and grumpy. Animated conversation ebbed early in the evening, replaced by snoring. Despite the British planes roaring overhead and searchlights beaming through the dorm windows at regular intervals, deep slumber came easily.

Neelie was surprised to learn that prisoners could send and receive packages and letters from loved ones, although they were carefully read and censored by the guards. Neelie had sent a few letters to Jan at their address, hoping he'd get them, and received a package from him, which delighted her to know that he was safe. Albeit, a favorite punishment of the guards was a mail-and-parcel ban. A wrinkle of a blanket could mean a month without letters. Of course, since the outside didn't know about the ban, the guards could open the mail and feast on the treats.

Daniel came to Barrack 24's rescue regarding outgoing mail. At great risk to the freedoms Daniel and Tamar enjoyed as medics, Tamar gathered letters from their barrack and sneaked them to Daniel. He dropped them in the mail bin in the administration building as he passed it. Thus, letters left the prison uncensored by Barrack 24's guards.

Neelie allowed Tamar to read her reply to one of Jan's letters.

26 July, 1944

Dear son,

I'm writing to you from the meadow where I spend hours on Sunday afternoons. It reminds me of the pastoral painting in the dining room. It's beautiful here, if you can believe that—although the morning air is getting chilly, so I'd very much appreciate a sweater when the parcel ban is up in September.

Our little opera singer is doing well. Give her regards to her family if you see them. It's good to have someone close who knows about sicknesses and their remedies. Her young man does what he's been trained to do. Our other bunkmate also works at the infirmary. She's been imprisoned longer than anyone and knows her way around a labor camp. She's a shrewd one for whom every object has a price. I'd bet that she'll walk out of here a rich woman. But when, son, will it happen? Is the end of the war at hand?

Last night, we were awakened by the roar of a tremendous number of planes flying over Vught. There seemed to be dozens of them. Any idea who they represent? Could it be the Allies?

We have all lost a lot of weight. Our daily dinner consists of a hard piece of bread and a bowl of weak soup with a piece of turnip and a shred of something that looks like gristle floating on top. No, I don't want you to worry. The Lord takes care of us. Our bunkmate sneaks us a bit of jelly, a peppermint, a piece of apple. I will never take food for granted again.

Have you any idea when our prison term ends? Some of the women in our barrack say we're fortunate because the train from Westerbork runs weekly to Auschwitz. They didn't have room for us in Poland, so we were sent here. Our labor is easy compared to that of Bergen-Belsen or Ravensbrück. I thank God every day for His goodness. He knows the future, and I am resting in His will.

I have gone on and on about myself, but I want to know about you and our friends. Even Maarika. I love you and miss you so much.

Your mam.

After weeks of work broken up by Sundays of freedom, Neelie received a parcel from Jan. Christmas-eager, she tore into the package, which had already been ripped open. Sugar, butter, sweets, well-filled sandwiches, and cake awaited her in a mushed pile.

The guards had examined each item in the parcel, running long knives through the butter, cake, and sandwiches to check for hidden messages. It didn't matter. The food hadn't lost its wonderful flavor. And at least it had been delivered rather than confiscated. The parcel gave her hope she would be reconnected with Jan. They weren't beyond communication.

On the downside of life at Vught, collective punishments were meted out for the most trivial acts. A child who cried during roll call. A blanket not perfectly folded into a square. A smile or a whisper when The General ranted.

One time, someone ran into line a few seconds late, and all the prisoners in her barrack were punished, which meant marching from twelve to one in the morning. The kapo, a former seaman, carried a rod, but Neelie didn't fear him. They hiked past areas previously undiscovered—an airplane graveyard, a grain field with a white steeple in the distance.

With gusto, the singing began, and the trustee prisoner didn't object. Hymns and patriotic Dutch songs poured out until they reached a building inside the barbed wire. A one-story brick building with a single, tall chimney sprouting from the roof.

"What's that?" Neelie knew, but she had to ask.

"The crematorium," said the woman in front of her. "I've heard they're going to start using it again, and there're going to be weekly outdoor concerts there starting next week. Guess they want to send them into kingdom come in style."

Neelie's breath caught, and she bent over in a coughing fit.

Weeks later, while Neelie worked in the barracks on a small jigsaw puzzle Hannie had traded for Neelie's shoulder pads, she described the twice-weekly performance to her bunkmates. They'd still seen no prisoners at the crematorium since she'd heard about the intention of the concerts, so she allowed herself to hope. Maybe the woman had been wrong.

"We've added Cole Porter's 'You're the Top' and Fanny Brice's 'Second Hand Rose' just for fun, but we're so far away from the barracks that nobody goes out that far. We even played the Dutch national anthem just to be naughty, but we stopped when The General came into view." Neelie released a small chuckle as she slid a piece of the puzzle into place. She'd become so quick at putting the puzzle together, she'd resorted to turning the pieces upside down and fitting them together without the benefit of their colors.

Hannie's eyes narrowed. "It's the middle of August. Awful hot to be playing outside without an audience."

Neelie nodded and shrugged. "We've seen the commandant and a few officers standing in front of the building pointing at it and discussing something, but they weren't interested in us. So we take advantage of our freedom to experiment with our craft when nobody's around."

"Sounds like a nice job if the weather cooperates, but why do you think they make you play out there?" Tamar's head tilted to the side as she rubbed ointment Hannie had given her on her hands. "Are they hiding something?"

Hannie belted out a smoker's cough. "It's a crematorium, sunshine. What do you think they're doing out there?"

"It is that," Neelie agreed. "But it's as though we're on hold—getting ready for something to happen, but no one's saying anything. What do you think, Hannie?"

She took a drag of her cigarette and blew out a smoke ring. "I think they're planning on using the crematorium, and your purpose will be to play as loud as you can to mask the noise coming from inside."

The chill that ran through Neelie silenced her.

Tamar didn't seem to want to believe it either. "Why? This is a transit camp like Westerbork," she said, throwing the ointment tube onto the thin sheet.

Hannie shrugged. "Neelie asked what I thought. The commandant we have right now is as mean as a coot. Whatever he decides will happen."

Neelie fit a grouping of two into the middle of her game. "We'll pray it will never come to that." She had to think about something else. "Tamar, tell me about your work."

"Tense. Daniel and Hannie spend most of the time checking on patients. My job is to clean up the infirmary area once the patient has been released. Sometimes, I get to visit with them while they wait. I try to help them feel comfortable. The officers don't want to be bothered with sick people, especially"—she paused, stared at her lap, then continued—"the ones the guards believe are trying to get out of doing work. They're not treated well."

Neelie covered Tamar's hand. "I'm sure the patients appreciate your kindness."

She shrugged. "I don't know what I'm doing. Daniel told me what to do when we visited families. He covered for me when I didn't have the answers. Now I just hope I don't hurt anyone."

"Have you thought of singing for them?"

"A few times, when nothing works to settle them down." Tamar grabbed her chest, her eyes widening. "I never told you two what happened that night the guard came to get me at Westerbork." She described the evening she wore the fabulous gown and sang for Hitler's birthday. "You'll never guess who I saw in the room behind the stage."

Neelie stopped and stared at her. "Do tell."

"Lieutenant Bergman."

"Who's Lieutenant Bergman?" Hannie looked up from cutting the filter off a cigarette with a nail file.

"He's a German officer who had a crush on Tamar, and we're here because of him."

Hannie lit a cigarette and spoke between drags. "You don't say. What was he doing at Westerbork?"

"I didn't stay around to find out. But that led to a whole other experience with a Nazi officer who died with his head on my lap." She went on to tell about the inquisition. "Daniel showed up just in time and deflected the officers' attention from me."

"God. God showed up."

"No. Daniel did." Tamar met Neelie's eyes. "I'm sorry, but I don't believe God involves Himself in every little thing that happens here on earth." Her eyes grew stormy. "If He does, why doesn't He stop all this? Why are we even here?"

Neelie fit the final puzzle piece in place and gave Tamar her full attention. "I don't know how to explain it to you. I know He's involved in the details. He's proven it time and time again. I wish that—" She felt helpless. It was hard to explain faith when sight sent a contrary message. It saddened her Tamar couldn't see with her heart. Had they taught her nothing in the months at her house? No. That was the Lord's job. Her eyes went to the gray underside of the puzzle, facing up. An idea quickened within her. "What do you see here?"

"Gray. The wrong side of your puzzle. I don't know how you can put it together without the picture."

Gaining enthusiasm, Neelie waved her hand over the surface. "Yes, this is Vught. Certainly, better than Westerbork, but still bleak because we're not free. The guards punish prisoners without reason. We're subject to their whims. You don't know where your family is. Now watch."

With her hand securing the puzzle from above, she flipped the blanket it lay on, then folded back the material. A colorful picture of Van Vreeland's well-known portrait of Holland's flowers faced up from her mattress.

Tamar clapped. "Bravo."

Hannie didn't say anything, but she'd been watching, listening, absorbing, and Neelie detected a slight, slow nod of her head.

"Thank you, but that's not my point. We see the jumbled gray pieces around us and wonder why, but God brings good out of the mess. We'll understand someday. That's faith. Having faith that God is good when circumstances scream otherwise."

Tamar nodded slowly. "What choice do we have, anyway?"

Neelie leaned forward, taking her hand. "But we do have a choice … in the way we look at it. In our attitude. Inside ourselves, where either turmoil or peace can reign. Our choice makes all the difference."

Tamar's lips pressed together, and three lines formed between her brows. She stared at her bed as if she was mulling over Neelie's words, then she looked up. "Faith," was all she said.

"Tante Neelie, wake up. We don't want to be late for roll call." Tamar reached down from the bed above to shake her shoulder, but Neelie, huddled toward the wall, was too far away, so she patted the edge of the bed. "Don't you feel well?"

Neelie waved her off but didn't turn around. "I'm fine. Just go. I'll be out in time."

"All right, but I'm going to tell Hannie to have a look at you."

"Just go." Her tone was harsh, but she didn't care.

Once Tamar's footsteps faded, Neelie forced herself to a seated position and wiped her eyes. With a shaky hand, she pulled out a handkerchief and put the breakfast that Tamar had left in it. Her appetite was gone, so she'd give it to one of the children. She doubted her appetite would ever return after yesterday. The shivering started then, and she grabbed her coat. It had rained during the night, and the September morning's chill still hung in the air even in the barracks, but it wasn't the temperature that was making her shiver. Still, she didn't want everyone in the barrack to suffer because of her tardiness. She lowered herself from her second-tiered bed and hurried to catch up.

Neelie slid into line just as The General strode up, tapping her baton against her hip. She did her morning walk up and down each row, poking her stick at anyone whose feet weren't in the proper place, whose chin wasn't raised and facing forward. Neelie tried to keep her lips from quivering, but the eyes of the prisoners—those frightened eyes—would never leave her memory. Thin women, a dozen or so, had marched past her and the other musicians yesterday. The guards made them march with the same kind of baton The General held.

Neelie had stopped playing her instrument. How could she? She'd glanced up at the chimney, then back at the women—some Tamar's age, some with white hair who could barely walk, much less march. How could she live with herself if her music was the last thing these women heard?

Katja's eyes had narrowed, and she'd motioned with her head for Neelie to pick up her bow and play. Felix continued to play his flute, but his eyes pled with her to join them. Wolf glanced over his shoulder from his piano, which they kept in the brick building and brought out for these performances.

Neelie had bit down on her lip so hard it bled, positioned her violin, and joined in, but then shook her head, tears dropping onto the instrument. Her breath had come in trembling spurts. "I'm so sorry," she'd mouthed to the last prisoner who passed, glancing her way.

An important-looking man in full regalia, hands behind his back, had stopped in front of the musicians. "Louder and faster." Then he'd clapped his hands. "This tempo. Keep playing until we tell you to stop, and none of those dirges."

"Yes, Commandant." Wolf had bowed slightly, suggested a gavotte, two concertos, and "Humoresque."

The officer had remained by Neelie's side for a minute, listening to the gavotte. She prayed he wouldn't notice her sniffing or shaky hand. Thankfully, he headed into the building without saying anything else.

They'd played the four pieces over and over. When shrieks came from inside the building, she bit her lip, prayed for the women's souls, and somehow made it through until a guard told them they could stop. Nobody else would hear the women—the red-bricked building with the chimney was far from the barracks. But Neelie had heard them, and then she didn't.

CHAPTER TWENTY-ONE

Tamar hummed the third-act chorus of "Gypsy and Picadors" from *La Traviata* while she washed spoons, cups, and syringes in a bucket of bleachy water. Whenever she failed to reach a note, she repeated the choral piece until it was perfect. Then she put words to the tune. Somehow, it connected her with her past and instilled hope she'd sing again.

One good thing about working in the infirmary—she had time alone in this supply room, interrupted only when a staff member rushed in and unlocked the cabinet for medicine. Tamar used every moment alone to sing. Five months had made her rusty, and she'd forgotten many words.

But she needed to hurry. The patients would wonder where their nurse was. Not that there was much she could do without adequate supplies or training. A gentle hand and a kind smile only went so far.

Daniel had told her on one of their Sunday walks that none of the staff were medically trained. Like most of the other guards and officers at Vught, the *oberen* in the infirmary were barely out of high school, inexperienced twenty-year-olds who had spent a month learning how to subdue large groups of people. Even Hannie had no experience except what she had learned by default during her years as a "nurse" at Westerbork.

What a spry little ferret. Hannie even looked like one with her sharp features, yet she could sniff out a deal like no other. She took advantage of her role as a medic to sneak medicine, bandages, and ointments—whatever meager supplies she could find—from the cabinets and used her stash to trade for money or goods. Tit for tat. A good friend to have in the barrack.

When the door creaked open, Tamar fell silent in mid-verse. Her mind went on alert even though she didn't whip around to see who entered. Better to keep a low profile in this place. That debacle of a night singing for the Nazis had taught her the value of not drawing attention to herself, and Daniel had shown her how to disappear in plain sight.

"I heard your singing, Tamar." The warm, deep-toned voice was low. Nobody called her by her first name except—. She whirled around.

Daniel.

Joy flooded her as he slipped in, leaving the door barely open a crack. He drew her close, breathed in her hair, and kissed her forehead. "I couldn't wait for Sunday," he whispered, his voice husky.

Tamar raised her lips, waiting for his to meet hers halfway. They didn't. Instead, he kissed her nose. "Can't stay long. I just came in to get some ointment." He pulled on the cabinet door. "It's locked."

"Yes, don't you have a key?"

"No, the ober keeps it on a chain around his neck. He lets me use it if he's in the room."

"How does Hannie get into the cupboards?"

"She has her ways." He pulled her close again. "Let me hold you for a second. It will get me through until Sunday. Did you give any thought to my suggestion from a few days ago?"

She rubbed her forehead against his coarse beard, drawing strength from his closeness. "You mean escape," she whispered. "How could it ever work? If we got caught, they'd shoot us like animals."

"Others have been successful. And if we made it, we could start over someplace—open a practice in our home when safe to do so and put all this behind us." He stepped back, his eyes searching hers. "Isn't it worth the risk to realize our dreams?"

"These striped blue-and-white uniforms—yours with the yellow triangle, mine with the red—would hardly camouflage us. We'd need clothes and money and so many things." She reached up and brushed a lock of curly hair from his face.

"Let me worry about that. The guards' locker room is close by. I could sneak in and nab two. You'd have to dress like a man unless I can find a female guard's uniform. Are you okay with that?" He nudged her chin with his knuckle.

"Of course. But then what?"

He glanced back at the door, then took a step toward it. "I'll hide them in here." He looked around, then pulled on the lower cupboard door in the corner. "Down there behind the cleaning supplies."

Tamar nodded. "We need a signal, a code word. Chocolate chip cookies." She closed her eyes and breathed in through her nose. "I can almost smell them. No, that's bleach."

"Don't joke. I'm serious. When the time comes, I'll find you with the code word."

Tamar's hand went to her hip. "Then what? We can't just walk out of here. It's too much of a risk."

"There's a pathway outside the infirmary. The oberen take girls down the path for … privacy. I've heard there are woods around the curve. If we're lucky, keep our eyes down, we can disappear there. Then we're on our own."

Could they make it? The uncertainty, the risks, swirled in Tamar's stomach. "Neelie thinks we'll be freed later this month or possibly in December if they don't count our time at Westerbork. It's already September. Shouldn't we wait to be released?"

Voices came from outside the door. Their eyes met, widened. He grabbed a bandage from a drawer. "Until Sunday." The door closed behind him.

"Where were you?" a gruff male voice demanded from the hallway.

"I needed some ointment. Could I have the key?"

"You know the rules. I'll come with you."

Tamar looked around, searching for another exit but not finding one. Her heart hammered. The guard would know. There'd be repercussions. New footsteps stopped outside the door. Muffled German, then the door creaked open.

Daniel. Alone. He lifted a key, opened a cupboard, and took out two used tubes of ointment, throwing one in her direction. With a wink, he disappeared out the door, and she let out her breath.

Escape. Of course, Daniel wouldn't be overwhelmed by the idea. Nothing scared him. When they'd been in hiding, he'd paced the rooms of the Visser house like a caged polar bear. Even when he'd been seated, his foot tapped, his hands fidgeted, and his eyes glanced at the windows. She wasn't like Daniel, preferring the safety of the familiar.

After Tamar disposed of the bleach, she hurried to her patients, having been gone much too long. The men would grumble, and the old woman in the second bed from the back would complain to the ober. Tamar couldn't lose this job. Whatever it took.

She slowed down and smoothed the rough fabric of her uniform, out of habit more than reason, grimacing at the smell of bleach on her withered, red hands. Strong enough to wake someone from a coma. In fact, one of her patients *was* comatose— the woman at the end of the row, who still lay with her back turned to the rest of the room as Tamar entered the infirmary. She'd been like that for a week. The woman would die soon without food or water.

Twenty-four cots lined the space, twelve on each side. Women filled one side, the oldest toward the back of the room, the newer arrivals—the acute cases—near the door. Four men lay on cots on the other side.

"I need something for the pain. Nurse, won't you help me?" the man in the second bed demanded. A gash on his shin, the effect of a guard's shovel, had become infected. Daniel had taught her how to debride the wound, but despite her care, it became worse. Pain medicine dwindled—Hannie said the staff helped themselves to the drawer.

Tamar squeezed the man's hand. "I will ask the doctor to visit as soon as he can."

She filled water glasses for some, used the ointment Daniel had thrown her way on small wounds, and dabbed cooled cloths on the foreheads of those with fevers. The medical staff called patients by the number tattooed on their arms, but when alone, Tamar asked for their names. Most were Dutch, though some didn't understand her question.

Coughing erupted at the far end. The weak, gray-haired woman, Mrs. Jaffe, struggled to sit up to quell the hacking. Tamar remembered that struggle—trying to catch her breath amid the compulsion to cough. She peered at the woman. The staff had reprimanded Tamar for spending too much time with hopeless cases, the ones who wouldn't be returning to the workforce. She hurried to the supply room to refill the water pitcher.

She rushed back to Mrs. Jaffe, who held a bloody cloth over her lips. So many people needed Daniel's expertise, but the job was too big for one person. Tamar poured a glass of water and lifted the straw to her shaky lips, pulling it away when another round of coughs came on. She handed Mrs. Jaffe a clean cloth and deposited the dirty one in a laundry basket to be bleached.

"Sing for us … Tamar. It always … helps settle me down."

Expectant eyes looked her way. Some of the patients propped up on one elbow. She thought of her mother, wondering if she was here, if she lay on one of these cots waiting for help. Soothing songs were sometimes the only medicine Tamar could offer. "*Nabucco*" came out unbidden—Verdi's chorus about Hebrew slaves. Not the best choice for a Nazi infirmary, but Tamar doubted that the twenty-year-old oberen knew Verdi from Broekhuizen. Still, it only took one. She lowered her voice and finished the melody.

Rustling from the end bed made Tamar swivel toward the sound. The comatose patient was struggling to face her, eyes open for the first time. A raspy voice called out, "Tamar."

She hurried toward the shell of a woman and grasped her hand. "Yes, I'm Tamar." The paper-thin hand felt as though it would disintegrate into dust if she held it too tightly. A small smile wrinkled the woman's cheeks—like the Chinese fans Tamar used to make in primary school when the May breezes failed to cool the classroom.

"Little Tamar, always singing. How could I forget such a voice?"

"Mrs. Betz? From the bakery? I didn't recognize you." Her hand went to her heart. "You've been here all this time?"

"I don't know. Lost track of time."

Tamar enveloped her neighbor's hand in both of hers, this connection with her past. Then she lifted a glass to her lips and helped her take a sip. "When you left in the middle of the night, Abba said you had gone to visit relatives. I believed him. He cleaned up the debris outside your bakery. Burglars, he said. But you were here?"

"Yes, and now you're here." She smiled. "From a wee girl, you always sang or hummed. My husband would say, 'That little Tamar's coming around the corner. I can hear her singing.' Your mother was so proud of you."

"Where is Mr. Betz?" Tamar covered her mouth. "I'm sorry. I should have thought before I said anything."

"That is all right. He was here for a while, then they sent him elsewhere. Bergen-Belsen, I heard from one of the guards." She closed her eyes. "I should rest now."

"Before you do, you need something to eat. I'll be right back." Quickly, Tamar rose from the side of the cot. She had so much to ask Mrs. Betz, but she'd wait until later. *Wait until Daniel hears. Maybe Mrs. Betz knows about Eema and Abba.*

Mrs. Betz's voice cracked behind her. "I saw your mother."

Tamar stopped, whirled, and almost fell over another cot. She edged back to her former neighbor's bedside. Time spent at this end of the room would mean dismissal or worse, but she had to know. "My mother? When?"

Mrs. Betz drew in a shaky breath and whispered, "Months ago. Your papa too. My abba was here then as well. They stayed in different barracks ... worked in different places, but we spoke to them on Sundays. Hand in hand, they walked. We talked by the fence."

"Here? What fence?"

"By the field. Behind the dirt. We'd chat. She talked about you, child."

"What did she say?" Tamar lowered herself onto the edge of Mrs. Betz's cot.

"Everything and nothing. About your singing and how you were always asking about your name. I remember asking the same question. Your mother said, 'The Tamar in the Torah rose above her circumstances. I want my Tamar to do the same.'"

Tamar clasped her hands over the painful thudding of her heart. Finally, she understood. And she'd decided to do the very thing her mother had wished. "What happened to my parents?"

One shoulder lifted. "I'm sorry, I don't know. I'm tired." She turned to face the wall.

Could they still be here?

Tamar hurried to the main hall of the infirmary and asked a guard for some soft food—soup or porridge, but he rolled his eyes and turned away. Mrs. Betz lay at death's door. She grabbed an empty glass on the counter and dipped it into the broth while the guard was chopping cabbage with his back to her. She managed to hide the cup behind her as he turned back to the pot of broth. Tamar returned to the sick room and headed to Mrs. Betz, who lay staring at the ceiling.

"Here, Mrs. Betz. It's just a little broth." She gently propped the woman's head and tipped the cup slightly up. Her former neighbor took a couple small sips, shook her head, and closed her eyes. German voices and footsteps were getting closer. More guards were coming. Time to leave. She took one last look at Mrs. Betz. She'd save some food and return as soon as possible, even if it meant sneaking back.

Back in the barracks, Tamar sipped her thin liquid containing a piece of cabbage and turnip. She ripped off a piece of bread for

Mrs. Betz and dipped the rest in the soup, waiting for Neelie to finish her prayer. They'd tried more than a few times to eat their dinner on the tables in the other room, but they filled up quickly, and fights broke out. It was easier and quieter in their corner of Barrack 24. "Guess who I talked to in the infirmary."

"Someone we know? Who?" Neelie nibbled on the crust of her bread.

"Did you know Mrs. Betz, the owner of the bakery across the street from our store?"

Neelie stopped eating and turned toward her. "Of course. I stood in line for their *duivekater* for the Feast of Saint Nicolas with everyone else in the neighborhood." She took a sip of her soup. "Oh, I remember their *sjekladebollen* and *sukerbolen*. I assumed she and her husband were able to escape with help from the Resistance. So she's not well?"

"No, she's been in a coma, but she recognized my voice and woke up. She saw my parents." The words fairly exploded from her.

"Oh, glory be." Neelie's hand went to her lips.

"She and her husband were both here before Mr. Betz was sent to Bergen-Belsen in Germany. They spent Sundays together, strolling by the fence. That's where she saw Abba and Eema."

"So they could still be here?"

"She didn't know." Tamar sighed. "If they are here, why haven't we seen them?"

"It's a big place. We don't know the people in the other barracks. How can we find out?" Neelie sat forward and covered Tamar's hand.

"That's all I've been thinking about since I talked with her. Maybe there's a list somewhere. Hannie can find anything." Tamar swung her legs over the side of her cot.

"Hannie can find what?" Hannie's face appeared from the bed above them. She and Tamar had traded beds when Hannie said having the top bunk gave her a better perspective on potential customers and the middle bed made her claustrophobic. "Cigarettes, vitamins, bandages, magazines, cards—you name it. Reasonable prices."

"The woman in the coma in the infirmary—do you know who I'm talking about? Mrs. Betz. She was our neighbor. She woke up today. Said my parents were here. Is there some list that might give me information as to where they are?" Tamar's words spilled out so fast, she had to take a breath.

"Easy, sunshine." Hannie climbed down to sit next to her. "I could access a list that might give me information, but honey, don't get your hopes up. Vught is a way station. People come and go all the time."

"But you could check the list? Jacob and Odette Kaplan."

"I'll see what I can find out. I accompany the guard to the other women's barracks—all eight of them. What does she look like?"

"Small, curly blonde hair. Smiling eyes—" Tamar bit on her lower lip. Hannie didn't appreciate tears, and she needed her help.

"All right, but it's going to cost you."

"Oh." Tamar's chin fell to her chest. She had nothing to her name except the small papers Neelie had given her. Not even a handkerchief. The jewels she'd grabbed from the store before she and Daniel left remained behind the bookcase in Neelie's home if the soldiers hadn't confiscated them.

Neelie removed the puzzle from underneath her pillow. "Will you take my puzzle as payment? It should bring a good price. You know how many times I've put it together."

Tamar gasped. "You don't have to give up your puzzle, Tante."

"If it will help find your parents, it's worth it."

"May I?" Hannie held out her hand, but Tamar shook her head, her lips parted.

"It is all right." Neelie reached up and laid the box in Hannie's open palm. "Tamar, you have been a joy to us. Please, it is the least we can do."

Tamar couldn't meet her eyes. She certainly didn't deserve her sacrifice. "Thank you, Tante Neelie. I'm sorry I've been so negative when you talk about God. You don't deserve that, after all you've done for me."

"Never apologize for honest feelings and honest questions. We can handle them, and God can too. Honest doubts are better than shallow acceptance." Sadness wreathing her face, Neelie took her soup cup and gestured for Tamar to pass her cup to her. "I've had questions as well."

Tamar managed a half smile, then leaned forward. They deserved to know. "Speaking of honesty ... Daniel is planning to escape. He wants me to go with him."

"Tamar, is that wise? You could be killed." Neelie glanced up, her eyes saucers of concern.

"I know. And I don't want to go, especially now that my parents might be here." She sighed. Tomorrow was Sunday. Often Daniel had to work on Sundays, but if not, she'd tell him what Mrs. Betz said. Together, they'd make a plan.

Tamar lived for Sundays. No loud voices startling them awake at five or six in the morning. No standing in the dark for roll call. No one checking their beds for wrinkles. Prisoners were able to sleep in until the glorious hour of eight, so the sun had already chased away the frost by the time they lined up for a quick roll call. Today there'd be no punishments meted out. The General always read through the list of people, departing quickly afterward.

The prisoners spent more time on their appearance, then sat on their bunks drinking coffee and nibbling on bread at their leisure. Lively chatter permeated the dormitory. Some women went back to sleep despite the noise. Others stood by the door or windows, smoking and chatting. Neelie always asked Tamar to join her for church, which met between the barracks. She turned her down with a single word, "Daniel." Maybe next week she'd go, if she were still here.

Tamar hurried to the tree by the corner fence where she always waited for him. Over the last three days, she'd managed to sneak Mrs. Betz a heel of bread, a few teaspoons of porridge, and a cracker, but each time the old woman was either sleeping or refused to talk, so she'd dipped the bread in the water and fed her, Tamar's eyes always alert for approaching guards. She'd also hoarded a bit of her food for today's date with Daniel. They'd find a quiet place and have a picnic. Today, she had two goals—elicit Daniel's help in finding her parents and see what he could do to help Mrs. Betz.

With no watch, it was impossible to tell how long she waited. She leaned against the trunk, staring at the wildflowers on the other side of the fence. A monarch lit on a purple flower, then moved to the next. The butterfly had more freedom than she.

Daniel didn't show up. It happened from time to time when they needed a real doctor, although the medical staff would never admit his value. He'd find her when he finished. She pushed away from the tree trunk and strolled along the fence. Soon the area would be full of people, but now she had it all to herself. The fence was such a popular Sunday destination. So close to freedom, to the world they remembered—a simple meadow on the other side of a barbed wire fence. Sometimes, she carefully poked her fingers through. For a moment, her fingers were free like that butterfly.

Tamar reached the hill of dirt Mrs. Betz had talked about. It offered a bit of privacy from the guards who stood in the courtyard. Her parents had stood right here, hand in hand, looking out at the meadow. If she stayed here long enough, maybe they'd show up. How she missed her father's deep voice and teasing humor, which had rubbed off on her brother. And her mother's worrying over every little thing. *Tamar, you must eat more. You're getting thin. Tamar, a career isn't everything. Before you know it, marriage will pass you by. How about the Dreyfus boy? Tamar, your eyes will fall out if you keep rolling them.*

"Hello." A young girl with blonde braids and a strip of freckles across her nose peered up at her from the other side of the fence. Tamar's breath caught. The girl couldn't be more than eight. She poked a stick through the fence holes.

"I'm sorry. I didn't see you. Hello." She smiled at the girl. "What's your name?"

"I'm Livia. What's *your* name?"

"Tamar." She bent down to the child's level.

"That's a funny name. Are you a criminal?"

What? Tamar giggled. "No, I'm not. I'm a prisoner."

The girl's forehead scrunched together. "Isn't that the same thing? Papa says this is where criminals live."

Much as she'd like to set Livia straight, she didn't want to cause a rift between the girl and her father. She changed the subject. "Do you live around here?"

The girl twisted around and pointed at a hill covered by large poplar trees. "I live up there." Tamar followed her finger and squinted to see the outline of windows peeking out from among the branches.

"That looks like a big house."

"We moved here last year. I don't like it here. Too many soldiers. My papa works at the prison."

"What does he do?"

"I'm not sure. The soldiers call him *Commandant*. Do you know him?"

She'd heard about the man called Commandant. The leader of the camp, he had the reputation of being a cruel taskmaster. "I've never met him," Tamar said. "Does your mother know where you are?"

"No, she's shopping. Again. My brothers won't play with me because I'm a girl, and my friends have gone to the seaside for the weekend."

Tamar posted her hands on her hips and nodded. "I have a brother, so I know about being left out."

Livia moved closer to the fence, her nose poking through the holes. "You're nice. My brother said everyone's evil in there. Are you scared of being with evil people?"

Evil? She thought of Neelie. How mistaken the girl was. "Most prisoners in here are nice. They're sad because they're away from their homes and their families."

"Maybe you can go back home when your punishment is over. How long do you have?"

She shrugged and tried to change the subject. "I don't know, but will your mother be upset if she finds out you came down here?"

"Prob-ly, but she won't be home for a while. Would you like some cake?" She removed a crumbled napkin smeared with frosting from her pocket and fit a piece of cake through the hole in the fence.

"Thank you. Won't you share it with me?" She felt sorry for this lonely girl and wanted her to think the best of those within the barbed wire. Tamar brought a morsel to her mouth, savoring its buttercream sweetness.

Livia took a bite, then licked her finger. "I grabbed this when Katarina turned around. It's from my brother's birthday two days ago. She made it."

"Who's Katarina?"

"Our cook. She's married to one of the soldiers that stands in our driveway. I don't like him. He never smiles, and he has creepy eyes."

"Your parents just want to keep you safe." Despite the lies the child had been weaned on, it felt good to converse with someone from the outside who didn't hate her for being a *Jid*. She stood. "You should go back. I don't want you to get in trouble."

Livia nodded and picked up her stick. "Do you sing?"

"What?" Tamar stiffened.

"Do you sing?"

"Yes, I do. Why do you ask? Do you want to sing a song before you go home?"

"I met a woman here." Livia tilted her head, her fair brows drawing together. "She said her girl looked just like me when she was little. She had long, blonde braids. You have blonde hair. The lady said her girl had grown up and sings songs. Is that you?"

Tamar's hand went to her chest. "Livia, when did you talk to the lady? Was it recently?"

The girl's forehead furrowed, and she bit a fingernail. "It was cold outside. There was snow. Well, I'd better go. Bye, Tamar."

"Wait." She knelt and grabbed onto the flat part of the wire. "What did she look like? Did the woman come with someone?"

"Hmm." The girl tapped a finger on her lip. "Older than you but dressed the same. She wore a cap and a big coat. She was nice and sad. I think she missed her daughter."

"Did she come with a man?"

"No, she came alone. The lady had a funny name like yours. She said her name was French."

Tamar's heartbeat galloped. "My mother has a French name. Was Odette her name?"

"Yes, I think so. Well, I'd better go. See you again some time." She skipped away.

Tamar leaned against the fence post. Her mother had been here. Maybe she still was. What were the chances of meeting this young girl at the same place that her mother had met her? Slim at best. This was no coincidence. For the first time in a long time, she prayed.

CHAPTER TWENTY-TWO

"Wake up, sleepyhead."

The voice made her start. Striped pants milling past her in both directions were the first thing she saw when she opened her eyes. How could she have fallen asleep in broad daylight?

"Tamar?"

Daniel sat next to her. She managed a smile in his direction. "Sorry. I must have dozed off. What time is it?"

"Near lunchtime. We have to talk." He reached up and dabbed at the edge of her lip. "You have blue schmutz on your face. Looks delicious." He tasted his finger. "Mm. Sweet."

"Icing." She shook her head. "Then it wasn't a dream."

"What wasn't a dream?"

"I have so much to tell you." She straightened, planting her palms on the ground, fully awake now. "My parents might be here."

"What?" He jumped to his feet. "Let's move to a more private place. We don't need extra ears overhearing. And I have something to tell you as well." He pulled her up and headed toward the birch tree they'd adopted, close to the fence but far enough away to give them some privacy.

"Who would hear?" She peered over her shoulder for the child.

"People will trade anything for cigarettes or extra food, including information." Daniel plopped down next to the trunk, then took off his jacket and laid it on the ground next to him. "I have a surprise." From his pocket, he took a dozen raisins.

Her eyes widened. "I haven't had fruit in months." She removed the food she'd saved from her pocket—a bit of plum preserves and half a cookie Neelie had given her from Jan's last package. "A real picnic feast today. But we must save some for Mrs. Betz." She sat next to him.

"Who's Mrs. Betz?"

Between nibbles, she told him about her conversation with the woman in the infirmary and her meeting with the little girl named Livia. "So, you see, my mother and father might be here now—or were when there was still snow on the ground. Can you find out?"

"You sure it was your mother?" He divided the raisins into two piles.

"Mrs. Betz said so, and the little girl talked about meeting a French woman with a funny name who had a blonde daughter who sings. I asked Hannie if she could look around and check the list to see if my parents are here. Would you help as well? See if you can find their name on a list?"

"They keep me on a short chain. Usually, they move people out before they bring new ones in." A furrow formed between his eyebrows. "By the way, the woman you speak of is still comatose. Nobody reported otherwise to me. Are you sure we're talking about the same person?"

"The woman by the far wall in the farthest bed from the entrance. The lady next to her, Mrs. Jaffe, coughed up blood. She asked me to sing. That's when Mrs. Betz woke up. She called my name. I hardly recognized her because she's so frail." Tamar huffed. Why didn't he share her excitement over finding Mrs. Betz and possibly her parents? This was the closest thing to God's hand in her life she'd ever experienced. There were lists somewhere. He could find a way if he tried. "What do you suggest we do to find my parents?"

"Aren't we getting ahead of ourselves? It's late September, a long time after winter." He pulled her close and put his arm around her. "I just don't want you to get your hopes dashed, and there's something else."

Tamar pulled away. "How hard can it be to look up her name? Odette Kaplan." She crossed her arms over her chest and stared at the meadow, anywhere but at him.

"The lists we carry only have numbers, no names." He heaved a sigh when he saw her sulking. "Okay, put the pout away. I'll think of an excuse to ask for names. Now get over here."

She exaggerated the act of pulling in her lip, scooted over next to him, and popped a raisin in her mouth. "Have you visited every barrack?"

"No, I've only been in the men's quarters with the guard, Wertz." He took her hand, folding his fingers gently over hers. So warm. "And no, I haven't seen your father, although in these uniforms, everyone looks alike."

She sighed. "So close, yet so far away."

"And listen, that little girl's father is no one to fool with. I've heard stories—"

She nibbled off a corner of the cookie, then fed the rest to him. "Livia was so cute, so innocent. How can a monster create such a normal little girl?" A rhetorical question. Lost in her own thoughts, she folded the napkin and put it in her pocket.

"Tamar? I have to tell you something."

"Hmm?" She didn't want to abandon her current daydream. Her father and mother had returned home and waited for her to come in. The house smelled of pot roast. *Pot roast.*

"Chocolate chip cookies."

"Stop talking unless you have one hidden in your pocket."

"You'd make a terrible spy. I said, 'chocolate chip cookies.'"

It was then she noticed his foot tapping the ground at high speed. She sat up. "The code word. What do you mean?"

"I hid the uniforms—one male and one female. We need to leave today when it's Sunday and everything is less rigid. Soon, before word gets out that the SS uniforms are missing." He straightened to face her. "Tamar? We have to go."

She stared at him, clenching her brows together. "How can I? I can't leave if my parents are here. Surely, you understand." Confusion filled her. How could she leave if even the tiniest possibility existed that Abba and Eema were here? What kind of daughter would do a thing like that? How could she choose? Her parents or the love of her life? Temporary safety in this evil place or potential freedom with the risk of certain death if they were caught? "Can't we wait until you check the lists? Or Hannie checks them?" A tear traveled down her cheek. "A day or two won't make a difference."

He traced a finger under the tear. "Your parents have moved on, I'm sure, or we would have seen them. They sent Mr. Betz to a camp."

"But what about Tante Neelie and Hannie? Do we just abandon them?"

His face tightened. "Neelie and Hannie can't keep up. We'll be running for our lives through woods, living on nothing. I'm sorry."

"But—" She chewed on a thumbnail.

"Tamar." Daniel gripped both of her hands, staring into her eyes. "I didn't want to frighten you or coerce you, but there's talk of a move tonight or tomorrow night at the latest. They need the space for new arrivals. We'll be moved out of this country, either to Poland or Germany."

Well, that did change things. She stifled a sob. "Not today. Give me until tomorrow morning. Please?"

"Think. If they move us tonight, it will be too late. We might not even be sent to the same camp. No. Our best chance of escape is now when most of the guards are off duty. No one would question us if we slipped down that path leading to the woods. They'd think we were two guards looking for some privacy." His eyes darted to the forest beyond the infirmary as his hands clenched and unclenched.

Trembling, she worried her lower lip between her teeth. He was right, but loyalty anchored her to this wretched soil. "At least, let me find Hannie and see if she's discovered anything. If my parents are here, I can't think of leaving now. I'm sorry."

He stared at her for a long time, his mouth tightened. She'd disappointed him. But she wasn't made from the same stock as her brother and Daniel, with their restless energy, their hunger for freedom.

Her fingers glided along the side of his face. How she'd miss him. "You go by yourself."

"I can't leave you here." His eyes closed against the touch of her fingers, and he drew a ragged breath. "Let's go find Hannie."

They located her between the men's barracks, bartering with an old man, poking her finger into his graying, grizzled beard, which reached his waist. "Five cigarettes are all they're worth. The playing cards aren't even real. They're homemade and flimsy." She shifted through them for emphasis.

The old man sniffed and shook his head. "Ten cigarettes. And flimsy? Who'll care that they're not real as long as there's fifty-two of them?"

Hannie's expression remained unyielding. "Eight is my final offer, and throw in something else because you're irritating me."

"Your cigarettes are homemade as well." The gnarled man lifted both arms. "All right. Deal, you old broad. I should give up the habit, anyways. It's making me hack."

"You're the hack." She counted out eight cigarettes.

Tamar waited for the man to shuffle away, then she leaned close to Hannie's ear. "Did you find out anything about my mother?"

Hannie ignored her, staring up at Daniel. "I thought you'd be long gone by now."

His eyes widened. "How'd you know? I haven't spoken to anyone except—"

"There's not a lot that goes on around here that I don't know about." She lit a cigarette and offered them a drag, which they declined. "You heard the rumors?"

"So it's not just idle talk?"

"Nah, they're shipping us out tonight. Germany, I heard—Ravensbrück for the ladies, Buchenwald for the gents. Tough place. Makes this one look like a day at the park." She shifted to face Tamar. "I can see by your expression, you don't want to go. Your mother's gone. I checked the list. Her name wasn't there. Leave."

Tamar fought to control her lower lip that quivered like a dry leaf in the wind. "What about you and Neelie?"

"Don't worry about us. We're in good hands. What is it Neelie always says? *The palm of God's hand.* That's why I stick close to her. But don't go telling her or she'll make me go to her church service." She chuckled. "But you two, you're young ... and in love. Go, child, while you still can."

Tamar pulled Hannie into a hug. Her voice broke. "Tell Neelie I love her, and I'll think about her every day. And find her—after this is all over."

Hannie pushed away and rolled her eyes. "We'll miss you, Tamar ... and Doc. Be smart and lay low." She pulled a can of sardines and some saltines from her shoulder bag. "Here, the best I can do."

CHAPTER TWENTY-THREE

After changing into their disguises in the infirmary supply room, Tamar used one hand to hold up her skirt. It still trailed around her feet, threatening to trip her with every step. Daniel's uniform hung on his thin frame like a tent, even though they both wore their prison clothes underneath for extra warmth—and to avoid having to dispose of the garments. The officers obviously enjoyed larger meals than they did. The only tight thing on her—the guard's hat that covered her thick hair. "Why don't I let my hair hang loose since I'm trying to look like a shiksa?"

"Right, but I want you to fit in, not stand out. How about putting it in a ponytail or a braid?"

Tamar nodded and fashioned her hair into a plait.

Meanwhile, Daniel opened drawers and grabbed gauze, tape, and pieces of cloth, and stuffed them into his pockets. Then he strode to the door. "The hall is clear." As she tied off the tail of the braid, he kissed her temple. "Ready for this? We're a loving couple out to enjoy an afternoon tryst, okay?"

She nodded, taking his hand. They made it through the exit, nodding at the guard who chuckled when they passed. His leer made her feel dirty.

They kept their eyes low, pretending to be in a conversation when they passed another guard. Daniel nodded toward the man but kept talking, interjecting a spurt of laughter as if they shared some funny anecdote.

After rounding the corner, Tamar saw the path, wide enough for a convoy of trucks. One hundred meters beyond, the dirt road veered to the left. But thirty meters before it disappeared, three guards stood, smoking cigarettes and chatting.

As they approached, Daniel whispered, "Keep your eyes on me." His arm circled her shoulder. Her breathing quickened with every step. "Smile," he said. "That's the way."

"You one of the new recruits for Scheveningen? What are you doing?" One of the officers stepped forward. "I want to get me some of that." The middle officer slapped his friend on the back. Then all three focused on Daniel.

"Wait your turn," Daniel said in German, his free hand brushing them off. He huddled over her, laughing, but his arm tightened around her shoulder, pulling her closer.

"Wait," one of them yelled. "Where you going?" Footsteps were catching up to them. "There's nothing up ahead."

"Play along," Daniel whispered. He stopped and turned toward the approaching officer. "Let us be. She needs privacy. Her friends don't know. *Verstehen sie?*" He propelled her forward with a slight shove on her back.

She ducked her head as she trotted along, but a sideways glance showed the officer backing up. Daniel's arm looped around her again. He nuzzled her neck. They'd made it past the first obstacle. She had the overpowering urge to run as fast as she could. Instead, she placed one foot in front of the other, counting the steps, matching Daniel's pace. Closer, closer to the curve that would bring freedom. But what waited around the bend?

"Good, stay with me. Laugh a bit, nod. Pretend we're having a fling until we reach the trees."

A couple passed them, the thin woman in stripes lagging behind the officer who jerked her forward every few steps. Laughter from the officers behind informed Tamar they'd already forgotten about her. Her heart sagged at the young woman's downcast face. Sundays had always been the best part of Vught ... but apparently not for everyone.

They rounded the curve and scanned the area for green uniforms. When they'd covered twenty meters, Daniel let go of her arm. "Ready?"

"Ready for what?"

"It's time to run. By now, the uniforms will have been missed. Their owners will think someone's playing a joke on them, but soon they'll figure it out. No turning back from this point on." He touched her cheek.

"No turning back."

They veered left and raced to the tree line. With one glance back, they entered the wood, their feet creating racket with every crunch of twigs and branches. She felt sure alarms would sound at any moment. Her heart raced. Dread filled her. What foolishness had she done?

Daniel pulled her forward, avoiding low-lying branches that threatened to whip across their faces. Slivers of light filtered through from above to show fallen trees on an uneven ground covered with moss, roots, and vines. The autumn chill was in the air, yet they were moving so fast she hardly noticed. The smell of decaying wood and leaves mixed with the pungent scent of pine needles. Nearby, a dove cooed a mournful note. A harbinger of things to come?

A rustling nearby made her tighten up. How could freedom seem so sinister?

"It's just a squirrel," Daniel said.

The hem of her skirt caught on the toe of her shoe, and she lunged forward. She managed to buttress her fall with her elbows. Daniel helped her to a stump, rolled up her pant legs, then kissed her forehead. She brushed twigs and burrs from her clothes but otherwise had suffered no harm.

"You're doing well, but we have to keep moving, okay?"

She nodded vigorously. "Where are we going?"

He lifted a shoulder. "All I know is, we have to put as much distance as we can between Vught and ourselves. And stay hidden."

Tamar brushed errant strands of hair from her eyes. "Do you know what direction we're headed?"

"No, except—" He pointed at the base of a tree. "This moss avoids sunlight, so it tends to grow on the north side of the tree.

We can use it as a compass, although Mother Nature isn't always trustworthy." He planted a foot on the stump she sat on.

"Do we want to go north?"

"That is the question, Shakespeare. What we want to avoid are natural enemies like the lakes and bogs that can show up unannounced, and human enemies, of course, that travel the main roads." He peered over his shoulder. "Soon they'll send the dogs, so we should head toward a town where we can shed these clothes. Tilburg is around eighteen kilometers from Vught. Let's head southwest."

They ran slowly but steadily, eyes focused on avoiding roots and rabbit holes. Had they escaped from Westerbork, Tamar would have found the trip an easier challenge. For the past few months, she'd stopped working on her stamina and had become soft. Her labored breathing and the stitch in her side protested, but she refused to be a hindrance. "Buck it up," she said between breaths.

"What?"

"I said, 'buck it up.' That's what Seth used to say when I complained. He learned it from one of our New York cousins."

"Good advice. You're bucking it up just fine."

When they'd covered what seemed like ten kilometers, she stopped and bent over. "I need a break. How far have we gone?"

"I don't know. Not far enough." He squatted next to her. "We have to go. Have you noticed the trees are thinning?"

"What does that mean?" She peered up at him.

"It could be natural causes like fires or insect infestation, or the area has been thinned for commercial or ecological reasons."

"So we may be close to humans?"

"Precisely. Let's go. We want to cover as much distance as possible before it gets dark."

They took off at a moderate pace, careful to sidestep exposed roots. The *rat-a-tat* of guns in the distance did little to allay Tamar's fears. Were they escaping one peril for another? At least Vught's danger was familiar. She tried to keep up, knowing Daniel could have sprinted through the brush if not for her.

An hour or two passed—she couldn't tell how much time had elapsed, but the shadows were eating up the sunlight. The stitch in her side persisted. If she could just rest for a minute. "Daniel? You should go ahead. I'm just slowing you down."

"Silly girl." He matched her speed. "Don't you know that life without you is mere shades of gray?" He drew to a stop and lifted her chin with his knuckles. "You make my life burst with vibrant colors."

And even in the midst of exhaustion and danger, that made her heart burst with love. Heaving another breath, she said, "But I'm holding you back. If it weren't for me, you'd already be safely hidden somewhere. Tell me where to meet you. The woods near Zandvoort aan Zee, or near your parents' house."

He pulled her close. "I love you, little non-flower. We will stay together, and we'll do it with cunning and careful thought. We're getting closer to Tilburg. Can you hear the jeeps?"

"Do you think we'll make it before dark?"

"Let's go another half hour or so, then we'll take a break." He took her hand, and they started off at a light run.

The stitch abated, but the impending darkness made it more difficult to see the ground. Her foot lodged in a rut. She fell with a loud grunt. Now she'd done it. Pushing herself to her knees, she tried to extricate her foot, but it had wedged in the tight space, like a peg in a hole.

"Don't move," Daniel said. "I'll try to ease it out."

Since she'd fallen headfirst, sitting proved impossible. She was forced to stay hunched on all fours while pain seared through her lower limb. Finally, he freed her foot and helped her limp to the nearest stump.

"I'm sorry. See? You should have left while you had the chance."

He sobered. "Don't say things like that. You and I will do this together. No matter what happens." He took a cracker from his pocket and gave it to her. "I wish I could offer you a drink."

She nibbled the corner of it, her appetite gone, and handed it back to him.

"You have to keep up your strength. Eat the whole thing." He removed a piece of cloth from his pocket and gingerly wrapped it around her ankle, which was already swelling.

Giggling came from somewhere close. Female giggling. Then a male voice.

Tamar glanced at Daniel. He helped her to her feet, her arm resting on his shoulder. They moved carefully toward the sound. Tamar winced with each step.

Birch trees provided little cover, but the shadows did. Daniel held her back when they reached a clearing. Hearty, green summer grass surrounded a perfect little lake, pristine and idyllic. A couple stretched across a checkered sheet, chatting, laughing. They couldn't be more than sixteen. A picnic basket sat next to the sheet, and the remnants of a half-eaten lunch sat at the edge. The boy teased the girl with a flower under her nose. She pretended to sneeze.

Daniel pointed at a truck peeking out from a knoll on the other side of the lake. "Come on," he whispered.

They were going to commit a crime. Tamar had never purposely broken the law. They'd go to jail for sure. She hesitated but he pulled her hand.

They slowly made their way toward the other side of the lake, remaining behind the trees, skirting the clearing. Darkness hid them. She glanced at the teenagers when the landscape allowed her to do so. Her foot screamed for rest, every step harder than the one before.

When they reached the closest point between trees and the truck, he pointed at bales of hay on its flatbed. Daniel crouched and gestured for her to do the same. She'd voice her concerns later, but for now, she followed.

He rounded the driver's door, eased it open, and fumbled inside. "Found the key. Get in and keep your head down. He could be a Nazi with a gun."

She pulled herself onto the seat, her foot throbbing with every centimeter of movement. Daniel slid in and started the engine, its loud bellow making her wince. He put the truck in gear and swerved onto a narrow, rough-hewn path. Acres of farmland spread out on both sides, fallow ground that had gone to seed.

She peered at Daniel's solemn expression and read worry in the craggy lines. The giggles outside the window had morphed into outrage. "What are we going to do?"

He glanced at the dashboard. "There's only a bit of petrol left. Vapors, really. We'll ditch the truck when we get close to a main road. We must be near Tilburg."

"What will happen to that couple?" she ventured. She hated to think of them stranded as darkness fell. Funny, when she considered her own dire straits.

"They'll be fine. It's probably walking distance to town, or they live on neighboring farms. If they're teenagers, their parents won't be too happy, but they'll get their truck back. By that time, we'll be long gone."

She studied him. "Doesn't it bother you to steal their truck?"

"Yes, unless they're Nazis. Then I hope they never find the vehicle." He angled her a look, then responded to her frozen expression. "We're not really stealing it if we leave it a bit up the road, are we, now? It's more like a loaner. Look around. See if there's anything we can use."

But *that* was stealing. Nevertheless, she felt under the seat, pulled up a change purse, and opened it. A few guilders, a school identification, and a tube of lipstick. *Lipstick.* How long had it been? "I don't feel right about this."

"Take the money." Daniel was no longer mincing words. A matter of survival, she reminded herself. He pressed her. "Anything else? Feel under my side."

Her foot pressed against the door so she could reach under Daniel's seat. She retrieved a pack of cigarettes and a billfold. "Want a smoke?"

"No, thanks. Anything in the wallet?"

"A driver's permit and some photographs of a family and a pretty girl."

He glanced her way. "Any cash?"

She ran her thumb behind the pictures, then shook the billfold. The clang of coins. Tamar turned it upside down. Out came four guilders, three Reichsmarks, and a silver note. She spread them on her lap.

With a shrug, Daniel said, "It's enough to buy us some food. Maybe even pay for train tickets."

Tamar shook her head. "I can't take it." She stared out the window.

"Do it," he said, swerving to miss a rock in the middle of the road. Then he sighed. "How about we memorize the license number, and when all this is over, we give the people their money back with interest?" He patted her hand. "Now we're coming up on some farmhouses. There's a grove of trees over there, big enough to conceal this truck. What do you say?"

"Good idea. But my ankle is the size of a melon. I'm not sure how far I can walk."

Daniel turned onto a narrow lane, barely wide enough for tractors. He pulled behind a thatch of poplars, then swiveled to face her. "Can you lift your ankle up on the seat?"

She held her breath and used her hands to gingerly raise it, then with a groan eased it onto the part of the bench between them. Daniel eased off her boot and lightly touched her ankle. "It's not broken. Looks more like a sprain." He gently put her boot back on. "Come on, you can lean on my extremely strong shoulders." He laughed.

She grinned back. "Isn't this a nice kettle of herring? Escaping from Nazis with a sprained ankle?"

"But look what God gave us? A truck and some cash." He opened the door and helped her out.

"He didn't give us these things. We stole them. We're thieves.

Are you saying that God helped us steal from that couple?"

He shrugged. "I'm just saying He knows we needed the vehicle and the cash more than they did. And we will return them."

She rolled her eyes. "You sound like Tante Neelie. She sees God in everything."

They started walking toward the nearest tree line, but her injury slowed their progress. The dark gray of dusk predominated, although outlines of trees silhouetted against the sky remained visible in the distance.

"He is. He's our Father. Think of your abba. Wouldn't he want you to escape a Nazi-run labor camp if you had the chance?"

"Maybe, unless we made a foolish decision. Did we?"

He didn't answer.

"What's our destination? The woods?"

"We really need to change clothes. As long as we're wearing these uniforms, the dogs can track us. I'm surprised we haven't heard their barking yet."

She tightened her grip around his back. "You're scaring me. And it's so dark it's hard to see."

With their slowed pace, they seemed no closer to the woods. Her foot throbbed, yet they had bigger problems. To take her mind off the pain, Tamar hummed a ballad from school, and then words followed. Music had always comforted her. She sang low enough that only Daniel could hear. He joined her, repeating the refrain with a breathless voice.

Suddenly, a silhouette appeared mere feet away. Tamar's heart jumped until she looked closer. "A scarecrow." It stared down at them, straw flapping in the wind from the cuffs of a denim shirt. A jaunty straw hat sat on his head. "Is this God's answer? If so, He has a sense of humor."

With a laugh, Daniel bounded forward, pulled down the stake that held the scarecrow, and relieved it of its clothes. "These dungarees look longer than your striped pajamas. How about I wear these, and you can have the orange hat." He held it up for her to see.

"No, thanks. I'll wait for the next scarecrow."

He circled his pointer finger. She faced away from him and waited. "I can't wait to see you in the morning light dressed like that."

"Okay, you can turn around."

She spun, then covered her mouth to suppress a giggle at his oversized pants. Even in the dark, he looked ridiculously handsome. "Are you going to dress the scarecrow in the striped pajamas or the Nazi uniform?"

"Neither. I'll hide them both someplace. Wish I had a shovel. Stay here. I'm going to look for soft dirt down one of these rows of corn and bury both of them." He headed right off the path. Meanwhile, Tamar lowered herself to the ground to rest her ankle. She slapped at a mosquito.

"Found a place. It won't take long." A slight rustling came from the direction of his voice. Minutes later, he trotted back. "Next, it's your turn."

"To bury me?"

He chuckled. "That humor of yours." He lightly cuffed her chin, then wrapped his arm around her, supporting her as he urged her forward.

They continued down the lane, which had narrowed to a path. The trees blended with the dark, moonless sky. Cicadas buzzed and a bullfrog croaked intermittently. The rustle of their pants and footsteps were the only other sounds.

"When we reach a safe place, we have to tell them." He readjusted his arm under her shoulder.

"Tell whom what?"

"About what we've seen at Vught and Westerbork. They'll believe us because we've been there."

She pondered his comment. "You mean the government?"

"No, they're just figureheads now. The newspapers aren't publishing, so that's out."

She cocked her head. "What about the Allies? If we can find a contact, they'd believe our eyewitness account. They'll tell our story."

He stopped and gently pulled her around to face him. "We've got to tell everyone."

"Do you think anyone will care?"

His jaw tightened, and his eyes held a determined glint. "There's got to be enough good people out there who will make sure it never happens again."

The throbbing worsened, but she focused on their new goal. *Beauty from ashes.* She hadn't thought about Daniel's epitaph for months. Neelie had described the crematorium in front of which her tiny ensemble played twice a week. Tamar had never seen it because it was located far from the barracks beyond an airplane grave. She'd spoken of the smoke and dust particles emitted from the chimney. The haunted eyes of prisoners in line. "Daniel, do you know anything about the camp Neelie and Hannie will be going to?"

"Ravensbrück? No, only that it's a female camp in Germany."

"Maybe we can tell the Allies about Ravensbrück, and they'll rescue them." That would make their fleeing from camp worthwhile. She could live with her conscience accusing her of selfishness if they helped her aunt, Hannie, Mrs. Betz, and her parents.

"Just a little farther. We'll look for a farm." Daniel broke into her thoughts. "Do you want to sing?"

She didn't answer right away, focusing on a small flickering in the distance. "Look over there. Is it my imagination, or is that a light?"

He leaned forward, his arm still around her waist. "I think so. If there's a farmhouse, there's a barn. If there's a barn, there's a place to hide and get some sleep."

They increased their pace, staying on the path to a slender dirt road that veered off toward the light. Tamar's pain subsided as her excitement grew.

The light shone from the second story of an old farmhouse. The barn on the right looked more dilapidated the closer they came. They froze when a dog's bark broke the night's silence.

"Nazis?" She eyed Daniel.

He waved her question off with his free hand. "Probably an old farm dog," he whispered. "There'd be more than one dog with the guards."

A silhouette appeared in the window, pushed it up, and yelled, "*Wees stil*, Boris." The dog whimpered.

They inched toward the barn, stopping every few steps. Tethered to a hook on the far corner of a building, its color nondescript in the dark, a large cocker spaniel pawed the ground, a tentative bark interrupting its whimpers.

"Hey, Boris." Daniel patted his leg and whispered in the spaniel's direction. "We won't bother you."

The barn door creaked with every inch they pushed it open. They slipped sideways through the slit into a dark cavern and moved blindly through the room, bumping into a trough of water. "I wouldn't want to drink it, but it might help the swelling go down. Look for a container."

She felt in the dark for something to hold water and found a crusty but empty bucket. "Here's something."

Daniel dipped it in the trough. "Let's find a corner to rest in for the night."

A nearby sound interrupted their movement and conversation. Tamar clenched her fingers around his arm, causing him to spill water on her shoes. "Did you hear that?"

"Sounds like a horse."

"Oh, sorry." She released her grip.

He moved away. "I'm feeling my way forward. Stay close." Then he stopped. "Ouch." Daniel toppled some more water. "Found a ladder. I'm going up." His voice came from above. "It's safe. Follow me."

Tamar started her ascent, favoring her sprain with little grunts and gasps. When she neared the top, the darkness deepened. "Can't see anything."

"Just a few more steps, but watch your head for a low rafter. Crawl until you feel straw. It's quite comfortable, and we'll be safe from the elements."

She responded with a high-pitched *ah-choo*.

"*Gezondheid*." Daniel let out a low chuckle. "You call that a sneeze?"

"I'm a soprano." She groped for the edge of the straw.

"Come, sit. Let's soak that foot." He patted the place beside him. She scooted to the edge of the straw pile, skirting its border until she reached Daniel and shifted to sit perpendicular to him. "Okay, this works." He carefully removed her boot, stopping with each gasp, then rolled up her pant leg. "Bend your knee and lie back."

She did.

He lifted her foot from the straw and lowered it into the frigid water. The pail proved too small for her whole foot to extend, so she curled her toes to the side. She closed her eyes. "That feels so good. Tell me a story, Daniel."

"What kind of story, darling?" His voice comforting.

"Something from your childhood." She yawned, gravity pulling her head to her folded hands.

"All right. When I was about eight, my best friend, Matthew Bloem, and I couldn't think of a thing to do one summer afternoon."

"So why didn't you get a job?" she murmured.

"I was eight. Do you want me to finish or not?"

"Sorry." She exhaled, allowing the darkness and peace to wrap around her.

Daniel gently massaged her lower leg, relaxing the tension in her calf. "We'd walked past this abandoned house on our way to school every day. One of those houses that's so covered with vines you can't see its color. Of course, we made up all kinds of theories about what went on inside—the owner had died, and nobody came to bury him, so his spirit still lived there. Or witches used it for a meeting place whenever the moon was full. That kind of thing."

"So ... did you go in? I would've." Shifting slightly, she turned her foot the other way in the pail.

"I know. You're no flower." He chuckled. "Matthew dared me to run up on the porch, then I dared him to open the door and stay inside for the count of ten. The door wasn't locked, so after Matthew had been in the house for ten seconds, I joined him. He suggested we play *verstoppertje*."

"Any sign of people living in the house?" Tamar asked, now too interested to sleep.

"Sheets covered all the furniture, and the air smelled musty, as though the windows hadn't been opened in years. Anyway, I said, 'I'll hide first,' and ran upstairs. I picked the last door on the left and went in. It had probably been a bedroom at one time, but now boxes filled the room. I found an antique wedding chest and climbed in. Then I pulled the sheet over it and closed the lid."

Tamar surrendered to a shudder. "Ugh. I hate closed-in spaces."

"So do I—after what happened. I waited for what seemed like hours, but Matthew didn't come. I tried pushing up on the lid, but somehow the lock had engaged. No amount of screaming and crying brought anyone to get me out."

Her eyes opened wide as horror swept her. "You must have been so scared. How did you breathe?"

"I don't know. Think I fell asleep. Hours later, Matthew returned with my father. It seemed my best friend didn't want to get in trouble for being late for dinner, so he conveniently forgot about me until my parents showed up at his house. Then he confessed. They followed my dusty footprints to the bedroom."

"How did they find you if you were sleeping in the chest?" The water had warmed slightly, so she withdrew her foot, and Daniel dried it with the tail of his shirt.

"I didn't wake up until the lid came off and my father said, 'Daniel?' I just remember jumping into his arms." Water sloshed as he emptied the bucket into some far corner. "Once assured I was okay, he gave me quite a licking."

Tamar stifled a yawn. "What happened to Matthew? Did he get in trouble?"

"His mother made him apologize, and they grounded him for … three—"

Tamar succumbed to restless slumber interrupted by her throbbing ankle. Sometime later, she shifted to her side, gingerly propping her foot on the overturned bucket. Dreams flitted in and out, each more confusing than the last.

When she finally opened her eyes, she peered at a slit of light that came through a shaft in the side of the barn. Daniel still slept, his resonant snore a bit louder than breathing. She could get used to it. Hay covered the floor, and several bales were stacked against the wall. Her nose scrunched up at the moldy smell. It must have rained, although their bed was dry. Should she wake Daniel? They couldn't afford to remain in the barn.

She was just about to whisper his name and shake his leg when she saw them. Two beady eyes peered at her from under the brim of a farmer's hat. But it was the rifle trained on her that made her gasp.

CHAPTER TWENTY-FOUR

"That's it. Stay where you are." The man's lips pressed together into a scowl. He climbed off the ladder, his eyes never leaving hers. His overalls draped over his thin, weathered frame. Suspicious, spry as a weasel.

Daniel sat up. Tamar glanced sideways at him, then back at the man whose rifle still targeted the space between her eyes.

"Don't move, I say."

"We mean no harm," Daniel said, his voice calm—the exact opposite of the way she felt. "Sorry we trespassed, but the lady sprained her ankle, and we needed a place to sleep. We'll be on our way now." He slowly lifted his palms in the farmer's direction.

The man took a step toward them with a click of the trigger.

"Take off your jacket," Daniel directed her between tightened lips. "Let him see."

"What?"

"Let him see the stripes," he whispered.

It was a gamble. Such a gamble. Yet she inched her hands up to undo the jacket's top button, then pulled the lapel sideways to expose the stripes. The man's beady eyes narrowed. The gun remained trained on them.

"Sir, will you help us?" Tamar ventured. "We escaped from Vught." Another sideways glance caught Daniel's pained expression.

Seconds passed without movement, without sound except for her heartbeat. Despite the brisk morning air, sweat dripped down her neck. They'd come to this moment. Faces flashed through her mind—her mother, her grandfather, Mrs. Betz, Neelie. A song Neelie sang when she did dishes—"It is well with my soul"—

played behind the kaleidoscope from her past, calming her spirit. The Nazi guards, this man with the rifle, could not take her soul. It belonged to the Lord. Her chin lifted. Neelie was right. The soul mattered more than anything. Fear ebbed away.

The rifle dropped to the man's side. "You're not Nazi scum, eh? The suit said otherwise. We've had a few prisoners from there, usually gone by the time I get up. Where ya headed?"

As Tamar drew in a deep, refreshing breath, Daniel rose to his feet, leaning forward to avoid hitting his head on the rafters. "Could you help us? Tamar needs to get out of that uniform, and we should burn it."

The man paused for a few moments. "For my son." He pulled out a handkerchief from his overall pocket and mopped his forehead. "Adrianus joined the Resistance. He left last November. Haven't seen him since."

Uncertain whether to offer sympathy or praise, Tamar settled for, "We both worked in the Resistance as well, based out of Haarlem."

The farmer gave an abrupt nod. "He'd want me to help you folks. I take it you're *Juden*. It's an honor, sir, ma'am. Follow me. I'll take good care of you." He removed his hat, lowered his head, then climbed down the ladder.

Daniel helped Tamar to her feet. She'd almost forgotten the sprain until she put pressure on it. The stabbing pain caused her to release a breath. Hopping to the ladder, she peered down. It seemed a lot farther in the light.

"Take your time. I'll go down first and help you down the last few steps." Daniel quickly descended. The farmer was waiting at the bottom. "My name is Daniel Feldman, and my fiancée's name is Tamar Kaplan."

"I am Jansen Bakker. It is a pleasure to meet you. Maybe I could offer you a change of clothes as well." He chuckled. "You might scare the birds with that outfit."

"That would be most welcome." Daniel turned and stood ready for her.

Tamar slid down a few steps, only slowing her descent with pressure on her good foot. Splinters caught her palms, but they were easier to handle than putting pressure on the sprain. Daniel caught her around the waist and eased her to the ground.

Mr. Bakker waved his hand toward the barn entrance. "Well, then, come. Boris won't hurt you. He's a good watchdog as long as the burglars stay at a distance. If they come too close, he'll roll over for a good belly rub." He disappeared out the door.

Tamar stared after their new host, blinking. "I can't believe this. What luck."

"Call it what you wish." Daniel took her hand and drew her forward.

Warm sunlight greeted them at the barn door. The smell of freshly cut hay and clover fragranced the air. She inhaled deeply, then sighed. The ubiquitous taste of fear lessened. Yet trust still remained at arm's length. She'd learned too well that people betrayed others for the slightest benefit. This farmer could be lying to trap them. Nazi soldiers could be sitting in the kitchen, waiting for Daniel and her to enter. Her hand tightened on his arm.

Daniel turned to face her. "You all right?"

She stopped. "Are you sure this isn't a trap?"

Daniel's arms crossed. "I don't think he's setting us up." He chewed on his lower lip. "He saw your Nazi garb first. When you showed him your stripes, he lowered his rifle."

Tamar scanned the area. The house and barn were the characteristic white of most Dutch farms—tidy, yet the paint was peeling on both buildings. A horse watched them from behind the corral fence. The farmer was cleaning off his boots at the back door, then opened it and went in.

"If you feel uncomfortable going into the house, we can leave right now, but there comes a time when you have to trust your instincts. What are they saying?" His head cocked to the side.

Tamar could tell he was becoming impatient with her. She smoothed back stray hairs and removed a piece of straw. "I believe him, I think. The problem is, I don't trust my feelings."

"Okay." He took her hand. "Let's trust him. What's the worst that can happen?"

Death.

Mr. Bakker exited the house, carrying kindling. "We don't need any more dogs here. Let's burn that uniform. Miss, you head on into the bedroom at the end of the hall and pick out one of my wife's dresses. Nothing fancy there, but it'll be more comfortable than what you're wearing. I don't want that disgusting green uniform in my house. We'll burn that one here and now."

With a sigh, she stepped out of the skirt and ripped off the jacket. "I feel like an onion, peeling away layers of shame and deceit from the last few months." She threw them in the fire, hobbled toward the door, and climbed the few steps to the kitchen.

Daniel saluted her. "Bring that lovely jailbird ensemble back for the fire as well."

The tidy room she stepped into held a small table bearing a single plate with utensils and a cup. Why not two place settings?

Tamar passed through the living room, down the hall to the bedroom on the left at the end. She opened the door, peeked in, then entered. A pretty quilt covered the bed. Two framed pictures—one of a woman about thirty, the other of a teenage boy with amused eyes and a full smile—sat on the bed stand along with a lamp and a Bible.

Tamar picked up the picture of the woman and studied her. She wore a long dress with practical lines, her hair piled high on her head. A natural beauty. A small boy peeked out from behind her skirt. Tamar would have missed him if she hadn't looked closely. The son who'd joined the Resistance? She hoped for Mr. Bakker's sake that his boy would return home at the end of the war.

The house was too quiet. Had the wife died? A single, unbidden tear fell onto the framed picture. So many families torn apart. Her family torn apart. Would she see her parents and Seth again? Or would she have to live the rest of her life alone? Would she even have pictures like this one to treasure?

If the farmer's wife still lived, she'd be about Neelie's age. Fresh guilt swept over her to the point she lowered herself onto the quilt. Would Neelie ever forgive her for abandoning her and Hannie? Tamar hadn't forgiven herself. Neelie would show her more grace than she deserved.

Tamar set the picture on the bed stand and opened the closet door. Tidy like the rest of the house, the closet held two simple dresses, a sweater, a robe, and a smaller pair of overalls, next to a man's suit and overalls. Black, sensible pumps, work boots, and gray slippers lined up with Wellingtons and a pair of Sunday men's shoes. Somehow, Tamar knew they could trust a farmer who kept such a neat house and let her borrow one of his wife's dresses, especially if memories were all he had left.

A door creaked open and brought the laconic voice of the farmer conversing with Daniel. She should hurry so they could burn her striped uniform.

Tamar chose the beige-collared housedress covered with tiny rose petals and a button-down bodice and the slip that was hooked to the hanger. Simple and roomy, the slip felt crisp and clean next to her skin. How she wished she could take a shower or a bath before contaminating the dress with a body that hadn't known a decent cleaning in months. But that luxury would have to wait.

Tamar eyed the pumps, longing to exchange them for her industrial boots, but it would be impossible to walk in them with her swollen ankle, so she closed the closet door instead. With her striped clothes held at arm's length, she entered the hall, then glanced into the bathroom. A private bathroom. Could she? She should ask. But first, she'd just take one look in the mirror. She tiptoed to the sink and stared at her reflection for the first time since singing at Westerbork. Oh, she'd caught glimpses in glass windows but hoped her reflection was distorted.

Now she faced the ugly truth. Her cheekbones protruded in a face angular and gray, and her eyes caved in, making her look twenty years older. But something else bothered her—a hardness, a lack of sparkle, a tightening of her jawline. The image looked more like her great-aunt Onalee than herself. Or Violetta. Gone was that fresh-faced girl of a year ago who aspired only to be the lead soprano. Back when life was simple. She shook her head to forget the image and hurried to the kitchen.

Daniel sipped a cup of dark coffee and grinned when she entered the room. "Throw your clothes by the door. I'll take them out and burn them as soon as I'm finished here. A cup of coffee? A piece of bread?"

Tamar surveyed the bare counter. "Just a cup of coffee would be fine." She managed an awkward curtsey. "What do you think? It feels so good to be out of those clothes."

Daniel nodded, his approval evident in his gaze, then pulled out a chair for her. "Mr. Bakker's going to let me borrow some of his clothes as well. It took you long enough."

Tamar opened her mouth to retort but changed her mind at the familiar wink he gave her. She took a seat, and he poured her a cup of coffee.

The farmer entered and removed his hat. "They turned off our water months ago. I've been collecting water in the well—enough for drinking and washing. It hasn't rained enough lately to catch any water, but if you want a bath, I can carry some in for you, but it will have to be a cold one. I don't want to keep the fire going any longer than necessary. Nazi varmints and all." He glanced at the counter. "Sorry, I don't have much food to offer you. We've a general store that accepts guilders under the table, but I ran out long ago." He pulled out his hanky and blew his nose. "I'll be back as soon as I burn this."

Once he disappeared, Daniel ran his finger down her cheek. She closed her eyes and leaned into it. "You look pretty."

She opened her eyes and frowned. "No, I don't. I look old enough to be my Aunt Onalee."

"Not to me." He grinned. "You know, we have that money. What say we give him some of it for food? He's sacrificing just by having us here."

"Of course. It's the least we can do."

"Do you still think this is a matter of luck?"

The chance of ending up in the barn of a farmer who sought to protect them was beyond coincidence. Tamar shook her head. "It's starting to make sense to me—all that Neelie spoke of about our people being in the palm of God's hand. I had expected Him to make all the bad go away with the flick of that hand, as if God were a fairy godfather. Evil doesn't vanish, but He's helped us more than a few times." She swept a hand around the room. "Like this place."

The farmer stomped through the door. "Well, I made short work of the uniform. Nothing but ashes now."

Daniel rose to his feet. "I have a proposal to make, sir."

"Yes, son, what is it?" He circled his fingers around the shoulder straps of his overalls.

Daniel pulled coins from his pocket and deposited them on the table. "We are so grateful for your help, and we have a bit of money here. Could you use some for groceries?"

The old man's eyes lit at the sight of it. "That'll buy some eggs and a hunk of cheese. Maybe some bread as well. I'll harness up Nico. He could use a good trot to Tilburg." He swept the coins into his palm, then his pocket, and tipped his hat to Tamar. "Be back soon. We'll have a feast tonight." The door closed behind him.

The house was quiet except for the tick of a wall clock. They stared at each other. Then Daniel grinned and shook his head. "Can you believe it? Yesterday we were running for our lives, not sure if we'd be torn apart by Nazi dogs. Today we stand in the kitchen of a man who wants to help us."

She looked away and fiddled with the handle of her cup. "He seems trustworthy. Yet I'm still not so sure. What if he went to town to alert the Reich? A person will do anything for money."

"He could have killed us up in the loft. I believe him." He regarded her. "But if you're unsure, we can leave right now. I'll change clothes, and we'll be on our way."

She shrugged. "I don't know what's best. This war has left me cynical about so many things. It's sad when I can't tell the difference between the good guys and the bad."

He kissed her forehead. "You've been through a lot in the past year, but we must keep our hope alive. Now what do you want to do?"

"We'll stay. Do you think Mr. Bakker would mind if I borrowed a wet cloth to help the swelling go down?"

"I'm sure he wouldn't. I'll go change my clothes." When he'd disappeared around the corner, she went to a chest of drawers in the kitchen and opened one after another until she found a dishtowel. Having seen a basin full of clean water in the bathroom, she headed in that direction.

The water felt cool to the touch. It would feel wonderful on her ankle. She dipped the cloth in the water, wrung it out, and couldn't resist wiping her face and neck.

A woman's robe hung behind the door. Maybe Mrs. Bakker was still alive, visiting a relative or working in town. Just because her husband didn't mention her, didn't mean she'd passed away. Tamar lowered herself to the floor and took off her boot, wincing with every movement. She wrapped the cold towel around her ankle, leaned her head against the wall, and closed her eyes.

A loud rapping roused her back to consciousness. Someone was at the front door. The farmer? No, he wouldn't need to knock. Maybe a neighbor. Where was Daniel?

She inched open the door. Daniel's head peeked out of the bedroom. "What should we do?" she whispered. The knocking started again. More urgent. Nazi urgent.

"We should hide." He pulled her by the wrist into the bedroom.

"Wait. I have an idea. I'll pretend to be a sick relative. You stay here."

"No, it's too dangerous." His hand clenched tight on her wrist.

"I can do this." She pulled free and grabbed the robe from the back of the bathroom door. Wrapping her head in the wet towel as if she'd just washed her hair, she hurry-hobbled to the door. Male voices came from the other side. Tamar swallowed deeply, hunched over, and adopted a tired expression on her face. Aunt Onalee's expression. She opened the door a few inches and peeked out. An officer in a green uniform and a man in a black suit stood outside. She jerked her head back. There was still time to lock the door and run. *No, Tamar, do your best acting.* "Yes?" she mumbled.

"Who are you? Where is Mr. Bakker?" the man in black said.

She took a few labored breaths. "He went to town. Now, if you'll excuse me, I need to lie down before I faint. Very sick. Virulent."

The man in the suit leaned close and studied her face with narrowed eyes. "I don't recognize you. Who are you?"

"I'm Ilse Bakker. My family sent me here. You should leave before you catch it." She pushed the door, but a green sleeve blocked her.

"You're hiding something." Shorter than the man in black, the uniformed officer's voice was gruff with a guttural accent. "What was burning behind the house?"

She frowned and exaggerated a slow shaking of her head. "I don't know and I don't care. Now leave me be."

The German officer's brows lowered. "I don't believe you. A farmer found two uniforms from Vught—a guard's and a prisoner's uniform." He opened the flap of his haversack so she could see them. "You wouldn't happen to know anything about that, would you?"

"No." Heartbeat picking up, she tried to close the door, but the man dressed in the suit blocked it with his foot.

"And do you know what else we found?" He fished out a small scrap of charred, striped material. "This came from the fire behind this house. You need to let us in." Fingers clenched around the door edge.

She feigned the urge to vomit and covered her mouth but aimed toward the gap in the door. "Can't you see I'm sick? I don't know what you're talking about." She slammed the door, and the moment the man jerked his fingers away, she engaged the hook in the hole, although the slightest force could still break the lock open. Her hands shook. Her knees threatened to give out on her.

A voice came from the other side. "When do you expect Farmer Bakker to return?"

"I don't know." Her voice came out in a rasp.

"We will be back." Footsteps sounded from the porch.

Tamar lowered herself to the floor and peeked through a gap in the curtain. The two men headed toward a motorcycle with a sidecar. They peered back at the house. She ducked. One of the men gestured toward the backyard. Her heartbeat raced. Had they believed her? She couldn't tell. Maybe her sickly face had scared them away.

Daniel's silhouette appeared in the hall.

"They're gone, but they'll be back. Did you hear what they said?"

"Yeah, they found my uniforms, and a bit of yours as well. That's not good." He joined her, careful to stay away from the window. "You ... were ... amazing. What an acting job. You might have just saved our lives."

"I didn't think it through. If I had, I never would have risked it, but I'd noticed a woman's robe in the bathroom, and if they'd broken in, we'd be caught for sure." She limped toward him and leaned her cheek against his chest. "I was so scared."

They stood in silence for a moment. "Did you get a look at the other guy?"

She shrugged. "He wore a suit. Probably an official from town who's cozying up to the Germans."

He unwrapped the towel and kissed her forehead. "We have to get out of here before they come back. I hate leaving the good farmer vulnerable, but if we stay, he'll be in more trouble."

She surveyed the neat living room, the colorful rug on the floor, the portraits of groups of people—probably relatives in happier times. It felt good to be in a house with doors that locked from the inside instead of cells that locked the other way. But it wouldn't bode well for the kind Mr. Bakker if they remained. "What should we do? The men might still be poking around outside."

"Let me check." Daniel moved the front window's curtain aside and peeked out, then hurried into the kitchen with her at his heels. He knelt by the window and peered out. "Coast is clear." He grabbed a hat from a post on the wall by the back door. In the flurry of events, she hadn't noticed Daniel's change of clothes. He wore a pair of overalls, a flannel shirt, and work boots. "How do I look?" He turned around.

"Like you belong on the farm, especially with that wide-brimmed hat. Much better than the scarecrow outfit."

"We still have some money. Not enough to afford passage out of the country but enough to get us out of the area. How's your ankle? Can you manage a walk into town?"

She swallowed, then nodded. "I can keep up. Shouldn't we leave a note?"

"We'd have to hide it." He pulled open drawers until he found a scrap of paper, scribbled a few words, then hid it under the teapot on the counter. "We should be on our way. We'll have to stick to the fields and avoid the roads."

With one last glance around the place, he closed the door behind them.

They headed in the direction from which they'd come, but as they reached the fence, Daniel stopped. "We can't go this way. They may be poking around back there someplace." He whirled. "Let's cross the road and stick to the fields on the other side."

They waited at the side of the farmhouse until they were sure no one would spot them, then hurried as fast as Tamar could manage to the nearest trees. The fear that had been part of her being for the last nine months returned twofold, yet she suppressed it and focused on keeping up with Daniel. "How far is it to Tilburg?"

"It can't be far. Come on."

"How do you know if we're going in the right direction?"

He shot her a fleeting frown. "You ask too many questions."

Tamar exaggerated zipping her lips, then they rounded a bend, and a church spire appeared in the distance.

"Where there's a church, there's people."

"And there's also a steeple." She demonstrated with her hands.

He shook his head. "Learned that from my uncle from New York. Can't believe you said that." He took her hand.

They walked in silence, Tamar's mind on the jigsaw puzzle of the past several months. How did it all fit together? How did good people allow a tyrant like Hitler to come to power? Where did the hatred for her people come from? "I wonder how Neelie and Hannie are doing in their new home."

"God will carry them through it, regardless of the circumstances. Those two are made of strong stock." He glanced at Tamar. "You still feel guilty about leaving them. The war may be over soon, anyway, so don't take on guilt that doesn't belong to you. Even if Neelie dies, she'll be in a better place. Do you believe that?"

"I don't know what I believe about the afterlife. We didn't cover that in shul. What do you believe?"

"I like to think of this life as the waiting room. Many are satisfied with being in the waiting room and want to stay there because it's familiar, because they don't know the next act is just beyond the door, and it's much better. The world to come."

"Is that where angels play harps and sit on clouds?" She imitated playing the harp.

He shrugged. "Who knows? What I do know is, every tear will be wiped away, and there won't be any suffering or sickness or death."

"So whatever happens to Tante Neelie, she'll be okay?"

"Yes, but we should continue to ask God to protect her and Hannie and Mrs. Betz. Shall we say a quick prayer for them now?" He adjusted the hat on his head, then turned toward her and took her other hand. They bowed their heads.

A sweet quiet settled in Tamar's heart during Daniel's short prayer. But as he finished, the engine of an approaching motorcycle made them pop their eyes open.

CHAPTER TWENTY-FIVE

Daniel tugged her into the ditch that ran alongside the road and pressed his hand on her back. "Keep down."

Tamar's heart raced under her thin bodice. "Do you think they saw us?"

"I don't know. Let's try to reach the trees."

Mud gushed around her knees as they crept toward a grove mere meters ahead. The rumble of the approaching motorcycle brought a new sense of panic. They'd come so far. Why did it have to end this way?

She stopped, as weighted as if a heavy hand bore down on her shoulder. Whether due to shock or weariness, Tamar couldn't make herself move another inch.

The motorcycle, with its sidecar, slowed to a stop. They'd been spotted. Daniel frowned at her and gestured to move. She shook her head and closed her eyes, so tired of being hunted. Tired of being treated worse than an animal. Tamar started to rise, but Daniel clasped her hand, forcing her low. "What are you doing? Stay down."

She couldn't ruin Daniel's chance of escape. She'd wait it out. He deserved her best efforts.

Daniel peeked between the reeds that skirted the ditch. He whispered, "One of the officers got out of the sidecar. He's by the trees, just standing there. Wait. Now he's going back to the motorcycle. Nature called." His eyes widened, and he turned to her. "Why did you refuse to move?"

She shrugged. "I just couldn't take another step. Like a weight clamped down on me."

"Well, girl, looks like that weight kept us alive for another day. Coincidence? Luck?" Daniel stared until the retreating motorcycle disappeared from view. He stood. "How do you feel? Can you move on?"

Tamar rose. "I actually feel invigorated, and my ankle hardly hurts." She crept up the bank, pulled a fistful of grass to wipe off her legs, then washed her hands in the muddy water. Daniel offered a hand up, and they headed to the next forested section bordering the road.

They made good time, despite the sludge of their boots with every step. The woods offered them safety when a rare vehicle passed, but most of the time, the even roadside surface made it easy to walk.

The clouds hid the sun, so she couldn't guess the time, but about three hours had passed when a vehicle appeared around the bend not far ahead. Close enough for the driver to see them. How foolish. They should have noticed the bend, but they'd grown lax.

Daniel leaped sideways into the woods, dragging her with him. Their eyes locked on each other. There were no words. The beat of their hearts thumped discordantly. They clung to each other and bent as low as they could. So close to freedom, yet so far.

German voices broke the silence. "They went in here." The thrashing of foliage only meters away made her cringe with each sweep of the cane or rifle.

"They can't be far," a man said.

Her forehead rested against Daniel's chest. It was almost over. They'd be taken back to Vught or sent to Ravensbrück or Buchenwald. She might see Neelie and Hannie again. Maybe even her mother. That would be good. And knowing Daniel, he'd find a way to cross the barbed wire from the male camp to Ravensbrück. And she could always sing, although her voice had been both a blessing and a curse.

"Psst."

The hiss right behind them triggered a collective gasp. They'd been found. Tamar's sliver of hope vanished, leaving her unable to lift her head.

"It's me, Jansen Bakker. Keep down. Follow my voice. I'll get you out of here."

Relief flooded her. She pressed to her feet and gripped Daniel's overalls, careful on the carpet of crunchy leaves. They moved stealthily deeper into the woods. Every few minutes, the farmer stopped, his head tilted toward the direction they'd come from. Then they moved again. It amazed her how quiet three adults could be when their lives depended on it.

"Just a short way." The farmer veered left toward a clearing and paused at the tree line where the horse and cart were waiting, Nico stomping his hoof. Tamar caught her breath as the late-afternoon sun broke through the trees. "All right, we should be on our way." He turned to face them. "Ready?"

"For what?" Daniel asked.

"We have to make it to Moerdijk. With the money you gave me, I secured your passage on a barge to England. It's leaving in two hours when the sun goes down. I also spent some of your coins on some food for Nico. It's at least an hour's trip to the sea. Follow me." He checked the surroundings, then started to move into the clearing.

Daniel's hand shot out and grasped the back of the man's overalls. "Wait."

Bakker turned. "Yes?"

"You can't go back to your house. A Nazi soldier and another man in a suit showed up at your door. They questioned Tamar about the fire. Found a piece of burnt material. Said they'd be back. Come with us on the boat." Daniel spread his hands. "You must come."

"I don't have the money for another passage." Brow wrinkled, Mr. Bakker mopped his forehead.

"We have a little bit."

"What about Nico? I can't just leave him."

Tamar touched his arm. "God will take care of him. Please say you'll come with us."

Their wide eyes met. The farmer paused, then with a lift of his shoulder, he nodded. "Follow me."

Daniel grabbed her hand. They sprinted toward the horse and cart, then climbed into the back.

From the driver's seat, the farmer glanced over his shoulder. "You'll have to hide under the blanket, especially when we pass through towns. Otherwise, you can come up for air."

They lay on their backs. Daniel covered them with a blanket that smelled of alfalfa. The farmer clucked at the horse, and they took off. Rescued again.

The gentle rock of the wagon and the rhythmic clip-clop of Nico's hooves lulled Tamar to sleep. She felt herself descend into oblivion despite inner warnings to stay alert. The past few days, weeks, and months had taken their toll, she reasoned, and Daniel could always wake her.

He didn't need to. The wagon stopped. Voices argued right above her head. Her breath hitched in her throat, and Daniel's arm tightened around her waist.

"We're just passing through," Jansen Bakker said.

A German-accented voice spoke in broken Dutch. "Your papers, please. And 'we're'? Who else is with you?"

A chuckle and a creak of the wagon as Bakker shifted his weight. "Oh, it's just my horse Nico and myself. I talk to him as we go along."

"Hmm. Where are you headed?"

"We're on the way to Breda."

"What is the purpose of your trip?" The voice moved closer to the back of the cart. Tamar could feel his eyes on the mysterious lump the size of two adult humans.

"To drop off the carcass of a dead boar. Getting it tested for rabies."

Tamar felt Daniel's chest quiver—fear or mirth? Definitely not mirth, though she had to smile. She'd never been called a rabid carcass before, but if it resulted in their freedom, Jansen Bakker could call them whatever he wanted. The soldier was less likely to touch the blanket covering a dead boar with rabies.

But the eyes of the German—Tamar felt them rather than saw them. She dared not move a millimeter. It took every bit of focus she had, and Daniel remained as still as she.

"Why take the boar so far? Why not bury it close to home? It makes no sense." A single pound on the side of the cart. "You're hiding something. Or someone. I don't believe you. Show me the animal."

Mr. Bakker's voice grew in intensity. "The boar's been dead for three days."

"I want to see it, not touch it."

"Maggots everywhere. You want to see that? And the smell?"— the wagon swayed with his emphatic gesture—"terrible."

"I don't believe you. I don't smell anything now. Show me the animal."

Tamar's heart thumped so loudly she was sure if they stopped talking, the officer would hear her. Still, she held her breath, managing only a shallow one when she couldn't stand it anymore.

"Very well, but may we do this around the corner?"

"We are not little girls. We can handle a few insects, no?"

"Away from any passersby. It would not be safe to expose them."

A pause.

"All right. Just around the corner."

The sound of footsteps and the rev of a motorcycle.

Bakker clicked his teeth at the horse, the jiggle of the reins sounded, and the cart lurched forward, then turned fifty meters or so to the right.

"Father," Daniel prayed slightly above a whisper, "we need Your protection. Jansen needs Your help. Amen."

"Amen," Tamar repeated.

They'd wriggled out of some tight spots, the two of them. Performing a German song while surrounded by Nazis. Slipping by the German guards at the ghetto's entry station. Neelie Visser offering them a safe place when they had nowhere to go. What was different about this time?

This time, they had no escape plan. She clenched Daniel's hand. He squeezed it back gently, and a measure of peace flowed through his touch.

They stopped. The motorcycle engine turned off. Nico snorted. Footsteps on the left side of the cart.

"Pull off the cover."

"No sir. I do not want to get a disease. If you want to see the dead animal, then you pull it off."

Silence. Then the click of the gun. "This is my last warning."

Please, Father, make us invisible.

A scuffling sound, something heavy falling to the ground, then a groan. "My leg. Help me up." Jansen Bakker's voice. The German response didn't need translating. More scuffling, a few grunts, and a thud, followed by silence.

The farmer hissed a warning. "We have to get out of here. Quick, before he wakes up."

Daniel bolted up and threw off the blanket. Tamar peered over the wagon's edge. "What happened?" she and Daniel said in unison.

Bakker knelt over the soldier, who had a patch of red seeping from one side of his head. "Help me drag him out of the way."

Daniel jumped down and placed two fingers on the man's neck. "He's alive. What happened?"

The farmer didn't answer. Instead, he grabbed the officer's legs. "We can talk about it on the way. We'll miss the boat if we don't hurry. Take his shoulders." They carried the man behind some trees and placed him on a bed of leaves, then the farmer steered the soldier's motorcycle into the woods beside him.

When he emerged from the grove, Daniel's jaw tightened, and a nerve ticked on the side of his neck. "His head is bleeding. Let me wrap it before we leave. It will only take a minute."

"Precious seconds are wasting." The farmer rubbed his hands together.

"Tamar, throw me your slip."

"What?" She pressed her arms against her chest, then understood. With a quick stroke, she tore a strip from the hem of her undergarment and handed it to Daniel. Tamar glanced over her shoulder at Mr. Bakker. "I'm sorry about your wife's—material."

"Quite all right."

She held back a grin. The farmer had seemed so meek once he'd lowered his rifle in the hayloft. A tall, thin reed of a man, simple stock, and a hard worker. Yet the gun in his hand—and his bold determination to save them—said otherwise.

Daniel wrapped the cloth around the officer's head. "At least that will stem the bleeding." He rose to his feet. "Let's go."

Within seconds, the farmer urged Nico into a trot. Tamar and Daniel lay in the wagon, but the blanket sat at arm's length if they needed it.

"So … what happened, Mr. Bakker?" Daniel asked, loud enough to be heard over the quick breeze.

He answered over his shoulder. "I got the idea to help you escape this morning, so I brought along the gun. Even thought to bring a horse sedative. Could make a human sleep for days. Almost needed to use it. That was close."

"I'll say. Did you pretend to fall or something?"

The older man chuckled. "When it got down to me pulling that blanket off, I said the quickest prayer known to mankind. 'God, help.' Then I pretended I got dizzy and fell sideways against the soldier. He was stunned and lost his balance, which gave me time to stand up behind him and hit him with the gun. Not hard enough to kill him but hard enough to give him a nasty headache."

"You've put yourself in danger." Tamar tilted her chin up to respond, a purpling twilight sky whisking past her gaze. "When he wakes up, he'll come looking for us."

"He never got around to looking at my papers. But you may be right about me joining you on the boat."

His words gave Tamar hope, but she didn't hold on to it. So many things could happen that were out of their control. The only sounds were the buzzing of nearby bees and the steady clip-clop of Nico's hooves. She fell asleep until a movement beside her jolted her to consciousness.

Daniel stretched his long arms. "How did you finagle us passage on the barge?"

"The boat owner owed me a favor. It won't be a luxury liner, but it will get us out of danger." He tossed two cards back at them. "Here are your new names. Marta and Willem Vogel. The pictures aren't too bad if you don't look too hard. We're getting close. Cover up with the blanket. I'll try to get as near to the barge as possible. Be ready to jump out when I tell you."

All traces of slumber disappeared as tension mounted between Tamar's shoulders Nico slowed to a trot. The sounds of a small town filled the calm. The squeak of a buggy wheel. The click of a cane along a sidewalk. The chatter of voices, a whistle, and a splash. All creating a new sense of panic, the all-too-familiar adrenaline coursing through her veins. Tamar found it hard to breathe. Daniel told her to inhale and exhale slowly. She counted to five. Concentrating on breathing helped.

The cart lurched to a stop. "Barge sixty-two, down a ways on the left. Captain's name is Jan DeVries. Time to go. I'll be right behind as soon as I find a safe place to leave the horse."

Daniel slipped over the side, then helped her down. He turned to the farmer. "How can we ever thank you?"

"When I did it for you, I did it for my son." He tipped his hat and turned the cart around. "Godspeed."

The wharf spread out in front of them, rows of fishing boats lined up along the boardwalk. Marine smells wafted in the air, and the Black Sea's waves lapped up against the pier. Nets full of fish sat on the deck by the boats, and fishermen smoked their pipes and chatted with their cronies as they parsed their catch into piles. People milled around. Seagulls soared above.

Daniel cupped her elbow, and they walked as quickly as they could without bumping into others or tripping over the nets. "Keep your head down," he said and stepped up his pace. They still had a ways to go since the numbers were low on this end.

"He's not going to come, is he?" Tamar said, concern filling her for the good farmer who had risked his life for them.

"Probably not. He's got Nico, and he wants to be there when his son comes home. The same as you when you knew your mother might be at the camp." He pulled her sideways to avoid a staggering drunk man. "Twenty-four numbers to go."

She raised her eyes. Two Reich officers stood chatting against the wall of a bait shop. A furtive cry escaped. "Nazis coming up on the right."

"Act natural. Do your best acting," he whispered. In a louder voice, "Oh, look at the herring. Nice ones. There're so many of them." He pointed toward the net ahead of them.

She played along. "That's nice. Wonder how much they cost." Tamar clutched his arm so tightly she was sure he'd have bruises.

"Price of herring—" He breathed out. "Okay, we're past them. Let's hurry. Thirteen numbers to go."

She had to run to keep up with his long strides, and her ankle throbbed with every step. Ten numbers to go.

Just then, "Halt, stop where you are." German accent. Footsteps. Fifty-eight. Four numbers to go. She could see the boat. She could see freedom.

EPILOGUE

Tamar stooped over the pram to place the pacifier in her daughter's mouth, the dappled shadows from the broad, green leaves of Fredrikspark's lofty oak trees providing some shade from the June heat for her twins. A bike wove around her and beeped. She pulled the pram off the red-bricked path just in time.

It seemed so strange being back in Haarlem after three years, mere blocks from her family's jewelry store. Yet nothing had changed. People picnicked. Children played on the swings. She'd done the same as a child and had walked in this park every week throughout her life until … This was the park where Seth had told her about his work in the Resistance. This was where her life had changed from being a naïve opera singer to an operative—is that what they called her?

A woman appeared ahead on the curved pathway. Her familiar gait caught Tamar's attention. Graying straight hair cut to her chin, sensible shoes, tall, thin, a jaunty, green hat on her head with a feather. "Tante Neelie, is that you?"

The woman lifted her eyes, which grew wide. Her hand covered her mouth. "Could it be? My Tamar?" Tamar pushed the pram toward Neelie, and they ran into each other's arms, holding each other in a tight, joyous embrace. "I can't believe my eyes." Tears brimmed on Neelie's lashes. "It is *so* wonderful to see you." She kissed Tamar's cheek, wet with her own tears, and then held her at arm's length. "You look beautiful … and happy."

"I am. Oh, Tante Neelie, you have no idea how I've longed to see you. This is my first trip back here to Haarlem. I haven't been able to … come here." She pulled Neelie into a hug again and swung her around, too choked up to speak.

A cry came from one of the twins. Tamar let go and turned to the pram. "Come and meet my children."

"Seth told me you and Daniel had twins." Neelie leaned over the buggy and looked in.

"Meet your namesake, Neelie Odette Feldman. She's almost two years old." She rounded the buggy and knelt beside the toddler with tight blonde curls peeking out from her bonnet. "This is Tante Neelie, the best aunt a girl could have."

Two little arms rose toward the older woman.

"May I pick her up?"

Tamar nodded. "Of course."

Neelie chuckled and picked the child up. "What a little beauty, just like your mother. I'll bet you can sing too." She sniffed. "I love the smell of children. Always have."

Another pair of arms lifted. Tamar bent over and picked up her son. "And this is our little boy. You'll never guess what his name is."

"Daniel?"

"That's his middle name. May I introduce Perez Daniel Feldman?"

Neelie gasped. "Tamar's son in the Bible. You remembered."

Tamar swayed back and forth with Perez on her hip. "Are you in a hurry? Do you have time to sit for a few minutes? Two children take a lot of energy."

"Of course, I have all the time in the world for my favorite niece—my only niece," Neelie said.

Tamar moved toward the nearest bench that sat by the path under a tree. With the children on the seat between them, Tamar took Neelie's hand and looked into her eyes. "I am so sorry I left you and Hannie in the camp. It was selfish of me and Daniel to abandon you. Can you ever forgive me?"

"There's nothing to forgive. God opened a door for you, and later, He opened a different one for me." She patted her hand. "We have much to share with each other. I spoke with your brother once at the market when I was in town to meet Jan. He told me you and Daniel were living in London, and he was going to get me your address, but I didn't see him again. You must give me your address so we can write to each other. So how did you end up in England?"

Tamar smoothed away a strand of hair the breeze had blown into her eyes. "A farmer near Tilburg, Jansen Bakker, helped us the day after we escaped. We hid in his barn to get some sleep and give my sprained ankle a chance to rest. I woke up to his gun pointed at my head. It took me a while to trust the man. Vught and Westerbork created that distrust in me." She ran her fingers through her son's hair.

"How did he help you?"

"He burned my uniforms, gave us clothes to wear, and bought us passage on a barge headed to England. We almost didn't get to leave. The false identification papers Farmer Bakker gave us were the only thing that got us past the Germans."

"Oh my. What a brave and amazing sacrifice." Neelie squeezed Tamar's hand.

"Yes. He said he did it for his son, who'd joined the Resistance. It was sad." Tamar smiled at her tante. Her hair was grayer, and a few smile lines framed her lips. But she had put on some weight and was prettier than she'd ever remembered Neelie, although she still wore the dark dress of a widow.

"Whatever happened to the farmer?" Neelie walked her fingers over Perez's arm, evoking a giggle from the boy.

It was so like Neelie not to talk about herself. "We begged him to join us, and he said he would as soon as he found a place to leave his horse and wagon, but that was the last time we saw him." As the familiar pain of guilt surfaced, Tamar squeezed her eyes shut to block the memory. Another person she and Daniel needed to visit, now that they'd finally made the decision to move forward with their lives.

"The man probably wanted to be there when his son came home."

Tamar dropped her chin, handing Perez his rattle. "I hope you're right. I pray the boy returned." She shifted to face her tante. "I never stopped thinking about you. You taught me so much. And I so wanted to find you. Seth told me he spoke with you, that you'd been to Ravensbrück but appeared to be fine, so at least I knew you were okay, but Seth also said you weren't living in Haarlem, and I didn't know how to get in touch with you. But in all honesty, I was ashamed." A shuddering breath released. She looked up. "Tell me about Ravensbrück, Tante Neelie."

Neelie sat Perez on her lap and rocked him. "It was as Charles Dickens said, 'the best of times and the worst of times.' Since the camp was in Germany, we met women from Poland, Russia, and Germany. We didn't speak the same language but managed to understand each other. And the best part was, our barrack was laden with lice." Neelie's face lit as though she was revealing a tantalizing secret.

Tamar's mouth fell open. "How could lice be for your good?" She'd told the guard at Westerbork there were lice in her bedding, but she'd never been certain.

"The *Aufseherinnen,* the female guards, avoided our building for fear of getting the pests in their hair, which allowed us the freedom to socialize. So, you see, lice were a godsend. Many people came to know the Lord because of those little insects." Two lines formed between her eyebrows. "I'm glad you left when you did. Unlike Vught, the work was hard at Ravensbrück, moving rocks from one place to another."

A trembling sigh escaped Tamar's lips. "I should have been there. Daniel should have too."

"Don't carry a weight you weren't meant to carry. I've never once resented your leaving. You did the right thing."

"What happened to Hannie?"

Neelie touched her arm. "She died a few weeks before Christmas 1944, right before we were released. Emphysema." She turned to face Tamar. "Now don't you worry. Hannie's no longer in the waiting room."

Tamar's chest squeezed. "Daniel talks about the waiting room." Neelie bounced her namesake on her knee. "Tell me, how is he?"

"He finished his residency in a London hospital. Today he has an interview for a position in the emergency department at St. Elisabeth Gasthuis and will meet us here in the park when he's done. Now that I'm here in Haarlem, it's not so bad." She lifted a shoulder. "Maybe I'll even get back into singing, and Seth will be close. Can you stay for a few more minutes? I don't want to keep you, but I'd love for you to see Daniel again, and I know he'd love to see you."

"Certainly. I am here until tomorrow, staying with Jan, though I live in Amsterdam now."

"Amsterdam? What do you do there?"

"I work with concentration camp survivors. So few returned, and they need help—" Her eyes took on a faraway look, then she roused herself. "So how is Daniel outside of work? The war can be hard on a man."

"Daniel's a doting father, of course, and little Neelie and Perez are the center of our lives." She paused. "He doesn't like to talk about what happened. Our plan was to tell the world what we experienced in Westerbork and Vught, but he's just not ready to do that yet. Neither am I. I use the excuse that the twins keep me busy, but if truth be told, the idea of talking about it repulses me."

Neelie patted her hand. "I understand. I work with survivors of the camps, and I see that reluctance all the time. Give him and yourself time."

"But we're here, and this was a big first step." Tamar broke into a smile. "Guess what? Thanks to you and Daniel, I'm a believer in your messiah now. Daniel showed me, as you did, how to see God in the circumstances of our lives."

"Oh, Tamar. I'm so glad." Neelie gave her a little hug. "It isn't easy to see God's hand when evil reigns around us. I'll confess that I had trouble forgiving the cruel *Aufseherinnen* with their dogs and whips and taunts." She laughed. "So you see, your Tante Neelie is not a perfect woman, only a forgiven one."

"That you are, and so am I. It's hard, isn't it, even though we know friends and family are in a better place?"

"It is. Seth told me your parents passed away in Dachau."

She lowered her gaze to her lap. "Yes, of typhus." She managed a smile. "I still have Seth, when we get him to settle down long enough to come for a visit. He's busy with a new project."

"What is that, dear?"

"He's joined the Zionist Movement. His goal is to move all Jewish refugees who survived the camps to Palestine. Can you believe it? Moving back to the land of Abraham?" Tamar shook her head in wonder.

"Your people deserve it after what you've been through." Neelie pushed to her feet. "Ah, this old body is stiff." She balanced Perez on her hip. "Tamar, you brought so much joy to our lives with your singing and your eagerness to help out at the house here in Haarlem. We were doubly blessed to have you and Daniel join us. Now I must ask a favor."

Tamar picked up her daughter, who rubbed her eyes. "Anything."

"Since we've both lost dear ones close to us, what would you say to me becoming a surrogate grandmother for these little ones and a mother to you and that husband of yours? I don't have any experience, but they tell me I'm a fast learner. I come to Haarlem whenever I can to see my son, and Amsterdam's only twenty minutes away on the train if you move back to Haarlem."

Tears rolled down Tamar's cheeks. She wiped them away with the back of her hand. "I can't think of anything better. You'd be the best bubbe ever." She settled little Neelie back in the buggy and enveloped her tante in a hug.

"Who is this vision from our past?" Daniel swooped in from behind and embraced both of them. "Tante Neelie. How wonderful to see you." He took his son from her, then placed his free arm around the woman's shoulders and kissed her cheek.

She pulled him into a hug, then backed up to look at him.

"Being a husband and father agrees with you. You've put on some weight—just the right amount. And with your dapper suit, you look wonderful. It is so good to see you."

"Guess what Tante Neelie suggested?" Tamar swiped a hand over her moist eyes. "That she could be a new bubbe for the twins and an eema for us."

"A grandmother for our children and a mother for us. I can't think of a better gift." He kissed Tamar's temple, then lowered Perez into the buggy beside his sister. He turned to face Neelie. "What have you been up to these past three years?"

She told him about her work in Amsterdam with survivors from the camps—how they provided psychological therapy to help the former prisoners overcome the nightmares, the bitterness, and the ensuing addictions. He listened with his hands steepled close to his lips.

"You know, that sounds like a place I should visit. It's been long enough. I could consider volunteering there, or maybe even sign up for a session or two. Tamar, what do you think? We've made it to Haarlem. Maybe we need to take the next step to Amsterdam."

Yes, she was ready for the next step. "I agree, and maybe I could volunteer there also—and sing. It's time my gift becomes a blessing, and no longer a curse."

Neelie clapped her hands, and Daniel grinned.

"How about I treat us all to lunch at Grote Markt, and we can catch up on the past few years? And I'll tell you about my chat with Maarika." He winked at them.

"Maarika?" Neelie and Tamar said at the same time.

"Yup. Hasn't changed at all." He smiled at Tamar. "Then you and I need to do some apartment hunting."

A rush of delight filled her as she realized what he was saying. "You got the job?" She hugged Daniel, then pulled Neelie into her embrace. "We're moving into the next chapter of our lives—a much better one."

AUTHOR'S NOTES

My first heroine was Corrie ten Boom. I marveled at her sweet and honest temperament. She didn't conceal her lack of self-confidence or minimize her anger at how the guards treated her sister, Betsie, at Ravensbrück. Nor did she conceal how difficult she found it to forgive Vogel, the man who betrayed her family and arrested them. But she did.

Corrie had a heart for the Jewish people as did her family, and she suffered through three labor camps for protecting them, her father and sister dying while in captivity. Yet after she was released in 1945, a sick, middle-aged woman, she spent the rest of her life traveling the world, speaking of God's goodness even when circumstances scream otherwise. That is the message of this book.

Though Corrie has been gone from this world since the '80s, her books are still timely, and I've read them all many times, listened to her speeches, and watched her movie. Not many Nederlanders protected the Jews, yet there were other people like Corrie ten Boom who sheltered God's people from the Nazis—members of the Resistance who hid them, took care of their needs, and transported them out of the country.

As a fiction writer, I always wonder *what if*? If a Gentile person from the Netherlands helped hide Jews, what if the story was told from a different point of view? What if a Jewish "guest" in her early twenties told the story instead of the host? I decided to write a fictional account from the point of view of such a woman, sheltered, naïve, just starting her career as a chorister for the local opera. Just falling in love for the first time.

Tamar Kaplan's world is limited to her work at the Haarlem

opera and her home life with her parents and brother, Seth. She's aware of the presence of Nazi soldiers who stand on sidewalk corners, but they're a nuisance at best. Until they close the opera. Then it gets personal.

Authenticity is important to me. All my characters are fictional, but the places that they inhabit and visit are real. Vught, the Grote Markt, even the Silveren Spiegel restaurant. My son and I toured the ten Boom house to get a feel of space in the narrow, multistoried houses of Haarlem. Imagine my joy to find a bakery across the Barteljorisstraat from a jewelry store! I'd written about it but didn't think it existed. Yet there it was—Kaplan's house across from the Betzes' bakery. That was a God moment for me.

My timeline might be off a bit, but I had to fit a lot of events into a short period of time since the war ended in May of 1945. The story starts in the fall of 1943. Tamar only worked for the Resistance for two months and only stayed at Neelie's house for two months. They were taken to Westerbork February 29th, 1944, and spent two months there, then were moved to Vught, where they stayed until Daniel and Tamar escaped in September of 1944.

I left holes to be filled with the second book. What happened to Job and Carina Hamel and Maarika? What if the picture of the girl and the violin showed up at Tamar's parents' house, which she saw when she sneaked into it? What if Daniel had to take care of Officer Bergman as a patient? If the first book in this series warrants a second, then I'll address those questions.

Readers who are familiar with Corrie ten Boom's stories and movie will recognize certain similarities. Her books were my primary sources for what life was like in houses hiding refugees and for life in concentration camps in the Netherlands. As said before, there were many families who hid Jews in the Netherlands. Some hid the people in barns. Some hid them inside walls. I chose the attic and I wrote about orphans. And because Tamar led such a sheltered life, her mentor would have to be either a relative or someone she worked with at the opera.

Readers may think I minimized the atrocities of concentration camps in the way I described Vught, but my description was accurate for the period. Remember that Vught and Westerbork were transit camps. Prisoners have even described them as resort-like, and many prisoners expected the same treatment at Auschwitz and Bergen-Belsen, but that was the Nazis' intent—to kill them with kindness, like the frog in the tepid water.

In *A Prisoner and Yet*, Corrie ten Boom is required to march at midnight as punishment along with others. They pass an airplane graveyard and then a crematorium quite far from the rest of the labor camp but within its fences. In reality, that crematorium is in the center of Vught, close to the barracks, yet I believe it was moved from its original place. Neelie is forced to play music with other musicians in front of the crematorium to mask the noise within. This did not really happen at Vught, but it did happen at Auschwitz. In fact, no one died in the crematorium during Corrie's stay at Vught. Yet many died at other times in Vught's crematorium.

Remember in *To Kill a Mockingbird* when Atticus Finch said, "Scout, simply by the nature of the work, every lawyer gets at least one case in his lifetime that affects him personally. This one's mine, I guess. You might hear some ugly talk about it at school, but do one thing for me if you will: you just hold your head high and keep those fists down."? *A Song for Her Enemies* is my book of a lifetime. I desperately want younger readers to know what it costs to be a true hero like Corrie ten Boom. I want all readers to know that God is good even when circumstances scream otherwise.

I can't wait to go back to Haarlem and other places in the Netherlands to capture the reality of the country. A land of beautiful cathedrals, but the country's faith in God is dead, replaced with a focus on tolerance, which is a good thing, but taken to the extreme, leaves people with tepid beliefs. I study the Dutch language every day but don't need to since it seems everyone speaks English. Still, it's the right thing to do.

Sherri Stewart

Please subscribe to my newsletter
http://eepurl.com/gZ-mv9

Amazon Author Page
https://www.amazon.com/author/sherristewart/

Website
www.stewartwriting.com

Facebook
https://www.facebook.com/sherristewartauthor/

Twitter
https://twitter.com/machere

9 781645 262831